The Sound Of Us

Jen Samson lives in Johannesburg, South Africa with her husband, three children and two Maltese poodles. Her love for reading began with her father, when she would check out Louis L'Amour books from the library for him.

Jen is an uncontrolled consumer of Chinese, Thai and Korean dramas. Her love for BTS is infinite. She is 99.9% OT7 but that 0.1% belongs to Park Jimin.

Also by Jen Samson

Say Yes: A D/s MM Lovestory
Behind These Eyes: A gay awakening college romance

The Sound Of Us

Jen Samson

ISBN: 978-1-7764430-5-5

Front cover photo: Canva Pro_Nuran Mammadov from Pexels
Back cover photo: Canva Pro_Stafichukanatoly from Pixabay
Fonts: Canva Pro_Coldiac ("The Sound"), Brittany ("of us"), Cinzel (Author's name)
Gay Pride Rainbow Fist Illustration: Canva Pro_copelandcreative
Formatting template: https://usedtotech.com/books/fiction-booklayout-template-in-word-for-5-5-x-8-5-digest/

To the girl who found the courage to say no after twenty years.
Now, live

To the survivors. You always deserved better. Right from the
start, you deserved better

To those still stuck. We know you're trying, and we're waiting
for you on this side. Don't give up

CONTENT WARNING

Please go through these content warnings carefully before starting *The Sound Of Us*. If you have questions, please reach out to me on Instagram, Facebook or in an e-mail: sharewithjen7@gmail.com, or talk to other readers first.

Graphic on page abuse (verbal/physical/emotional/ psychological)
Suicidal ideation
Sexual assault (between MC and abusive spouse)
Grief
Narcissistic behavior patterns
Life-threatening illness
Cheating (MC cheats on abusive spouse)
Rape (The end of Chapter 49 / between MC and abusive spouse / about 20 lines / not gratuitous but descriptive enough to cause discomfort. Please take care.)

If you have experienced a trigger and it is not listed here, please let me know anywhere on social media or via email. Again, please take care.

ABOUT THE BOOK

The Sound Of Us was difficult for me to complete. I considered canning everything right up until the formatting stage. It didn't feel like fiction; like something to escape to. Axel's story felt too real.

I witnessed a tremendous amount of domestic violence growing up. It was all around me—neighbors, family members, church members. The abusers were often well-known, respected members of the community, the *good guys*.

Some stories were so unbearable it seemed easier to pretend these things don't happen in real life to real people. Some events in this book may seem a little farfetched or over the top. Please believe me when I say that these types of abusive situations are very real for some people, as ludicrous as it may sound to those of us fortunate enough to have never experienced such pain.

There is nothing glamorous or sensational about this story. It is just one perspective of a very painful and, sometimes misunderstood, act of betrayal and is not meant to invalidate the experiences of those who have been cheated on.

I wrote this story to honor someone very close to me. To tell her that her story matters, even if people don't believe her. That her pain is valid, even if she stayed as long as she did.

PLAYLIST

My playlists always include books that comforted me during my time writing. My reading tastes are vast but I've contained my reading within the MM world for the last few years. These are the books I loved recently. The first two share themes with *The Sound Of Us*.

UNTIL I SAW YOU by Dianna Roman
THE GOOD LIAR by C.P. Harris
FIERCE by Lola Malone

Now, an actual playlist. I usually fall in love with one song during my writing process and it goes on repeat until my family begs for it to stop. If you know me, especially on Instagram, you might know about my undying love for the Korean pop band, BTS. I beg you to look up this song and listen to it. I *promise* it'll leave you in tears.

EPIPHANY by Jin of BTS

ACKNOWLEDGMENTS

To my sister, Lynette— let's do it one more time and see how it goes, even if this one flops

To Stefka— you are the star that shines in my dark world as I approach publication and all I want to do is cry. I love you SO MUCH

To Lola Malone— thank you, not just for catching me when I fall, but also, for pulling me to my feet and showing me I can still run

To C.P. Harris— I don't know how to ask for help but you come looking for me to offer me something I need. It's a little dramatic to compare, but it's like when Clint goes looking for Raven. Thank you for your guidance, help and encouragement. Thank you for letting me mention your work in this book

Bookstagrammer JamieReadsRomance for allowing me to immortalize you in this story

Garry Michael, for allowing me to reference your beautiful book, *All The Battles We Surrender*, in this publication

My beta readers: Julie and Tatiana. Special thanks to Tatiana for all your help with Eli, my deaf character.

The Sound Of Us

JEN SAMSON

CHAPTER 1
Axel

When the cold weeks following Christmas and New Year make promises of turning our small town of River Valley in Eastern Kentucky into a (poverty-stricken) winter wonderland, you know it's time to start chopping the wood. You didn't want to get caught without proper heating during this year's winter in these parts.

I'm outside, axe to wood, when I see the big piano.

Not all of it, since the wet winds have uncovered only a portion of the magnificent instrument as the moving truck upon which it stood eases its way past our house on the corner of Alice and Third Road.

There isn't much of the piano to see, but it's enough to know that the instrument isn't from this age. A vintage masterpiece.

My curiosity has me straightening my back, watching the truck until it disappears around the bend.

There's only one house at the bottom of the bend. It belonged to Mrs. Johnson, who'd left River Valley about a year ago. She'd been sick for a long time and we heard she went to stay in one of those fancy retirement homes in Louisville. A maintenance company takes care of the house here.

Sadly, Mrs. Johnson died soon after she left River Valley and our local radio station dedicated a ten-minute segment to her each week, calling for information about any extended family.

Of course, the station was broadcast only to the two thousand-three-hundred and sixty-four people who made up the population of River Valley, and we all already didn't know anything.

We're a town starved for any kind of entertainment and would turn anything and everything into town news and, usually, we made things bigger than they actually are.

We all knew Mrs. Johnson had gone to Louisville to be closer to her family, but we had to go and sensationalize it by acting like we had no idea what had happened and what was going to happen to her property.

David Shapiro, River Valley's only lawyer, was quick to burst our bubble, assuring us that there was no need for an investigation into Mrs. Johnson's mysterious extended family. It's a simple story, he'd said, to the dismay of the townsfolk.

According to David Shapiro, someone from Mrs. Johnson's very affluent family was going to upgrade the old house down around the bend and turn it into some sort of guest house.

Not that many people would willingly pass through these parts, let alone sleep here voluntarily, but we admired their optimism and who were we to turn down something as exciting as the grand opening of our first guest house since the last one got destroyed in a fire about seven years ago?

I already knew all of this before it became public knowledge, because my best friend, Benson Turner, works at the town's only bookstore, named *Till Books Do Us Part*, which is next door to David Shapiro's office, and he always got the juiciest news first, straight from the horse's mouth.

I already knew the new resident was arriving today, but no one ever said anything about him owning the most exquisite thing I'd ever seen. Imagine owning a baby grand like that.

I sneak a look over my shoulder, where my golden retriever named Pepper, is busy sulking.

She's a therapy dog, and I got her as a gift from Mrs. Dalton. *It's to help with the cancer*, she'd said, but I was sure it was also because of the *other thing* that had started happening. Pepper isn't a guard dog, but she still protected me as best as she could.

Sometimes I feel sorry for Pepper. Her purpose in life is to watch her owners die. It sounds a little dramatic because she's actually meant to provide comfort and love to terminally ill patients and I guess we should look at the glass as half full and all that, but ultimately, those people need her comfort and love as they approach *end of life.*

She's been through it twice already. Her soft, gentle temperament is meant to ease the pain of her companion and then she's shipped off to another terminally ill patient who was *approaching end of life.* Apparently she'd been a puppy when she'd started and neither owner had lasted more than a few months.

I'm her third owner and well, I'm still here. I decided that I'd be the last person Pepper would have to watch die. I already stated in my will that I want her to go to a perfectly healthy child somewhere in the suburbs, who'd love her and who'd live to eighty at least.

I definitely don't want Pepper to stay with my husband, Frank. And he wouldn't want her too, anyway.

"It's five o'clock, so no, Pepper. You'll stay right there. You're a dog. Not a race car, so you stay inside until the evening traffic subsides," I tell her now.

And by *traffic*, I mean the two or three cars that need to get down to the front of Mrs. Dalton's house, to drop off perishable items like milk and cheese, or, as of the last few weeks, to drop off renovation supplies to Mrs. Johnson's house.

Pepper whines, telling me exactly what brand of asshole she thinks I am (the stick-in-the-mud-no-fun kind). Especially since I destroyed her deepest, darkest fantasy of chasing a giant moving truck down the road toward the woods by keeping her locked behind the old picket fence.

Another low rumble carries through the evening air and Pepper spins in circles, whining like a wolf calling to the moon.

"No fuckin' way, Pepper." I chuckle at her dramatics and go back to my chopping. We need this wood out of the wet weather immediately.

I hear the soft click of the gate latch about the same time another rumble of a car engine grinds through the air. And then—

"Pepperrrr!"

Fuck. Her golden hair flying behind her, Pepper bolts out of the gate, racing for the sleek, black SUV as it glides up the road.

Maybe some people let their dogs chase after cars. I'm just some crazy, overprotective dog-mom, right?

But I watched Mrs. Dalton cry for months after her giant schnauzer got run over by some city folk who got lost while passing through. I'm not prepared for that. Pepper is not just a therapy dog. She's my best friend, even before Benson most days.

"Pepper," I yell, as I take off after her.

Her excited barks give me heart failure. She runs and I run behind her. It's like a comedy show, where everyone is laughing at a racist or homophobic joke, but it's actually not funny.

The SUV comes to a halt just as Pepper leaps forward for a nip at the wheel.

"Pepper, I swear to god—" I yell with my hand pointing upward like I'm on the frontline of a war and the captain just yelled *charge!*

I'm winded, more than usual, when I get to her. I don't like how tired I am after a ten second run.

The driver steps out of the car and I— I—

I just—

Breathing hard, my chest burning, I come to a dead stop two feet away from the driver of Pepper's dream car.

Although I'm standing still and at a reasonable distance from him, it feels like I've been flung right into him. The pull to him is instant and shocking to my nervous system.

He's tall. Not as tall as Frank, but I still have to look up to get a good look at his eyes. I don't know how to swim but if I ever tried, now I know what it would feel like to drown in the palest blue ocean. My thumb grazes over the inside of my ring finger, where my wedding band digs into that finger as well as my conscience.

One time, nine years ago, when I was nineteen and married for one year, I didn't look into the mirror for ten months because I hated the sight of my face (*god, your face is like a fuckin' Chihuahua, Axel*).

First of all, I didn't even know at the time that a *chi-hua-hua* is a tiny dog with a skinny face. Secondly, I guess the price you pay for chemo is looking like a dog whose name no one can spell.

But now, even from this distance, looking into this stranger's glassy stare... I'm *captivated* because I'm convinced that if I were to step closer, I might see my reflection in those eyes and I might never want to *stop* looking.

He's wearing professional-looking clothes—black dress pants that sit on him so elegantly. Shiny black shoes. A white button shirt with the sleeves rolled up. He must have good heating in his vehicle. No one can dress so scantily and get away with it over here.

His short brown hair catches some flakes of snow and, sadly, for my confused, married brain, he runs his hand through his short strands, dampening and spiking them slightly and turning himself into the most handsome man I've ever seen. *Even more handsome than Frank* is my next horrifying thought.

He makes some signs with his hands, snapping me out of my shameful, inappropriate observations.

What? I must look as confused as I feel.

He makes another sign, pointing to his ear. Then, when he gets nothing but crickets from me, he retrieves his phone from his pocket. I'm ashamed of how much I notice that elegant slide of his hand.

He types and turns the screen to me. *"I'm deaf. Speak. I can lip read."*

I'm so flustered. I've never met a deaf person before. Do I just... *speak?* Like I normally would? He's so gorgeous. My thoughts are as scattered as the flakes of snow falling around us.

"I'm sorry," I say slowly. I don't know if I should round my words carefully? "My dog. She likes to chase cars."

Pepper gets one of my covert glares, but she doesn't care. She's sitting next to this exquisitely beautiful stranger as if she belongs to him.

He smiles and dips his head. He understood me. I'm inexplicably pleased that I spoke clearly enough and so I offer him my own smile without meaning to.

He bends and ruffles Pepper's fur. She's all over him, pawing and licking.

"Pepper," I call. "Come here, girl."

Nothing.

She'll keep him there until it gets dark if I let her, and when she shows no signs of letting the stranger go, I step forward to pull her away. The man chooses that moment to rise.

I'm face-to-face with him. God, those eyes.

My thumb grazes my wedding band again, and the reminder helps me get Pepper away from her new crush without turning myself into a fool, too.

He lifts his hand in a wave, his face breaking out into a smile that has me hypnotized all over again.

He's going to get his own welcome party just for looking like that. Mark my words.

What the fuck am I thinking?

Like me and my disgusting thoughts, Pepper has no shame, whining and wriggling to get out of my grasp as the truck eases back onto the road and takes the bend.

With Pepper secure between my legs, I steer her back into the front yard.

It's Friday, after all.

NO LUBE FRIDAYS to be precise, and there are chores to be completed.

CHAPTER 2
Axel

I stare after the black SUV long after it's disappeared. That's the new resident. Benson didn't say anything about him being deaf. How could he leave out such a pertinent piece of information?

As with all new things in River Valley, he'll be smothered. Already I can see it. The girls will swarm for sure, and honestly, with a face like that, I wouldn't blame them.

The *Mom's Club* will definitely be all over him, trying to get him involved in their community programs. And most certainly, we're going to have sign language classes.

When I was diagnosed with Acute Lymphoblastic Leukemia during senior year, the *Mom's Club* was formed to raise money and awareness, and everyone had to attend a class at the library twice a month to educate themselves.

We didn't raise much money, but that was okay. River Valley was not known for its wealth, but we sure knew how to support each other with what little we had. We have our problems, one being that we are one of the poorest, most forgotten towns in the whole United States. The other is that we have a slight problem with prescription drugs and most of the two thousand three hundred and sixty-four of us are high on (illegally obtained) prescription drugs at any given time of day.

Not me, though. I've had enough of *legally* obtained prescription drugs to last me a lifetime. I never want to see another pill ever again for as long as I live... which might not be very long but that's a story for another day.

The soft fall of snow litters my face, reminding me of the task at hand. I'd been chopping for an hour before Pepper's Great Escape and my Highly Inappropriate Moment, but I hadn't gotten much done, since my mind had been on the evening ahead and my movements had been slower than usual.

Fridays, as it happens to be today, are reserved for all-night fights and drunken sex without lube because *real men took it straight.*

But before you feel too sorry for me, I should tell you that Frank, my husband of ten years (and fifteen years older than me), is big in many ways but not in the way that counts for most men.

He's six-foot-five, attractively muscled with broad shoulders, thick thighs, and a mouth as big as Texas, especially when he'd had one too many and the filth to come out of his mouth was enough to make you want to take a three-hour shower.

But I'm the only one who knows about Frank's filthy mouth. The people around town loved him because usually, he's charming and kind. Happy and playful. So *handsome.*

Anyway, down there, there wasn't much going on for Frank. On non-Fridays, he brought the lube to our marriage bed himself, shoved his thin, short penis inside me and was done in record time: eight seconds.

On those days, after it was over, I'd lie next to him with a cock as flaccid as it had been eight seconds earlier and with tears of sorrow falling down the side of my face and seeping into my ears, listening to Frank's snores and wondering how I allowed my life to become what it did.

NO LUBE FRIDAYS was a different matter altogether. There was something about Fridays that got Frank going.

Maybe he was extra tired from the work week. Or maybe it was that all those hours he worked amounted to 'a pittance' as he liked to call it, at the end of the week.

Sometimes I think it starts when he and his buddies got together (Friday night usual) and they all got drunk and started talking about the things that drunk men talk about: whose dick is bigger, how many notches they'd gained on their belts and how lucky Frank was that he got to *bust that pussy* every night.

It's a term I've gotten used to over the years. I've even begun to suspect that Frank secretly enjoyed being teased like that.

I may *look* like I *get my pussy busted* every night with my five foot eight frame and looking like every pretty boy ever, but I'm the opposite of Frank in one particular way. I'm small in most ways except one.

If you can imagine it, picture Frank towering over me in the shower (the top of my head not even reaching his shoulder).

He's hard and I'm flaccid.

We won't get into too much detail about Frank's disapproval that it takes me more than one second to produce an erection (*you been gettin' your cock hard somewhere else, Axel?* And *you been jerking off by yourself? Disgusting fuckin' bitch*).

Half the time I wished I could tell him if he treated me good, maybe it wouldn't be like this.

The other half of the time I swallowed my sneers, knowing the only reason he's mad is because even flaccid, my dick is bigger and thicker than his fully erect one. Not that I care, but after all these years, after all the poison-filled lies, the bruises, the threats with that fucking gun, and the humiliation, you learn to hold on to anything that feels like power.

When you've been stripped of every teenage dream of love and romance, every hope for a happy future, stripped of every shred of the person you were and thought you'd become, all you have left are the splinters, embedded deep enough to be a constant reminder of all you'd lost even before you could *have* any of it.

It's a dangerous place we've come to, me and Frank. Me, especially. These days, I'm suspicious about his erratic behavior. Some days he's nice, but most days he's just... monstrous. And the nice days have been getting fewer and fewer. *Now* is nothing like *then,* when we first met.

We had what people would call a whirlwind romance. Frank was large and grandiose about how he felt about me, telling everyone who'd listen how much he loved and wanted me. Big promises of loving me for the rest of his life were declared to the church members every Sunday during *Personal Testimony* time:

—*"What are you thankful for this week, Frank?"*
—*"Well, I'm thankful for my wonderful husband, whom I love with all my heart. Taking care of him is such a privilege."*

Then the gifts, big and small. His unwavering dedication to me while I underwent treatment. My mother had been dead for six months. My father was on his umpteenth promise he'd come home after he suddenly disappeared one day when I was ten and I was just... so fucking *alone.*

No one had ever *loved* me like Frank did, so big. Frank had loved me *big.* I'd been *love bombed* and I couldn't get enough.

The town adored Frank for how much he loved me. How much he'd sacrificed for the sick love of his life, even marrying me when I was given a death sentence with the cancer.

Once or twice, I'd wondered if Frank was more in love with the admiration he got from the people around town than he was with me.

But how ungrateful does that make me sound, right? I made the mistake of making a casual joke about it once, and Frank ripped into me about being ungrateful. And after slamming my head into the headboard, he went out and bought me a forty-eight pack box of Ferrero Rochers, which we couldn't afford. All I could think about was the sacrifice he's made to get me the chocolates and I remember how grateful I'd been for that sacrifice.

Two weeks later he bashed my head into the headboard again and reminded me about how much he does for me, and didn't I remember the chocolates he'd gotten me two weeks earlier?

You're so fucking ungrateful, Axel. You could have at least made an effort for all I do for you.

I'd just completed chemo, and sex had been the last thing on my mind. I couldn't even get it up for a few weeks because of the meds.

Then there was the issue of faith. In the beginning, when I was eighteen and on fire for The Lord and I knew I would sacrifice my life for Him the way He sacrificed his life for me, it seemed a small expression of my gratitude to agree to marrying Frank.

You see, Frank wasn't the first man I'd been with. And as a devout Christian, I understood the importance of 'remaining pure'.

Here in our own little forgotten part of America, only two things were intolerable: promiscuity and painkillers. Both were problems we, as a town, were struggling to keep under control. We had a special Thursday night spiritual warfare prayer meeting for these two sins alone.

Gay rights were well received, as long as you remained pure: have only one partner until death do you part, no premarital sex (marriage is encouraged as soon as possible after the engagement), no extramarital affairs (immediate shame and disgrace).

Poor Olivia Dawson, who cheated on her husband with the deacon from the church, ran away in the middle of the night after the whole town found out about it. The deacon stepped down, went on a six month *Daniel Fast* and returned ashamed, but forgiven, and on fire for The Lord. Abstaining from meat and alcohol and generally every good thing you could eat was apparently a great way to get closer to God. *Consecration* they called it. We never saw Olivia Dawson again.

Sometimes, I think about her and wonder if she's happy. Then I wonder what it would be like if I just left one day, never to be seen again.

It didn't matter the iciness sloshing through my blood the day Frank asked me to marry him, turning my body cold as death. I knew that since I was no longer *pure,* it was best that I get married quickly, while someone was still willing to have me.

It was that, and the fact that, at eighteen, I was truly alone in the world. Frank's attention and declarations of love and forever meant I'd never be alone again.

Back then, I never knew your body could speak to you in certain ways. Could warn you about impending doom with icy goose bumps and rocks inside the bottom of your belly. I just knew to look for the still, small voice of The Lord. I'll never have the courage to admit it out loud, but all I ever heard was my own voice inside my head screaming at me to run as fast and as far as I could. Of course, the flesh is weak and can't be trusted, so I banished those thoughts, sending them right back to the pit of hell where they belonged.

Before Frank there was James Hubble. And James Hubble was one half of the reason I was no longer pure.

He was one of those *bad boy* types—cigarette-smoking, class-skipping, rough, loud and popular kind of bad boy. I didn't even really like him to begin with and I don't think he felt any deep connection to me, either. We hooked up in junior year, before the cancer.

I didn't know it at the time, but James had made a bet with his friend, Donny (who was only slightly less bad-boyish than James) that he'd *get that cute little twink with the gray eyes* before Donny did. I also didn't know at the time that being bet on wasn't exactly the way to start a relationship.

Anyway, James and I began dating during the summer. It lasted one-hundred-and-twenty-seven days. And by the end of it, I was so deeply in love with James I became convinced I would die from heartbreak when he broke things off.

Looking back, the only thing I was in love with was the idea that someone was willing to sit in the park across from school and just talk to me for two hours and then kiss me sweetly for a few minutes. James was a good kisser. I loved every minute of kissing him. That, and the other things we did together.

But hold on. I'm digressing.

James had an older brother named Kenny. Kenny worked at the lumber store across the river with Frank. And one day Kenny told Frank that James had told him I had the biggest dick he'd ever seen and even though he topped in every single hook-up, he'd wanted to bottom for me just to experience my cock.

And that my cock was still too big for his mouth, even though he didn't even have a gag reflex. Also, that no one had sucked his dick the way I did.

I didn't even know that I was that good. I mean, it hadn't been *that* difficult to give a little head. I didn't—still don't—get the whole big hoo-haa about it.

Frank and I weren't even together at that time (we knew each other from church and just barely, too) but Frank never lets me forget I was already 'second-hand-goods' when he 'accepted me'. *You remember that time you were sucking James' cock in the park like some whore?*

In my head, I tell Frank it's none of his fucking business the things I did before I met him but, on the outside, I just hang my head and hope he drops it. You see, the butt of Frank's illegally acquired gun is harder than it looks when it's connecting with your cheekbone.

CHAPTER 3
Eli

Seven months and thirteen days.

Will I ever stop counting? They don't prepare you for the counting. Yesterday was seven months and twelve days. Next year this time it'll be one year, seven months and thirteen days. Last year this time, he was still alive. The most alive eighty-nine-year-old to ever live.

Turning away from the floor to ceiling window of my seventeenth floor office, I allow a sigh to escape my clogged throat.

Death should be easier to accept when the person has lived a long, fulfilled, happy life, as my father had. But I don't know a more devastating feeling, knowing that I'll never see him again.

Never again. The finality of it all cuts today as much as it had seven months earlier when my mother and I had watched them lower him into the ground.

Flanked by friends and family, holding us together like glue while we fell apart, mourning the death of a man everybody had loved as their own.

My eyes drift across my office, inherited from my father seven months earlier. His beloved bookshelf is exactly as he'd left it—an old, tattered children's book of fairy tales still lies face down on the third shelf. He often read from this book long after I'd grown up. A way to reminisce about the days he'd read to me when I was a child. Books had been my father's life, after his family and his work.

Trailing my fingers over the oversize oak desk, I bring to remembrance the old days, when I would sit next to him right here, pretending to do important work with his discarded notes and papers, and then at the end of the day he's say, *well done, Mr. Saxon. Good work today.* Not long after that, he'd had to sign those words, and I'd sign back, *Thank you, Mr. Saxon. You're a great boss.*

My eyes settle on a frame on the left wall, a little bigger than the size of a regular piece of paper. It's new amongst the various other frames my father had collected and hung up over his fifty-year reign over Saxon Intel Inc..

Robert Saxon foresaw the need for qualified cyber specialists when computers were still making waves as *new technology* and had dedicated his life to preparing Americans for the kind of cyber security now required to protect our interests in cyberspace.

I studied hard alongside him for as long as I can remember. His *prodigy,* he'd called me so many times as I grew. He had so much faith in me and the need to excel under his instruction fed my obsessive need to study.

Nothing was going to stop me from walking in my father's giant shoes. I'd spent my life growing, learning from him, emulating him.

Slipping my hands into the pockets of my black dress pants, I stand in front of the framed picture in the middle of the wall. This is the only change I made to this office, moving some paintings around to make space for this one.

It's a handwritten note. Wrinkled and yellowed with age at the edges. The fold lines are visible, but the handwriting is still crisp and clear, as it had been twenty-seven years earlier, when it had been written.

You're a good boy, Eli. If choosing children was an option, I'd choose you over and over again.

The words of a father, written on a piece of paper, dated the year I turned five. The year I lost my hearing. *Profound deafness as a result of bacterial meningitis.*

I don't remember much of it, the time I lost my hearing. I have one vague memory of sticking my fingers into my ears and shaking them incessantly. But nothing more than that, no matter how hard I tried to remember. And I *wanted* to remember. Not the time I lost my hearing, but the time when my father had been an energetic sixty-one-year-old and age had not yet become a thing that would tear us apart.

Even when they told me I'd never hear again, I hadn't quite grasped the idea that I would never again hear the rough, gentle voice of my father saying *I love you*, as I had every single day of my life until then.

Never again hear, *why grandma, what big TEETH you have*, followed by a loud *ALL THE BETTER TO EAT YOU, MY DEAR*, and then screams of laughter as a little boy tried to get away from his father's tickling fingers. I mean, I was already nearly five by then and had wanted to move on to other books, but my father loved *Little Red Riding Hood* because then he could make all those growling sounds.

Sounds.

Now I hear them in my head, and when it comes to my parents, in my heart. My ears are now just for aesthetic appeal.

Tracing the calligraphy with my fingers, I reach for the memory of the day my father had written this note. He'd folded it and placed it at the back of a picture frame of the two of us and took it out again for the first time when I was an angry thirteen-year-old, ranting in sign about some hearing idiots at the bowling club who'd laughed when I tried to speak to them with my voice.

Till today I don't know what they'd said exactly, but their pointing and laughing had been enough.

I don't remember what my voice had sounded like, but even if I had, it would have been the voice of a child. I don't know what I sound like as a man. Sometimes I think I would sound like my father.

I still remember all the words from when I was a kid, but practicing them had become second to learning to lip read. My lipreading skills are higher than the average deaf person and I'm better than most at inference and context clues. So lipreading is easier for me than most. Unless the speaker is mumbling or has speech issues, I can lip read with relative ease. Being able to hear until the age of five makes it easier, too.

My internal vocabulary is something to be proud of, but forming words with my voice quickly enough for hearing people is difficult and frustrating. So, even though I *know* the words, it's hard to *speak* them. And hearing people aren't always very patient. It's faster and easier and far less chaotic to navigate the hearing world using sign language. So, I don't speak.

My eyes are drawn back to the framed note. After all my years of study, my life will now be dedicated to filling my father's enormous shoes.

Already, words used to describe him over his fifty years in business are being transferred onto me: strong, calm, diplomatic. Grounded. Empathetic.

But the one I hold most dearly to me is *strength of mind.* He has *strength of mind*, just like his father, they'd said.

That's what I'd wanted of my father's all my life. His strength of mind. Not easily swayed by the outside world. Quick but careful decision maker. Immune to naysayers who said something couldn't be done. In a world where my hearing loss could have placed me at a significant disadvantage, it was this strength of mind that ensured I was never underestimated in business. There is power in silence, too.

The light flickers above me and I turn to the door.

My mother enters.

Five-foot-one in heels, silver hair brushed neatly to one side and touching her shoulders, and a smile that made the whole world right, she defies her seventy-nine years in every way possible.

My mother had the spunk and enthusiasm of someone half her age. Not even a surprise baby when she was forty-seven (and my father ten years older) could have deterred her from running Saxon Intel with my father.

Childless, not by choice and educated despite the obstacles, she was everything not expected of a woman. In a time where women were muzzled and ignored, she rose to the uppermost ranks of a male dominated world, standing alongside my father as an equal. She had been magnificent to watch while I was growing up.

And as of seven months ago, she stands alongside me, supporting me as she had done with my father.

"He was always proud of you, Eli," she signs when she joins me by the framed wall.

"I know," I sign back.

She faces me, using her voice. "Are you ready?"

I nod.

"The last of the promises made between father and son." She smiles, rubbing her palms up and down my arms. "He always wanted to go back, but life can run away with you sometimes."

River Valley, Eastern Kentucky.

My truck had arrived at the airport just outside River Valley about two hours ago, waiting for me. I had already dispatched electricians to the house a week ago to make the house deaf-friendly and a cleaning company has already deep cleaned the place.

A moving truck is already on its way to the tiny town in the middle of nowhere where my father had been born to humble, penniless parents who'd dreamed big for their only child.

Both had died when he was thirteen years old, and my father had been raised by his aunt alongside his cousin, Alberta, who had lived in River Valley her whole life until she became ill and came to live in a nursing home near us.

My father and I planned last year to go back to his hometown and restore the home he'd grown up in with Alberta, so she, too, could see the restored home where her mother had raised both her and my father.

But things don't always go as planned. And sometimes, putting things off for a couple of weeks or months can easily turn into a couple of decades without you noticing.

Alberta passed away nearly a year ago, and then, my father, a few months later. She'd had no children of her own, so she left the house to me.

"Have you sent over the piano and the coal stove?" my mother asks.

I sign, *"Yes."*

JEN SAMSON

The piano and the coal stove had belonged to my father's mother. He'd had it moved when he left River Valley, but he often mentioned that the two items belonged in the coal town of River Valley.

"Aren't you going to go home and change first?" My mother frowns, indicating that she's not just asking. She's scolding.

"No need," I sign. *"Everything is on its way. My truck is already waiting for me."*

"Don't get too lonely over there," she says, switching from scolding to worrying.

"I'll bring back a son-in-law for you," I sign with a grin.

"If I should be so lucky," she signs back, laughing. Then, with a serious face again, she says, "Travel safe, Eli. I wish I could visit, but I'm getting old and traveling isn't easy for me anymore. Come back home if you finish sooner, okay? Your staff will miss you."

"And you? You won't miss me?"

"I'll miss you the most. Take care of yourself and don't spend too much time alone. And don't think too much about things."

"Okay," I sign.

"Have you eaten?"

"I'll eat on the plane."

She somehow manages to bury my six-foot frame inside hers, hugging me tight.

"I love you, Eli. So much," she says when she pulls back. "You deserve all the happiness in the world. Go and fulfil your and dad's last wish; grieve him the way that feels right to you. You deserve to grieve your father, Eli. But I also want you to *live*. Find a husband who'll love you and then be happy with him, my son. I love you, Eli."

"I love you too, Mom," I sign and pull her back for a hug.

24

I'm grateful for the family I have. For the life I have. I have wanted for nothing. I've been loved and cherished and guided my entire life, and I am grateful for the privilege I'd been born into.

It's true that I'm struggling with expressing the extent of my devastation. To adequately describe just how shattered I am for the loss of my father.

I have so much to be grateful for. It seems unfair that I should ask for more. It seems selfish to wish for just one more day with him after the life I'd lived alongside him.

I've been given so much. How could I ask for more?

CHAPTER 4
Axel

My musings about my life, my town and my (almost non-existent) future are periodically interrupted by flashes of the new resident's face stealing through my mind.

"Axel, dear, you'd better hurry and get inside. We haven't had a storm like this in thirty years." My next-door neighbor pulls me out of my runaway thoughts with her worried tone. I set down my axe and give her my biggest smile.

Elizabeth Dalton, a rising star in Hollywood during the eighties, and who, to her eternal regret, chose a husband over her career, peers at me from under her white woolen hat.

"I'm almost done, Mrs. Dalton." (Thankfully, otherwise she'd have stood out here in this cold to keep me company).

"You got yourself some nice warm pants?" she asks.

"Yes, Mrs. Dalton."

It may have seemed like an odd thing to ask, but do you know that saying about neighbors being your *first family*? I can't remember the exact words, but it means that if you were ever in trouble, it was your neighbor who would be the first to help you, since they're the closest.

Mrs. Dalton's question is very valid. She's the one who gave me the idea for the double and triple layering about two years ago.

She knew the drill. Not just from watching me and Frank for several years, but because we'd watched her and Mr. Dalton for the same amount of years, too.

Mr. Dalton hit his wife regularly right until the day he died. The last hit meant for Mrs. Dalton's delicate face had frozen mid-air, while Mr. Dalton's heart pumped for the very last time.

"Axel, darling, why don't you just leave? Run away where no one knows you. Start a new life. Find someone who will love you so much you'd die for them," she'd said one time.

I would've smiled that day if it hadn't been for the unbearable sting coming from my split bottom lip. Mrs. Dalton was a hopeless romantic.

"He said it was the last time." I'd spoken straight out of the *Most Unconvincing Excuse For Abuse-Victims* handbook.

With a sigh, she'd filled my cup up again and said, "You need at least three pairs of sweatpants and sweatshirts. We can't do anything about the face—" she'd touched her fingers to the rise of her cheekbone, as if she could still feel the slam of Mr. Dalton's fist— "but the bruises everywhere else are much better if you're well padded."

"I have enough, Mrs. Dalton," I call back now, as if we're talking about whether I have enough sugar, and not about my upcoming undeserved beating. "Four more months, huh?" I say.

These last few months, if you wanted to distract Mrs Dalton from something, all you had to do was bring up the topic of how she's going to be a grandma for the first time in a few months.

"Almost there, Axel, honey. Can you believe it?"

"Time sure flies, Mrs. Dalton. You go on inside, now. This snow is really coming in."

Her head bobs with a quick nod and I head inside with Pepper trudging behind me. She's still so mad at me she won't even talk to Mrs. Dalton.

"You'll be fine," I tell her cheerfully and then try to bribe her with a snack. She turns her nose up and *tick-tick-ticks* to the bedroom. I need to get her nails cut. That *tick-tick-tick* of Pepper's overgrown nails tapping against the floor drives Frank mad.

"And not on Frank's side of the bed, don't forget," I call after her. She stops at the doorway and gives me a short bark. She's talking to me again.

"Good girl."

After washing up, I begin preparations for *NO LUBE FRIDAYS*: Beef stew, still warm, half a teaspoon of sugar to cut the acidity. Wood in the fireplace.

The blue duvet over the red one (*"Fuck, but you weren't this stupid when we got married, Axel. It's blue over the fucking red"*).

Three pairs of sweatpants.

Three sweatshirts.

Four pairs of socks because the heel of Frank's boot over my toes is nothing to joke about, even when I'm wearing shoes. Then, with my heart bouncing off the walls, I move to Frank's side of the bed and quietly open the drawer on his nightstand. It's stupid. I'm alone here. I could yank the drawer open and nothing would happen.

Except, maybe I pull too hard and the loaded gun in there goes off suddenly. I don't actually know if it's loaded. Frank always tells me it's loaded and, well, if ever there was a something I chose to believe Frank about, it would be this.

The small weapon lies inside, like a sleeping viper. Sometimes, I imagine picking it up and burying it in the backyard. I'd never have the guts. Frank would make me bring this house down brick by brick and then build it back up again if that gun went missing, and he decided that I was responsible.

I don't know why I do this every Friday, opening that drawer and looking at that gun. It's not like seeing the gun makes me any less terrified about the possibility that today will be the day Frank makes good on his promise and actually kills me with it.

I curse the gun softly and close the drawer again.

Lastly, and this is one of my many secrets, I slip into the bathroom to lube myself. But not too much because the last time Frank noticed... well, he also has very big hands. Hard and calloused from his twenty-five years of service to the lumber store.

Unfortunately, my face doesn't carry the same toughness. One swing equals a split lip immediately. Two equals a bust-up eye. And then I have to miss church for three weeks because of Frank's obsession with his image.

The bathroom is my favorite place in the house.

If mirrors and showers and linoleum floors could speak, they would tell tales of unstoppable tears and unspeakable anguish.

Only the cascading waters from the showerhead truly understood the brokenness of my heart in those minutes taking us from Friday night into the dawn of Saturday.

There's something else I keep in the bathroom, in the bottom drawer, where Frank usually won't look. I keep old razors and medication in there.

About six months ago, I found a pack of four condoms stuffed into the corner of the couch. When I confronted Frank, he'd just rolled his eyes and said it must have slipped out of Peter's pocket or something.

I hadn't known whether to believe him because it hadn't been the first time I'd found condoms in the house. But it was always the same story with Frank—it must belong to one of his friends. It was a plausible explanation because it really could have belonged to any of the three friends Frank had, especially Peter, who was an insufferable creep.

This last time I found condoms, I hadn't thrown them away like all the previous times.

I don't know why I kept them. Maybe I was some lowest form of a masochist, keeping the evidence of my husband's possible infidelity so I could always have a reminder of how pathetic I am.

They now lie in that bottom drawer with the old razors and medication and I get tested regularly because Frank never uses a condom with me. So far, I'm clean.

I head back to the bedroom where Pepper is lying on my side of the bed. "Good girl." I give her a scratch behind her ears.

Then I check the drawer at the bottom of my nightstand, making sure anything of sentimental value is hidden from drunken, raging hands.

Once I left a Christmas ornament with my and my mom's name on it out in the open. Frank had crushed it under his boot. *Where the fuck is* my *name?* He'd growled the whole evening. And then he held me all night telling me how much I mean to him and how he sometimes gets a little jealous. I'd felt so special. How stupid of me.

The bathroom worked overtime for a lot of weeks after that episode.

Dropping to my knees, I take the old wooden box out. I like to look inside, especially on Fridays, to remember that I had not always been alone. Picking out the handmade beaded bracelet from the box, I close my eyes and reach for that feeling of closeness. Of safety.

Frank likes to tell me my mother killed herself because she couldn't stand to have a cancer patient for a son, but I know the truth. She loved me as much as she could. It's true that I'd *hated* her those first six months after she'd died, but I didn't really.

I'd just been so damn scared.

She'd been addicted to painkillers because that's what happens to people sometimes when their sadness overtakes them.

She thought she could handle the pills that day she took too many. It had been an accident. She hadn't deliberately left me.

Maybe the pain had been too much that day.

Frank may tell me a lot of things and most of them may be true—I look like a *chi-hua-hua* when I'm sick; my curly blond hair is too girly when it's grown out; my father didn't even want me; why bother with finishing school or getting a driver's license if I have a terminal illness *(what's the fuckin' point, Axel, and besides you have me)*.

But this one thing that my mother had left me? I'll never believe that. My father, yes. He definitely left me. He left *us*, me and my mom. And went gallivanting across the state in search of his lost youth or whatever. But my mother never left me. She'd made a mistake. A fatal one, but she never deliberately took those pills to kill herself.

She wasn't much different from most people in River Valley, you know. It's just the way it is around here. People can't afford treatment for mental illness, let alone proper illegal drugs. So, we have a sort of system going.

For example, I have a regular supply of pain medication from my last chemo, which Frank sells to the guys at work for extra money.

The broken public healthcare system allows me to get medication for an illness I hadn't needed treatment for in recent years, and I know that's illegal, but for Frank, it's *good business.*

I can't believe we can actually get away with crap like this and that I actually do it, but I had come to some sort of agreement with the barrel of Frank's gun.

I haven't needed the pills in years (praise Jesus), but I still collect them at Frank's insistence (*what if you need them one day?*).

I once asked Frank exactly that (what if I need them one day) while he sat at the kitchen counter, repackaging the pills. "You've been in remission for how many years now? If you were going to die, you'd have done it by now," he'd replied. I almost felt bad about not dying when he said that.

My mother got caught up in prescription drugs and she just could never get out of it. But she never *left* me.

I replace the beaded bracelet carefully, my fingers grazing the pieces of paper folded neatly at the bottom of the box. Letters my mother had written to me in the early years of my life and during her pregnancy. I think it's common for new mothers to do that sort of thing in the beginning.

Grow up strong and brave, Axel, one letter had said.

Know that no matter what, I'll always be with you.

I believe her, you know. That she's always with me.

The front door creaks open. I shove the box back into the cubicle, making sure my other secret is also hidden from plain sight: a pair of black silk ladies' underwear.

The particular way in which the door creaks makes my heart leap with hope. *No Lube Fridays* usually begins with the front door slamming into the wall behind it. I reach for my shoes anyway, so my toes are covered.

"Axel?"

I detect a slur but still, no door slamming. I leave the shoes and step out of the bedroom, pasting a smile on my face.

Pepper whines softly behind me.

"Hey, you're home." Soft, gentle voice. The way he likes it.

"Something smells good. Better taste as good." Words that begin as a compliment and end as a threat. Only I understand the paralyzing fear from those words.

"Beef stew," I tell him. He hands me his gloves and the evening newspaper. I set them down on the kitchen counter.

"You hungry?"

"Starvin'."

"Blue plates or the white ones?" I ask, watching him from the corner of my eye, praying he'd say blue. His fists clench and unclench. Bad sign. I inhale carefully so it doesn't sound like a 'fed-up sigh' on the exhale. Because *what the fuck do you have to complain about, Axel?*

"Blue."

My out-breath sends relief skittering down my spine. You see, the blue plates were thinner, lighter. And had little impact when flung across the room. Also, I was able to dodge them easily enough. The white plates are large and if I was close enough, like I am now, a cut to my chin is inevitable.

Frank settles into the chair at the four-seater dinette just next to the kitchen.

Clench. Unclench.

Another careful in-breath.

"You remember James?" Frank asks, grabbing his blue plate of food from my hands.

Pepper comes to stand next to me. Frank glares at her. She bit him once when he hit me, so now she has to stay outside when Frank feels like it. Pepper is one of the reasons I spend so much time outside, especially at night. I hate that she has to sleep outside sometimes.

"Get this mutt outside," Frank growls.

Pepper growls back. She has no self-preservation. I stroke her discreetly, urging her to stop.

Thump. Thump. Thump. My heartbeat races out of control. Maybe they did some drugs after work. Frank likes to work up to the beating when he's high on my pain meds and whatever else they mix together. Frank says he's not a drug addict *(don't reduce me to the likes of your mother, Axel)* but I don't know if I believe him.

"Yes, Frank." My best non-confrontational voice, answering both his question and his statement.

"He came by the store this afternoon."

Thump. Thump. Thump.

"Couldn't stop talking about how pretty you are. Get this fuckin' dog outside."

I send a protesting Pepper outside and shut the door. She scratches and whines, but I don't want her getting Frank's boot too.

Sliding into the chair next to Frank, I scoop three medium size hard-boiled eggs into his plate.

Someone might wonder why I chose to sit close to him when it's clearly the most dangerous place for me to have chosen, but you have to understand that Frank is very watchful.

If I sit across from him now that he's mentioned James' name, he'll think I have something to hide. Sitting close like this gives my husband some comfort, knowing that no matter what happens, I'll always be here like a good Christian husband should.

There isn't a correct response to Frank's statement. Nothing I say will be good enough when he's decided that today wasn't going to be my lucky day. Right now, I choose silence. I need more time to assess this situation. To predict the outcome of whatever it is Frank is thinking about.

It isn't by choice that I keep the air trapped inside my chest while I wait for the consequence of my silence. I simply can't breathe.

"You know what your problem is, Axel?"

Silence was the wrong choice.

"You think you're *too* pretty."

I touch the tips of my fingers to his clenched fist. A smile I don't want to give him, a smile he doesn't deserve, touches my lips. "If I'm pretty at all, it's only for you, Frank."

He sneers, nasty and ugly. "You need a haircut. Walkin' around with those curls like fuckin' Goldilocks."

"Okay. Tomorrow. More stew?"

"Not tomorrow. The boys are comin' over." And then, "Yeah. Why is this food so acidic? How many times did I tell you to cut the acid with sugar?"

"I'm sorry, Frank."

"Don't be sorry. Next time, don't be such a dumbass. My money don't come easy. At least cook us a decent meal every now and then. Is that too much to ask for around here?"

"No, Frank." I rise from my chair. "Here, let me try to fix it," I say as softly as possible, while reaching for Frank's plate.

I'm not sure how I'll fix it since I already cut the acid with sugar earlier and if I add more, he'll say it's too much sugar, but I'll think of something.

Frank shoves my hand back. The screech of the chair as he pushes away from the table hurts my ears.

I haven't yet had a plate thrown at me at such close range, not even a blue one, but something tingles at the base of my spine and bile churns sickeningly low in my stomach.

I sit back down, keeping my eyes fixed on the table.
It's *NO LUBE FRIDAY.* Let's go.

CHAPTER 5

Axel

Frank's big, fat fingers sink into my hair, yanking my head all the way back. My skin stretches over my Adam's apple. It's hard to swallow the lump of fear in my throat.

In the absence of the usual stench of alcohol, it occurs to me how much worse it is when he's not drunk enough. That there is an element of *clarity* in Frank's actions. That he *wants* to do this.

"Why do you think James is still talking about your cock after all these years?" Frank hisses in my ear.

"I don't know, Frank."

"You know what your problem is, Axel?" Slobbering words. Spit leaks into my ear.

"No, Frank."

"You think your cock is too good."

He means *too big*. He's just too mad to say it. Before Frank, I couldn't have cared less about comparing dick sizes.

But these last ten years, Frank's hostile obsession with my looks, the size of my penis, the color of my eyes have become unbearable. All the things about myself I can't change have, over the years, become a spark quickly exploding into an inferno of rage.

I hate everything about me now. I wish I had no eyes, since my gray ones, too big for my face, make me look like a wolf in lamb's clothing—innocent on the outside but a *filthy whore* on the inside.

I hate my blond locks, since they make me look like a girl. I should have been born taller than my meagre five foot eight inches.

Lips less pink, so I wouldn't look like I'm wearing makeup because make up is for girls, not real men. I hate the deep dimples that won't stay away, even if I just press my lips together. Even now, they must be on full display to make Frank even angrier.

"Frank, please don't be mad," I beg like a dog.

With my curls still bunched inside his fist, Frank shoves my face into the table. My well-developed reflexes kick in and I miss my still-full plate by an inch, and my nose, this time, remains intact.

"Why not, Axel? You like it when I get jealous, don't you? When I have to be reminded of how you used to suck James' cock."

My cheekbone throbs against the table and my upper lip slides up comically. I can't breathe through my left nostril.

"You like it when I'm like this, all possessive of you, don't you, Axel?"

Tears during a beating have long since dried up, stolen years ago by hopelessness. By *helplessness*. Tears are now reserved for the unjudging toilet seat and all-forgiving shower, where the only one to judge me for what my life is, is me. "Yes, Frank," I whisper.

He eases his grip, but I know the drill. I keep my head close to the table. It takes a second and then it comes. *Boom.* Frank slams my head into the table a second time.

Fear breathes through the pores on my skin, pulsing with anticipation and priming me for the coming onslaught. Alive and alert, my body engaged in full survival mode. My chest closes up, like a demon is sitting right over my heart, sucking all the breath out of my body, forcing me to breathe in short, controlled gasps until the heavy thump of my heart begins to calm down.

It'll be some time before my heart eases itself out of the terror so I focus on controlling my breathing. My finely tuned ears are alert to Frank's movements: the thump of his boots means the gun. The drag of the boots means more of his hands.

Please let it be the drag of his boots, I beg internally.

It is, and my relief is profound.

Still unmoving, I listen for his breathing. Harsh and heavy means the dishes will also suffer his wrath. That's also okay. If he breaks the dishes again, I'll just clean it up when he goes outside for a smoke.

But it's not the breathing that makes me tremble inside my skin. It's the low mutterings that are most dangerous. Like he's having conversations with some invisible person. The low mutterings are the reason for the three pairs of pants and sweatshirts and socks.

Frank once told me that his father had lost his mind. If you look through our house, you'll find the windows barricaded with iron bars. The front and back doors have three different locks.

That's because Frank's father used to think people were coming for them, so he turned this old house into a kind of prison. The big window in our bedroom has been sealed shut for probably thirty years. Only the smaller window on the side works, but that one also has those iron bars. If you came into our house and we didn't want you to leave, you'd be stuck.

I'd begged Frank to seek therapy after things started to change early in our marriage. He just barked at me, saying he was *not* mad like his father.

Now, his low mutterings increase in intensity:

"You little fuckin' liar."

"I'll bet you want James' cock."

"Do they know how fuckin' useless you are? You're like a fuckin' corpse on that bed every fuckin' night."

My toes curl inside my four pairs of socks, instinctively recoiling from the memory of the heel of Frank's boot. God, why didn't I put on my shoes?

My head is still pressed to the table, my mouth dry. Terror snakes its merciless arms around me. Pepper whines from the other side of the kitchen door.

Then I'm dragged out of my chair. My slight frame crashes into the wall. Scrambling to my feet, I swallow lumps and lumps of terror, bracing myself for the first real blow. My hands come up on instinct to protect my face. I can't have visible bruises. Not this week. I'm starting a new job on Monday.

Frank's open palm connects with my ear.

The ringing. God, the fucking ringing. I lose my balance with the force of the hit, sliding across the floor once more.

Just a few more. Then I can beg him to stop. Just a few more before his ego is filled to capacity that he is indeed stronger and better than me. Until he's satisfied that I look as much the useless, cancer surviving corpse of a husband as he thinks I am, lying on the floor like this. So weak I can't take a few hits like a man.

"I'll bet you sucked his cock like a real bitch," he spits above me. Curling my legs underneath me, I keep my head down and take two more open palmed slaps across the side of my head.

It happened more than ten years ago, I want to scream. *And what I did before this marriage has nothing to do with you.* The screams for justice lie trapped inside my chest, fear chasing away any courage I might have been able to conjure up.

Frank pushes his fat index finger into the center of my forehead, forcing my face up and the back of my head into the leg of the chair. A wince escapes my lips, and that earns me another resounding hit to the side of my face.

Head bowed like a pious nun, I whisper as if praying, "I'm sorry. Please, Frank."

"Do you see what you made me do?" Franks huffs, short of breath.

"I'm sorry, Frank." *I fucking hate you.* The screams inside my head drown out the rest of Frank's heaving breaths.

"You always do this, Axel."

One boot lifts. The pain, from memory, registers in my brain and my body before he even strikes. My toes curl inside my socks and this time I can't stop the tears. I feel the excruciating pain even before the heel of Frank's boot comes crashing down on my toes. A howl flies out of my mouth, weak and helpless.

"Why do you always fucking do this, Axel?" He swipes my plate of food to the floor. Beef stew lands on my three-layer sweatpants.

Frank stalks across the kitchen. His breathing has changed.

The scrape of his boots across the floor is calmer. The fridge door whines with the fast yank. Clink of beer bottles. He'll be gone for at least fifteen minutes. Enough time to clean up.

Part One of *NO LUBE FRIDAYS* is over.

I survived. Again. It's all that matters.

I spring into action the second the front door slams shut, holding the tears back and ignoring the pounding in my head and the sides of my face, and the throb of my toes.

First, the food. I scoop the bits of beef and vegetables back onto the discarded plate. Then the gravy, wiping the remaining mess on my sweats and thanking Jesus in quick, short prayers that I don't have to clean up pieces of glass this time.

And once that's done, the toilet seat bears the weight and burden of my sorrows. Locked doors are not allowed for the bathroom, so I cry quickly. It isn't with much effort that the tears fall.

I'm not the choking, heaving sort of crier. If you can imagine it, picture me sitting on my beloved toilet seat, my back rounded with sadness, my temples pounding with rage I'm not allowed to feel or express, and tears dripping down my cheeks while I stare into the light bulb hanging from the ceiling. I don't wipe the tears away. I just sit there, stiff and unmoving, while my sadness and rage fall from my eyes and onto the floor.

And when the time on my phone says my crying time is over, I stand under the shower, letting the spray join my hopelessness. And even that is on a tight timeline.

By the time the front door jerks open again, I'm warm inside the duvet—a false sense of safety—secretly re-lubed and wearing only one set of clothes. Different outfits for different forms of abuse and all that.

Pan lids and plates clink in the kitchen. At the sound, renewed tears fall down the side of my temple and seep into the pillow.

I don't know what I hate more: Frank's beatings or his affection afterwards. Acquiescing to his affection always feels like I'm betraying myself. Betraying all the secret tears.

Like a tape on re-run, Frank enters the bedroom and flicks the light on. The bed dips with his weight on my side. Covertly, I wipe the side of my face. I've cried many tears on this side of the bed with Frank lying next to me, oblivious. But on the rare occasion he's caught me, what I got was a shove between my shoulder blades and *fuck, but you and your crocodile tears*.

Sliding a plate of food across the duvet, he reaches over and runs his finger over my hair and down my face, hooking his index finger under my chin and forcing my face up.

"I brought you food," he says. A smile tips the left side of his mouth upward, gentle and kind.

I ignore the food. "It hurts me when you do this, Frank." This small window of freedom to say how I feel will last only as long as the smile on his face.

"I just get like that sometimes, Ax. I don't know why. Maybe I need therapy, like you're always telling me."

A sliver of hope blooms in my chest. But wait. He's said this to me at least three times in the last few months. Is this another *tactic*? I can hardly think straight when Frank goes from cold to hot to cold again.

"I brought you your food," he says again.

"I'm not hungry."

He reaches over the food and pulls me into a seated position, and shoves the plate on my lap. "I warmed it for you, and I also added some sugar to cut the acid."

With the worst of it now over, I try hard to hold my ground. "I'm not hungry, Frank." My tone is soft but laced with as much sternness as I can get away with while there is still time.

Frank walks around the bed. My eyes track his movement and my heart begins to thump.

Time's up.

I lift a spoonful of beef stew to my mouth, still watching Frank.

With his back facing me, he fiddles inside the drawer on the nightstand on his side of the bed. I chew and shovel more food into my mouth. The stew is sweet. The oddness of the sweet taste mixing with the spice makes me gag, but I swallow it down.

Frank looks over his shoulder. He still has a smile on his face, but it's turned nasty. "What? I'm not gonna shoot you for saying you're not hungry, Axel. I'm not a pyscho."

I don't need to see the gun to know it's sitting on his lap. And I know he's not going to shoot me for saying I'm not hungry. He just knows how terrified I am at the sight of that gun, and this is his way of letting me know who's in charge. He always plays with the gun when I'm 'being difficult'.

I comply. When I'm done, Frank sets the gun back into the drawer and takes my plate to the kitchen. When he returns to the bed, my back is facing him, my body curled in a fetal position, closing up as much of my body as possible.

Frank's arm slithers around my waist, yanking me against him.

"So, the new neighbor. He's deaf," I say. My way of delaying the agony.

"Yeah." He snickers. "I heard about that. Also heard he brought a big-ass piano and what not. The fuck a deaf guy doin' with a fuckin' piano is beyond me."

"I think they can feel the, uh, what is it? Vibrations?"

"Stupid," he mutters.

I wish Frank wouldn't be so nasty about things.

CHAPTER 6
Axel

NO-LUBE-FRIDAYS: Part Two.

I force my body to relax when Frank slides my sweats down my hips. The move is meant to be sensual. I can feel it in the gentleness of his movements. The soft brush of his lips across the back of my neck. The trail of his fingers over my ass and the press of his naked body against the length of mine.

It all makes my skin crawl and I have to grind my molars and take deep, calming breaths to stomach the bile rising up from my belly.

I search my brain for something to turn me on and give Frank the erection he believes he deserves. While Frank's touch eats away at my body and his heavy breathing bears down on my neck, I escape into the deepest recesses of my psyche.

Detached from the things being done to my body, I run away to a place where I'm safe inside the arms of a beautiful stranger. The perfect man made up in my head. Where the touch of this stranger's fingers brings me excruciating pleasure and untold happiness.

I learned this *technique* after coming across some erotic art in Mrs. Dalton's attic one day. Sketches she had to hide away after she got married. Mrs. Dalton's choice of art was *disgraceful*, according to Mr. Dalton.

The sketches were of two men, doing exactly what Frank is doing with me right now. Except, in the sketches, the men were... enthralled with each other. Their passion forever captured in the intensity of their gazes and the lust swirling around them, created by the strokes of a graphite pencil.

Now, as Frank inserts his penis into me, uncaring for my physical comfort, I sink deep into the canvas of my imagination.

My imagined lover, gazing down at me, his eyes filled with awe and love as he gently enters my body. His lips lower to mine, capturing me in a kiss so soft and angelic.

And when he knows I'm ready, he moves inside me with sure and hard strokes. Because even though I crave the sweetness and gentleness of love, my starvation for the uncontrolled wildness of *lust* is undeniable. And with the lover of my dreams, I can have both.

My erection grows with each thrust of my imagined lover, and Frank reaps the benefits. My fury, caused by his grunts of approval as his fingers close around my erection, threatens to pull me out of my secret place but I hold fast to the images spinning in my head and count down the eight seconds needed for Frank to take undeserved pleasure in my body.

It's over.

NO LUBE FRIDAY is over.

Frank rolls over and within minutes, he's snoring quietly. I wait longer still, just to be sure. And when his grunts and half drunk mutterings have subsided, I quietly slip out of bed.

In the bathroom, cleaning up is quick and exiting the house with a heavy jacket, a novel, woolen hat and boots is quicker.

This is the best part about *No Lube Fridays*. After sex, Frank sleeps like the dead.

My feet move quickly through the snow with Pepper. I drag a shovel behind me, covering up my footprints. Not that Frank has ever caught me, but I learned not to leave anything to chance, and I know how to, well, cover my tracks. I'm only allowed to go down to the lake to read when Frank says so. It's not that I can't go. I can. But only when he says so.

Like my single lace panty hidden in the bottom of my nightstand, my midnight rendezvous with my books at the lake after Frank's eight second marathon is my secret.

Dropping the shovel at the edge of the property, I step onto the main road, walking briskly down the road and around the bend, with Pepper trotting quietly next to me.

The road leading down to the Johnson house becomes filled with bramble the further in you go. That's because the house sits next to the woods.

Since the arrival of the new neighbor this afternoon, I might be in trouble for trespassing, but Mrs. Johnson had no fencing to differentiate their property from the woods. So, it's hard to tell if the spot near the lake where I'd spent many middle-of-the-nights these past few years belongs to the town or the new owner.

I take my chances.

When I pass the house, a soft yellow light from the kitchen side casts some light onto my path. The light dims as I make my way to the lake, further away from the house.

A boulder sits near the lake and has, in the recent years, come to be known as my *boulder of shame.*

Here, all the parts of me that I hide from Frank can be set free. My dreams of wanting to be loved, cared for. My dreams to play the piano. Of running away from this place.

I hide all my secret wishes from Frank, just like I hide my beaded bracelet and my mother's letters, my single lace panty and every square inch of my heart. Frank can't touch any of those as long as he has no access to them.

Gazing out at the lake, I let my most shameful thoughts run rampant. I watch the gentle ripple of the lake and wonder what it would be like to stand out there with a bottle of Frank's vodka, drink until I can't stand up straight and just accidentally fall into the water. There're some smooth rocks just inside the water's edge. Easy to slip and fall in.

It would have to happen in the springtime. I'd choose the month of May, when River Valley gets the most rain and the lake has swelled.

It would be an accident. I wouldn't just jump in. But if I was drunk enough, I wouldn't be able to save myself. It would be a terrible tragedy.

On my boulder of shame, I contemplate all the ways I might die. How ungrateful I might seem to others, if they knew. I've looked death straight in the eye when I was diagnosed with cancer. I should be grateful to have been given a second chance.

Yet, here I am, wishing every day I could just close my eyes and never open them again.

Only one way to die is unacceptable to me: staring into the barrel of Frank's gun. The deeply hidden rebellious part of me refuses to die at Frank's hand. I would rather fall into this lake during the spring than die just because Frank declared it so.

Tonight I add to my sick fantasy about accidentally falling into the lake, changing the narrative.

This time, something else happens. A pair of strong arms slip around my waist, pulling me back, and out of danger. A soft, soothing voice in my ear, whispering,

I was so afraid you'd fall in, Axel.

What would I do if I lost you?

And then this nameless, faceless lover would pull me deep into his arms, shielding me from the world and telling me over and over how much he loved me. How empty the world would be without me. How wanted I am. How *needed* I am. That my death would mean something to him. I'd be missed. I wouldn't be forgotten.

No longer amused by my morbid thoughts, I switch on my flashlight and open my book.

Eighty-five pages later, when I look back towards Mrs. Johnson's house, the dim light from the kitchen is still on but this time, movement behind the curtains disturbs the still night. I look closer, focus on the outline of a man's upper body.

Heart pounding, I hop off the boulder of shame and creep in a semicircle until I'm behind the big, old Scarlet Oak tree. *What the fuck am I doing?* Pepper whines softly. We don't usually do this.

The side window, which has no curtain and has not had one for as long as I can remember, faces the oak tree. If the man moved into the kitchen, it would be impossible not to get a glimpse of him. I hold my breath, my body engulfed in a thrilling freeze. "Come on," I murmur, excitement building with fascinating momentum.

It's as if he hears me. An unsung melody between us, pulling him to me. A thing without the need for physical hearing. I call him with my heart and he... hears me.

I give myself a hard shake. What melancholic garbage am I making up in my stupid brain?

The man steps into view. His back is facing the window. My chest suffers from the savage beating of my heart.

He's shirtless.

He stands in front of the pantry, reaching up to place two tins of canned food on the top shelf. A swell of pride joins the discomforting bang in my chest. The man could place a hundred tins on that shelf and it would be as sturdy as this oak tree since I was the one who fitted it for Mrs. Johnson about five years ago.

But all thoughts of my superior carpentry skills vanish when he reaches up to place more food items on the shelf, and the ripple of his back muscles causes dips and bulges along his sides and shoulders. Indentations on his lower back. And something happens in me.

It isn't just the whoosh of air exiting my body and refusing to re-enter, leaving me breathless.

It isn't even the burn of my eyes because I can't bring myself to blink, fearing this image might disappear if I closed my eyes for just one second.

It's the unmistakable hardening of my cock at the sight of this stranger that has me reeling back so fast I stumble on some loose rock and land on my ass a foot or two away from the oak tree.

What am I doing? My life must be a dozen shades of pathetic if this is what brings me excitement. Despite the cold, my face is hot with guilt. What was I thinking, ogling a half naked man from behind a tree like some creep?

But there's more than excitement here.

What *is* this? Besides the thrill of breaking some moral rule, there's a sense of ... longing? But for what? I've seen Frank's friends lie around shirtless in our backyard hundreds of times. Not once has any one of them ever inspired such a... reaction from me.

Suddenly, I have the urge to cry.

Inside of a single second, the briefest of time, the story of my life, all twenty-eight years of it—the everlasting cancer, my dead mother, my very much alive father, my marriage, my devotion to a God I'm yet to understand—all come crashing down onto me.

And for one second, the hopelessness closes off the air supply to my body. Chest tight with regret. Stomach unable to contain the rare fury felt for a mother who was stupid enough to accidentally kill herself. For a father who disappeared in the middle of the night. A thousand wishes to have never been born in the first place. A single moment where I see the entirety of my life and all of it, *all* of it, makes me want to wail in despair.

The moment dissipates immediately, as fast as the snowflakes disappearing into the ground the moment it touches the soft earth.

Scrambling to my feet, I dust my hands on the side of my sweatpants. I've been out here too long. It's never happened before, but I can't risk Frank waking up and finding me gone. Pepper jumps, placing her paws on my chest, trying to lick my face. "I'm okay, girl," I whisper.

My feet move quickly and quietly through the path back toward home, determined not to look back. I count my steps to keep myself from turning back.

One to sixteen—up the path.

Seventeen to fifty, the backside of the Mrs. Dalton's vegetable garden.

By step sixty-six, I've lost the battle.

I turn, far enough away to not look like a Peeping Tom but still close enough to catch the corner of the side window.

What carries me home faster than the birds leaving Kentucky for the winter is the absolute devastation crashing over me that the man is no longer by the window.

The disappointment is so frightening and confusing all I can do is race home, focusing on the lingering pain in my toes where Frank smashed them with his boots just less than two hours ago.

And when I lock the door behind me with the stealth of an old crook, and then creep into bed next to Frank like a cheating son of a bitch, logic makes a fool out of my earlier emotional ramblings:

River Valley has not seen a new resident in nearly three years. It's natural to be a little excited over a newcomer. He'll have a dozen residents at his doorstep in the morning with homemade pepper steak pies, piping hot coffee and freshly fried donuts.

And then, he'll get asked to be the guest of honor at the reopening of the fire station next month. He'll be the town's shiny new toy for a while. It's nothing out of the ordinary. Even Pepper had been excited to meet him.

So it isn't just me. I'm not immune to the excitement of it all.

But, as I drop off into sleep with the occasional grunts and farts from Frank's side of the bed, it's hard to explain away my *body's* wildly inappropriate response.

CHAPTER 7
Eli

I haven't been able to sleep much since the death of my father, but being here helps fill the time with a different kind of melancholy.

Here, I search for my father when he was a different man. Not even a man. A boy. It's sobering to imagine how much of life my father had lived before I was born. Here as a child and teenager and then back home, where he created a legacy unmatched for men of his time.

Now, as I walk through each room, I look for signs of life. *His* life. Aunt Alberta was a sentimental woman who kept everything. I hoped to find memories of my father in the weeks to come while I restore this old house.

The house looks as old as it is. Apart from the lighting that's now connected to the doorbell, everything else looks like I'd walked into a nineteen-fifties middle-class home. Even the piano and coal stove fit right in.

The house contains four large bedrooms, three bathrooms, two living rooms and a massive kitchen.

It has the potential to host at least twelve guests if I work the space properly. It's what my father and Alberta had wanted—to have as many people who pass through this small town enjoy their childhood home as much as they had.

A new bed had been delivered along with the piano and coal stove, and installed in the main bedroom.

A quick look outside—it's still snowing. I'm a little tired, so I take a shower, hoping to get some sleep as I crash on the bed with just a pair of sweats.

Four hours later, my grumbling stomach wakes me up. I've slept more than two hours after a very long time.

The fridge produces fresh fruit and beer. The note I'd found on the door lies on the counter:

Welcome to River Valley, Mr. Saxon. Please join us for a welcome breakfast on Sunday at the River Valley Public Library. Our dedicated and wonderful mayor will personally escort you. We look forward to meeting you.

I'm not extremely social, but I appreciate their efforts.

I go to switch on the living room lamps since the light from the kitchen is still very dim (I'll have to get new bulbs) when a flash of light across the property catches my eye.

The snow has calmed down, leaving the outside in a soft blanket of white.

Someone is sitting out there. I can make out the silhouette, but not much else. I leave the lamps off.

Why would anyone be out there in the snow at this hour?

I watch for a while under the safety of the darkened living room and after a while I can make out that he's reading with the flashlight. Every so often, the light hits his face, illuminating it, and I get a brief glimpse of his features.

The third time he does it, I realize it's the neighbor I'd passed on my way in. Curly blond hair. Lean, slight frame. Red, red lips and beautiful dimples.

He sits far back on the boulder, his back against the trunk of the tree, hunched over. His dog sits next to him on the boulder.

This town is nothing like I'd imagined. I might even go to this welcome party tomorrow, although I'm almost sure I wouldn't be given a choice in the matter, anyway. The people here seem a little... enthusiastic.

I stand at the window and suddenly he looks up and right at the house. It's dark enough, so I'm confident he can't see anything, but I still take a step back.

I'm not sure what just happened, but there's a curiosity here that feels... comforting. It's new but not unwanted.

Leaving the light off, I head to the kitchen and look for the pantry and find it in the corner of the kitchen next to the window. I must make a note to have a blind installed on that window.

I find every kind of non-perishable item of food in the pantry. So well stocked by the housekeeping staff that they didn't find space for the ones still on the counter. I reach for the remaining tins of canned food and place them on the uppermost shelves.

There's nothing here I feel like eating. I was told Uber Eats doesn't come this far out, so cooking for myself is going to be the way for now. I don't think I've cooked a day in my life, but trying new things and all that, right?

Hold on a second. I'm *freezing*. Oh. No shirt. I switch off the lights and, with a beer in my hand for dinner, I head back to bed.

CHAPTER 8
Axel

The morning after *NO-LUBE-FRIDAYS* always begins with the bang of pots and pans.

Frank wakes up early, fresh faced, well rested and extremely remorseful that, once again, he was forced to react the way he did because 'who asked me to have such a pretty face and make him so jealous that other people still *simped* for me'.

I cringe inwardly at the use of the word *simp* since even I'm too old for such terms, but I sip my coffee in bed silently like a good husband, grateful to have a husband who brings me coffee in bed and who 'doesn't drug it up with painkillers like those other men down under the bridge near the town square'. And can I just let him have a few drinks in peace without 'my past' being rubbed in his face every time?

"The things you said hurt me yesterday, Frank," I say in a neutral tone now. You see, on Saturdays there's no danger, and that is why Saturdays are my favorite days.

Frank spends most of the day making up for *No Lube Friday*. He's usually distracted enough by trying to deny everything to let me get a few words in.

Now he sits on my side of the bed, rubbing my leg through the blanket. Gentle circles. I've come to hate Frank's gentleness. His gentleness, like his kindness, comes at too high a cost.

"What things?" he asks, as if he *truly* doesn't know what I'm talking about. He says it with a smile. And that tells me he *knows*.

But according to Frank, since I never finished high school, and actually hardly ever went to school at all because I was 'sickly', I'm not smart enough to catch and correctly interpret his every nuance. He's wrong that I hardly ever went to school. It had only been senior year.

He thinks his smile means he's innocent.

I know his smile means he knows he was fully in charge of his faculties last night, but he's really going to sit there and actually act like nothing happened and Saturday is the only day of the week I can speak my mind.

"You said I was useless and a corpse in bed." Among other things, but I choose the best ones.

Another grin meant to make me feel stupid. "No, I didn't say that. You heard it wrong. I would never say that to you."

"You did say it, Frank. You could just say sorry, you know."

"Okay. If that's what you heard, then I'm sorry. And you know I don't mean anything I say when I have a few drinks."

I finish my coffee and Frank takes the mug from my hand. His movements are gentle, his voice light and upbeat. I take liberties.

"I hate it when you're like that, Frank."

He turns at the door. "Okay. I said I was sorry you misheard me. What else do you want, Ax?"

A tiny edge accompanies his tone. I bow my head. "Nothing."

Frank remains at the door. "What, you're angry now?"

"No." I'm almost shaking with fury.

"You gonna walk around with that long face all day then and make me feel like I'm the bad guy? After everything I do around here?"

The shirtless back of the deaf neighbor flies through my head, a lightning bolt piercing through my conscience. My eyes fly to

Frank, almost expecting him to have looked inside my head and found that last night I had an unaided erection for the first time in a long time and it was in response to a man who is not my husband.

It's enough to force a smile out of my face. Bright and cheerful. "No, Frank," I say. And it's only because it felt like I cheated on him last night, and no one deserved that. Not even Frank.

CHAPTER 9

Axel

I hate the cold, except of course, on Fridays, when I can wear multiple sets of clothes. On ordinary days, I much prefer the sun warming my face while I sit on my boulder of shame, waiting for Frank and his boys to finish watching their game.

Frank has exactly three friends, if you include James' brother, Kenny. The same three friends from kindergarten. You already know Kenny. The remaining two are Peter Gibson, who packed the shelves at the big supermarket in town. Married, with three adult daughters. Straight, obviously, right? Yeah. Right.

Then there's Scotty Scott. Really, that's his real name. Scotty isn't married but after he got kicked out of his mom's house for stealing her high blood pressure medication, he moved in with Audrey Vincent, whose husband died two years ago.

Audrey's two adult daughters left River Valley last year and Frank told me that one of them was pregnant and didn't know who the father was and that's the reason she left. The other one did good. She got an actual job in Ohio and sends money back home to her mom every month. Sometimes I wonder if I could have left River Valley if I'd finished high school. The thought used to sicken me as much as it excited me when I would fantasize about it in the early years of my marriage.

Anyway, 'thick as thieves' Frank and his friends were, all four of them (sometimes, three when Frank got tired of Kenny). An unbreakable bond between *brothers*. Because the blood of the covenant was thicker than the water of the womb and all that. Closer, actually, than brothers. Frank loved his friends and they loved him.

Last Christmas, Peter had drank himself into a stupor after his wife sent him packing for being drunk at nine a.m.. He then decided he wanted to explore a bit of a bi-awakening. With me.

Until that point, I usually hung out with them, watching the game, drinking some beer. Frank watched me like a hawk, so I made sure to always remain sane, never drank too much. Never talked too much with the three.

That day, after Peter, without hesitation or fear, ran his big, fat palm over my ass and squeezed it like he owned it, and then propositioned me right there in our kitchen, Frank threw him out. So, Peter got kicked around a lot that Christmas. Not that he didn't deserve it.

"Don't you have a fucking wife?" Frank asked him. To which Peter just lifted the side of his beardy mouth and said, "Hey, just wanna get a lil' taste of that pretty pussy."

I suppose if he'd just kept his mouth shut, he wouldn't have had to spend Christmas night under the bus shelter.

But that wasn't the worst part.

"Do you have to go around ruining everything, even on Christmas?" Frank had asked in my general direction. I'd looked over my shoulder to see who Frank was talking to, since Peter had already been booted out the front door.

"Maybe if you cut off those fucking curls and wore some collared shirts instead of looking like—"

He waved his hand in the air up and down the length of my body, and that's when I realized Frank was talking to me.

"—like a fucking third grade bitch, then maybe the boys won't look at you like a piece of meat all the time."

I'd stood there with my mouth hanging open. In the first place, I had no idea what a *third grade bitch* was. Maybe it was a term they used from the nineties when Frank was a teenager. But it didn't matter because the message was clear. Whatever a third-grade bitch was, it was the reason Peter had grabbed my ass and asked me if I'd let him suck my cock since everybody always talked about how juicy it was.

My fault. *It was my fault.* My curls, and my sweatpants, which happened to fit my body the way it's supposed to—it was fucking *my* fault.

Peter finally got let back into his house the day after Christmas, but Frank forgave him only after six months.

During those six months, after *No-Lube-Friday*, when Frank was asleep even before he'd fully rolled off me, I'd fantasize about how much Frank must love me to actually choose me over his childhood buddy. Over his *blood covenant brother*. How he threw Peter right out of our house on Christmas day... for me. For *me*. Maybe Frank just needed some time to realize how happy we could be together if he just stopped being so angry all the time. Stopped acting like it was my fault I was born with this face, this body. Maybe he'd go see someone, a professional, about some of his issues.

It turned out Peter wasn't allowed to come back to our house because he owed Frank a hundred dollars and could only get back in the covenant brothers' circle after he paid Frank back.

These days, I make sure there's enough food for all of them and then I escape to my boulder of shame or I remain in our bedroom. It's the only time Frank doesn't check upon me.

"Everything is still warm, but if you all decide to eat later, then you can just heat it up in the microwave," I say as I zip up my parka.

Frank stands in the kitchen doorway. "You don't have to go every time they come over, you know," he says kindly.

The newly developing creases around his eyes soften, and the tone of his voice almost sends me to my knees. I'd give anything for this gentleness, this softness to last more than ten seconds. I'd forgive and forget every blow, every awful word, every bruise if he would be like this forever.

But that's not how it works. Frank is making yesterday go away. He's not sorry. He's bent on making it like it never happened. Since he's being nice *now*, what does yesterday matter? *'Stop living in the past, Axel. You're so pessimistic.'*

It's no use. I know this circle of insanity, this push and pull, so well. He's not asking for me to stay. He's just making sure it's 'not his fault' that I didn't stick around if it comes up later.

In the old days, maybe five years into the marriage, I'd be so shocked by the way Frank treated me, I'd just scream. And not in that *oh stop, Frank* way. I'd scream in that *aaahhhhhh haaaaaaa* way that made you think you've actually lost your mind. Tears streaming down my cheek, snot dripping into my open mouth, I used to just scream into the void.

I don't do that anymore. I hardly ever get angry these days, not outwardly anyway. I'm too afraid I'll go mad again like that and this time Frank would really get me on a video and send it to everyone. But it was his mocking that had got me every time. *Oh my God, Axel, you're acting crazy.* And then he'd laugh. Actually laugh and mimic me. *Aaahhh haaaa.* And then he'd laugh some more.

"It's okay. You guys have fun. I'll take a book down to the lake," I say now.

The book I intend to read is tucked away inside the oversize pocket of my parka. Frank doesn't usually care about my reading habits, but he'd sneered once or twice at book covers with shirtless men on them when we visited the book fair. My reading material today has a picture of an insanely handsome man, thickly muscled upper body and a chest and arms full of tattoos. Yet another thing I hide from Frank.

"I'm glad I let you go up there for some alone time. You're happy I let you do that, right?" Frank says.

Like a betrayal to myself, I answer, "Yes."

Frank shoves his hands into his pockets. "You're not still mad, right? I mean, it's all in the past and I just got a little jealous, right?"

"Right." I grab my book with a discreet cover from the table and shove it under my arm. It's my diversion book.

"And I don't remember saying all those things. I guess you heard it wrong, yeah?"

"Yeah." And since things are calm between us, I take advantage of the situation and say, "Ben wants to have a beer next week."

"You want a beer? I'll buy you some. Don't worry."

"I mean, he wants us to meet up at the bar."

"You don't need all of that, Ax. And if you do, I'll take you. Who else do you need but me, right?"

I'm boiling inside because I can't remember the last time I went to the bar with my best friend. "Right," I say, anyway.

"Why don't you give me a smile?" He steps forward, and it takes a grandiose effort to keep still and not shrivel away from his kiss.

I smile, and save myself by saying, "Don't forget I'm starting my new job on Monday."

He gives me my space again. "Why do you need that job? My money not good enough for you? I don't give you fancy enough things? And I told you so many times I don't like that Ben character."

It's said with a smile. A teasing note to hide the nastiness just underneath. Two shots of vodka would expose the fakery. Luckily for me, Frank won't start drinking until his buddies get here.

Anger and resentment, my ever-loyal companions, rise like devils, but I manage to keep any response trapped inside my mouth. I don't want to reassure him that his money is good enough, even though I know that's what he wants. *Especially* because I know that's what he wants. I don't want to give him what he's asking for.

"Oh, I'm going to get a wall phone installed at the house."

"A what?"

Frank laughs. "I always forget how young you are. A wall phone, Axel. When I was growing up, we didn't have cell phones like you spoiled kids. We had a wall phone. So I'm going to get one installed."

"Okay?" I'm not sure where this is going. And I mean, I'm twenty-eight. I'm hardly a kid.

"So, from Monday, I'll call you every day at six p.m. If you answer, it means you're home from that job you insist on having."

Oh my god, *what?*

"If you don't answer, it means you're not home and *that* would mean you're out doing something you shouldn't be doing."

I've never—

I'm shocked beyond words. "I—I wouldn't—I'm not..."

"I guess I can admit I get a little jealous sometimes. You're so young and beautiful. And here I am, pushing fifty, almost."

"You're only forty-three, Frank," I say softly, hoping he'll drop this ridiculous plan.

He laughs. "That's a long way away from twenty-eight."

"I won't even see forty, probably, so count it as a blessing."

Frank sighs. "Fuck, Axel. Do you have to turn everything around and make it about you? So you had cancer. No need to bring it up when I'm sharing my feelings with you. Fuck, you're so inconsiderate."

"Sorry, Frank."

"This whole wall phone thing. I'm doing it for you. I just don't want to be angry with you, okay? So, if I know you're home, safe and sound from other men and their fucked up minds, then I'll be happy."

I hold my breath, releasing it only when he steps back and tosses a woolen hat at me. "Get back before dark," he says. "You can't read in the dark anyway, and besides, that deaf neighbor... we don't know him. He might think you're a trespasser and with him being all deaf and what not, he might do something."

I'm confused by what he means, but I keep it to myself. "Okay, Frank. But I took a flashlight to read, just in case I get too absorbed in the story, okay?"

He considers my request and, after a beat, nods and pats his cheek with his index finger. *Give me a kiss.* Every cell and atom in my body rebels, but if I'm going up to my boulder of shame with the precise intention of staying there till after dark so I can see the new neighbor, then the least I can do is give my husband of ten years a kiss on his cheek.

As Pepper and I walk, all I can think is, *a fucking wall phone?* I can't fucking believe it.

I'm just curious, like everyone else. It's easy to reason with yourself when you can get lost in the crowd, so to speak. I'm not interested in the rippling of back muscles. Not in the curious indentations above his waistband. *Back dimples.* I have them too. I never understood Frank's fascination with them in the early days.

Now, as I settle on the boulder, I guess I can see the appeal. It's... sexy. The thought makes me choke on my saliva. I'm not saying *I'm* sexy—that's just embarrassing.

Except for James (and even that is a stretch of a comparison), I've never found a single man in this town *sexy.* Back when I used to imagine being miraculously cured of cancer, I fantasized about finishing high school and moving away; about meeting someone who knew nothing about River Valley. Someone who was nothing like us.

I don't know what I'm doing, sitting here trying to get a glimpse of a perfect stranger. The gentle swish-swish of the lake bears witness to my self-inflicted humiliation.

Turning to the page in my book where my grocery store receipt serves as a bookmark, I conclude that, just like everyone else in this town, I am, indeed, *just curious*, and then I put it all out of my mind.

The book I'm reading is called *All the Battles We Surrender.*

After I interviewed for the assistant position at the *Till Books Do Us Part* bookstore last week, Benson gave me a complimentary copy from the new shipment that had just come in.

Third shipment this month for this book, Benson had said. "Might as well let you have a copy of our fastest selling book, yeah?" And then, more seriously, he added, "it's about a guy who has cancer."

"Does it have a happy ending?" I asked immediately. Because that's all I needed from a book about a guy with cancer. I don't care how it happens, I just need for the guy with cancer to get the love of his life and *live*.

Benson hadn't answered me because a customer had walked into the store just then, so I took my chances, hoping this author—Garry Michael, from Seattle who has a background in medicine and academics (he's an actual doctor, apparently)—wouldn't actually let the main character die. Right?

The book is about a couple that had split up over some disagreements about their future. Sawyer goes back to his husband to make things right when he learns he's dying of cancer, before it's too late. I don't know how this book is going to end, but I know I need for Sawyer to survive. I need to see someone like me get the future they dreamed of.

And if this book ends badly, then this author won't be 'skiing or surfing or playing tennis' ever again since I'll find him and personally relieve him of his arms and legs.

I'm nearly at the end when the words begin to blur into the darkness.

I check my phone for any texts from Frank. Nothing. The light at Mrs. Johnson's house remains off.

Maybe Sawyer is going to be okay. Maybe he'll get back together with Hawkins and they'll make it work this time, even if Hawkins is being a complete asshole at the moment.

But... what about me? What about *my* happy ending?

The darkness from Mrs. Johnson's place eats away at me with a ridiculous amount of unease. My boulder of shame feels too small to hold the weight of my troubles. I pull back my tears, resolving to stop reading for a while. I hate the way books make me long for a life, a world different from the one I live in now. I hate getting lost in love stories I can never have for myself. Happy endings, not written in the stars for me. Fantasies that run away with all my secret dreams, only to return with the crushing reality of my life.

When I've pitied myself enough, I wipe my tears, tuck my books into my pocket and make my way home with Pepper.

The cold air is soothing tonight. I keep my head down so my cheeks are not too red when I get home. Red cheeks with overgrown golden locks and dimples and a red mouth isn't Frank's favorite version of me.

You look like one of those dolls, Axel.

You need a haircut. Get a soldier style like me.

No, Frank. I like the way I look when you're not around.

I like the panties I hide from you.

I like my big, fat cock when it's not for you.

When I turn the knob and enter the house, not one of those thoughts enter with me.

Pulling back the bedcovers, I slip into bed and lie next to Frank, listening to his garbled breathing and cursing the day I was born.

CHAPTER 10
Eli

It turns out the people of River Valley have no concept of words like *boundaries*. Or *personal space*. Or *no, thank you*. And they do it with the most incredible amount of politeness and happiness. Sometimes, they're high on painkillers (according to David Shapiro, who we'd worked with after Aunt Alberta's death), but man, they're nice.

So, I graciously accept their apple tarts and cupcakes. The most delicious pasta I've ever had. Freshly squeezed juices. Homemade pastries I've never tasted before. Each container has a label on it with the name of the owner and their address, and a note asking for the dishes to be kindly returned.

Later on Sunday morning, a text comes through from David, saying that the Mayor Harebell asked him to pass on the message that he'd be around any minute to pick me up for the Welcome Party. I text back, asking if I could rather follow with my truck. David tells me I can 'discuss it with the mayor' and that just sounded like code for *no*.

The mayor is a man of round proportions and a kind smile. A moustache that covers his entire upper lip. Graying hair around his head, except on the top (there, it's shiny and smooth).

Mayor Harebell had been briefed regarding my ability to lipread, so he creates all sorts of theatrics with his mouth, letting me know how happy they are to host me for the next few months. And that some of the older folk remember my father from the old days and how sorry they are to have lost one of their own. I thank him for his condolences in sign and he panics, so I type it out for him on my phone.

"It's an honor to have you here, Mr. Saxon," he says dramatically, returning my thanks with one of his own in sign, looking very pleased with himself for it.

I might have taken some exception to the whole thing if David Shapiro hadn't given me the heads up on what to expect.

To the unsuspecting person, one might feel like a circus act passing through the way this town 'welcomes' new people. But if you've been given fair warning, like I had been, you'd see that this is a town starved for life. For anything new. Their enthusiasm is only an expression to be a part of something new and exciting. And renovating Aunt Alberta's old house is about the most exciting thing to happen to this town in years, David had said.

I was told my new neighbor, Mrs. Dalton, who I am yet to meet, went through the same thing in the eighties. She was followed around and showered with all kinds of gifts for months. Until the new pastor came into town from the city. And on it went. And so, here I am, the latest shiny new toy.

I take everything with a pinch of salt and choose to appreciate their hospitality and their intentions and make the most of it while I'm here. This is, after all, the town my father had wanted to come back to for so many years.

It's humbling to see people with so little go out of their way to share what they have with a complete stranger.

So, I ride with the mayor in his '74 Chevy. Sometimes he forgets that I'm deaf, and he speaks while looking straight ahead, and I can't get any of what he's saying. Then he looks over at me, apologizes and focuses on the road again.

The library is small, with a small lawn space at the front. Kids run about with balloons and teenagers huddle together, their faces buried in their phones. Every single one of them waves at me in greeting and I return each one with a smile on my face. And I'm not faking it too. I... I'm genuinely enjoying this. Why don't we have this in the city?

Inside the library, I'm given a seat right at the front, with Mayor Harebell, his wife and their three teenage daughters. I pretend not to notice their mother giving them several side eyes whenever one of them stared at me too long. Sadly, although I can't hear them, I can read their lips very well. *He's gay, you idiot,* the one at the end of the rows says. Apparently news travels fast in these small towns.

After that, I focus on everything else but those three, my eyes roving every now and then across the room looking for blond curls.

I must be in the favor of the gods because not only does he appear, but he does so right in front of me. He comes from behind one of the bookshelves carrying what looks like a bible and places it on the podium. A reed-thin stick of a man comes up behind him. Immediately, I know with his formal pants, shirt and tie, he's the town pastor. I was told this was a gay friendly town, so I don't put my guard up.

The blond boy jogs down the step separating us from the pastor. I can't tell how old he might be. He looks young, but I don't think he's a *boy.*

His eyes lock on mine as he walks, his gaze grabbing me by the throat and squeezing the air out of my body. He's not smiling that friendly River Valley smile. In fact, his eyes—and they're so damn pretty—flick away from mine and back again like a nervous teenager. I follow his movements, uncaring about the fact that I'm openly staring at him. Unblinking, because I find the idea of missing even one millisecond of his face inconceivable.

He shoves his hands into the pockets of his sweats. The movement causes his sweats to stretch in the front enough that I'm forced to look away. But I'm not fast enough. He's caught me looking at his junk.

Well, fuck. What a creep I turned out to be on my first day. I'm not usually like this, but that guy is just so... interesting.

The pastor starts talking, his face turned slightly away from me. A woman—his wife, I assume—sitting on the chair to the side gets up and whispers something in his ear and he casts several apologetic glances in my direction. She sits down again, and he lifts his head high, turns his body so it faces me and says, according to his lips, "Thank you, Mayor Harebell, for letting me open this morning's breakfast celebration. I believe our special guest and our newest resident for the next few months can read lips—"

He looks at me for confirmation. I nod and give him a thumbs up for good measure.

He beams and carries on. I dare not look backwards to see where the blond guy went.

The pastor looks at the crowd. "This is okay, right? He's fine if I talk like this, right?"

When he looks at me again, I give him another thumbs up, but I'm less enthusiastic or impressed this time. It's only the horrified look on his wife's face that allows him an inch of mercy for speaking about me as if I'm not here. The ignorance is unintended but still irresponsible.

With a smile in my direction, he continues with his speech. "Ladies and gentlemen, as you know, River Valley is a town that welcomes all people. No matter where you're from, you'll always feel at home in River Valley."

He pauses and, with a raise of his eyebrows that produces thick lines on his forehead, he seems to ask me if I'm still okay. I'm not entirely sure, so I give him a vague thumbs up.

"We welcome everyone to River Valley with open arms, even the gays—"

A quick glance at his wife's scowl tells all of us she's furious and embarrassed for what her husband is saying up there. The flustered pastor wipes his forehead with his handkerchief and smiles awkwardly at me.

I mean, I must be a double slice of strange and wonderful for this town, being gay and deaf at the same time.

The microphone stops working, it seems, because the pastor taps on the head several times and screws up his face. The blond boy walks up to the front to help him.

I get a good look at his profile while he fiddles with the mike. He's a little skinny but with enough muscle on him to pass as lean. His clothing hangs a little loose on him. I don't know if that's for style or if he really can't find clothes that fit him.

His nose is straight and from here I notice he has freckles on his nose and the part of his cheek I can see. A chin that points out slightly and long, slim fingers. He pulls his lips into his mouth, concentrating, and all that does is bring his pretty dimples out on full display.

He finishes with the microphone and walks back to his seat somewhere at the back. He doesn't look at me when he passes.

The rest of the agenda passes quickly. According to the next speaker, whose name and title I've forgotten (I think she's the librarian, the way she keeps scolding the children for pulling books out of the shelves), sign language classes will commence immediately as of next weekend. A qualified teacher from the neighboring town has agreed to lead the classes. She comes very highly recommended and at least one person from each family must attend. It's the least they can do for Mr. Saxon and could Mr. Saxon please attend some classes to advise on the progress of the learning.

Then, apparently, there's a book fair coming up and could Mr. Saxon please hand out the Benson Bookworm award for this year? I agree because the pressure of the mayor's wife's enormous smile was stifling, and I'd forgotten how to say no. There's also the grand reopening of the fire station later in the month.

I'll have to admit, for people who don't have much, they sure know how to have fun.

We're dismissed after that, and the crowd disperses for some cake and tea. I'm ashamed to say I ate everything on display, much to the delight of the members of the *Mom's Club*, but I drew the line on choosing the best cake. I wasn't about to upset whatever hierarchy might exist in this club.

I look for the blond guy outside while eating a dozen samplings of different cakes and pies. I spot him on the far side of the building and before I could decide my stalking boundaries, I'm already across the parking lot. His shoulders are hunched over and his head is bowed. Another man comes into view. He's massive. Well-built and, well, handsome. The blond man walks up to him and stands close.

I can vaguely make out what the other one is saying. Did he say *can't* or *cunt?*

Something's wrong with this scene. The blond man is standing too close for them to be just acquaintances, and the other man's body language is just too aggressive. He has something bunched in his fist and he shakes that fist in the blond's direction. Whatever is in his hand seems to be the cause of his hellish behavior. After some more spitting out whatever words, he flings the thing in his hand to the ground.

Then, out of nowhere, the other man pulls his hand back and slams it across the blond boy's cheek. The impact is so powerful, the boy spins a full three sixty and smashes into the wall next to them.

I've never in my life seen anyone get assaulted. My father never laid a finger on my mother. My parents never touched me like that. School bullying was heavily controlled and dealt with, so we experienced hardly any physical fights at school.

I'm stunned into a frozen stupor. That someone could be on the receiving end of such a brutal action is shocking. The man stalks off in the opposite direction before I can recover from my shock but I regain my senses quickly enough to make my legs move in the direction of the man just as he picks himself up, also picking up whatever the other man had thrown on to the ground. He's brushing dust from his pants when I get to him.

His eyes round in shock when he sees me. He stuffs whatever is in his hand into his pocket, but not before I see the object of all this inhumaneness.

A pair of black lace panties.

I look away to give him that one second to think I hadn't noticed.

For someone who'd just been hit as hard as he was just hit, there's not a single tear in his eyes. But his cheek where he'd been hit is red, the finger marks from the other man's hand are clear as day.

He smiles at me. A soft, beautiful smile that meets his exquisite gray eyes, and made even more beautiful by the appearance of his dimples. I don't understand how he's standing here, smiling at me like this with a five finger mark on his face.

"Are you okay?" I ask in sign. If he doesn't understand, I'll type it for him.

He's not sure. "Am I okay?" he asks.

I nod.

He glances in the direction the man had disappeared and then back at me. "Yeah," he says.

I reach up to touch his cheek. He jerks back like I've burned him and I drop my hand immediately. *Fuck.* What am I thinking?

"See you," he says, and he brushes past me.

I return to the crowd in search of the other man. And then I find David. "Who is that? I type on my phone, pointing at the man who'd assaulted the blond guy.

"That's Frank Davis. Nice guy."

Nice guy? I only just manage to keep the disgust out of my face.

Then I point to the blond boy. He's now standing next to an elderly woman who looks like a movie star. She looks concerned as she inspects his face. He plays with his dog while he tries to get away from the older woman's inspections. "And who's that?" I ask David.

"That's Axel." His name warms me up inside. Putting a name to his sweet face sends my heart skittering.

Then David says, "Frank Davis' husband."

If you didn't think it was possible for your heart to plummet and rocket to the stars at the same time... well, it is.

CHAPTER 11
Axel

If River Valley was not put on the map a hundred years ago, no one would even know we exist. We'd be these weird cave people out in the middle of nowhere, getting high on painkillers and cheating with the deacon. Not much happens here and so we go big on what we *do* have. For example, a welcome party for our new resident.

My skin pebbles with goose bumps when I think about him. The way he looked at me. But more than that, it's the way he wouldn't *stop* looking at me.

I don't know how much he saw of what happened at the library with Frank, but what else could I have done but smile and pretend it never happened when he showed up? The lace panties were safe inside my pocket by the time he got there.

It's not that Frank had been upset that I like to wear women's underwear sometimes. The problem had been that I hadn't asked for his permission first when I bought the pair. And if Frank was not the center of attention for *everything*, he bashed it down. *You couldn't even ask me how I feel about it, Axel? No fuckin way you're gonna wear them. You're so damn inconsiderate.* It's why I'd hidden it in the first place. I hadn't wanted Frank to contaminate something about myself I'd just recently discovered.

I think the thing that bothers me the most is that he'd found my secret hiding place. It's hard to tell when I'd pay for *that*. I'll need to find a new hiding place. Especially for my beaded bracelet and my mom's letters.

Anyway, we went to the evening church service together after that welcome party and praised and worshipped God like good Christians. I had a hard time because of how many sins I've committed since Pepper chased that black SUV.

I put all thoughts about this weekend away and jog the few steps left to the bookstore.

I'm starting my new job just in time for our annual book fair, an event attended by every single resident for a small entrance fee of one dollar. Besides books being sold, you could buy every kind of beer, wine and spirit with money you don't have, after which husbands went home and beat their spouses for 'being too chatty' with the town folk or for 'acting like snobs with the town folk'. When alcohol was involved, the nondrinkers unfortunately arrived at the same outcome.

Till Books Do Us Part opened fifteen years ago and is River Valley's pride and joy. The story about how it got its name is that Deborah Flannigan quietly divorced her husband when he complained that she read too much. She gained half of their small fortune in the divorce settlement, sent him packing, and opened a bookstore aptly named *Till Books Do Us Part.* There is a rumor that Mrs. Flannigan had kissed the librarian's husband at that year's Christmas lunch and that was the real reason for the divorce but it was never clarified and everybody loved Deborah and her seventeen-year-old daughter, Casey, too much to dwell on it. In any case, it was bad enough that she was a divorcee, so everyone left it at that.

"You're early. I like that." Benson, my best friend, and, as of eight o' clock, my boss, claps his hands when the tinkle of the doorbell announces my arrival for my first day of work.

"Hey, Ben."

Benson throws his arm around my shoulder and pulls me inside the store. "Why didn't we think of this sooner?" he asks.

"Because you needed someone who wasn't going to die suddenly." It was meant to be a joke, but Benson has never been fond of my dying jokes. I give him a playful shove, but he's not buying it.

"That's not funny, Axel."

"Okay, okay. Sorry. Thanks for giving me this job, by the way. I was going to die of boredom otherwise."

"Axel!"

It takes me a minute to figure out I'd done another dying joke. "Sorry."

Benson takes my coat and places it behind the counter. "Okay, so first rule of the job. No death jokes, ever, okay?"

"Okay."

"Do I need to put that in your contract so I can fire your ass if you do it again?"

I hold up my hands. "Okay, okay. God, so serious on my first day, Ben."

"Come on. I'll show you around. I'll manage the front ninety percent of the time, but you'll still need to know how to work the register, look up titles, put in requests for new titles, that type of thing."

I follow him to the back of the store, passing the self-help and religious section. Funny how the books that tell you that you need no one but yourself and the ones that tell you that you're nothing without God sit side by side like that.

"How's that husband of yours?" Ben asks once we're inside a backroom. But he says it like, *herrrrsssbin*, just in case I missed his sarcasm because Ben couldn't care less about how Frank is doing. "Luke said he got employee of the month again?"

Luke is Ben's brother, and he's a supervisor at the lumber company Frank works at.

"Yeah. Last month. He's okay."

Ben faces me with his hands on his hips. "That man can fool everyone else, but not me. What's the latest disgusting thing he's done?"

"He's having a wall phone installed today."

"A what?"

"A wall phone. He said he'll call me every day, so he knows I'm home."

"What kind of controlling bullshit is that?"

"Right?" I make light of it, but Ben won't let it go so easily.

"I hate that fucking guy," he mutters.

I look away because I don't want to encourage another useless conversation about my terrible life. And today isn't about Frank. This job, getting my own money, it's all about me.

Ben gets the hint and swiftly moves on. "This is mostly where you'll work. Sorting through new arrivals, stocking the shelves, removing and reporting damaged books."

His eyes scan my face while he talks, and although he's extremely discreet about it, we've known each other long enough for me to see through his covert inspection. He's looking for bruises.

Luckily, the slight swell from Frank's palms on Friday night had settled down pretty quickly. Can't say much for the bruises on the parts of my body that are covered.

By Saturday afternoon, according to Frank, nothing ever happened. And by Sunday evening, we were like newlyweds singing hymns at church. At least that's how Frank acted. The bruises on my hips are still bad. I'm worried that they're taking longer than usual to heal.

"You know what I wish?" Ben says. He points to three large boxes in the corner. "New *Garry Michael* shipment came in this morning. Put five up by the window, four flat and one standing up facing outside."

I drop onto a chair and get to opening the box.

"I wish you'd have fucked it up properly with James and then left this town before Frank ever got his claws in you."

"This cover is gorgeous," I say, admiring the copy of *All The Battles We Surrender*. I finished my copy at the lake the other day just before I ogled a stranger from behind a tree.

"Yeah, you know who else is gorgeous?"

I roll my eyes and focus on the cover of the book.

"You, Axel. You're as gorgeous as that tattoo covered hunk of meat on that book cover. More, maybe. You could have had anyone."

"The book was good, by the way." I set five copies on my lap. "And are you sure you're not gay?"

"You liked it? I knew you would. And I don't need to be gay to appreciate an attractive man, okay?"

"Yeah, yeah. If you ever want to experiment though—"

Ben raises his eyebrow and a stupid grin forms across his face.

"—don't ever come to me. I'm not your science project."

I laugh when he tackles me playfully. "If I ever want to experiment, you're the *first* person I'm coming to. I don't care that you're married. I'll show you what a nice, young, fresh body feels like."

I shove him away from me. "That was a horrible thing to say, Ben. Take it back." I'm not mad and he knows it, but it still feels awful hearing the insinuation about Frank.

"Stop defending him," Ben says, serious now.

"I'm not defending him."

"You are. You're young and beautiful and kind and sweet. He doesn't deserve you."

"He's not always bad."

Ben rolls his eyes and then moves to the door. "Come on, I'll show you the new gay fiction aisle."

I follow him out with the five copies for the window display.

Ben continues with his speech. "Just because he's sometimes good to you doesn't change the fact that he's an abusive, controlling piece of trash and you deserve better. I don't even know how you got away with taking this job. You usually have to lie if we want to hang out. Being a decent human being is like the most basic requirement. He doesn't get extra points for being nice sometimes."

"Don't say he's trash, Ben." Really, I don't know why I do this. I don't know why I defend Frank.

Ben levels me with a glare. Someone watching us may have become alarmed, thinking we're about to throw hands, but Ben and I have been having this argument for nearly ten years. I understand and respect his concern for me. It's hard to explain my sympathy for Frank when someone points out his bad side. I don't understand it myself.

Ben finally says what he's been trying to say since I walked into the store.

"He isolates you from your friends. I'm lucky I get to see you sometimes. He made you stop playing the piano at church and he *knows* how much you loved playing. He's so fuckin' jealous. He still berates you about James, for fuck's sake, and your phone never stops ringing when we just go down to the bar for a fucking beer. He blows up for no fuckin' reason. And don't think I've forgotten about how he always calls you names. And anyway, what did he say about going to the bar?"

My answer is a sigh.

Ben shakes his head. "The fact that you have to even ask for permission in the first place is fucked up."

I dream every day of running away from Frank and starting over somewhere where no one knows me. But I just... *can't*. I'm totally dependent on him. Without him, I have no home, no one to check on me in the middle of the night if I suddenly got sick. But most of all, the thought of being all alone all over again makes me want to vomit. And if those were not good enough reasons, then that damn gun sure is. Frank isn't shy about telling me he'll shoot me if I leave him.

And then there are those times when he's so good to me.

"You've been through so much, Ax," Ben says. "You fought so hard to just *live*. Why don't you have a husband who *worships* you? Because that's what you deserve. I hate how he treats you."

"Maybe in my next life." My way of acknowledging that my current life is nothing like I'd imagined it would be without directly throwing Frank under the bus.

Ben slaps the back of my head.

"Hey, that was not a death joke. I really do believe in the afterlife."

"Okay, I'll let that one go."

The gay fiction section looks like Disneyland. Not that I've ever been, but I'd imagine it would be as colorful and... happy as this book aisle.

There's a shelf with a sign that says WARM AND FLUFFY. Another shelf says YOU'LL STILL BE CRYING NEXT YEAR. Behind me—

I laugh. Ben throws me a rotten grin. "You'll love everything from there," he says. The sign over the shelf I'm laughing about says NO AMOUNT OF SOAP WILL HELP. SORRY NOT SORRY.

"Guess whose titles go there?" he asks.

"C.P. Harris."

"You know it."

Across the space, near the window, is a display table. Above it is a sign that says, *JamieReadsRomance FIVE STAR READS.*

"You have a bookstagram corner too? That's so fuckin' awesome!"

"Yeah, I did that one for Casey. That girl worships that bookstagrammer so I started stocking her five star reads. Casey's going to make a career out of reading romance novels, I'm telling you."

Ben moves to the calendar stuck to the side wall. "Okay, next up. If either of us needs time off, we'll add a note here. Like, see here—" He points to a date a couple months from now "—I have my exam in a couple months, so I made a note for you." *Ben's entrance exam.* "My exam is late morning but I'll be leaving early so you'll open the store on that day, okay?"

"Okay. I can't believe you're gonna be a whole ass lawyer one of these days."

"Me either," Ben laughs.

There's a tinkle at the door.

"Let's get to work," Ben announces and heads to the front.

When I look up, it's like the world slides into slow motion and I'm in the middle, spinning off my axis at an unearthly speed.

Ben greets the new customer using sign language.

CHAPTER 12
Axel

It's almost like a salute, what Ben does. His right hand touching his forehead and then moving outward.

Eli Saxon repeats the sign. When the fuck did Ben learn sign language? We're only starting classes at the library next week. And how did he miss such an important detail when he gossiped all the juicy details about it to me a few weeks ago?

But Ben's newly acquired skill isn't important right now. From where I'm standing, almost behind the *JamieReadsRomance FIVE STAR READS*, I'm able to study the new customer without feeling like a psychotic creep, since I've already ogled him half naked while he packed his pantry inside his house and possibly before that when Pepper ran off and claimed him as her own, and maybe even at his welcome party at the library.

Now that I'm able to look at him in the light of day without him looking back at me, the most striking thing about him is that he looks like a soldier. A very pretty soldier.

Tall—six-two would be my assumption—straight backed, squared-out shoulders. Short, neat hairstyle, keeping his straight black hair away from his face. And his face—he turns at just the right angle for one second. It's all the time I need to devour every inch of his face and burn the image deep inside my psyche.

Elegant is the only way I can describe his face. A straight nose reddened at the tip from the cold. Square chin. I manage to catch a glimpse of his light eyes before he turns back to Ben, who's now talking.

"What can I help you with?" Ben asks.

Eli Saxon curls his fingers and thumb, then makes various signs. Ben laughs nervously and shakes his head, showing he doesn't understand. The man drops his hand and smiles.

If, at the end of my life, whether it be a month, a year or eighty years from now, I were to think about a moment my world stood still, I'd think about this moment. The moment a stranger parted his lips, tinged pink with lip balm, and smiled at my best friend. A smile that made the room brighter and warmer. One that reached inside some unknown part of me and shook me alive. Like all this time, these last twenty-eight years of my existence, I'd been asleep. Or dead. And now—

My stack of *Garry Michael* books slips from my hands, landing with a loud thump. I scramble to pick them up, cursing internally for the noise, only to realize that the noise wouldn't make a difference.

The man takes his phone out of his pocket, types and turns his screen to Ben.

Ben nods and smiles just as the door tinkles with a second customer. Ben steers the man in my direction.

"This is our store assistant, Axel." Ben points to me. Then, to me, while still facing the customer, he says, "Ax, this is Eli Saxon. Please assist him. He's looking for cookbooks. Aisle seven."

Every feeling crashing through me is foreign. This impossible thump of my heart. The lack of cohesive thought, like when you've had too much to drink and the world suddenly begins to move in slow motion and words are an illusion. The sudden dryness of my throat when he turns his eyes on me.

I get to look at his beautiful eyes again. The color of a tidal pool on a bright day: light, glass-like almost. His lips shine with pink prettiness as they lift upward. And within a space of two minutes, this stranger's smile takes my breath away once again.

He lifts his hand in a wave. I'm not sure what to do so I mimic his action, hoping it means the regular *hello* that it means to audibly enabled people.

He turns his phone screen to me where it says *cookbooks*.

As if being shaken awake from some strange dream, I set my stack of books on the *JamieReadsRomance FIVE STAR READS* table and stupidly move my hand in a *come* action. I hope he'll know what it means, but just in case, I stand there until he takes a step toward me. Then I turn and walk down aisle five and left toward aisle seven, turning back every other second to make sure he's following me.

I know deaf people are capable of maneuvering the world with ease, but to be faced with someone who can't hear you and whose language you don't understand makes me nervous. Like I'll mess it up somehow. I may have googled a few things about it over the weekend.

I stop at the cookbooks section and turn around. Palms sweaty and lost for how to communicate with him, I point to the shelves. He lifts his hand, places his fingers to his chin, and then tips his hand toward me. I fidget, my fingers playing with the hem of my jersey, and smile awkwardly. What does that mean? It could mean *you're an idiot* and I wouldn't know the difference.

I pull my bottom lip into my mouth and glance around like a nervous wreck before returning to his smiling face, and if I'm not mistaken, it's a *playful* smile. He types on his phone and turns the screen to me. "That means *thank you*," he says.

I offer him a smile that says *I'm sorry I'm so stupid* in any language, in exchange for another of his cheeky grins.

"What kind of cookbooks are you looking for?" I ask slowly, making sure my words are perfectly pronounced. I may have spoken louder than necessary, which doesn't make any sense.

He holds both his hands up, palms in a fist with his pinkies sticking out, and then he makes circles with both hands in front of him.

I blink. His smile widens and I swear to God he's playing with me. It's just the way his eyes twinkle. Reaching forward, he grabs both my hands, closes my fists and pulls out my pinkies. Then, he moves my hands in circles like he did a second ago.

I have no idea what it means, but my ignorance is second to the baseline instinct to continue touching him like this. It strikes me like a lightning bolt. Two things send real electrical charges through my body. The first, the feel of this man's big hands engulfing my fists. Warm and hard. But also soft in the way he handles my hands. The second thing is the absence of something important: my wedding ring. I hadn't realized I'd left it at home today.

Both send my mind reeling in opposite directions. Stunned by my response to his touch, I keep my hands up, frozen in the way he left them. He shows me his phone screen. "Pasta."

He puts his phone away again and repeats the sign and, if it were physically possible, his glass-ocean eyes sparkle. A stirring low in my belly, foreign... except it isn't all that foreign.

I know exactly what this is.

I'm fucking married.

I'm also a customer service assistant. This is stupid. No one goes around feeling insanely attracted to a complete stranger just because they got taught the sign for *pasta*. But those eyes. So bright and playful. So transparent it's like you could see right into his soul—or your own—if you got a chance to look long enough. So... not like Frank.

I give myself a mental boot and get on with doing my job. I nod to indicate I understand and drop to my haunches to go through the middle shelf while he looks through the top shelf.

I find one that says *101 Ways to Make Pasta in under Fifteen Minutes*. A hundred and one? Geez, is it even possible to make pasta that many ways?

Eli Saxon chooses three cookbooks, including the one I picked out, and I lead him to the front to pay. He pays with a black card and I watch him leave, wondering why, of all the places in the country, he had to have an aunt who'd once lived in River Valley.

CHAPTER 13
Axel

"You're staring."

My head snaps back to Ben. He has a stupid smile on his face.

"No, I—"

"I don't blame you. There are a lot of reasons to stare, especially from the back."

"Shut up, Ben," I say, hoping he'll drop it because it's true. I *was* staring. "Anyway, where'd you learn sign language?"

Ben hands me my *Garry Michael* pile and I take them to the table at the window while he packs the *JamieReadsRomance FIVE STAR READS* table.

"I learned a few basic words after I heard he was moving into town. You should learn, too, for like, when he comes in here again. We can go to the classes together."

Done with my display, I go to help Ben unpack his box of books. "But you never said anything about him being deaf."

"I didn't? I thought I did." Ben stops and puts his hand to his temple, like a salute the way he did when the customer came in. "This means *hello*." Then he places his fingers on his chin and moves it toward me. "This means thank you or thanks."

"Yeah, let's do the classes together," I say, trying out the ones Ben just showed me.

"He's gorgeous, right?"

Guilt hits me immediately like a bucket of ice cold water. My fingers still tingle from the time he showed me how to sign *pasta*. I know I'm a little naïve and I rushed into a marriage I've regretted since the first moment I said *I do,* but I know right from wrong.

"And he's got such a cool name, right? Eli Saxon. Sounds so... upper class," Ben says.

Eli and Axel. The thought comes from nowhere and I immediately feel for my wedding band, sickness pooling low in my stomach.

Axel Saxon. Too many *x's.* Dread fills my belly, mixing with the sickening feeling already present.

"Not married, no children, no ex in the last two years. Owns a tech company in Louisville, inherited from his dad. They basically work for the government. Cyber security *something-something.*"

"So, why don't they just sell the old Johnson house?"

Ben perches on the table. "According to David Shapiro, his dad was born here, and he had, like, some bucket list with his dad, and one of the things they'd planned to do was upgrade the old house. But his dad died before they could."

"Oh, that sucks. So he's here for like, how long?"

"Not sure. Couple months, I think. You wanna know something else?"

I scrunch my nose up at him. I don't trust that face.

"He's gay."

I have to fight through the electrical surge that begins low in my belly and shoots up to my chest, exploding there and sending my heartbeat into a hundred horsepower sprint. I manage to catch myself in time.

"Okay," I say without commitment.

"You deserve a guy like that."

I laugh. "C'mon, don't start, Ben." I grab the flattened boxes and carry them to the back room. Ben follows.

"You deserve a guy who'll make all your deep, dark fantasies come true."

I dump the boxes in the corner of the room, against the wall. Ben leans against the door frame with a rotten smirk on his face.

"Firstly, I was *drunk*," I say defensively. "It doesn't count. And secondly, you were just as drunk. How the hell do you remember when I don't?"

Ben laughs and mimics my voice. "I want a guy who will fuck me right into the stratosphere. I want him to eat my ass like it's the last meal he'll ever have. I want it dirty and nasty and hot and—"

I pick up a book, aiming at him.

"Hey, hey," he wheezes. "We don't throw books around here."

"Then shut up. I don't remember saying those things and even if I did, I was stupid and young and drunk out of my mind and I just got the green light from the doctor that maybe I wasn't going to die immediately, okay? So, I got a little carried away."

Ben turns serious, and honestly, I prefer him making fun of that stupid drunken incident than when he gets serious about it.

"It was a few months after you got married, Ax. You knew you shouldn't have gone through with it even then. He stole your light, Axel. You weren't like this. Even when we thought you wouldn't make it, even when we thought for sure you were on your last days, you were—you were fucking *alive*. The day Frank came into your life, it was like something worse than the cancer got you. You know, it's almost like you were forced. The Axel I knew would never have chosen a guy like Frank."

Ben isn't wrong. And while my best friend knows every tiny thing about me, who refused to leave my side when I got so sick, there is something—one tiny little thing—Ben doesn't know.

There's a term for it. I learned it on a YouTube video: forced choice. A choice you make because it's the most right thing to do, even if everything in you says it's wrong. The lesser of two evils.

"Come sit by me," Frank had said that night at the park. It was New Year's Eve, and the church had been camping out at the park, going into the New Year with outdoor praise and worship. A bonfire had been going on in the area demarcated for such things, and I'd been on the grass forcing back tears, thinking about my mother.

The weather station had predicted the best snow-less New Year River Valley had ever seen and, being the devoted Christian community that we were, we all made an event out of it.

I should have been at home, sleeping my way into the New Year. My mother was gone. I'd finally gotten a response from my dad on a message I'd sent him on Facebook, telling him I was sick. He'd said he was sorry but he couldn't make it home and that he hoped I'd get better soon. Like I had the flu.

I'd felt so alone.

I shake the memory away, but it persists.

"Hey, Axel," Frank had called again.

I'd smiled and waved him away politely. I'd have been useless company. Frank was a good guy. He checked up on me a few times at church. Even got me McDonald's on two separate occasions when he gave me a ride back home after band practice.

I used to play the piano at church every Sunday until Frank decided that too many people were ogling me from the pews and he didn't like people looking at *his boy*. I'd been shocked at the endearment. I hadn't even been aware there was something between us.

I'm a little ashamed to say I found his attention a little... off putting. He was a good-looking guy—nice and tall, a nice neatly trimmed beard, and all-round nice guy. Plus, he had a good job across the river and one of the nicer houses up on the hill that he inherited when his parents died. He'd told me all about it while we waited in line at the drive thru.

And, I had eaten his McDonald's twice already, so when he'd called me a third time to join him under his blanket at the back of the park, I'd agreed. And then we listened to the reverend deliver his last sermon for the year. Good meat for the seasoned Christians and strong milk for the still-growing ones:

Be faithful to your spouse because only when the sanctity of marriage and family is upheld can the world be a better place.

Cast the devil from the high places and resist his temptation as Jesus resisted in the wilderness. Sometimes the Spirit will lead you to the wilderness to be tempted, the reverend had said, *to test you, but you* must *resist, as Jesus had resisted.*

And:

Your body is the temple of God Almighty, consecrated to God and to the one partner intended for you.

I'd thought back to James then, and wondered why it was so bad that we responsibly enjoyed each other's bodies for a moment in time. Even if we'd broken up, I didn't regret that part. But listening to the reverend, I'd begun to feel that I should have. If James and I had been intimate and we didn't end up together, then we'd *defiled* each other. I didn't think James cared much, but the more the reverend spoke, the more convinced I'd become that James and I should've gotten back together, especially after what we'd done together.

The reverend must have gone on for a while and Frank's blanket had been warm and soft. I'd dozed off and somewhere in that time, I'd gotten myself in a comfortable sleeping position.

It had been this feeling of warmth that roused me from my sleep. At first, it was so good, somewhere between dreams and waking and then—

The unmistakable grip of a man's hand around my cock registered.

I don't know all the psychological words to describe why people react the way they do in these types of situations. On the surface, it seemed obvious what the reactions of a person being violated ought to have been. Scream. Push the person away.

Tell someone.

I'd done none of those things. I'd pressed my eyelids together, made sure not to breathe too hard, and remained perfectly still while Frank stroked my dick.

Over the years, the only explanation I could provide myself with was that I was hard, so I must have wanted it. A fact Frank never allowed me to forget when he was drunk. *Don't act like you didn't want it, Axel. Right there on the grass with Reverend Baker preaching, you got so excited, like some whore. I only gave you what you wanted.*

We never ever talked about how I had never given him permission to touch me in the first place. That I had woken up to his hand in my pants. Unfortunately, I could never explain why I had an erection, so Frank won the argument every single time.

I went into the New Year that year with the reverend's words ringing in my ear: *commit your bodies to the Lord. Your body is the temple of God, not to be handed out to every person that comes along.*

And whatever *purity* I could find in me and between me and Frank became the foundation upon which I began to build my life with Frank. After James, I figured this was as good as it was going to get. That I should be grateful that Frank wanted me.

That *someone* wanted me after I'd defiled myself with James.

Over the years, the fire I'd had for The Lord had been doused and I became suspicious of this Being who we went to church for and worshipped every Sunday.

"Whoa, hey, where'd you go?"

Ben's voice brings me back. I'd even forgotten what we were talking about. But before I can answer, he checks the time on his watch and dashes out of the storeroom like he's being chased by hound dogs.

CHAPTER 14
Axel

I dash out after Ben.

Are we being robbed? Why would anyone rob a bookstore? And anyway, we might be the poorest, most backward town in the whole United States, but we don't have a lot of crime around here.

I stop short when I find Ben slamming the glass door shut and locking it with so much force it's like we *are* being robbed.

Then I catch a glimpse of Casey Flannigan pressing her face and both palms to the glass window. Ben steps away from the door and claps his hands together like he's dusting something off them, looking pleased.

"Dude, what are you doing?" I ask, my head swinging between him and a furious Casey.

"You know what's the first thing I'm gonna do when I take over this place?" she yells.

Ben laughs and points to his ears. "Can't hear you," he sings.

Casey bangs on the window again. We *can* hear her, but even if we couldn't, it's clear she wants to murder Ben.

"I'm gonna fire your crusty ass. That's what I'm gonna do." And then when she sees me, "Hey, hey new guy. Axel, right? I know you from church. You got sick that one time and I was the one who brought you water. Open the door." Her head bobs up and down like there's a spring at the back of her neck.

I remember that time I passed out in church. "That was you? Thanks."

Her smile almost cracks the glass. "See, I'm a good person, right? Tell that big ogre over there."

"Ben, come on," I say, making for the door. "Technically, she owns this place."

Ben hauls me back. "She's not allowed in here. Her mom's— *my boss's*—instructions."

"Why?"

Casey was now on the floor with the back of her head banging against the glass. "Open the door, Ben," she wails.

"She's failing every single one of her classes. You wanna know why? Cos all she does is read. She doesn't study. And last week, she pretended to be sick, so she didn't have to go to her uncle's birthday party—"

"—I would have been sick if I'd gone, by the way," Casey calls out from outside. She's still knocking the back of her head against the window. "So, I saved everybody the trouble and just called it before it happened."

She jumps up and presses her face against the glass again. "And tell me something, Oh, Great Ben, god and gatekeeper of bookstores, when has a birthday party ever been better than reading a book in your bedroom?"

Ben falters. I'm finding this exchange hilarious.

"Okay," he says, defeated. "Okay, but what about your grades? Your mom says no more books until you get your grades up."

"I'll get them up, Ben. Please?"

"She said you need to get them up *first*."

"I just want one."

Ben rolls his eyes at me. "She's lying." And then to Casey, he says, "Which one?"

"Bad Wrong Things."

"You already have that one."

"Not the special edition illustrated cover."

Ben checks that the door is still locked. "The story is still the same."

"Benson Turner, how dare you say something so vile?! I'm going to kill you right now." And then, with the puppiest puppy dog eyes, she tells me, "Axel, please open the door. I just need that one. I already have a place on my shelf for it. Just that one, I promise. Just that one and *All The Battles We Surrender.*" She points to the window display I'd just set up with stars in her eyes.

"Ha!" Ben shouts triumphantly. "You said one." And then to make sure everyone knows he was right, he tells me, "You heard me say she's a liar, right, Ax? I just said it, didn't I?"

"There's hardly a difference between one book and two books, Benson. It's not like I was asking to buy twenty," Casey counters.

"C'mon Ben. Let her in. No matter what, she's still a paying customer."

Casey's smile spreads across the glass. "See, Benson, that's the kind of customer service assistant I want working for me when I take over this place. You—you—I'm gonna fire you. That's the first thing I'm gonna do. And I'm gonna give Axel a nice big promotion to *manager* and you'll be just some bum snorting up fake cocaine under the bridge downtown."

"Wow, Casey. That got dark real quick," Ben says dryly.

"Fake cocaine?" I ask. God, I'm really out of the loop with things. Ben laughs. "Don't ask."

"Hey, Benson," Casey calls out in a sing song voice. "You have a customer."

Ben growls and moves to the door. It's Meribeth Collins, assistant to David Shapiro, from next door. Casey stands so close to

Meribeth you'd think they were two easels stuck together. Ben tries to pry Casey away when Meribeth crosses the threshold, but Casey just grins and slips inside.

"Only one book," he tells Casey grudgingly after greeting Mrs. Collins.

"Mrs. Collins, I have your order ready," Ben says, reaching over the counter for a box. "Three psych thrillers and one Louis L'Amour."

"Any manager recommendations from your *JamieReadsRomance* section this week?"

"Oh yeah," Ben says while his eyes follow Casey as she browses the NO AMOUNT OF SOAP WILL HELP SORRY NOT SORRY section.

He picks up two books from the table and adds it to the box.

While Mrs. Collins waits to pay, Ben snags my attention, and points his index and middle finger at his eyes and then at Casey. *Watch her.*

It occurs to me we'd all still be okay if we had to use signs to communicate with each other.

Casey slides up next to Mrs. Collins. With two books in her hand. Ben smiles at her, but his eyes are shooting daggers. Can't go crazy with an actual customer in the store, I guess.

"What?" she hisses. "I was just looking. I'm not actually taking both." And then she leaves *All The Battles We Surrender* on the side of the counter.

Once Mrs. Collins has paid, Casey moves up, looking between me and the door nervously. I round my eyes, shaking my head. *Don't do it.* I look at Ben. He hasn't seen anything.

Just as Mrs. Collins reaches the door, Casey grabs both books, throws a bill at Ben and sprints after Mrs. Collins. She miscalculates the timing and ends up flying into the glass door and then landing flat on her back.

Nothing can stop this book addict, though. I can barely contain my laughter. She scrambles to her feet, yanks the door open and flies out with Ben hot on her heels.

"You'd better get those grades up, Casey, or we're both dead, you hear me? And you're not getting your change," he shouts. Casey just waves her books in the air and continues to sprint down the street.

"It's that JamieReadsRomance. This happens every single time she posts something," Ben says when he comes back in.

"But you're the one who made a whole table for her," I point out.

Ben gives me a bored look. "Yeah, okay? So? That Casey is going to get me fired."

"Or she's gonna fire you." I laugh.

"One way or the other, I'm screwed then, huh?"

"Looks like it."

"But you'll bring me some good soup when I land up under that bridge, right?"

"Yeah, sure. If I'm still alive."

Ben slaps the back of my head. "Shut up, Axel. You're fired."

CHAPTER 15
Eli

My life falls into a weird yet comforting routine. I get about three hours of sleep, which is a step up from the two hours I've been getting these last few months.

Mrs. Dalton makes me tea every single day at ten a.m.. She brings it to me and we sit on the front porch like two old friends. We don't talk much because she hasn't been able to get around to attending sign language classes because of her bad knee. It's hard to get up the steps, and she doesn't like to be a burden to people if Axel isn't around to help her.

I know all of this because Mrs. Dalton writes me letters along with making me tea. That was in her first letter. Subsequent letters included how her flowerbeds are doing now that winter was in full swing, how much Axel helps her and have I met Axel yet? I answer her questions in each letter with notes of my own.

I learn that her daughter is having a baby in a few months and that she'll be flying to England to meet her first grandchild soon.

As best as she can, she tells me stories about Aunt Alberta. They were, after all, neighbors for a long time.

As for meeting Axel, I simply say yes, but I feed her obvious affection for him, trying to get information about him. The most I've been able to gather is that he is a beautiful soul with a heart of gold, but I'd kind of suspected that already.

Then, there's the weekly check up by the mayor, who's always impressed by the progress I've made with the house, judging by the number of thumb ups he gives me.

I'm the 'honored' guest every Saturday at the library, but I think they've given me the title to make sure I attend sign language classes and assure them that they're doing a good job. They are. Doing a good job, that is. What a dedicated bunch of people. Their effort is endearing.

My days are filled with working outside while the renovators work inside, driving into the town's center for food and supplies and making as much chit-chat with the people as can be allowed between a deaf guy and people who are still learning sign language

Then, apparently, as the newest resident of River Valley, albeit temporarily, I get to help in the celebration of the newly reopened fire station.

"After three years, can you believe?" the reverend's wife says when I arrive early on Saturday morning.

Sign language classes had been moved to the afternoon so everyone could attend the grand re-opening. Everyone had clubbed together to serve food, including me. It wasn't that I was in my kitchen cooking up a storm. I chose the simplest way to solve that problem, and that was to pay for everything. So, out in the back, rows of casserole dishes line up on makeshift tables, already hot and tempting everyone.

After an eternity, speeches are finally done. Some of which I got and some not. I missed some of the speeches because the speakers were mostly facing the other side, but really, the reason was that Axel was standing just in front, off to the side.

I found myself watching him too intently sometimes and had to force my eyes elsewhere. His husband stood next to him, his hand wrapped around Axel's waist. Frank Davis felt like a loud person. His mouth opened too big when he laughed and the playful slaps he gave the people around him—his friends probably—felt large and unnecessary. To my dissatisfaction, people around him seem to like him.

Axel mostly didn't participate in their theatrics, but he did smile at Frank every so often when Frank leaned over to say something to him.

They seemed like any normal couple. Although, I can't imagine anything normal about being slapped across the face, for any reason.

When it's time to officially open the fire station, I do my honorable guest duty and, together with the mayor, I help cut the ribbon with a huge pair of scissors. Everyone claps and Axel stares at me from the crowd below. I return his gaze because I want him to know that I'm looking at him, too.

Everyone cheers when they hear the food bell. It's time to eat. I join the *Mom's Club*, dishing up for the people. I'm in charge of the sticky wings.

It's still early, so most of the residents are sober and sane and in need of a wholesome meal. *Thank you* was last week's word in sign language class, so every single person who came up for sticky wings said thank you in sign, including the smallest kids.

I watch for Axel the whole time. He finally joins the line with two plates in his hand.

Either he is a picky eater or Frank is. By the time he gets to me, one plate is filled to the brim with everything and only enough space for one or two wings. The other contains only a piece of steak, some baked potato and a salad. I watch him as covertly as possible and am shocked to see that the full-to-the-brim plate isn't for his huge husband, but for him.

A smile touches my lips. So interesting. He loves to eat. He sits down next to that Frank and they eat together. My smile slips when I see Frank lean over and kiss the side of Axel's head. And my blood starts to boil when Axel smiles back. A *happy* couple. That's what they look like. They're *both* acting like Frank has never put his hands on Axel. I don't understand it.

Axel comes back twice more for chicken wings. He gives me these quick glances. Uncomfortable, like he's afraid to look at me. I try not to look at him too, so as to not make him even more uncomfortable. It's suddenly important to me not to make him uncomfortable. I don't know why an effort is required at all. We're just neighbors.

The wings are a hit because they're disappearing faster than any of the other food items. Another covert glance in Axel's direction. He's finished with his wings and is getting up. But he's not moving toward the trash can to dump his throwaway plate. I have only a few wings left and a couple of teenage boys are making their way to me faster than he is.

I need a plan. Grabbing a paper plate, I throw five wings onto it, cover it, and set it to the side.

Sure enough, the boys clean out the last of the wings and when Axel arrives behind them shortly afterward, he looks devastated. It's so cute, I consider letting him suffer a little longer, thinking all the wings are finished.

He catches me watching him and, fuck me, his whole face blooms the sweetest shade of red. I smile at him. He doesn't return the smile, but he doesn't turn away either. For one second, everything around me disappears, and it's just me and this strange man. Not a boy, I've since learned, but a man, despite his very youthful face.

I wonder if he feels this invisible pull, too. He looks as transfixed as I feel.

I reach over and pull out the plate of wings and extend my hand to him. He looks at the plate and then back up at me and back down at the plate. For a second, he looks so shocked I become convinced no one has ever dished him a plate of food before. He takes the plate, offers me a rushed *thank you* in sign and without looking at me, rushes off.

I follow him with my eyes. He returns to his husband, this time choosing to sit on a chair where his back is facing me. I can't help thinking how disappointing it is that I can't watch him eat.

And my next thought is how deflated I feel that I did something nice for him, but he won't even look at me, yet he smiled so sweetly for his husband, who hurt him so badly not long ago.

When did I start becoming so petty and unreasonable? It's irrational. Crazy, at best. I don't know where these thoughts are coming from. They're so inappropriate and out of line, I feel my face heat up with embarrassment.

CHAPTER 16
Eli

He comes to the lake almost every night. And every night, it's with a book. I've noticed a pattern: he comes every Friday, usually at midnight. Some Saturdays and at least three times during the week. On Saturdays and weekdays, he's out there not long after dark and he stays late into the night.

I keep the lights off so I can watch him. There's no shame in the darkness.

I have at least one person come by every day to see how my renovations are going. But not him. Never him. My interest in him is odd. I'm not usually so... smitten. My relationships in the past were simply enjoyable. But there were no... feelings... like this.

This excitement to see him come down the path with his dog. The uncomfortable anger when I think about what happened to him on the side of the library a few weeks ago. Uncomfortable because I've never felt this kind of anger before. I'm taking what I saw so *personally*. And then... I just feel so *sorry* for him. But not just pity. More than that.

Sometimes, I imagine taking his face in my hands and looking into his eyes with the hope of finding the thing that draws me to him like this. I could tell you it's his gray eyes. Or the humble way he carries himself. Or the way he looked at me in the library. Or the way he looks back to the house when I'm watching him in the dark. Sometimes his stares become so intense, it makes me want to bring him inside.

Despite these things, I can't provide a decent enough explanation for this interest in Axel Davis. More so because I know to stay away from married men. That's just not something I've ever had the inclination to do. I provide my conscience with several justifications: there's no law against *looking* at a married man; I have no intention of becoming some kind of home wrecker. Although, I'd like to wreck that Frank Davis' face for putting his hands on Axel.

Now, he sits on the boulder, his back rounded, his head buried in his book and his flash light accidentally illuminating his face every so often.

The sudden rapid thump in my chest is in response to my unconscious move toward the front door. And then I don't stop moving. I can't. I need to look at him up close.

I take the path that will let me come up on the side of him. When I get close, he's set his book down and has his phone in front of his face.

His profile is... just fucking gorgeous. How is this man so gorgeous?

He looks up. Maybe my footsteps alerted him and his dog.

I manage a glance at his phone. He's playing some kind of game? There's a piano on his screen.

I lift my hand in greeting. Mine is just a small wave. His is the proper hello they were taught at the sign language lessons on the first day.

He gives me a small smile when I approve of his sign.

His dog is much more extroverted. She circles me excitedly and then rolls over on her back. I drop to my haunches to give her some love.

"What are you up to?" I ask in sign, after I'd rubbed his dog enough. That was last week's lesson. He was there, but he'd left before the lesson was over, so I don't know if he'll recognize it.

He does. He brings his phone close to his face so I can see his lips. "Nothing much," he says. Then, with a worried frown, he says, "Did I disturb you with my flashlight?"

I shake my head and then get my phone so we can communicate faster. *"Are you playing a game on your phone?"* I type.

He shakes his head and then turns his screen to me. It's a YouTube video of someone playing the piano.

"Do you like the piano?" I type.

A nod with another hint of a smile.

"Do you play?"

He holds his hand out, palm facing down, and turns it from side to side, indicating, so-so. "I used to play at church, but that was a long time ago," he says.

"I have a piano. You can practice on it if you want."

His eyes light up and then dim again almost immediately.

"No, it's okay. I have an app on my phone."

But the way his eyes lit up for that one second...

"You should use it. No one else will."

He thinks for a long minute and then, as if he was choosing his last meal before his execution, he nods.

I gesture for him to follow me. When we get to the house, he hesitates at the doorway. His dog trots in ahead of both of us. I love this dog already.

I lead Axel into the living room and point to the piano. He looks like a shy kid in a toy store. Excited, but still afraid to touch. When he just stands there with stars in his eyes for the piano, I grab his wrist and pull him further into the living room.

He pulls his hand out of my grasp immediately, his eyes flying to my face. Then, his face goes red. "Sorry," he says, and then hurries to the piano.

He doesn't sit down immediately. He first inspects it from every side. Runs his fingers over the shiny surface. I stand back and watch him, fascinated by how much I like this perfect stranger. He carries a certain innocence that I find endearing.

He finally sits down and tests the keys. Then his hands move slowly across the keys, playing something. I move closer and place my hand on the top of the piano, palms flat down.

Axel smiles, his eyes on me, and his fingers moving more confidently now over the keys. "Are you feeling the vibration?" he asks, his smile widening.

I nod.

"So cool," he says, looking impressed.

I smile too. I like that I've impressed him.

He closes his eyes, and with languid movements, he plays.

It's a slow melody, thrumming softly against my palm. Almost... sad. It feels like a sad sound. It seems strange to think about it, but I come to the conclusion that perhaps it sounds like him. For all the small smiles and innocence, there seems to be a sadness about him that pulls on something inside me.

I think he plays the same melody twice. The vibrations feel the same.

His phone, which he'd set down on the bench next to him, lights up. He doesn't see it, but my eyes fall on the screen involuntarily. The text notification pops up.

Sweetheart, where are you? There's more, but it's hidden from the notification bar. His phone must be on silent.

He continues playing. I debate whether to alert him to his text. The picture of his reddened cheek that day at the library flashes through my mind and I decide against it. His wedding band, dull against his finger and infuriating, serves as an unwanted reminder that this man is not available.

He finally notices his phone flashing and his mood plummets immediately.

Grabbing his phone, he looks at me, apologizing. For what, I don't know. "Thank you," he says and hurries out of the house with his reluctant dog. I watch him leave, and an unfamiliar heaviness settles in my chest.

CHAPTER 17
Eli

Without realizing it, I've planned my nights around Axel's visits to the lake.

His dog, Pepper, is always with him, so I made sure to get some dog treats the last time I went to the grocery store.

I think he's fallen in love with my piano. When he comes to the lake, he reads for about an hour. Pepper sits near him and waits. Then, I go out to them, give Pepper a treat and the three of us go back to the house so Axel can play on the piano.

Some days he'd rush out like he did the first time, and other days he stays till past midnight.

The routine has become so predictable he even comes by on Friday nights around midnight. It's a strange routine but I know nothing about his life so I try not to make judgements. But one thing is clear: he's always on edge. He might struggle with anxiety because I've also noticed Pepper nudging him or placing her paws on his chest sometimes.

We never, ever talk about his husband. It feels stolen, these moments he comes to play on the piano. But we do nothing else. Nothing's *going on.* He sits at the piano, playing, and I make sure I'm barefoot so I can feel the vibrations, or, I sit next to the piano and place my hands on it so I can feel the sound of his music.

Sometimes, he gets so lost in the music he seems to forget about his anxiety and even Pepper settles down under the bench.

He never accepts anything from me. Not food, not water.

Definitely not wine. Nothing.

One day, I went to get a treat for Pepper while Axel played. When I got back, he had a piece of chocolate in his hand. But he wasn't eating it. He was picking out the nuts from around the chocolate, eating them and discarding the chocolate into the trash can nearby. When he saw me watching him, he'd laughed with embarrassment and I got him an actual bag of nuts from the pantry. He accepted those.

I show him old albums with pictures of my dad. His fascination with the old photos is curious, and he tells me that he's always loved history and when he was younger, he'd read through the obituaries in the newspaper and wonder what kind of lives those people had lived.

He's fascinated with sign language, but not everything he wants to learn is innocent. Last week, he wouldn't leave me alone about swear words. We sat in front of the fire, crosslegged and facing each other, and Axel made me teach him how to say *motherfucker*.

So, I held my palms out facing each other, my index and middle fingers making a V shape and the rest of my finger tucked in. Then, when Pepper came to sit next to me and refused to leave when it was time for them to go home, he told her she was a motherfucker in sign. It left me breathless to watch him laugh his head off for cursing at his beloved dog.

His happiness over learning swear words was so endearing I'd spent the whole week teaching him.

Asshole.

Fuckface.

Fucking cunt

But *motherfucker* was his favorite. Poor Pepper.

It isn't long before I have to come to terms with the fact that Axel's importance in my life is becoming increasingly concerning.

For two people, one of whom couldn't hear and the other was only starting to learn to sign, we 'talk' for hours.

With Pepper sitting quietly beside one of us near the fire if we're inside or at the foot of the boulder if we're outside, I got to learn that he started reading so he could live in another world sometimes. It still helps him escape sometimes, he'd said. I asked what it was he wanted to escape from and he just shook his head and smiled.

I told him about my father, showing him online articles which documented my father's contribution to the protection of American cyber borders.

He'd looked so impressed and then he googled me, which I'm not sure was a good idea. Luckily, he didn't look into articles about previous partners I'd been linked with.

He was most interested in how educated I was. "You're so smart," he'd said. I told him it was all because of my father and somehow I also managed to tell him that I struggled to shed tears over his death. Axel had smiled then, and typed a note on my phone, telling me that the best gift I could give my father was my tears. I saved the note.

Then, he told me he got sick in his senior year, but he didn't tell me what kind of sickness he had and I didn't pry.

His mother had died when he was still in high school and his father had left when he was still a child. He's been married for ten years and... maybe it's my deafness and the subsequent fact that I might be more sensitive to body language and mood changes, but Axel's visible anxiety is disturbing, especially after he mentioned his husband.

And it gets worse with each day that passes after one particular Friday two weeks ago. Two weeks ago, I noticed the first bruise on his cheek and that was when I decided I didn't care that Axel was married.

He was already inside my skin. My fascination with him escalating to a kind of possessiveness that should have had me booking the first flight back to Louisville. Instead, the more I convince myself that I don't get to just embark on an affair with a man like Axel, especially because he's not once given any indication that he'd be willing to cross that line, the less sense it makes that he should be with someone like Frank Davis.

Tonight—Friday night—I watch him walk down the path with Pepper by his side. But instead of turning left toward the house, since it's extra cold today and we've gotten used to the fireplace on days like this, he makes for the Scarlet tree.

I watch him for a while from the window. He passes the boulder and heads to the lake.

He doesn't have a book with him as far as I can see. Or flashlight. Even Pepper seems confused. She stops at the boulder, looking between it and the lake.

My palms tingle. Something doesn't feel right.

Axel steps close to the lake. Too close. There's a smooth rock near the water's edge. Big enough to stand on if you kept your feet very close together, but even then, it's not a good idea. The rock doesn't offer a good grip.

Axel steps on it.

I race out of the house. It takes me less than sixty seconds.

I grab him from behind, my arms gripping him around his waist and pulling him away from the water's edge.

He turns in my arms and that movement changes everything. He doesn't just lean into me. He makes himself small, burying his face in my chest. I think he's drunk.

He's so hidden inside my body it's like he wants to get lost in me. My arms come around him, pulling him in closer. And when he shifts, letting our lower bodies press tightly together, I gather him closer still. Pepper sits obediently next to me while Axel shivers inside my body.

I stroke his curls softly, praying to all the gods to help me ignore the way our hips and thighs are connected, and fighting demons to keep an inappropriate erection at bay.

Axel lifts his head after a long time.

I search his face. I don't know what happened, but I've never seen him—or anyone ever in my life—look so sad. He's not crying. There's just... nothing... nothing but sadness.

I want to kiss him. I want to pour some of the happiness I've experienced throughout my life into him. My eyes linger on his mouth. He follows my gaze, parting his lips. My head drops and I swear to all the gods, for one fraction of a second, he tilts his chin upward. I can almost taste him.

Axel drops his head, ending whatever could have been between us. He takes a step back and the cold air separates us like mountains.

And then he turns and walks away. Pepper hesitates, but eventually, she too walks away.

It may look like Axel has ended something, but it *feels* like he's started something and if he'll let me, I'll be the home-wrecker.

I'll be the bad guy as long as I can take away all this sadness he keeps inside him.

Fuck Frank.

CHAPTER 18
Axel

One time, when I was twenty-six, I didn't shower for a week. Frank gave me money for a haircut, since my hair had reached my shoulders, and I spent the money on books.

My birthday was on a weekend that year and Frank had invited some of his friends over for a get-together to celebrate. It was a little strange to have a birthday party without a cake or a gift. Or a happy birthday wish, for that matter.

All night long, Frank and his friends drank and smoked and talked about all the reasons Frank had married me: I was *cute*. And *pretty*. And *sweet*.

Frank seemed okay about having his friends drone on and on about it, so I accepted their compliments, smiled and laughed with them even.

And then when they were all gone, Frank rearranged my face because *you like them ogling you, don't you, Axel?*

That was the thing with Frank when we were with friends or in public. The very things I was beaten for in private were the things he praised me for in public.

So, after that birthday weekend, I did everything I could to become as unattractive as possible. It was nasty but also liberating in a way, not taking a shower for a whole week. Looking in the mirror every morning and admiring my stress induced breakouts. My chapped lips and the peel of my skin from my recent sunburn.

I wanted Frank to look at me and regret the day he ever met me. I wanted him to lose. He wanted a husband he could show off to people, and I didn't want him to have that. I didn't want Frank to have all the things that led him to me. I didn't want to be pretty for him. Didn't want to be sweet. Or cute. I wanted to be the opposite of everything he thought he deserved to have from me.

I wanted to be all the things he accused me of being behind closed doors and none of the things he praised me for in public.

I wanted to be all the nothingness he accused me of being. All the uselessness. If I was ugly, then I wanted to be the ugliest one of all. If I was worthless, I wanted to be as worthless as they come.

I wanted to embrace this nightmare. Become its loyal companion, so I wouldn't have to be this powerless bystander, watching my life disintegrate before my eyes.

Sometimes, I think about if the cancer came back. I wouldn't tell Frank. I spitefully didn't want him to be treated like a grieving spouse while I lived out my last days in some cancer ward. Because he'd love that. He'd love the attention.

Now, sitting on my boulder of shame, I gather my hair into a bun at the top of my head to keep it off my face while I read with a flashlight in the dark. I rebel at the idea of cutting it.

You see, for someone who's been through the horrors of chemotherapy, your hair becomes a sort of measuring stick. It isn't even about the aesthetic appeal of having thick, healthy long hair. It's simply the fact that you *have* hair at all and that having all this healthy hair meant that maybe I wasn't going to die soon. I don't want to cut it off because I don't know how long I'll get to keep it next time.

Next time... *next time* is like a monster waiting for you around every corner. When will the cancer come back? When will *next time* be the last time? How many lucky breaks do I get before all this hair falls off and never grows back?

And as for that fucking wall phone, it's driving me crazy. Some days I'm home way earlier than expected and I get Frank's call easily. Other days, if I get distracted with the books at work, I barely made it through the door and the phone would be ringing.

My eyes drift across the black water, snaking its way to some distant destination.

Perhaps life is like that, too. No matter what, you just keep moving. Sometimes you trickle along, sometimes you flow with ease. Other times, you gush forward with the momentum of a storm.

Like the pull of the river to the ocean is inevitable, I guess our pull toward death is the same. We think we don't want it. We think we want to remain an endless flow of nothingness, but the truth is, we're all looking for that end, where we can reconcile with some greater part of us. Streams and oceans. Life and death. One is intrinsically a part of the other. And the lesser is always pulled toward the greater.

You might think it's extremely melancholic that I'd be sitting here on my boulder of shame, thinking about all these things. You can call it a benefit to having an illness like cancer. With death walking alongside you daily, it isn't hard to contemplate life in this way.

In any case, I don't want to cut my hair. The last time I refused, three years ago, Frank sat me down and cut it himself. I did so well, hiding my tears, until Frank started sweeping the discarded locks into a dirt tray. Something in me snapped when I watched my hair get thrown away like that.

I got embarrassingly dramatic after that. When Frank went outside for a smoke and a beer with Mrs. Dalton's husband, I dug through the trash, looking for my hair.

Can you imagine trying to pick up hair strands from the trash? It's not easy, firstly, if the strands came apart once it was dumped. Secondly, if the previous night's dinner was spaghetti, which Frank dumped in the trash can because it was too saucy, try extracting strands of hair from spaghetti sauce.

Crying like a baby, I finally gave up and lived with my *soldier style*.

A crunch sounds behind me.

Eli's lights have been off all evening and well into the night. I'd read almost two hundred pages and didn't detect a single movement from there.

I wanted to go over there a hundred times and Pepper has been whining about it since we got here. But the truth is that I don't know how to face him after last Friday. I don't think I would have actually jumped into the lake, but it had been *No Lube Friday* again and after all the time I'd been spending with Eli, the thought of being with Frank had become unbearable, worsened even more still by that one tiny moment when I thought Eli was going to kiss me and how much I'd wanted it.

I turn at the second footfall.

I can't get past this man's striking beauty. In the light of day, like at the bookstore, he's beautiful, like an angel. But now, with nothing but the moon to show me his beauty, he is absolutely breathtaking.

The silver light from the moon glitters in his eyes. His lips, so pink and full, open slightly to release air.

He lifts his hand in a wave. I reflect the hand movement, but something has me frozen in that position. He comes closer and with each step, he steals the breath from my body. I have never laid my eyes on a man as captivating as him.

He points to himself, and then to the boulder, where there is ample space next to me. I nod.

I press my thumb to my ring finger, feeling for my wedding band. Because the depth and height of my elation at Eli being here feels dangerous.

My heart shouldn't jump like this. My stomach shouldn't twist like this. My instant desire to learn his language so I could *talk* to him shouldn't feel this urgent. But I know now what it is to be held in this man's arms and I don't know how to exist without it.

He sits. The boulder is big enough to provide a decent space between us. He takes out his phone, types and turns the screen to me.

You don't want to play today?

I chew on my bottom lip. His eyes drop to where I'm playing with my lip. "Maybe later," I say. Because I'm afraid of myself when I'm alone with him inside his home.

What are you reading?

I'd already finished the novel and had started with the new book before he arrived. I hand the new book over to him, uncertainty laced in my movement. I'm struggling to look at him without staring. He pages through the book and then hands it back to me. He doesn't look impressed. How can a person not be impressed by poetry?

"You don't like it?" I ask, making sure the flashlight provides enough light to my lips.

He shakes his head. "Why not?"

Too depressing.

"It's real life," I grumble while I pick at the threads on my pants.

His fingers, cold at first, and then burning into my skin, lift my chin until my face is lifted up to his.

Eli drops his eyes to my lips, studying them with a frown.

If someone asked me what I would have given for just one moment of a tenderness like this, my answer would have been *anything*. I would have given *anything*.

The catastrophic impact of this gentle touch has me reeling backward, my body unable to contain the easiness of it. My back hits the bark of the tree behind me.

Eli seems a little shocked at the wholly unnecessary dramatics on my part. His hand remains in the air and he looks at me curiously. His expression cuts between reality and all my imagined ramblings, and I realize he was just trying to read my lips.

My face heats up, the burn amplified by the cold night air.

The thing about trying to talk to a deaf person is that you can't hide behind mutterings under your breath or selfish words spoken into the air. You had to look them straight in the eye if there was something you wanted to say.

"I'm sorry," I say, facing him when all I want to do is hide my face.

He shrugs, but the frown on his face remains.

I should leave. I like being here, with him, too much. I'm going to get us both killed with Frank's gun. I turn to leave but he puts his hand over mine, stopping me. Despite my dangerous physical response to this man, I manage to remain calm, even though the feel of his hand on mine has set my heart beating wildly.

He types on his phone. *Don't go yet.*

This is a bad idea. "Okay," I say.

Eli's hand moves from mine upward. His fingers graze the tips of my hair. I try hard, but it's impossible to stop the visible tremble of my body.

It's pathetic, but no one has ever touched me like this. So... gentle. I should turn away, but this tenderness is too much to give up. So foreign to me, but still, it's as if my body recognizes it and lays immediate claim to it.

So, instead of turning away, and with a shaky inhalation, I turn into his hand. He shifts forward until he's close. So close I can see the vapor releasing from his mouth with every outbreath.

His fingers move deeper into my hair, entwining with my locks. Curling thick strands of my hair along his finger, letting it go and then doing it again.

I sit there, stiff as a frozen corpse, but my insides are burning hot as hell itself.

He removes his hand from my hair and I immediately feel the loss. He makes a sign with his hand. I don't know what it means. I frown and give my head a small shake.

He types on his phone. ***Your curls are beautiful.***

Someone else might've been pleased to receive such a compliment. But for me, something happens inside of me that is so fearful, I shake my head vigorously.

No. It's too girly. But how do I tell him that? I don't speak his language. I feel so useless. For some inexplicable reason, I want to speak to him in sign.

He just smiles and nods, countering my denial of his compliment. And then he touches his index finger to my cheek and makes the same sign. *Beautiful.* He thinks my dimples are beautiful.

My eyes drop to his mouth. I reach for my wedding band, rubbing it with my thumb while I watch this man's mouth with fire inside my soul. I'm trapped in a nightmare. Only, in this nightmare, I embrace the demons like old friends. And in fact, it's not a nightmare at all. This is my deepest, darkest dream.

The one I escape to when Frank invades my body.

My cock gathers blood with unstoppable speed and there's no denying my sexual response to Eli. The light of fidelity begins to dim as I fall into this liquid, silky darkness.

Eli watches me for a second, and when I lift my eyes to his, he drops his to my mouth.

Whoever said you need words to say all the things in your heart? Words are not needed. Not for this and not for the unspeakable things that come to the mind of someone about to do something immoral.

Guided by the softness in his eyes and the gentleness of his touch from moments earlier, I shift a fraction forward. My thumb pressed to my wedding band, holding on to it like a punishment for my pending sins, I inch closer to Eli.

He has no wedding band to hold on to, yet he hesitates.

Somehow that makes me want this more than before. I read his hesitation as some kind of loyalty or care for me. That he wouldn't want to cause me to fall. But he doesn't know it's too late. I fell that night when he held me from behind and pulled me away from the water. Maybe even the day Pepper tried to chew the wheel of his SUV.

He stares at me.

Kiss me, I cry silently. He doesn't. And so I reach forward and press my lips to his.

If there was anyone to blame for my sin against God and my husband, it would be me. *I* caused it. *I* made the first move. Eli only shared his gentle soul with me, and I devoured it. And him.

At first, I only just press my lips to his. It's quick, so quick it might as well not have happened. Shock sends me flying back. In one second, I've betrayed God and Frank.

But it isn't enough. One second isn't enough.

Eli pulls me back to him and I thank him internally for not leaving me with only one second of this unspeakable pleasure.

His lips descend on mine, kissing me like no one ever has.

Not even James had kissed me...

... *like this.*

Soft lips moving over mine. His warm wet tongue playing inside my mouth. I kiss him back, tangling my tongue with his, and he doesn't feel like a dirty, filthy sin.

He feels like the most ardent prayer falling from his lips and mine. He tastes like worship being carried up to God by angels.

And I eat. With every moment that passes, I partake and the more I eat, the hungrier I get. The further I fall into this darkness, the easier it becomes to ignore the light of reason. Of purity. Adultery engulfs me like a blanket of lust, and I give in to every single ounce of carnality.

The kiss is no longer a kiss. It bears no resemblance to the tentative, hesitant exploration of moments ago. Eli slips his fingers into my hair with both his hands, anchoring my face between his palms. His grip is firm. Hard. But there's no fear here, like when Frank holds me down. Instead, my body aches for more of Eli's touch.

And so I kiss him back, this man who is not my husband.

CHAPTER 19
Axel

I can't bear this tenderness.

The soft strokes of Eli's fingers across my cheek. The press of his thumb to the corner of my mouth, encouraging me to open wider for his tongue. And then the whisper of his lips along my jaw. I can't bear this.

But it's all I've ever wanted. To be adored like this, even for just one moment. This is all I've ever wanted.

Eli pulls away gently, his hand still in my hair. I try to follow him because the thought of being away from his mouth feels like a death sentence, but he stops me with a soft cup of my cheek.

He makes the sign again. *Beautiful.*

I drop my gaze. What if he's like Frank? What if he's interested only in my outward appearance? I don't value compliments about my looks. My face is the cause of the way my life turned out.

Eli makes another sign. It frustrates me that I don't understand. He makes it again, slower this time, and then picks his phone up from the boulder.

I'm sorry.

My eyes fly to his. Sorry? No. I can't let him take the blame for this. I made the first move. I shake my head. "No, I'm sorry," I say.

A smile settles on his wet lips. Wet with my— I look away again. I wet his lips like that.

Where is the agony over what I've done? Where is the outrage from my conscience? Sitting so close to Eli like this, there's no place for regret. Only... only a need for more.

He feels it, too. Just as I lean into him, unsure of what exactly I want, Eli grabs my face between his palms. His wet mouth fuses with mine once more, but this time, he kisses me like God ordained vows don't sit heavily between us. I'm no different. My cock throbs inside my pants, demanding to explore this new sensation it's being fed.

Is this what a kiss is? Eli pulls me to him until I'm straddling him. The first contact with his erection sends shockwaves through my body. I press into his hardness with mine.

What is this? This... this feeling that if I breathed my last right this second, then this life would have been enough. For just this moment, I'd give up every second of my life before this. I'd break every vow I made for this one moment.

I've never been so hard. So full of need. Never had an orgasm chasing through my body like this, demanding for release.

The newness of it makes me sloppy. I kiss Eli back like I'm eating him. He reaches for my belt and fuck me to hell, I let him. Not only do I let him, I beg him with my body to continue.

To never, ever stop.

But Eli's hands on my stomach, slowly moving down, his mouth on mine... it's too much.

When he slips his hand into my boxers, I've already spilled my seed. I couldn't stop it.

Eli pulls back, his eyes filled with wonder and his fist working my softening cock. My breathing comes in short gasps. Eli brings his semen covered fingers to my lips.

Brushing slowly across my lips and my chin. Then he leans forward and licks across my parted lips. I groan with the salacity of it. Then he slips his tongue into my mouth. I gasp. I've never tasted my own cum before, but I suck my own semen off Eli's tongue now with no consideration for the vileness of it.

Frank and I never did these things.

Frank.

I push off Eli, stumbling as I scramble to get away.

What have I done?

My pants undone and my cock still half hard make me sick. What have I *done?* What if Frank finds out?

Eli stands. He signs furiously, his forehead creasing severely, like he's worried. I don't understand.

All I can do is turn and flee like a coward. Pepper chases after me.

The discomfort in my pants is the last thing on my mind as I half sprint back to our house.

I grab a pair of sweats from the mobile clothes dryer on the porch and reach for the doorknob. The light from the bathroom offers some light into the darkened kitchen.

On the table is a plate of food, covered and next to the plate, a bag of nuts. Bile rises fast through my chest, sitting high in my throat. That bag of nuts usually cost a fortune, so I can have them only every couple of months. Frank knows they're my favorite.

I rush to the bathroom, trying to be as quiet as possible. Frank must be in bed. He must have spent some of the gas money on that bag of nuts.

What have I done?

I study my face in the mirror. Flushed pink. From the race home or the evidence of my betrayal? My freckles stand out like accusing dots. I go to wash my face but—

My hands cupped with water below my chin, I pause. I don't want to wipe away this... this... This what? This evidence? This aliveness on my face? My bright eyes? My reddened, swollen lips? My accusing freckles? It doesn't make sense, this unwillingness to wash away my sins.

Just like I couldn't bear the softness of Eli's touch, now I can't bear to erase the evidence of it.

I let the water fall through my fingers.

Reaching down to remove my pants and underwear, the unwillingness to get rid of the most damning evidence persists. My heart beats a mile a minute. There is no guilt. Fear exists, but not for what I've done. It's for what Frank might do if he ever found out.

I dump my pants and underwear into the laundry basket and then snatch the items of clothing back.

What the fuck is wrong with me?

With a sickening pit in my stomach, I realize I don't want to wash this evidence off, either. How sick am I?

I pull on a clean pair of sweats and, rolling the soiled clothes into a ball, I creep into the bedroom. The closet door creaks. *Shit.* Frank's grinding snores continue without interruption. Like a psychotic fool, I shove my dirty clothes, covered in my semen, to the back of the bottom cubicle, my new hiding place. The evidence of my sins lies next to my single black lace panty and my box of my mother's memories.

And then, I creep into bed, a shameless cheater, rounding my body in a fetal position and facing away from Frank.

Frank stirs. "Axel, sweetheart. You're back," he murmurs. His arm curls around my midsection, pulling me flush against him. I dare not breathe. What if he smells the sex on me? What if he smells *Eli* on me?

"Did you finish the book?" Frank nuzzles my ear.

"Yes," I whisper. Does my voice sound like a cheater? It must. How can it not after what I've done?

"What happened at the end?" Big, rough hands slip into the waistband of my sweats.

"He died."

"That's a stupid story." Frank's fingers close around my cock. His hand feels like a violation. Like he has no right to touch me like this. It was different when Eli touched me. I hate myself. I reach to the nightstand and grab a bottle of lube. I have to fix this. But how, when only the thought of Eli makes my body burn while I lie right here next to my husband?

"They were happy, so I guess it's okay."

"You gotta stop reading that nonsense."

I reach back and press the bottle into his stomach.

"Hmm, what's this?" Frank strokes my growing erection. I don't know if he's referring to the lube or my hard-on, but it doesn't matter. Frank doesn't wait for an answer. He pops the lid off the bottle and slips his lubed hand between us. Within seconds, he's inside me.

This is how it's supposed to be between husband and husband after ten years of marriage. Quiet, predictable sex. A few problems every so often. But all in all, a quiet, decent life somewhere in the world where nobody cares.

But as Frank fucks me, the faceless, nameless stranger in my fantasy begins to take shape. With every stroke of my imagination's paintbrush, his face becomes more and more clear. My mind is wild with this conjuring. So wild, it sends bolts of electrical charges slicing through my body.

Eli Saxon.

Eli Saxon is the one holding me to him, back to chest. Eli Saxon's stubbled chin digging into my shoulder, scraping my skin there. *His* mouth on my bare skin. Biting, sucking. It'll be red in the morning and I'll admire it.

Deep inside my secret mind, in the depths of my secret heart, it's Eli Saxon who is fucking me. It's Eli Saxon's cock inside me. His hand around my dick.

And I come.

For the first time in so many years, my orgasm with Frank is full and satisfying and impressive.

Frank's voice in my ear yanks me away from my beautiful darkness and brings me back to reality. "You liked that, huh?" he says.

Horror engulfs me once more. My mind is a turbulent ocean. I'm an erratic wave, crashing this way and that, capable of creating nothing but destruction.

I'll cut my hair.

Frank doesn't like my long hair. So, tomorrow I'll cut it.

CHAPTER 20
Eli

I don't regret it. Kissing him. I don't regret it.

I'm on my thirty-third variation of *101 ways to make pasta in fifteen minutes.*

I don't regret it. And I don't think he does either. I know he acted like he did, but the way he felt in my arms, the way he responded to me... so sweet and sincere. So unsure but his passion was undeniable.

You made him cheat.

The newly renovated living room listens while I ramble on in my head and eat my spinach and Parmesan cheese pasta.

He's married.

I don't care. Fuck Frank.

I'll find a way to get Axel away from Frank. I'll take him back home. I'll teach him sign language. I'll listen to the vibrations of his music. I'll hold him when he cries about betraying Frank, because I have a feeling he's that type.

And I'll buy him books. I'll buy him so many books he'll still be reading them when he's ninety. He could live in my father's library if he wanted to.

A gust of wind blows out the curtain, as if to disagree with my plans. I get up and close the window. Any disagreements will be shut out in the same way.

I put the dirty dishes in the dishwasher after eating and, while I walk through the house, I think about how big and lonely it suddenly feels. When I got here, I enjoyed the solitude.

I liked walking through the house, imagining my father as a little boy. But now... I want to lie on the couch and talk with someone about books and life and art. Make love on the carpet in front of the fire.

What I want is *Axel*. I'll pursue him until his heart beats only for me. I will selfishly have him, one way or another. And my justification for all of it, all these thoughts so out of character for me, is that Frank Davis doesn't deserve his husband.

I catch a movement outside the kitchen window. Axel, dressed in sweats, jogs along the edge of the property. Pepper trots leisurely next to him.

An evening jog? Is he also having a hard time sleeping? Slipping into my sneakers, I grab my phone and a light jacket and step outside.

Axel slows down when Pepper stops every five seconds to sniff the flowers and pee on every tree trunk. It gives me time to catch up.

He lifts his hand in in proper sign language. I greet him back. *Hello.*

His eyes dart away and back to me several times. After several awkward moments, his lips move. His frown adds distress to his face.

He drops his head and I have to lift his face to mine to watch his lips. "Oh, sorry. I was saying, I'm sorry. About last night."

I smile. His eyes drop to my lips. He's as unsorry as I am, but I've gotten over the mandatory guilt trip. *I'm not,* I type on my phone.

"I'm married." His lips tremble after that declaration.

I nod, indicating that I know.

"I won't do it again."

I nod again. But his eyes devour my face. His lips tell me one thing, but his eyes speak a language we both understand.

His lips are lying. His eyes tell me a hundred truths.

So, I reach over, pluck his woolen hat off his head, releasing his pretty curls, and touch the pad of my thumb to his lips.

They part for me, blowing warm air into the cold.

Pepper nuzzles my crotch. I ignore her.

When I drop my hand, Axel screws his eyes shut and then presses his lips to mine. It's a fraction of a second and not enough time for me to return his kiss. His lips move against mine. I can't read his words—we're too close—but I'm dead sure he said he's sorry.

I watch him scurry away with Pepper, trying hard to hold on to the feel of this man's lips on mine.

CHAPTER 21
Axel

What am I doing? Like a fool on a loop, I ask myself this question all the way to the barbershop in the morning.

Frank had left a fresh cup of cappuccino on the table for me before he left for work and a note reminding me he's on an early shift today because of a swap out with another colleague.

Make us some good spicy pasta, the note had said.

This swap out meant Frank will be on overnight duty on Friday. And *that* means *NO LUBE FRIDAY* would be postponed until the following week.

As I hurry for an early spot at the barbershop, the question bangs around inside my head. *What the fuck am I doing?*

Who goes around kissing strangers like this? Anyone could have seen. Okay, that's not true. If anything, if you were a married man wanting to kiss a stranger, then Eli's property near the lake is the least likely place you'd get caught.

The bookstore opens at nine a.m. today, which gives me enough time to get a haircut.

"Axel, you're up." Harold, the guy who's been cutting my hair since I was a kid, holds up his scissors and shaving machine. Harold is a reed of a man, thin and long, with kind brown eyes and a neatly styled afro. He's almost eighty years old, but no one would ever guess. I think someone fed him water from the fountain of youth when he was born.

I take a seat in front of the mirrors.

"Are you sure, honey?" Harold asks. He always asks. Even when my hair was falling off during chemotherapy and it needed to be shaved, he still asked. I think it hurts him as much as it hurts me to put a pair of scissors to my hair.

"I'm sure, Harry."

He doesn't believe me. "Why don't you go to work and come back in the afternoon? Sometimes, we just need to stew on things a little, you know?"

I almost believe him, but then I remember the press of Eli's lips on mine. The indescribable pleasure that raced through my body. The stench of betrayal entering and exiting my body with every breath.

"No, I'm sure."

Harold scrunches my curls in his palm. "I'd hate to cut off these beautiful curls, son."

"It's just hair, Harry. It'll grow back."

"Why cut it if it's just gonna grow back?"

Honestly, I don't have an answer. But this is the only way to make amends for what I did. I need to renew my devotion to my marriage and hope that no one ever finds out about what I did over there on Eli Saxon's property.

"Last chance, Axel."

"Cut it, Harry." Cut off my curls that Frank hates so much. Cut them because Eli Saxon said they were beautiful and the last time a man told me I was beautiful, I married him and then he changed. Cut them because Eli Saxon touched them with a kind of tenderness that terrifies me.

"Do you want to keep them?" Harold asks thirty minutes later.

"Yes." I want to keep my curls. Harry places a plastic bag on my lap and begins to dust off my neck and shoulders. Yes. I'll take my hair home and every time I feel like I'm going to die of cancer, I'll take out this plastic bag and remember that one upon a time, I used to be healthy, with thick, luscious golden curls.

"You're still a gorgeous boy," Harold says, smiling at me in the mirror. Famous last words by your barber. Harold has ended every haircut I've ever had with those words.

I stare at the mirror, studying my soldier-style haircut. I look like I did when I was on treatment. I look like a cancer patient. *We can't tell if it will work, but we'll try*, the doctor had said the last time. *But we can't guarantee it won't come back.*

At eighteen, being told that if the cancer comes back, I will die, is the best way to marry and remain devoted to the person who held your hand while you were given a provisional death sentence.

You'll get through it, Frank had said. And I did, didn't I? I've been well for nearly ten years. And Frank stayed with me the whole time. So what if he got a little angry sometimes? Everyone is entitled to a few bad days. And besides, if Frank stayed with me through sickness and health, the very least I could do was love and cherish him.

Frank likes my hair like this. I should have had it cut when he told me the first time.

Frank will be happy.

It's my duty to do what makes my husband happy.

"You're fucking kidding me." Ben slams a stack of paperbacks onto the counter when I walk in.

Ben is like a big mother hen, clucking and fluttering and checking everything.

"You said you're never cutting your hair again," he says.

"Hey, be nice to the books," I say lightly, hoping to distract him from starting a conversation that always ends badly.

"I have some money saved up," he says. He rounds the counter and inspects me. "He hit you again, didn't he?" I try to squirm out of his grasp, but it's no use.

"What's this?" He grabs my hand and pulls up my sleeve.

"Nothing." I pull my hand away.

"What's nothing, Axel?" He jerks my hand back. "When did this happen?"

I sigh. This bruise isn't from Frank. I'd genuinely hurt myself while chopping wood. It just hasn't healed. But even if Frank had hit me, I'd have deserved it because I'm a cheater.

"Take my savings. It's enough to start over. It'll be a pitiful start, but at least you'll be free. I can't believe he made you cut your hair again. Does that man just not *get it?*"

"Stop it, Ben," I say softly. I appreciate his concern. His anger, even. "It's not that simple, you know that."

Ben plants his hands on his hips. "I'll come with you. If you get sick again, I'll help you. I'll take care of you." And then, with a drag of his hand down his face, he says, "What is there for you here, Axel? Just go. Be free enough to let your hair grow if that's what you want. Be *happy.*"

I know what he means. Be happy while there's still time. But I'm not... unhappy, right? Maybe I'm not filled with joy for my life, but at least I'm not dead or something. I'm just... nothing.

"Even if it were possible, Ben, I'd never take your money or ask you to leave your home just because Frank gets out of hand sometimes. Besides, he didn't make me do it."

"Oh, then you just decided you don't want your hair anymore?"

"Yeah." Because I cheated. I let another man touch me. No, I *begged* another man to touch me.

"I don't buy any of that bullshit. And don't talk to me about Frank *just getting out of hand.* That man is an abuser. He's a fucking narcissist."

"A what?"

"A fucking narcissist. If I wasn't your best friend, even I would have a hard time believing some of the things he does to you. He's such a fucking snake. You need to stop defending him."

I consider just telling Ben the real reason, but I... I like this secret.

"Do you want more hardbacks out front?" I ask.

Ben sighs and shakes his head. "Yeah. Line up the new Booktok ones on the left."

CHAPTER 22
Eli

I haven't seen Axel since he kissed me and apologized for it. Or, I think he apologized for it.

He hasn't been to the lake to read, and he hasn't brought Pepper out this way.

I had to stop myself from visiting the bookstore every day this week. This quiet man with his curious but fearful eyes has crept right through my skin and lodged himself deep inside a place I never cared to fill. My heart. That's where Axel is right now. Deep inside my heart. And not only that, he's seeped into my pores, into my very bones. There's no part of my body, physical or ethereal, where I don't feel him.

I can't shake him. Can't stop thinking about his lips on mine. The more I think about him, the less it matters that he's married. That he shares his lips with a man I despise for owning him.

The reasons that brought me to River Valley are becoming less important as the days pass and my grief for my father begins to feel easier to bear. Axel is beginning to fill spaces I never knew were empty. He's brought light into places I never knew were dark.

I've become so obsessed with him that I've resorted to bribing his dog with meaty bones, so she'd come over here more often. My grand plan is to lure Axel into the woods looking for Pepper.

It pays off on Friday evening.

Axel walks along the edge of the property. He must have been calling out her name because Pepper's ears prick up and she listens carefully but then simply goes back to her bone. She's sitting on the sectional like an entitled queen without a care in the world for her master. I'll worship at her feet if it means having Axel near me.

Dusk has fallen, leaving the earth with a red-orange hue, now that the snow time has passed. I'm able to see Axel from the bay window where I'm standing.

Pepper suddenly jumps off the sofa and lifts her head in the air, yapping her mouth. She's barking.

Seconds later, the light in the kitchen begins to blink rapidly. Doorbell.

Pepper weaves between my legs as I get to the door.

Axel stands there, a woolen hat covering his head.

"Have you seen—" His lips move and then stop when Pepper pokes her head out from between my legs, wagging her tail. She dashes back through the kitchen and into the living room. I won't lie. The bones I bought for Pepper are like drugs.

Axel's eyes widen in horror and I stand there examining his face, trying to figure out what's different about his look.

"I'm sorry," he says, facing me.

I think I'm getting tired of Axel apologizing for everything in his life. I wave my hand, dismissing his apology and then make a sign easy enough for him to understand, inviting him in.

He hesitates, licking his lips. I track the movement without any shame. He isn't oblivious to my observations. A pink blush creeps into his face. I have never seen a man so handsome in my life.

I sign again. *Come inside.*

Axel contemplates the decision the same way someone might if he was given a bomb and didn't know which wire to cut.

He looks past me and then back at me.

I help him decide. I step aside, turn and walk back into the living room to give Pepper another bone. That way, she'll stay for another hour at least.

A few seconds later, Axel is standing in my living room. He looks good here, like he belongs in this house. With me. Not with his asshole of a husband.

His curls. That's what's missing. His locks usually peek out from under his hat. I walk over to him and, with a dangerous amount of what feels like ownership, I slip the hat off his head.

He's nearly bald.

"My husband doesn—"

He's mumbling with his head bowed. I can't read him. His husband what? I capture his chin between my thumb and index finger. He jumps back, like I've burned him. Maybe I have. I'm burning too.

He seems to realize the reason for my touch; his face flushes with embarrassment. Maybe he laughed. But it's not a good smile or laugh. Tension radiates from his body, rolling off him in waves.

"My husband doesn't like my long hair," he says clearly.

What a fucking shame. Because if Axel were *my* husband, I'd have used that hair as leverage while I fucked him from behind. I'd press his face into the bed or the floor or the kitchen fucking table and yank all those curls back while I drilled his ass.

I'd have sunk my fingers into those curls and held them back while I watched my cock fuck his beautiful mouth. And then, after I'd fucked him into a limbless, post-orgasmic mess, I'd play with his curls and tell him how beautiful they are. How sweet his face looks, surrounded by those pretty fucking curls and how gorgeous they look lying against his dimples. My blood boils inside for this simple thing.

I sign. *I liked your long hair.*

He doesn't understand. His confused frown makes me want to pull the skin right off Frank Davis' face. Why couldn't that undeserving bastard just leave Axel's hair alone?

"Do it again," he says.

I sign again. He frowns and then shakes his head with a tiny lift of his mouth. "I don't understand," he says.

I take out my phone and type it for him.

Axel's discomfort increases tenfold when I turn my screen to him.

"I'm married," he says.

I nod. *I know.* For the first time in my life, I regret not being able to speak like a hearing person. To tell him in elegant words everything I want to say.

I want to touch you.

I want to taste you.

I want to own every inch of your body.

I don't care about that ring on your finger. I don't care about the vows you made. I care nothing for a piece of paper that says you can't be mine.

His body speaks volumes, contradicting his words. He speaks again, and I read him clearly.

"Kiss me," he says.

I don't think he's finished speaking. I swallow his words into my mouth, kissing him with all the liberties offered to me by his permission.

His lips part beneath mine, warm and wet. He tastes of sweet tea and life itself. Of hope and happiness. My palms capture his face tightly and my tongue assaults his. He tangles his sweet tongue with mine, kissing me back harshly.

My hand moves to his neck. His groans vibrate in his throat, thrumming against my fingers. He sounds so beautiful.

His hands remain at his side until I try to break the kiss. Then he leans into me, his arms coming around my waist, holding me to him.

I smile against his mouth and kiss him again.

Pepper jumps off the couch. I kick a new bone to her. She's my queen and I, her humble servant, but even Pepper won't break this moment.

Axel's body vibrates. His whole body sings to me. A melody I understand inside the blaring silence of my inner world. Vibrations call to me from his throat, so I kiss him there, careful not to suck too hard. His heart beats too fast beneath my palm, so I kiss him there too, through his shirt. His abs dip when I slip my hand inside his shirt and so I run my hand over the muscles there before moving to grip his hips, pulling him to me.

My lips return to his. I listen to his body with my hands. Committing to memory every tremble, every groan vibrating in his throat. Every beat of his heart and the pacing of his breath.

This is the Axel I want. The one who wants something more than what he'd been given. The one who *asks* for more. Who *demands* it with his body.

He breaks the kiss and falls into my chest. My arms encircle him, holding him close. His chest moves with harsh breaths against mine. I'll have to learn the difference between his breath of ecstasy and his breath of shame and fear.

My hand moves to his hair. Soft strands, impossible to hold.

I stroke his short hair.

I can't hear his words, but his body is speaking clearly. Axel wants this as much as I do.

CHAPTER 23
Axel

I'll grow it out again for you.

The thought is a ton of bricks crashing down over me, burying me underneath a mountain of awful contradictions.

The desperation for this man's touch and the betrayal of my vows.

The lack of guilt and the horror over that fact.

The sadness that I wouldn't even be here if my marriage contained even one iota of happiness and safety, and then the inconceivable thought of never knowing the taste of Eli's lips.

And now all I can think about is how sorry I am that I'd cut my hair. That I disappointed Eli. My need for his approval slices through me, the sharpened edges of a sword bringing the truth of what is happening into stark focus. I want him. I want him more than I've ever wanted anything in my life.

Eli's kisses are accompanied by the wet sounds emanating from between us. He can't hear what we sound like together. He can't hear my uncontrolled, lustful groans of encouragement, but he touches me as if he *can* hear. He hears what I'm asking for without words.

Eli holds me firmly in his arms. Close, so close there isn't a sliver of space between our bodies.

I've never been held like this. I feel *consumed.* Absorbed into his very pores until every molecule contains both him and I.

Pepper barks, the sound crashing through this bubble. I startle and Eli lifts his head. I can't get over how sexy his lips are after he's been kissing me. After he's been kissed... after *I've* kissed him. He stares at my lips and I wonder if he's making the same observation. Does he like how my lips look after he's kissed them swollen?

"Pepper's barking," I say.

Eli turns and pretends to scold Pepper by wagging his finger at her. I laugh when all she does is jump up, place her paws on his chest, and try to lick his face.

Then he takes out his phone and types. ***Where is your husband?***

"He's working overnight."

Eli nods once and grabs my hand, dragging me to the kitchen. Pepper follows us and earns another bone to keep her quiet. If Eli keeps this up, I won't be able to maintain Pepper's newly acquired upper-class lifestyle. She settles under the table, happy.

Eli retrieves a bowl from the cupboard and sets it on the counter. I inspect the new kitchen while he dishes up food into the bowl.

He's done a great job. It has that same rustic feel, but the new, updated appliances give it a modern look. The floor's natural hardwood seems to have been given an updated shine too. Only the stove stands out. It looks so old but it works with the new design, somehow.

Eli catches me looking. He slips his phone out of his pocket and types. ***This stove belonged to my grandmother when she lived here, my father's mother. And the piano too.***

"I love old stuff," I say. I want to ask him about his family, but I'm also scared of knowing too much about him.

Eli slides the bowl of spaghetti close to me and points to the chrome bar stool. I sit and he sits next to me. Close. I don't hate how he sits so close.

"What about you?" I ask, pointing to the bowl.

He grins. It's a cheeky, sexy thing he does with his face that I have never seen on a man's face before.

He picks up the bowl, wraps the spaghetti around the fork, and holds it to my mouth.

My heart beats, tossing back and forth inside my chest, unsure of the direction to beat in. Slowly, I open my mouth. I don't know why, but this feels so... sexual. Eli concentrates on feeding me and his eyes on my mouth feed my already unbearable hard-on. My erection from earlier when we'd kissed had sent my body into overdrive, and now this food situation was threatening to blow me apart.

Eli slides the fork into my mouth. A stray strand of spaghetti falls over my chin. I laugh and go to put it in my mouth, but Eli gets to it first. But he doesn't simply use his fingers. He leans forward and sucks up at the strand and then slides it into my mouth with his tongue.

It's a small mouthful of food, so I chew it quickly and watch Eli take a bite and chew.

In the grand scheme of things it means nothing, this sharing of food. But this is not the grand scheme. This is a tiny moment inside my tiny, unpredictable existence. And in this tiny moment, what Eli is doing with the food right now is changing my whole world. He's turning the insignificant act of sharing food into an expression of... care.

Care. Yes, care, but also more than that. There's a lightness here. A sense of *contentment.* Like there is nothing more that is needed for this moment to be perfect. Like the world is right and nothing more is needed to make it *more right.* Because *more* is not needed.

I give myself a shake. My overdramatic analysis is way out of hand. I should get over this over-romanticizing nonsense.

Eli continues to feed me his spaghetti and after the third bite, I become convinced that he deliberately allows some strands to fall to my chin.

By the fifth bite, my eyes drift shut in anticipation of his tongue on my chin, dragging up and into my mouth. And after I've chewed my next bite, Eli's mouth is on mine again. The food is forgotten and I have a fleeting thought that I've never been so happy that Frank is working the night shift.

Pepper seems to have licked off all the meaty bits of her bone. The grinding of her teeth against the bone reaches my ears. But I want to be like Eli, where nothing exists but him and me. No sound from the outside world exists. Only the sound of our hearts beating, a sound heard clearly through our touch, as Eli pulls me close to him, chest to chest.

I go willingly, falling into the great expanse of darkness where wedding vows and husbands, loyalty and fidelity are swallowed whole and such things as sin and betrayal do not exist.

Eli's hand moves down, his fingers caressing my throat. I moan loudly and he moves his fingers across my Adam's apple. I don't know how I know this, but I make an instant connection in the movement. I groan out loud again. He tracks his thumb across my throat again.

He's listening to me.

I don't know why tears spring to my eyes. Is it because I don't know a single time when Frank has been this attentive to me? How is it possible that I can say that this man, who cannot *hear* me, is now listening to me like no one else ever has?

The thought sends ripples of *something* through me. I can't name it. I don't know what it is. All I know is that it feels like the earth has disappeared from underneath me and I'm falling without the need for a safety net.

Eli's hand drifts further down to my chest. He presses slightly. Is my heartbeat another way he listens to me? It must be, because as the rhythm of my heartbeat increases, so too, do the intensity of Eli's kisses.

But my need for release overpowers my awe and wonder over his ability to listen while he can't hear, and I press my body closer to his, somehow conveying to him that I need more of him in places far more demanding for touch than my throat or chest.

Eli obliges me, sending his hand flying to my crotch. He palms my erection through my sweats, and I press up into his touch. He strokes me hard, rubbing my length, grabbing as much as the material would allow.

Then, I can't bear the excruciating pleasure any longer. I hump Eli's palm shamelessly. Finally, when his elegant, slender fingers slip inside to encircle my cock, I throw my head back with a deep groan.

Eli fists me. Lazily at first as he leans forward and sinks his teeth onto my shirt covered nipple, biting hard enough for me to lose half my mind.

Then he lifts his head, pushing me back gently. I'm on the edge of the seat, my hands behind me, providing support. My head falls back as Eli straightens and continues to work my dick. My eyes drift open. He's watching me. His blue eyes, like glass, studying my face as he gives me this excruciating pleasure.

I should be embarrassed, exposed under the harsh light like this. That I'm not tells me how far gone I am. How desperate I am for the kind of orgasm only Eli can give me. The kind of release I have only ever felt once before, near the lake, at Eli's hand. The desperation to feel that again has me jerking up into Eli's hand.

Eli bends. I pull him up again and he looks at me curiously. I detest breaking this moment but it's important. "I'm clean," I say. "I got tested recently."

He nods and drops his head to my chest for a kiss there. And then, further down.

It must have been a fraction of a second, but to me it happened as if in slow motion. Eli's lips slide over my dick. And all the fucking way down.

If I had possession of my rational mind, I'd have thought James and Frank were lying this whole time. Eli has no problem taking my cock.

Ahh, it's beyond what I could have ever imagined.

Eli's saliva glides over my dick, lubricating me. My pre-cum is licked off, followed by Eli's probing tongue along my slit.

Ahh, fuck. I push up, praying he'd do it again. Fuck, he does and then he swallows me again. His throat squeezes my dick and when he's deep throated me straight into the fucking abyss, I press up until his chin grazes my balls, and for the first time in so many years, I come inside a man's throat, pouring my semen into him like his throat was made for my dick.

CHAPTER 24
Axel

Pepper's incessant barks for more meaty bones cool the air around us. Eli can't hear her, so he's not distracted from what we're doing. I feel a little jealous that he doesn't have to deal with the distractions of the outside world in this way.

I decide to ignore Pepper. Act like I can't hear her.

Eli brings his lips back to mine, pressing softly. White liquid remains at the corner of his mouth. Still drunk on my orgasm, courage is in abundant supply. I lean forward and drag my tongue over the corner of his mouth.

He exhales harshly. I can't stop the smile that creeps into my face. I'm not the only one losing my mind here.

There's no need to clean up. Eli was meticulous when he swallowed. He slips my underwear and my sweats back over my dick and comes back for another kiss.

I wait for the onslaught of guilt. I'm not surprised when it doesn't come. Still, I have the need to acknowledge what this is.

"I'm married," I tell him again. I sound less convicted now than I did when I said it before we came into the kitchen.

He nods again.

"Doesn't that bother you?" I ask.

I must have dropped my head because he lifts my chin. This is becoming easier. I can now tell the difference between when he touches me like he wants to fuck me and when he touches me because he can't read what I'm saying.

"Doesn't it bother you?" I ask again.

He shakes his head. *No.*

"Why not?"

He signs for me, but I don't understand. Both our phones are in the living room, so he reaches over to a drawer and takes out a pen and a piece of paper.

Pepper whimpers at my feet. She wants to go outside.

Eli slides the piece of paper over to me. His handwriting is impeccable. ***He doesn't deserve you***, it says.

"I'm betraying him," I mumble. He frowns at my lips, so I say it again.

You're betraying yourself.

I pick up the paper and read it again. How am I betraying myself when I'm the one here, practically having sex with someone who is not my husband?

It doesn't matter how you dissect it: Frank will always win.

He will always be the scorned one. I'm the villain in all of this. Because no matter what, Frank deserves a true relationship. Whether he's a good or bad husband, he doesn't deserve a husband who creeps around behind his back.

My mind goes to the condoms inside the bottom drawer in the bathroom. But I don't have proof that Frank ever cheated. He denied it every time I found the condoms, and it's not impossible that they could have belonged to one of his friends. In any case, even if Frank did cheat, that doesn't give me the right to do it, too.

All the arguments swirl in my head:

But what if he cheated? Then you should have left him.

But he's not good to you. Then leave.

But I never wanted the marriage in the first place. Then you shouldn't have married him.

But I tried so hard to make it work. Then leave.

But he's abusive. Then leave.

But he'll kill me if I try to leave. Then leave to a place he'll never find you.

Nowhere in the rules does it say that the decisions I've made in the last few weeks have been or could ever be Frank's fault. With no proof that Frank ever cheated, he becomes the innocent husband in this situation, oblivious to how much he's being duped. Lied to. Cheated on.

Yet still, as my gaze upon Eli's face intensifies with the way he's looking at me, I cannot find a single shred of regret.

And that makes it so much worse.

Pepper barks and whimpers again. She needs to go outside. I slip off the bar stool. "Pepper needs to go outside," I say.

Eli dips his head and lifts his hand, indicating goodbye. He walks us to the door. I turn on the threshold. "I don't think I should come back here," I say, facing him. It feels like the right thing to say, but I don't know that I mean any of it.

A frown creases his forehead. He leans forward and kisses me again. A deep, soul shattering kiss that sends shockwaves to my dick, detonating my heart on its way down.

Even if he could speak, words wouldn't have been necessary.

Eli's message is loud and clear. He disagrees.

He leaves my lips and I whimper at the loss. He wouldn't have heard me, but he senses my unwillingness to end the kiss, even though my words are a total contradiction. So, he presses another short kiss to the corner of my lips.

Pepper barks again.

I step outside, following Pepper as she takes our path into the woods. When we're up near the road, I turn back. Eli is still at the doorway, his hands shoved into the pockets of his sweats and his shoulder leaning against the door frame. I could be wrong, but I think he stayed there until Pepper and I were out of sight.

Pepper stays close for most of the way, giving a few squirrels heart attacks, as she chases them back up the trees. A few flowers catch her attention and I leave her to track dog scents while she looks for places to pee.

The time on my phone says ten p.m.. Frank will be home at four a.m.. He'll be hungry. I suspect sleep will evade me tonight, so I make plans to make something special for him to eat. Usually, I leave out the previous night's dinner for him, but I have the sudden urge to do something more.

My hand hovers over the sign language app icon on my phone. I tap on it and swipe to the screen for beginners. I need to learn faster than the weekly lessons at the library.

It's not that hard to learn. It doesn't seem harder than learning any other language. Like, if I'd met someone who spoke French, I'd need to learn French in order to communicate with them. It's no different.

Anyway, Eli already understands my language. He learned how to navigate my world. It doesn't seem like an unfair thing that I learn his language, too.

But what if Frank finds out? I could just say that he's a regular customer at the bookstore and Ben asked me to learn a few basic words for when he comes in. It's not a lie. That part is true. The problem is with my *intention*. My intention is not to provide Eli with good customer service when he comes into the bookstore. My intention is to get close to him. Know him.

Understand him. I want to *talk* to Eli.

Pepper christens a few shrubs of plants, then digs a few holes and barks up at me. I pick up a few rocks and drop them into the holes. Pepper wags her tail and pounces onto the first hole before covering the rock with soil.

While Pepper buries her rocks, I mimic the signs on my screen.

Hello.

Goodbye.

Hot.

Cold.

Then I search for signs of the things I want to tell Eli.

How old are you?

Where are you from?

Tell me about your family.

Were you born deaf?

You're beautiful.

When can I see you again?

I love the way you touch me.

I want to touch you the way you touch me.

I want to taste you.

What would you feel like inside me?

The admission of the last one jerks me out of my nonsensical fantasies. I search the app for a search history. I find none and hope the search doesn't show up somewhere else. Frank likes to go through my phone from time to time. *If there's nothing to hide, what's the problem?* He said one time when I asked why. So, I make sure my browsing history is always clear.

Pepper appears to be satisfied with her rock burials and sits in front of me, panting and wagging her tail.

"You done?" I ask, scratching behind her ears.

She barks. *Yes.*

I don't think you need to hear or speak to understand someone. Because understanding someone, *knowing* them, doesn't need words.

Frank and I talk all the time. He's heard every word I've ever said to him about the state of our marriage, how much it hurts me when he treats me bad, but he's never understood a single word I've said.

Pepper and I walk back home.

I'll learn sign language.

I'll grow my hair back out.

I'll cook Frank something nice to eat for when he gets back.

CHAPTER 25
Eli

I can't get the feel of him out of my mouth. It's been hours since Axel left, hours since I had him in my mouth, but my mind won't let me forget the thick ridges of the veins along his cock. The thickness of his penis pulsing, jerking in my throat.

I don't give a fuck that he's married. As long as Axel comes to me, as long as his answer isn't no, I'll pursue him.

I consider walking over to their side just to check on him. Frank might be back home from his shift, but that doesn't matter. I'll just check if Axel is okay. Make sure there's no trouble over there.

I give myself migraines trying to figure out how to get Axel away from here.

I consider telling my mother, but things feel too chaotic. Too messy.

At five a.m. the flicker of the bedroom light tells me someone's at the door. I jump out of bed. The pounding at the back of my head moves to my temples.

There are only two people who could possibly be ringing my doorbell at this time of the morning, and one of them isn't a human.

It's the non-human that's ringing my doorbell. I can't believe how smart this dog is. I love her.

Pepper bolts into the house, heading straight for the kitchen where I keep her bribe snacks, but before I can go give her a treat, movement catches my eye from just up the path.

But it's not Axel coming down the path looking for Pepper.

Frank Davis' mouth moves, but he's still too far away for me to make anything out. He might have called out to Pepper because she races back to the front door, wagging her tail. She could also be reminding me that I need to give her a treat. I don't know and, either way, I don't know what Frank is saying.

Soon, he's standing in front of me, making grand gestures with his hands and pointing to Pepper, who's bolting between the door and the kitchen. She's more playful than usual.

I want to ask him where Axel is, but he won't understand and I refuse to make the effort with him that I do with Axel.

He gives me a broad smile. I'm barely able to stomach half of one. He lifts his hand and says, "Sorry," and points to Pepper.

Then he bends at the knees, tapping on his thighs, calling her.

Pepper sits in front of the cupboard that contains her treats and rests her head on the floor. She's not going anywhere.

I walk to the cupboard and open it. Pepper jumps up and circles me like a vulture. But even after I've given her a treat, she still won't go. Frank stands there awkwardly and I make a point of not making things easier for him. Let him stand there and suffer trying to communicate with a deaf guy. Right now I'm twelve, not thirty-two.

Pepper circles me and I give her a second treat and no matter how many times Frank bangs on his legs, she doesn't go to him.

Eventually, I walk to the door, Pepper hot on my heels. I decide to walk them back home. Maybe I'll get to see Axel, although it's still early.

Frank gives me an elaborate pat on the back when Pepper follows obediently up the path and all I want to do is break his neck. I keep my distance after that and make no attempt at small talk.

When we reach their house, Axel is on the porch draping a towel over the clothes dryer.

His beautiful eyes widen when they collide with mine. He's so beautiful, even with his buzz cut and his eyes bugged out like that.

He's frozen in place, horror creeping into his face, so I offer him a light smile to calm his nerves. I think it helps. I love how I'm able to communicate with this sad, beautiful man without words, without signs. It's as if his heart has become connected to mine and we speak a language created only for us.

Frank jogs up the steps to Axel and makes a few quick gestures at Pepper. His body language and the slow bow of Axel's head tell me that Frank isn't happy.

Axel's eyes dart between me and Frank and occasionally at Pepper, who's turning out to be a big cheater, sitting at my feet like she belongs to me and not to the two men on the porch.

After being sufficiently chastised, as it appeared to be, Axel walks down the steps.

"I'm sorry about Pepper coming to your place so early. It won't happen again," he says.

I wish I could tell him that I would steal Pepper away if it meant that he would follow.

I dip my head instead and sign *you're beautiful.* I've never used my deafness to my advantage like this before but fuck Frank. I tell Axel he's beautiful right there in front of that deadbeat cunt of a husband.

Axel recognizes the sign because his face lights up into a soft pink and he casts a quick glance back at Frank, who's already gone inside.

I could say *beautiful,* which involves waving my fingers over my face in sign, and I still don't think Frank Davis would get it. He behaves like he's too above deaf people to bother with our language. He's doing me a favor with his giant ego.

Axel puts four fingers to his chin, taps and extends his hand. *Thank you.* He's a little dramatic about it, but I think he just wants to make sure he's done it right.

I laugh and give him a thumbs up.

He beams and I fall in love with him immediately. It's instant and I don't bother denying any of it.

Last night I was prepared to steal him away.

This morning I was prepared to steal his dog with the hope that he would follow.

Now? I would burn everything to have him.

CHAPTER 26
Axel

There are a dozen things I should be agonizing over. A dozen things worthy of my anxiety.

Things such as how I, a married man, had my dick sucked by another man. How I've kissed another man half a dozen times. The fact that I am now officially cheating on a man who would think nothing about blowing my brains out with his illegal gun. A man who would turn my face into a piece of trashy art if he knew I even had thoughts about another man.

But all I can think about is the look on Eli's face when I signed *thank you* and when he realized that I understood what he'd signed. He looked *impressed*. He approved. Of me. He looked at me and there was something about me that he *liked*.

Somehow it's different from someone being impressed by my so-called pretty face. Different from that first time Frank had told me I was the handsomest boy he'd ever seen.

Back then, something told me that Frank's motives were questionable. There were no words to describe it. Only that feeling of... unease. But with Eli, there was a sliver of pride on his face that made me bloom under his gaze. Instead of wanting to shrivel up and hide, with Eli I wanted to grow and expand. With Eli, I wanted to be *more* of myself, not less.

"You just gonna stand there?" Frank demands. I jump a little, remembering I'm standing by the kitchen sink with my empty cup still in my hand. The truth is that I stood over by the sink with my coffee because from here I could watch Eli make his way back up the road without looking like an adulterer.

"Uh, no. Let me just wash up these cups." Which I proceed to do now that Eli had long since disappeared down the road.

"Keep that dog on a leash, Axel. I can't be runnin' out at five o' clock in the morning after that mutt."

"I'll keep a better eye on her," I tell Frank, because I can't exactly tell him that Pepper has found a second home on the property round the bend and I don't know how to keep *myself* out of that property, let alone Pepper.

"And that deaf guy is something, ain't he?"

My hand pauses on the last cup. "What do you mean?"

"He's just got that thing about him."

"What thing?" I set the cup on the drying rack and turn to Frank. I shouldn't be this interested.

"Like he's better than everybody else."

It almost makes it out of my mouth to tell Frank that Eli is the most easy going person I've met, but after what I've been doing the last few weeks, the last thing I need is to draw attention to myself by defending Eli. But not defending him feels like a... betrayal. I don't like how it makes me feel to sit back and let someone misjudge Eli, but I guess this is how it is when you're cheating.

I choose the option of self-preservation. I remain silent, not defending Eli, even though it sours my stomach.

Anyway, I get the feeling Frank doesn't like the fact the Eli isn't so easily impressed by him.

"Do you want me to put out another blanket for you?" I ask instead.

"Yeah, it's gotten pretty cold this morning."

"Okay." I gather his breakfast dishes from the table and lay them in the sink.

"And anyway, where'd you get money to cut your hair?"

"Uh, from my week's pay." I smell trouble, so I add, "Do you want some tea before you turn in?"

"No. I thought your week's pay was for the overdue gas bill."

My eyes flit from Frank to the window with the sickening hope that Eli would magically reappear.

When you've never known safety, it's easy to navigate through the world. You just keep your guard up. But what do you do when you've tasted that elusive sense of safety and then you have to leave it behind? When you know what it is to be seen, to be kept safe with not even one word spoken? Knowing how I feel when I'm with Eli makes being with Frank a hundred times harder. Every nuance of his is amplified because now I have something to compare it to.

"Ben gave me a little extra last week, so I could still get a haircut after I paid the bill."

He sneers. And this too, a month ago, would have been just another normal twist of Frank's mouth, his usual display of his disapproval of me. But today, that twist of his mouth feels... ugly. Not that it *looks* ugly, but that it *feels* ugly. Uglier than usual.

I feel it in the tighter knot in my chest. In the increased heaviness at the bottom of my stomach. The churn there is that much worse today. Because this is not how Eli is.

"You couldn't have waited one more week to get the haircut? My money not worth waitin' for anymore?"

I can't tell for sure what caused the sudden change in Frank's mood but if I were to guess, I'd say it's because he felt a little small when he went over to Eli and doesn't have to courage to deal with his own insecurities. And so, my haircut is the only way out.

"It's not that, Frank." I'm surprised at the firmness in my voice. Where has this courage suddenly come from?

Frank notices it too. He gives me a sharp look. "Don't take that tone with me, Axel. Just because they throw some peanuts your way over there at the bookstore doesn't mean you get to wag your little tail over here."

Fear is there. I can feel it. But there is something else sitting next to the thing that keeps me bound to Frank. I don't have the word to describe it, but maybe it feels like rebellion.

Like something shooting up inside my chest, causing me to inhale sharply and deeply through flared nostrils. This feeling scares me. I am not strong enough inwardly or outwardly to beat Frank at anything. Where is this *rebellion* coming from?

"Sorry, Frank. I meant to say you asked me to have the haircut ages ago already. I didn't want to burden you, so I decided to do it on my own."

"You've been burdening me ever since you got the cancer, so what's the difference now?"

My mouth falls open. And it's not over the fact that he doesn't even recall that I 'got the cancer' even before he fucking slipped his hand into my pants at that fucking church event and I thought I had to fucking marry him over it, since I'd be 'damaged goods' if I hadn't.

It's not even that he was the doting, supportive husband through chemo only when he had an audience, but he never let me forget behind closed doors how tiresome I was.

It's the fact that a lucid, functioning adult would actually believe that he had the right to utter those words to another human being.

To another human being who he promised to love and cherish in fucking sickness and health. He's sitting there acting like he's the sole reason I didn't die of 'the cancer' when I was eighteen.

His face suddenly breaks out into a broad smile. "What? You're angry now? I was just joking, Axel. You don't have to take everything so seriously."

That unfurling in my chest again and along with it that inexplicable courage. "That was a horrible thing to say, Frank." *Also, if I knew how to make myself do it, I'd run so far away from you, you'd never be able to find me.*

"God, you're so sensitive. Can't you take a joke? Just get my permission first before you spend any money. And you can start paying for the life insurance and groceries from this month. Also the credit card."

"But if I pay for all of that I won't have anything left over." What is Frank trying to do?

"Yeah, well, I've been paying for everything until now. It's your turn now. I'll be the pampered princess for a while."

The chair scrapes against the floor. Frank rises, drawing himself up to his full height, his eyes boring into mine and a smirk on his face. He acts like it isn't the case, but I know he's showing me who's boss around here. *Put your head down and shut your mouth, Axel,* is what he's saying without saying a word. He doesn't have to. I hear him loud and clear.

He throws a kitchen towel over my shoulder. "The boys are coming over later," he says, squeezing my shoulder a little too hard. "Cook us something nice and you can go over to the lake and read for the evening."

It's the best thing Frank could have ever said to me.

CHAPTER 27
Eli

Axel said he wouldn't be coming around anymore. I don't believe him and I'm not going to help him with that, so I stock up on meaty bones and dog treats. Because if I can't have Axel, then I'll take his dog with all the charm and flattery I can muster.

And since there is that chasm of possibility that Axel's moral compass is leading him away from me, I work on the house to pass the time. And since I can't sleep, I make a list of things to do that would have me working well into the night.

Then when I no longer have manual labor to distract me, I pore through old newspapers dating back sixty years, when my father was a young man, trying to capture what living in his time might have been like. I can't help thinking how much Axel would love sifting through history like this. I set the newspapers aside to show him when I see him again.

The weather is perfect for me to do some work on the outside today and, because I'm tired of the raccoons, I get back to working on the fencing.

I was only halfway done before the snow came in last week but now I can finish it.

By midday, I've managed to put up enough fencing to take me all the way to the lake.

The boulder that Axel reads on every night falls within the property's perimeter. If I fence it in, he might never come back here to read. If I fence it out, he'll think I don't want him here.

I go with the lesser of the two evils. I fence the boulder out. At least he can read without worrying about trespassing.

By evening, I've covered most of the property line and Axel's boulder sits outside the fencing. I'll leave the installation of the gate for another time.

Heading back inside, I grab a beer, down it in three gulps, and strip out of my clothes for a much needed shower.

Later, because it's such a still, calm night, I grab the rest of the six-pack and a container of cold pasta salad, and make my way back outside, toward the lake.

Sipping my beer, I gaze out at the lake, thinking back to the time I thought Axel would fall into the water.

I'm still suspicious of his intention, even if we never talked about it. Nobody stands on those rocks like that without a plan to fall in, especially if they're drunk as hell.

The night is black. Starless. It's perfect. I enjoy this stillness. This nothingness.

My father loved these starless nights. A blank canvas, he used to say, speaking of the night sky. A canvas where you could hang up every dream and desire and watch it come to life. And then, when the stars were out on another day, he'd point up and say, *"there Eli, don't you see all your hopes and dreams shining down on you? Let your dreams be as vast as the stars in the sky and may they all come true and shine like this night sky."*

My father was from another time and he spoke like it. The decades separating us could be observed in the simpleness with which he viewed life.

I'm sitting sideways on the boulder with my back leaning against the tree trunk. A movement along the path catches my eye.

If my back had been facing the path Axel usually takes, I wonder if he would have quietly left, knowing I wouldn't have heard him.

I unlock my phone and face the lit up screen in that direction. He can't back out now.

Even from this distance, I can see the uncertainty in his eyes. He takes a step back, lifting his hand in that *I'm sorry* way. I'll never teach him the proper way to sign *I'm sorry* and I hope he never learns it on his own. I've never met anyone who's always so sorry for everything.

When that foot of his moves back, I spring from the boulder, eating up the distance between us, and grabbing his wrist.

He turns back to me. He has a book in his hand.

Don't go, I sign. His forehead creases, but it's okay. I'll teach him the sign for *don't go* later. For now, I gently tug his hand, pulling him in the direction of the boulder. But... where's Pepper?

I type on my phone and ask him.

"I had to put her on a leash," he says.

Why, I type.

"Frank says she's too free, going into people's houses."

I shake my head, making sure to convey my disapproval.

Let's go and get her, I type.

His eyes light up. And it takes my breath away.

I take his hand in mine. He lets me. And we walk together up the path. At the first sliver of light from the house at the end of the path, Axel tugs his hand out of mine. I let him. He turns to me. "I'll go get her," he says.

I nod. I can see the front of his house from here. It's obscure, but I can see enough to make out Pepper's shape sitting on the porch.

Axel hurries down the road and within a few minutes, he's walking quickly up the road with Pepper trotting alongside him. I think she knows this is a covert mission too, because she doesn't go crazy when she sees me. She just nuzzles my crotch and walks between me and Axel. Her body language tells me she hasn't barked.

Soon, we're back at the boulder and Pepper is happily devouring her bone next to us on the ground. I resume my position on the boulder, my back against the tree trunk and my knees propped up. Axel sits next to me, facing the lake, his legs dangling over the edge of the boulder. I study his profile while he studies the sky.

For the second time in my life, I regret the limitations of being deaf.

I wish I could lean over to him and whisper sweet nothings.

I wish I could lay my ear to his chest and listen to his heartbeat. Would it sound the same as it feels beneath my palms, strong and steady? I wish I could hear the sound of his voice to see if it would sound as it does vibrating against my fingers.

But I'm not the type to dwell on what cannot be done. So, I lean forward and trail my fingers along the sleeve of his jacket, pulling his gaze away from the moon.

Turning my palm over, I offer him my hand. *Come here.*

Hesitation pours out of him. He looks at my hand for a long time. It's not like me to wait like this. To have my heart in my hand and my breath trapped inside my chest, waiting for him to choose me just one more time. But, it seems, I could wait forever if it promised me just one more moment with this man.

In a world like mine, where time moves too fast to appreciate just one single moment, here in this world, in *Axel's* world, he slows me down. Makes me savour each moment.

The uncertainty of my victory in this situation with Axel— whether I can have him—hasn't deterred me, but it has forced me to be more careful with each moment. Treat it with care because I don't know if it would be the last.

Like now, watching Axel war with his heart and his morals, I respect his battle. I remain inside this moment, forcing out the intermittent need to simply take what I've already claimed as mine.

He slips his hand into mine, choosing me.

I pull him up between my legs and into me, his back to my chest. With my face to the sky, I thank whatever powers exist that this place is so secluded, we don't have to worry about being caught.

Axel's body is stiff against mine. Tension causing his muscles to harden beneath my hands as my fingers trace the outline of his arms. My hand snakes around his waist, pulling him further into my body. My dick, hard and ready, presses up onto his back while my hands glide over his abdomen.

It's beautiful to witness the moment he lets go. To observe the second time tonight when he chooses me. His head falls back onto my shoulder, his fingers, laced with mine, guiding me underneath his shirt.

My hand moves up his chest to his heart so I can feel the rapid rise and fall of his chest, my way of hearing his breaths. I imagine them to be harsh; loud maybe.

I feel for the beat of his heart and know with every quick, strong thump that his need for me is as desperate as mine for him.

And then his mouth is on mine. He makes the first move. Turning his head, he slips his hand around my neck and pulls me down to him.

The gentle brush of his lips against mine is another of the many compromises I make for him. At another time, with another person, I wouldn't have bothered with such gentle strokes. But now,

I savor his gentle exploration of my mouth. Encourage him with equally gentle licks inside his mouth.

His tongue comes out and I lick across it. I feel his gasp in the vibration of his throat, against which my hand currently rests.

And all I can think of as I follow him into this gentle bliss is how I could make this man truly mine when he belongs to someone else.

CHAPTER 28
Axel

I'm drowning in this chaos. This push and pull of my conscience. I'm entirely responsible for this complication in my life. And I've dragged two people into it. My desperate need for this physical pleasure I've never felt before... paid for by Eli and Frank. Both innocent bystanders in this hurricane ripping through me.

It's the desperation. It's the *desperation* I can't get past. This inability to walk away, to say no, is shocking and terrifying.

But my curiosity over what it feels like to be near Eli has turned into an uncontrollable need to *feel him*. And as his hand now travels down my chest, my stomach, and moves lazily along the waistband of my sweats, I begin to wonder if I have a death wish. If this one moment is worth dying over if Frank ever found out.

I find myself gripping Eli's hand at my waistband, moving with him while he sucks into my mouth and his other hand rests lightly over my throat. I crane my neck, wanting more of his mouth without wanting to disturb his fingers tracking my waistband.

He gives me more. Jesus fuck, so much more than I've ever had. And I risk my life a little bit more. Entwining my fingers with Eli's at my waistband, I guide his hand into my sweats, widening my thighs for him.

He shifts, leaving my mouth and pulling me to him until his chest is pressed to my back. He spreads his legs, causing my legs to fall even more open for his hand. His other hand slides down from my throat and into my pants and—

Ah, fuck. Eli's hot palms glide down over my hipbones, his thumbs meeting at the root of my dick. He presses slightly there, and my hips jerk upward, asking for more.

But he doesn't give me more. Instead, with his fingers splayed over the inside of my thighs and his thumbs grazing the innermost part of my thighs, he moves his hands up and down. Massaging the insides of my thighs, fluttering touches to my balls but never to my cock.

I'm leaking, desperate for this and more, the back of my head digging into Eli's chest and my hips moving of its own volition as the moon and the starless sky witness the gasps and moans being pulled out of my mouth. Eli's harsh breaths join mine, unafraid of our spectators.

Then Eli brings one hand up my chest, pulling at the sleeve of my sweatshirt. I help him, desperate for whatever plan he has to touch me more.

With one hand now free from its sleeve, Eli has unrestricted access to my body. His hands race up and down, from my neck, down my naked chest, over my abs and back into my pants.

But this won't do, too. Mindless, and with no value for my life or for my godly confessions to Frank on our wedding day, I lift my hips and slip my pants down over my ass.

Eli groans. I wish he could hear how beautiful he sounds.

Almost lying flat on the boulder now and cradled tightly to Eli, I writhe beneath his touch.

Yes. The answer is yes. I would face the barrel of Frank's gun for just this one moment. If the price for this one moment is death, then it's a price I'm willing to pay because nothing, *nothing* I have ever experienced or ever dreamed of compares to how this man makes me feel.

If I whispered his name, if I told him to never stop touching me, he wouldn't hear me, so I move his hand to my cock so he would know.

"More, Eli," I whisper, turning my head so my lips touch his throat. "Fuck me with your hands," I gasp out, my breath against his neck.

He responds as if he has heard the words. Listening to my breath against his neck and the vibration of my voice against his fingers, his other hand closes over my cock.

I cry out from the contact and Eli's fingers stroke my throat, as if pleased with my response.

His thumb strokes over the head of my dick, spreading thick pre-cum over the top. It's unbearable, this sensation. His hand stroking me like this. I want more. I want it harder. If this is what will bring me to the barrel of Frank's gun, then I want *everything* this moment has to offer.

As if he knows, Eli's fingers tighten around my cock and he begins to fist me. From root to tip, he draws my lust through my body. His downward stroke ends in an open palmed roll of my balls and four flattened fingers rubbing down my taint. The upward stroke follows the same path until his hand caresses my dick again, pulling upward, hard and sure. I swell under his confident strokes, so ready. And I tell him so with my body.

I tell him with the vibrations echoing from my throat, my breath falling onto his neck. I encourage him with my arm snaking back and around his neck and my fingers clutching at his hair, pulling him closer to me. I tell him in all the ways I can how much I want this. How much I need this. Need *him*.

And he hears me. He responds to me as if he's heard these prayers.

Tears gather at the back of my eyes as I come face-to-face with my orgasm and my unbearable need for Eli.

He sends me over the edge and I'm falling, safe in his arms. Falling into this sin. Falling in love with him.

He holds me like that for a long time. We have nothing to clean up with, so he drags his hand up my chest, my cum beneath his palm, hot a second ago, now cooling quickly. But Eli's warm hand alleviates some of the discomfort as he rubs my semen into my abdomen, up into my chest and whatever is left disappearing into my skin at my neck. Eli has lathered me with my own cum.

It should feel nasty, what he's doing. But all it is, is sinfully erotic. I bask in it, fighting off the reality of what I'm doing.

My self-loathing can wait until I get home.

CHAPTER 29
Eli

I'm addicted to him.

I'm not officially working, but I'd asked to sit in on some meetings from time to time. I missed a board meeting this morning. I have never missed a meeting, ever.

I slept through the night.

It isn't rocket science, what's happening. There's a shift here. The earth's plates moving beneath my feet, cracking down the center and I'm stuck in the middle. My life as I know it—predictable, easy and under my absolute control—is slipping away from me as Axel, inch by inch, begins to take center stage.

Thoughts of him consume me. Dreams of him hasten my sleep, pulling me into a kind of rest I haven't had in months.

He's everywhere. His breath whispering across the skin on my neck. His heartbeat against the palm of my hand even when it's been hours since I last saw him. I feel him long after I'd let him go.

I stand at the kitchen window, willing Pepper, at least, to make an appearance. My coffee, long since forgotten, is cold between my palms.

I set it down and check my phone for messages. My assistant, Theresa: *we don't mind, but you missed the board meeting. Is everything okay?*

Is everything okay? Since when do I skip work meetings? And in which universe would the reason be that I *overslept*?

I respond to Theresa: *I'm fine. I'm sorry I missed the meeting. Send me the minutes.*

My eyes are still on the path outside. Pepper is nowhere to be seen. I hope she's not tied up. I should check up on her. Axel must be on his way to work. The morning is still, making the emptiness that much more unbearable. I play with the idea of going to the bookstore.

The bookstore wins and an hour later the bell above the door sways, announcing my arrival.

The manager, Ben, greets me in sign language. I return the greeting while my eyes quickly scan the space. Axel is nowhere in sight. Maybe he's at the back.

"What are you looking for today, Eli?" Ben asks. He pronounces his words clearly enough. I guess some hearing people do listen to us.

I take out my phone. *A few mystery books to pass the time.*

Because the mystery books are all the way in the back.

Ben guides me happily, reaching for several recommendations. I covertly investigate the back room.

Ben is an excellent customer service agent. After a few minutes, he goes into the storeroom and comes out with my prize.

Axel looks tired, but the light in his eyes when he sees me is unmistakable. He masks it quickly when Ben turns to him. He listens to whatever Ben is saying to him, nodding and with periodic glances over Ben's head at me. He chews the corner of his bottom lip and he catches me watching him play with that lip every time he looks up.

It must have been fifteen seconds, but it feels like an eternity before Ben finally heads back to the counter with a smile and a wave at me.

Axel takes a tentative step toward me. The downward turn of his mouth, his fingers fidgeting with the cuff of his sleeve and his hesitant steps combine and produce a myriad of panic and confusion, but his eyes tell me a thousand things to the contrary.

In this harsh light of day, of reality, without the moon to protect us under the old Scarlet tree near the lake, our situation slowly morphs into something else. Dirtied by the light, by social norms and secret abuse that prevent Axel from simply walking away from a life he doesn't want. From walking into a life he *wants*.

I know he's feeling this unwanted intrusion of reality, too, pushing its way into the secret places we created only for us.

He comes to stand in front of me. "Mystery books?" he asks.

I nod.

"Any favorite authors?"

I shake my head. *You're beautiful,* I sign.

A smile teases the corner of his mouth. He drops his head. Glancing over to the front, I make sure the store is still empty and Ben is still hunched over some paperwork at the counter.

The tall bookshelves provide sufficient privacy.

I hook my finger underneath his chin and lift until his face is close to mine. His eyes shine and he gives into his smile. And then he lifts his hand and signs. *You're beautiful.* He falters on the last movement, but I hear him loud and clear.

He peers at me after that and so I cradle the side of his face with one hand and sign *thank you* with the other.

His smile grows, contagious. I'm infected. I return his smile. He can't seem to stop smiling, looking away from me, trying to hide it. It's beautiful. He's *beautiful.* This is our first full conversation in sign language and *that* is as beautiful as he is.

He drops to his haunches and selects a few books. I drop to the floor too, so close to him he's startled when he looks up again.

I take my phone out of my pocket and type. *Are there cameras?*

He shakes his head. *No.* And then his eyes widen adorably when he guesses my intentions. But he leans forward anyway, giving me permission, choosing me.

My lips fuse with his, a sweet, deep lover's kiss. Stolen behind the bookshelf. Stolen from Frank. Stolen from a piece of paper that prohibits him from being entirely mine.

I don't know how I'll bear it but if I can't have him openly and freely, and if I can't have him all to myself, then I'll share him. It sickens me, but what other option is there? I'll share him for now. For now, I'll take only half of him while he gathers the courage to give me all of him.

CHAPTER 30
Axel

The first major headache comes on Monday morning while I brush my teeth. For most people, two Tylenol is all that's needed.

I know that there is a difference and what lies between my kind of headache and the normal kind of headache is the word *relapse*.

Now, I just can't ignore the bruising from a few weeks ago.

Or the fatigue.

Despair snakes up through my feet, the blackest darkness swirling around my legs and moving upward to settle in my chest, choking me. Choking the little life that I have left in me.

I drop onto the toilet seat, my head in my hands, willing the headache to disappear. For it to have been just some tension knotted up in my head, easily taken care of by a light painkiller.

My helplessness consumes me. I sit there, grieving for my dying body. This flesh and bone that does its best but still it's not enough.

I sit in the bathroom with my husband in the bedroom, getting ready for work, and feel the loneliest I've ever felt. Rushing out to him in tears to tell him the headaches have returned isn't an option I can consider.

I get up again, wash my tears away and step out of the bathroom without a hint of what happened ninety seconds earlier.

Ben notices that something is amiss when I get to the bookstore, but I'm convincing enough that he leaves me alone after a while.

"You'd better promise you'll tell me if something is wrong, okay?"

I promise him, but I don't know if I have the strength to admit even to myself that the cancer might be back. All the way home, I avoid thoughts about it.

I think about Eli instead.

It's not that hard, you know. To fall in love with someone while you're married to someone else. And it doesn't make you a worse partner. Better, in fact, has been my observation.

My fear of getting caught and my need to never let Frank become suspicious has made me extra meticulous about keeping the house in order. Never, ever messing up dinner. Keeping my voice down. Smiling more, but not too much more because that might be more suspicious than if I behaved like a cheater, whatever that meant. In some fucked up way, I've become a better husband.

I don't know if it's because I feel less and less resentful with each day my feelings for Eli grow. Or if it's because I was starting to not need Frank's love. I just know that I'm not so *angry* anymore. I don't think about the past as much, wondering what would have happened if I hadn't married Frank.

Don't get me wrong, I'm not thinking about the future either. Despite my numerous poor choices so far, I'm not so far gone to imagine any kind of future for myself.

Being a cancer survivor will do that to you. You live only in the moment, and only on special occasions, when the anger at the hand you've been dealt becomes an uncontrollable fury, do you allow for those moments of *what if.* What if I could live to thirty-five? What if the man in my imagination found me and took me away from here?

And then you look in the mirror at your hairless head and tell yourself how grateful you are that you are alive for just that moment, at least. And if you're still around tomorrow, that would be something amazing, too.

I haven't yet reached the place where Eli had become entwined with the words *what if.* Eli is always a *now* moment. Maybe that's why it's not that hard to do what I'm doing.

And I know all the clichés that ring true and lessen the authenticity of what I feel for Eli:

Starving men will eat from any hand.

To him who is denied true love, the basic principles of humanity will feel sensual.

The thirst for love ... blah blah.

And that's when the anger rears its ugly head, helping me deflect responsibility, if only for a time. When my need for Eli becomes too much to bear, I hurl blame at Frank.

While I prepare dinner—sticky chicken wings and fried potatoes—my opposing thoughts give me whiplash.

I have a ball of cotton wool stuffed into each ear while I cook. I can still hear the sizzle of the oil in the pan and the whirr of the refrigerator so I stuff another ball of cotton wool in each ear. I can still hear but I keep them in, anyway. I want to live in Eli's world. Not mine. My world feels dangerous. And lonely. So bleak and lifeless. In Eli's world, I'm safe. Free. Happy.

The whole time it takes to prepare the chicken is spent advocating for myself.

Why couldn't Frank just love me?

Why couldn't he keep the promise he made to cherish me?

Why did he insist on professing his love for me when all he'd wanted was someone to control and abuse?

If Frank had just kept his promises, none of this would have happened. And if he didn't want me, then why couldn't he just let me go?

And then, while I fry the potatoes, sympathy for Frank drowns me.

He doesn't deserve this.

He's a lot of things, but he's not a cheater. Not one I can confirm, anyway.

No matter what, he deserves the truth.

There is no sympathy for adulterers.

I don't know why people cheat on partners they claim to love, or why they cheat on partners who are good to them in every possible way.

All I know is that Eli gives me everything I have ever wanted. Nothing of what Eli gives me exists in my marriage. Respect. Care. Kindness. Eli is breaking me with his presence in my life, but it's the kind of breaking that brings you relief. Like having someone slowly chip away at the boulders you'd been carrying on your back.

The scruff of boots outside has my heart racing. Like Frank can pry into my mind and see all the things I've been thinking and doing.

The door opens with a bang.

I'd forgotten it's *NO LUBE FRIDAY* again.

Frank is drunk. He can hardly stand up straight. I slip into my pious husband role.

"Frank, let me get your jacket," I say, hurrying to him.

"Get the fuck off me," he growls, slamming his forearm into my chest. If I stop, he'll accuse me of not caring about him. I stumble but manage to get myself back up and hook my hand under his arm, helping him to the bathroom.

He mumbles and grumbles all the way, but his words are unintelligible. I can't gather enough to gage what the night will bring or what brought on this mood.

Once Frank is settled in the bathroom, I return to the kitchen to dish up his food, stopping by the fridge to make sure the beer is at the back, where it remains cold. We really need to get a new fridge.

With seconds to spare, I rush to the bedroom and pull on a second pair of sweats and socks.

The toilet flushes and when Frank returns to the kitchen, I'm already laying his plate and the beer on the table.

"The fuck is this?" Frank slurs, pulling the cotton wool from my ears. My blood turns to ice, my body stone cold, and I prepare to die. He must be able to figure it out. And when he does, he's going to kill me.

"You got some kind of ear infection or something?" He drops onto his chair in front of his food.

My body sags with relief. "Yes," I lie. "But it's nothing serious."

"Good, cos we ain' got no money for those ear drops."

"Don't worry about it, Frank." I rub my hands up and down my thighs, making sure the barrier between my outer sweats and my skin is at least a little bit thick.

"And it better not be the cancer. One time was enough, fuck. I can't deal with that again."

A lump thickens in my throat. I shove it down. It's nothing new. Why should I cry about it?

He mumbles some more incoherent words and as rare as it is, I might be able to escape *No Lube Friday*. He's too drunk.

Frank is almost asleep at the table. "Should I help you get into bed?" I ask as gently as possible. Like soothing a rabid dog.

"Can I eat my fuckin' food first, you dumb fuckin' third-grade fuckin' bitch?"

I slide into the chair next to him. My stomach grumbles. I'll eat later, when he's asleep. It occurs to me that Eli wouldn't be able to hear my stomach growl with hunger, but I'll bet he'd just *know* if I was hungry.

"Yes, Frank."

He falls asleep over his food after two bites. If he wakes up hungry, he won't remember that he didn't finish his food. He'll say I didn't dish up for him.

In any case, I coax him half awake. Enough to hook his massive frame over my body and help him to bed, removing his socks and shoes as lightly as possible. I leave him with his jacket and pants.

All I can think about is that he won't hit me tonight. I contemplate removing the extra clothing, but at the last minute I lose my confidence and keep them on.

I fall asleep next to Frank, dreaming about the stranger in my imagination. The man who is now anything but a stranger.

CHAPTER 31
Axel

I'm pulled out of my sleep at some point during the night, and I'm sleepy enough to let my defenses stay down when I'm manhandled from behind. A sharp tug of my sweats, both of them. An intrusion between my ass cheeks. It must have been the grogginess of sleep that made me push Frank away. He's done this before, but I've always been on alert for it. Tonight I'd slept more soundly than I usually do. And so, without thinking, I push him away. It's the first time.

"The fuck you doing?" Frank's hoarse grunt near my ear. "You don't want to give me some ass?"

My body, stiff with uncertainty, doesn't help the situation.

"You too good for me now since you started earning some money?" He grabs my hair, but there isn't much to hold on to since I shaved it all off and for that, I'm grateful.

Still, I can't answer him. The thought of fucking Frank makes me sick. Revulsion clogs my throat.

He shoves my pants further down and yanks my hips back against him. I don't know where the courage comes from. Maybe it's the overwhelming feeling that it's *Eli* I'm cheating on right now. "No, Frank," I whisper.

"*What?* You're gonna hold out on me like some prissy virgin?"

"It's rape if you force me," I whisper.

Frank yanks up my sweats. "I ain't no rapist."

I can hear the twist of his lips in his voice. A horrible sneer, reserved for the meanest words to ever be uttered by him.

He shifts away from me and slams his palm into my back, between my shoulder blades. "The fuck you think you are? Some sex god or something?"

Terror is a living thing, uncoiling inside me and threatening to crush me from the inside.

"You think I need sex from you?" A second shove between my shoulder blades.

The nightstand drawer jerks open. Every inch of my body pulses. Heat and goosebumps gather at the bottom of my spine and I just can't breathe.

Just turn and give him what he wants.

But I can't. I can't move. And I can't let him touch me after Eli has touched me.

The cold metal of Frank's gun digs just above my spine. Silent screams gather in my throat, ripping through my esophagus like wild banshees.

I'm going to die. My mind scrambles for the date so I can die knowing the date I took my last breath. I can't remember. I don't know what day it is. I don't know if Frank will let Ben come to the funeral. Will they arrest Frank? And then... *Eli.* I'll die knowing his touch. Isn't that enough?

Frank's harsh breath flies into my ear and then the gun slams into my shoulder.

He's only going to hit me.

Relief floods my body as tears leak from my tightly shut eyes. It hurts so bad. Pain explodes with each hit. One. Two. Three.

The bruises won't heal. They haven't been healing recently but I can't think about that now.

The bed dips with the weight of Frank moving away.

Curled up in a ball, I press my fingers to my ears as covertly as possible, but it doesn't help. I can still hear him.

"I don't need you, you stupid fuckin' cunt. I can go anywhere and get it. You're lucky I come home every day to you."

I think it's my silence that sends him over the edge more than my rejection. Frank lands his fist into my head. I know I should defend myself. Put up a fight and let him win so he would stop.

But as images of Eli race through my head, providing an anchor I've never had before, all I can do is hold myself in this ball, in this fetal position, and let him hit me. My non-response is my defiance. For me. For Eli. I can't let Frank feel great after doing what he's doing to me right now. I refuse to satisfy him and his sick need to control me. I can't let him inflict wounds, only to come back later and try to heal them as if he hadn't been the one to cause them. Not this time.

His feet connect with the small of my back, kicking. My body slides closer to the edge of the bed. He doesn't stop. And I don't beg him to. Not this time. It's almost euphoric, this small victory, no matter how fucked up it is. The more he hits me, the more I dare him to with my silence.

A final slap across my head and Frank's foot connects with my lower back, sending me flying off the bed.

Even then, I don't utter a single sound, only making sure that the hits were superficial and that I don't have a concussion.

Frank pulls the blanket I fell off the bed with back up.

"Nobody needs you or your fuckin' pussy, you cancer-ridden fuckin' cunt," he says and turns over on his side of the bed with all the bedding wrapped around him.

I remain there on the floor for a long time. Tears slipping down the side of my face, trickling into my ear and wetting the short strands of my hair on their way down.

I've mentioned before that I'm not a dramatic crier. I possess the ability to break into a million pieces without so much as a twitch of a muscle.

Now isn't any different.

The floor is cold, made worse by the draft coming in from the crack at the bottom of the window. I lay there, grateful that I have two sets of clothes on to ward off the cold and that my head is still intact.

I close my eyes and listen for Frank's breathing. I can pinpoint the exact moment he drops off into sleep, the kind of sleep he's not likely to rouse from until tomorrow morning. His breathing evens out, his inhales noisy and his exhales coming out in sputters. At that, I rise from the floor.

The left side of my face is wet. I let it dry out while I quietly move around the room. The gun is still in Frank's hand, almost at the edge of the bed.

I think if I were to mark the exact moment I made the most terrifying decision of my life, it would be this moment. Standing at the foot of the bed, watching Frank grunt and click and sleep peacefully with a fucking gun in his hand.

The audacity pushes bile up my chest and, like being engulfed in a tornado, I'm confronted by what the reality of my life is and what it should have been... and then what it could be.

My heart, broken for my own life, moves my feet, in search of my sneakers.

Rage sends me to the bathroom, rummaging through the bottom drawer between old razors and medication. I get how bad it looks, stealing the condoms that may or may not belong to Frank, but is there ever anything *good* about having an affair?

Regret for the last ten years hastens me to the front door.

The realization of what my life could have been if I'd met Eli first has me sprinting up the road and around the bend with Pepper hot on my heels.

And it's the single, almost unformed thought of *what if* that gives me the courage to ring his doorbell, with a foil packet hidden in the pocket of my sweats.

I need him. Tonight, I need *all* of him. And the threat of that gun be damned. I'm dying anyway, and I cannot die without knowing Eli like this. Without giving myself to him in this way. To be known by Eli has become unbearable. I'll turn every sacred vow into meaningless syllables for him. My marriage papers be damned.

Frank be damned.

His gun be fucking damned.

CHAPTER 32
Eli

I sit at the counter with a dozen photo albums. These from the very back of the attic. I found them only just this afternoon. My father had been a great tennis player, although their idea of tennis had been handmade rackets and bouncy balls. Not actual tennis balls.

The incessant flickering light above me indicates an urgent ringing of my doorbell.

I fly to the door. That can be only one person.

Yanking it open, my eyes focus on the man standing in front of me.

He's been crying. His eyes are red. His face... devastated.

Pepper wags her tail and sniffs up into the air. I pat her head absently, my eyes fixed on Axel.

He lunges forward, propelling us both into the warmth of the house. His lips, crashing over mine in a kiss that steals my soul.

Something's happened, but he's not giving me a chance to find out. He bites and pulls, his desperation making my concern for him override my desire for whatever he's offering with his body at this moment.

But he won't give me an inch, sucking at my tongue, tugging at my hair. He's losing control in a way I've never seen before.

I kiss him back on instinct. There's a wall coming down from between us, crashing at a phenomenal speed. A line being erased. Boundaries breached. Vows being broken.

I don't know who deepens the kiss and takes us to the other side. I'd like to think it was me so Axel wouldn't have to bear the burden of taking us to that place of no return.

I suck into his mouth, pulling his tongue into mine. His hands rush up and down my back and I place my hand on his throat to hear his need. The vibrations thrumming against my fingers harden my cock. I drop my hands to his hips, slamming them against me.

He's so fucking hard, rubbing against me, so hot and needy.

But I need to know what this is.

I rip my lips from his and, with his face captured between my palms, I search his face for answers.

He pulls me back and I allow another hard kiss, but then I hold him back once more.

His hands move, both palms facing each other, his index and middle fingers pointed outward, and then he points to himself. I lift my eyes to his face. His mouth moves. Even if I hadn't understood his signs, I'd have heard him in my soul.

"Fuck me, Eli. Please."

I frown, trying to convey my concern. I don't have my phone or a pen and paper nearby, so I sign, hoping he'll understand.

"What's wrong?" My palms cup his face.

"We can talk later. For now, please, Eli, I—"

The desperation in his eyes is too much to bear. I slam my mouth over his, kissing him like he belongs to me. He does.

He's brought the walls down. Nothing exists between us now.

He's *mine*.

My hands, previously restricted by that fucking ring on his finger, now move with a ferocious possessiveness, demanding to know every inch of him.

He revels in my touch, dipping his head backward, pressing up against my dick, carnal and full of sin.

I lift him up. His legs come around my waist and I carry him to my bed.

He slips down my body, standing in the middle of my bedroom. My lips connect with his again, biting into his mouth, sucking at the corner of his lips while I undress him.

I'm half naked, wearing only a pair of sweats, so when his hands flatten against my chest, moving up and down, any doubt about doing this with Axel before knowing what brought him to me like this flies out the window.

I may be *grounded* and *diplomatic*. Cautious. But not tonight.

Tonight, I'm a selfish asshole.

I reach for his jacket, stripping him of it. Underneath is a jersey and, underneath that, a sweatshirt. I frown. It's cold, but not *that* cold. The light is still on, so when I remove all the layers of Axel's clothes, the red smudges on his shoulders scream back at me.

My eyes widen, meeting his. He drops his gaze and reaches for me again, but this time I'm not giving in to his desperate search for my touch.

I sign furiously. *"This? What happened?"*

He shakes his head, trying to kiss me again. I hold him at arm's length, turning him around slowly.

A sledgehammer of fury blasts through my chest. The same red marks follow along his back. His lower back is completely red. The area near his left ear is also red. I lift my hand to touch the side of his head. He winces. I'm going to tear something apart.

"Doctor," I sign urgently.

He shakes his head. Then he signs, *I'm fine*, and he does it perfectly, except he also includes, *how are you?* at the end. Another time, I would have lifted him in the air with joy over his attempt to communicate with me like this. But not now.

He's hurt. In pain. I can't bear it.

I grab my jacket and head for the door. Axel pulls me back.

"Where are you going?" he asks.

Angry that I can't communicate with him fast enough, I sign harshly. *I'm going to kill him.*

He frowns and I'm angry at him for not understanding. I jerk out of his grasp, but I think he's figured out what I'm planning.

He turns me back to him, his palms on my cheeks, holding onto me tightly. Shaking his head desperately, he says, "No, Eli. Stay, please. Make it right. I'm like a corpse. I'm not any good at this but please, Eli, make it right."

I don't understand. Corpse? Did that fucking cunt down the road tell him that?

I *am* making it right. I'm going to pulverize that bastard's face and have him thrown in jail, and then I'm going to take Axel back home with me. Marriage or not. Vows or not.

But he holds onto me tighter. "Make it right," he repeats.

I don't know another way to protect him. Defend him. Give him justice. He drops one hand and when he brings it up again, it's to press the square packet of a condom into my hand. Tears fall down his precious face. "Make it right, Eli. I beg you. Make everything right."

I can't get past the lump in my throat. Make it right? Make *this* right? Make what exists between us right? Touch him, claim him and make him mine even when he belongs to someone else?

No. He belongs to no one but me. I take the condom from him.

I'll make it right. Reaching down, I slip his sweats off. Seeing he has two pairs on makes my blood boil. I drop to my knees. Two pairs of socks. I'll kill that fucking cunt.

My lips graze his thighs. Lightly muscled, light dusting of hair. I press my lips to the juncture between his thighs. My cheek brushes against his heavy erection.

When I drop my head to rub my nose against the base of his cock, his fingers sink into my hair, pulling.

I bury my face in his groin, rubbing up and down, side to side. Round and round. His cock is so beautiful. So perfect. Full and thick. His balls, big and heavy. My chin rubs up his balls. Up, up to his beautiful penis. Memories of what he tasted like, how he felt in my mouth, force my mouth to seek out another taste.

But I want to savor this, so I ghost my lips over the crown of his cock. I'm rewarded with a sharp tug of my hair.

Axel's fingers dig into my scalp. His thighs tremble. Pulling back, I look up at him. His forehead is creased, his eyes on me and his mouth open. His chest moves up and down rapidly.

I rise, backing him up until we get to the bed. Pushing slightly, I urge him onto the bed. I stand back, admiring his nakedness. Lean and strong. Sinewy muscles. But has he lost some weight?

He watches me watching him and then looks away, grabbing the edge of the blanket and pulling it over his body.

I drop onto the bed, between his legs, spreading them wide. He bites his lip, uncertainty dancing across his face. I tug at the blanket he's got captured in his fist and then give him a questioning look. He lets go, allowing me to see his nakedness once more.

Axel's dick lies proudly against his stomach. I lean forward and lick slowly over the crown, taking all his pre-cum into my mouth. His body bows off the bed, and when I look up, his head is thrown back and digging into the bed, his hands spread wide out. He's a fucking wet dream. So open and exposed to me. *For* me. *Because* of me.

I suck the crown into my mouth. Another jerk of his hips.

He leaks into my mouth.

With his cock in my mouth, I reach underneath and rub his balls between my fingers. Flattening my palm, I rub him, then hold all that heaviness in the palm of my hand. He writhes under me.

He's not a goddam fucking corpse. He's so perfect. So beautiful. So *alive* beneath me.

I'll make every fucking thing right.

CHAPTER 33
Axel

There is no guilt.

I can't explain the feeling of freedom from... yourself. From your beliefs, your values, your ideologies. When seeking comfort from someone—from Eli, in my case—who makes you feel safe and is no longer regulated by hollow vows and empty promises, it's easy to clutch the sheets in ecstasy while he wraps his mouth around your cock and takes you in so deep you might die from the sensations wracking through your body.

Eli's bed smells of him. I lay sprawled like it's where I belong, inhaling him from the sheets. Never have I ever offered my body up to someone like this. Never before has my body responded to another human being like this.

Thoughts of Frank waking up and finding me gone, of him barging through Eli's door come and go like little sparks, shocking me for just a millisecond, but when Eli takes me deep into his throat, he chases away these intrusive thoughts.

My tugs of encouragement on his hair demonstrate my need to let him know with my body what this is doing to me. What *he's* doing to me. He reads my body like an open book.

I'm left writhing on the bed, begging him to give me more. I, a married man, am lying here in another man's bed while my husband sleeps in ours down the road. Panic threatens to rise, but then the image of Frank punching my head and kicking me off the bed overpowers my anxiety. His words ring inside my head.

*Nobody needs you or your fuckin' pussy, you cancer-ridden fuckin'
cunt.*

Nobody needs you or your fuckin' pussy.

You

cancer-ridden

fuckin'

cunt.

And just like that, I erase Frank from my head. My hips lift,
encouraging Eli. He sucks me deep and then lifts his body, resting
on his knees between my legs.

With the light still on, I'm self-conscious, but with the way he's
staring at my body, I can't bring myself to hide.

He signs, *Beautiful,* running his palm over my calves and up my
thighs.

I lift my hand and sign. *Thank you.*

Eli's hands continue to run up and down my thighs, sliding his
thumbs along the juncture of my thighs, massaging. I raise my hips
to his hands, thrusting upward with every stroke of his fingers.

My cock is thick and big, standing up and beading with precum.
He isn't touching my cock and that drives me insane, but to have
him touch me like this is equally maddening.

He encourages me onto my stomach. I turn hesitantly. Under
the bright light, I don't know how to hide. Eli comes to settle at my
side. His fingers trail from my nape, down every knob along my
spine, to the small of my back. Over my ass.

He bends, licking along the small of my back. Soft, petting kisses
there. Then his mouth moves down.

His tongue glides over my ass. My dick swells, painfully so.

Eli moves between my legs again, gently shifting my left leg until
it's bent at the knee. His tongue swirls along the crease of my ass.

Moves across each ass cheek kissing, biting, sucking. Then he pushes my ass cheeks apart and slides his tongue from my taint all the way up and then back down. Eli licks my ass, lapping along the inside of each cheek.

I moan loudly, engulfed by my lust, lifting my ass, offering more of it to Eli's sinful mouth. I want his mouth on my hole. I need it right there. How long has it been since someone loved my body like this? *Never.* I have been married for ten years and I have *never* been loved like this.

Eli's tongue swipes at my asshole. I still, pulling in with the sensation. He licks again, upward and hard this time.

Ah fuck, yeah.

I reach down, pulling my ass cheek further apart. Eli gets it and flattens his palm over each cheek and pulls apart until my asshole is stretched for his mouth. Then he covers my hole with his mouth. Tonguing me and sucking, then kissing like it's my mouth he's kissing.

The thought of Eli kissing my asshole like this fucks me up so badly my balls prepare to shoot. I stave it off with only shreds of willpower.

Oohh. Eli buries his face into my ass, rubbing his nose up and down my hole, his strokes long enough for his chin to graze my hole.

Fuuck. *Again,* I scream internally and push back, telling him to do it again and I know I will never be able to walk away from this. Like tasting the forbidden fruit, I'm drunk with lust. Free from my vows.

With low, lustful moans, I move my ass round and round, inviting more of Eli into me.

His chin scrapes down my hole. The prickle of his clipped beard is fucking heaven. Or hell. Whatever it is, I'll die for it. When he scrapes up, a loud groan leaves my mouth. I rotate my ass and he mimics the action, rotating his chin over my asshole. The prickliness of his facial hair massaging against my hole is fucking insane. I'm so far gone, my moans loud and my vulgarity the worst shade of unholy.

"Fuck, Eli," I chant, but he can't hear me. So, I turn on my back and pull him up to me. Wrap my legs around his waist, bring his hand to my throat and I eat his mouth. Vulgarities fly out of my mouth between bites.

"Fuck me, Eli. Fuck me like I'm your last fuck." Because he might be mine.

His fingers tighten around my neck.

"I need you inside my fucking hole right fucking now."

He pulls back, and I repeat the words for him to see. He grabs the condom from where it's lying on the pillow above us.

I reach down, yanking until he's free of his sweats. His cock is the most beautiful thing I've ever seen.

I've changed my mind. Pushing him back into a kneeling position between my legs I take the condom from him. I need to taste this man before I take him inside me. I stand on the precipice of yet another secret to make and keep. Leaning forward, I take him inside my mouth. His head drops back, and loud grunting sounds escape his throat.

Eli's voice, his lust, sounds so fucking beautiful.

His dick swells in my mouth, and I eat him up, feasting on his pre-cum. But he pulls my head back and brings the hand holding the condom to his dick.

I sheath him slowly, reveling in the newness of this. I'm dying only to be reborn, over and over again.

Eli pushes me back onto the pillow and I lift my knees to my chest. Frank hated missionary style. He always wanted me facing away from him. Never wanted to be face-to-face. Something dark moves inside my chest, moving down to fuel my erection. It must be some kind of evil force making me fucking love what I'm doing. Fuck Frank.

Eli anchors himself, his hands at the back of my thighs, holding me in place, and then he breaches my hole.

Fuck. I'm doing this. Another man is fucking me and I fucking *love* it. I *want* it. I'll burn in hell for this. I'll deny God for this. I'll die for this.

Eli pushes all the way in, pauses, and then begins to move.

Ah, fuck. He massages me so well. In. Out. In and fucking out. *Give me all of this fucking dick, Eli.*

He watches me. I pull him to me until we're nose to nose, and then I kiss him while he fucks me so fucking deep and hard. My own dick suffers, smashed between our stomachs.

But I don't need much.

I'm a starved man. I've been on a lifelong fast.

He thrusts once. Twice.

And fuck if I don't wake up the whole of fucking River Valley with my shouts as I come between my and Eli's stomachs.

His orgasm chasing mine, he comes with loud grunts.

It's the most beautiful thing.

CHAPTER 34
Eli

He's beautiful when he comes. Does he know that? Will he understand what I mean if I tell him nothing on this earth comes close to how beautiful he is in this moment?

Axel's chest heaves with his pleasure. I pull out of him gently, remove the condom, and discard it on the nightstand.

Then, I reach down to his stomach, trailing my finger over his cum stained skin. My head dips, swiping his cum into my mouth.

His hand tightens in my hair, pulling at my scalp.

I rise to meet Axel's lips. His shocked face makes me smile as I slip my tongue into his mouth, depositing his cum onto his tongue.

He sucks hard and greedy. The length of his body smashes up against mine, his legs wrapping tightly around my waist as we kiss and he eats his cum out of my mouth.

It's Axel who pulls away first but only to say, "Pepper is scratching at the door."

I roll off him, pulling him close to my side, and then reach for my phone.

You'll have to divorce Pepper, I type. He watches me type, so by the time I realize what I've written, it's too late. It was meant as a joke, what with Pepper interrupting us but I know what it looks like. Not that I don't agree with the idea that Axel should divorce Frank too, but I don't think this is the way to begin such a discussion.

His eyes look worried again, and he lowers his face.

What happened, Axel? I type.

"He hit me." He presses his lips together, and his dimples deepen with his shaky inhalation.

Why? Not that it matters, but when I kill Frank, I want to be able to say why.

Axel's answer causes a kind of fury I've never experienced before. "I don't know for sure," he says. "I didn't want to have sex with him."

And then, when I can't imagine a fury greater than this, he adds, "With the gun. He hit me with the gun again, Eli."

I pull him into my arms, my mind racing. I'll get him the best divorce lawyer in the country. I'll ask my mother to speak to one of the judges in our circle to see if they can speed things up. The upgrades to the house have been completed. We can do an official opening because I know this town won't let me leave without one, and I'll ask Mrs. Dalton to manage everything.

We'll also need a restraining order. Not just so Frank can stay away from Axel, but to make sure I don't get near enough to Frank to actually kill him.

I have it all worked out. It's so easy. I'll have to communicate all of this to Axel as soon as possible. Maybe not tonight. He's still shaken up, and I don't want to overwhelm him.

Tomorrow. I'll tell him everything tomorrow and I'll start making enquiries then, too.

Axel shifts, moving away. I let him go, but only so I can get a good look at his face.

"I have to go," he says.

I give him my most clear *you're-fucking-kidding-me* look.

A smile ghosts his face when I turn my phone screen to him.
Stay here.

He shakes his head. "I can't. I have to be there when Frank wakes up."

What? Absolutely not. I won't allow it. I type. ***Fucking why?***

His face brightens at my words and his shoulders shake with laughter.

"I love the way you curse," he says with a smile.

My lips pull upward despite my growing concern over Axel wanting to return to Frank.

He answers me after a long time. "He'll probably kill me as soon as he finds me if he wakes up and finds that I'm not there." His teeth clamp over his bottom lip and his eyes search mine. Fear radiates from him. "He'll kill us both if he finds out."

I'm not letting you go back there.

Axel stares at my phone screen for a long time. When he lifts his eyes back to mine, I'm surprised by the worry there.

He won't lay another hand on you.

"Please don't do anything, Eli. I'll find a way to handle this."

I shake my head and his worry expands in his eyes. He gets up. I grab his wrist, pulling him back, but when a flicker of shock and fear pass through his eyes, I drop my hand immediately. "*I'm sorry*," I sign.

"I'm just going to get Pepper."

I nod.

He pulls the light blanket with him, wrapping it around his body. So different from the uninhibited man he was when his body was underneath mine just a few minutes ago.

Pepper comes bounding into the room, landing on my side of the bed. I shift to the center to give her space. Axel comes to sit on the edge of the bed close to me.

My plans, which sounded perfect in my head a few minutes ago, now seem less than simple.

I'll take you away from here.

Axel takes my phone from my hand and types. ***Will you steal me away in the middle of the night?***

I don't know why we're communicating like this, but I type back. Maybe we need to see our thoughts. For them to exist in this world. Not like words or signs that can't be looked at again.

Yes. If that's what I have to do.

Promise me, when the time is right, he types.

My eyes search his for this new way he's being. I can't gage it. Why won't he just leave? What is he so afraid of? Bullies and abusers use fear like a weapon. All Axel has to do is show he's not afraid and that bastard won't come near him. He can simply walk away. Isn't it *that simple?*

I can't yet figure out how to navigate this differently from how I'd handle any problem I'm faced with, so I let my instincts guide me. ***I promise***, I type.

"I have to go back tonight," he says.

I take a screenshot of our conversation. I don't want to lose it. I want these words to always exist.

I squeeze his hand and he squeezes back. "Trust me," he says. "Nothing terribly bad will happen to me."

I shake my head. *No.*

"If I know something very bad is going to happen, I'll find a way to come to you, or I'll send Pepper."

Do you promise?

He takes my phone. ***I promise.***

I watch him get dressed into his two sets of clothes. He notices and with a sad smile, he explains: "It hurts less when I'm well padded."

The restrictions Axel has placed on my role in all of this make me rage. But I force myself to trust his promise. I move to the edge of the bed, helping him dress. Kissing him as I do so wherever I can find naked flesh. His thighs. His thick, flaccid cock. His abdomen. His chest. His neck. Then his eyes, the tip of his nose and finally, his lips. He deepens the kiss. So deep that when I reach up to touch his face, I find tears there.

He tears his mouth away from mine and, with a signal to Pepper, he rushes out of the room. I follow, watching him hurry out the front door and up the pathway.

And for the first time in my life, I feel utterly helpless.

CHAPTER 35
Axel

"How long you gonna sleep like the dead?" Frank's raspy voice sounds close to my ear.

My eyes fly open and I'm immediately awake and on high alert. But my body remains frozen in place, braced for pain.

Frank yanks the blankets off me and drags me off the bed.

"Get up and make us something to eat," he grunts.

Silently, I walk to the bathroom to wash my face. Pepper follows me inside. As I brush my teeth, I ground myself with thoughts of Eli. His care, his gentleness. The feel of his hands on me while he tongue-fucked my ass.

My cock stirs.

When he put his mouth on me, sucking and biting at my asshole before fucking me into a place where only he and I exist.

Thoughts of Eli fucking me give me the courage I need, and my expectations begin to shift.

I don't need Frank's love. I don't need him to be the man he promised to be. I don't need to obsess over what I could do to please him, how I could change myself, how I could understand him more so he'd be better.

I have Eli.

I don't need Frank.

I just need to figure out how to not die at the hand of my husband.

I listen for noises. The scrapes of Frank's boots come from outside. He's having a smoke.

I urge Pepper to the door, making sure her heavy body is flush against it.

Then, sitting on the toilet seat, I rub my palm over my erection. Dark thoughts unfurl in my head. These thoughts bring with them courage and an uncaringness for my vows. I tilt my hips forward, imagining Eli inside me.

Fuck Frank.

My hand slips inside my sweats and I wrap my hands around my dick. Pre-cum oozes out, a testament to my lust for Eli. With blood rushing in my ears and my dick begging for release, I pump fast and hard, swiping at images inside my head.

Of Eli with his face in my ass.

His mouth on me.

His cock buried deep inside my hole.

Thick cum flies over my fist and my abdomen. I massage my dick, milking my orgasm.

A sheen of sweat covers my upper lip and I tilt my head back while my heart rate slowly descends to a regular pace.

I wash my hands and then I leave the bathroom, prepare Frank's breakfast and call him in to eat.

He eyes me all through breakfast, watching me push my eggs around my plate. "Stop wasting the fuckin' food, Axel." And when he doesn't like my silence, he adds, "What're you, deaf and dumb, like that neighbor of ours?"

Without speaking, I lift a forkful of eggs to my mouth.

That deaf and dumb neighbor's dick was inside me just a few hours ago, is what I tell Frank inside my head. Outwardly, I settle for, "Do you want more eggs?"

CHAPTER 36
Eli

I haven't seen Axel in two days. I'm out of my mind with worry. I've driven past there more times than I want to admit to. The bookstore is closed this weekend so I can't see him there.

He wasn't at sign language class today. I'm distracted, and it's showing.

A touch on my back draws me out of my rushing thoughts.

Are you okay? Mrs. Dalton signs when I turn around.

I nod and sign back. *I'm okay.*

She leans in close, her face turned up. "Is Axel okay?" she asks with her voice. I look around me to see if anyone is around. The library has mostly cleared out.

I lift my shoulder in a shrug. She frowns and takes my hand in hers, leading me to the back of the library, where it's quiet.

Then she takes out a notebook and a pen and writes.

Are you taking good care of him?

I don't know Mrs. Dalton well enough to trust her with this. Morning teas don't qualify as a factor to share with her something as big as my affair with Axel. When I don't answer, she writes me another note.

Will you take him away from here?

Leaning into my instincts, risking everything because those words make her sound like an ally, I nod slowly.

Her wrinkly face lights up. She writes again. ***Don't make him cut his hair, it's cruel.***

I frown. What is she talking about? Is she also mad about Frank not liking Axel's long hair? My confusion is evident because she starts talking instead of writing. "His hair is the only thing he has when he's well."

She drops her head, shaking it sadly. I don't know what's going on here.

I take the notebook from her and write. **What do you mean, not well?** I recall Axel saying he'd been sick when he was younger, but...

A frown crosses her face to match mine. "Uh, well."

I take her by the shoulders, my frown deepening. She seems to have caught herself before she could give me some important information.

She slaps her hand to her mouth, her eyes wide. I pull her hand away and cock my head, indicating for her to repeat herself or explain.

"He was just... just very sick at one point," she says.

From the way Mrs. Dalton is reacting, I don't think it's a small matter.

I run my hands through my hair, frustrated.

Mrs. Dalton rests her fingers on my arm. "Just take him away, Eli," she says with imploring eyes.

"And let him keep his hair. That Frank makes him cut it every time, but you don't do that to him, okay?"

I nod. What else could I do? My thoughts are all over the place. I have to get to Axel. He needs to tell me exactly what's going on. I don't like Mrs. Dalton's concern. It feels too heavy. I have so many questions, but the one that's bothering me the most is what this deal is with Axel's hair.

At first it sounded like such a mundane thing, but Mrs. Dalton is acting like it's the most important thing she could tell me about Axel.

My stomach twists. Because I can think of only one common denominator if Axel used to be *very, very sick* and if his hair was the only thing he had when he was *well*.

And if I'm right, Axel's life is much worse than he lets on.

I write in the notebook. ***I won't do anything to hurt him.***

She smiles radiantly and writes me a note back. ***I just want you to take him away.***

"I've told him for years to find someone else and just run away," she says. "And I don't care that he's doing it this way. Sometimes, you're left with no choice."

She searches my face for understanding. I give it to her and she gives me hers for what Axel and I are doing.

But I have to find a way to talk to Axel. This isn't a simple game. Not some small-town fling.

So much is suddenly at stake here. I don't know how it got so big so quickly, but one thing remains: Axel is in trouble and I'm not going anywhere until he's safe with me.

CHAPTER 37
Axel

The headaches are getting worse and I just know my anemia is getting worse, too. If I don't schedule a visit to the doctor soon, I'll be dead sooner than necessary.

Frank makes us coffee on Monday morning, before work.

"I'm swapping a few shifts again this and next week," he says. There's no reference to Friday's episode. It's like it never happened. Frank is nonchalant. Friendly, even. Anyone looking into this scene would see an ordinary couple doing ordinary things before leaving for work.

But Frank is not the only one. I, too, am behaving like nothing happened on Friday night.

I just can't decide which one of us is worse. Abuser or Adulterer?

"Okay," I reply. While I'm able to ignore the growing ache in my head, I'm not able to ignore the leap of my heart that Frank won't be here some nights.

He hands me a cup of coffee, a gentle gesture offered with a kind smile. I search my conscience for some measure of guilt for Friday night and I find none.

Frank being nice to me like this makes me even angrier than when he's abusive. The absolute dismissal of what he's done to me makes my blood boil. Only to be cooled down by the fact that there is something that I've done that could get me and Eli killed.

Frank comes to stand in front of me. The urge to step back is frightening. And when the back of his fingers graze my cheek, I brace myself.

"You're so beautiful, Ax. I love you so much."

If I thought Frank's open palm slicing across my cheek was awful, this is worse. Frank's 'love' for me is worse than anything I can imagine. I'd begged and pleaded for ten years for him to love me. Yet now, it feels *vile.*

He leans forward just as the honk of a horn sounds outside, indicating his ride. I turn away under the pretence of being distracted by the horn. Because to kiss Frank is to betray to Eli.

He pulls my face back to his and pushes his lips hard onto mine, and then leaves them with a smacking sound. He gives me a broad smile and heads for the door. "You're the best thing that ever happened to me, Axel," he calls from the door.

I drop onto the chair, wondering how people who cheat usually navigate through their affairs.

All I know is that Eli consumes me. Nothing else exists. I'm in so deep I don't care for consequences anymore.

Eli lifted the veil, showing me what it could be like to be happy. He *removed* the veil and let me see myself. The *good* me. The *me* that's worth it. The *me* I'm not allowed to be when I'm with Frank. In Eli, *through* Eli, I see the *me* I've never met. And to see that me is so heartbreaking, I can't bear to look sometimes. I'm afraid that Eli might love me. And then, I'm afraid of *how much* he might love me. But the thing I'm most terrified of is how much I might love him if I let myself.

But I'm so starved for it, I'll drink from this well of infidelity like a dying man.

With a sigh, I grab my umbrella and follow Frank out. There is a slight drizzle outside. Nothing to worry about. I've walked in this weather several times.

Frank is getting into Kenny's car. Kenny greets me from the car and leans sideways. "Hey Axel, you want a lift? James says hi, by the way."

The drizzle has picked up, but only slightly. "You sure?" I call back. I ignore his comment about James and I don't even dare look to see what Frank thinks about it.

"It's just a slight drizzle. He'll be fine," Frank says as he climbs into the passenger seat. "Besides, you know how people become brain dead on the road when it's raining and forget how to drive. Let's go; we'll be late."

But before Kenny can back out, a black SUV swings into our yard, blocking Kenny in.

Eli hops off the vehicle and walks around. I stand there stupidly with my umbrella over my head, alternating between terror and elation. It takes superhuman strength not to behave like a cheating asshole. I avert my eyes, keeping them off Eli.

He walks around the hood and heads straight for me. My heart thunders in my chest. What is he doing?

He signs to me as he walks, his gait confident and relaxed.

Hello beautiful, he says with his hands.

If Frank had not exited the car right then, I might have allowed the stars in my eyes to shine.

"Did Pepper get away again?" Frank asks me and then flicks his eyes between me and Eli.

I cast a gaze around the yard. If Pepper ran up to Eli's place, he'd have brought her back. So, she's probably out in the woods chasing squirrels.

"No, I don't think so," I say.

Eli frowns. Frank is facing away from him; he didn't catch what Frank said.

"Is it Pepper?" I ask Eli.

He shakes his head.

I look at him enquiringly, indicating that I'm confused about why he's here, while also trying to tell him how happy I am to see him.

"Is there something he needs?" Frank asks me, his eyes bouncing between me and Eli once again.

"Is there something you need?" I ask Eli. And then to Frank I say, "Eli can lip read."

Frank frowns like it's the stupidest thing he's ever heard.

"Well, can you tell him he's blocked us in?"

I face Eli again. "What did you need, Eli?" I try to keep the softness in my eyes and not my voice.

He signs first. I recognize only a two words. *Rain. You.*

I frown and shake my head, telling him I don't understand.

With a relaxed smile, he takes out his phone and types.

I saw it was raining, so I came by to give you and Frank a lift to work.

I lean forward to read it, but he pulls it back and types again. *Just trying to be neighborly.*

Me *and Frank?*

He holds it up to Frank, who reads it and then tells me, "Tell him to move so we can go. He's making us late. And no, you can't ride with him."

Eli can read his lips clearly. Only I notice the clenched fist at his side. He drops his phone back into his pocket, heads back to his car, and backs out.

Frank gets into the car with Kenny and they drive out.

Alone with Eli now, I watch Kenny's car until it's disappeared down the road. Eli circles his vehicle and stops next to me.

Frank's confidence in my obedience to him, and his over inflated ego making him believe he can issue an instruction and simply leave like that, provides the perfect protection for my affair. He'll never suspect that I would disobey him.

His parting words infuriate me. Does he really think I'm so easy to control? Has he always thought this lowly of me?

But I'm the cheater here. Frank is absolutely right about not wanting me to ride with Eli.

Eli drops the window and leans over the passenger seat, opening the door.

I wait a beat, double check down the road. Then, I climb in.

"I'm sorry Frank ignored you like that," I say, facing him. And then, "That was a dangerous move, Eli."

He takes my hand in his for a second. Then he signs and I understand him perfectly. *"You are mine."*

My eyes flick up to fuse with his and then, without meaning to, they drop to his lips.

Even though he can't hear my response the way I can, I need to hear myself say it, even if it's barely a whisper. "Yes."

He signs again. *"You belong to me."*

Again, without hesitation, I answer. "I belong to you."

He smiles and I find myself returning it with some degree of confidence.

I wish he would kiss me and, with his eyes locked on my lips, I know he wants it, too. But it's too risky so we settle for holding hands. The fact that I had been instructed not to ride with Eli finds a place somewhere at the back of my mind.

Eli pulls our entwined hands into his lap, his thumb sweeping over the back of my hand.

And for these few minutes, I pretend that we have the right to be like this. The right to have this moment.

The ride is over too soon. Eli slows down to a stop as close as possible to the entrance of the bookstore. The rain is coming down stronger and the fact that Eli had noticed enough to park so close to the entrance makes my heart swell.

He squeezes my hand and I return the action.

Neither of us moves, but the street is already busy and someone is bound to notice if I stay inside Eli's car for longer than is deemed polite. I have no reason to stay in this car as long as I already have.

Finally, Eli releases my hand and reaches over my knee for the glove compartment. He pulls out a phone. It's an iPhone. It looks brand new.

I look at him sharply. *"Keep this at work,"* he types on his phone.

He places the phone on my lap. It vibrates with a text immediately.

A secret phone.

I close my fingers around the phone and slip it into my pocket, signing, "*Thank you.*"

I exit the car with yet another tool to help me with my affair.

Another way to cheat on Frank.

Another way to be with Eli.

Another way to experience the most incredible thing in my life.

A secret phone to provide a lifeline directly to Eli. Not an ounce of guilt rises in me.

Today, I feel justified. Why shouldn't I have this? Why shouldn't I be happy too?

I unlock the bookstore, keeping the *closed* sign facing outside. I'm grateful for the thirty minutes I'll be alone before Ben arrives, because I'll need to figure out how to use an iPhone.

CHAPTER 38
Eli

I'd never thought much about how my life would end up when it came to love. Like everything else in my life, I knew it would work out based on how much or how little work I put into it.

I'm not the guy that obsesses about things. I *expect* things to work out. Relationships have been relatively easy for me. There aren't many to speak of, being the main reason. But even the few forgettable ones had come and gone without much drama. We met, had a good time, things changed and then we went our separate ways.

I don't regret them but walking away had been the same as walking away from a business deal that didn't work out. It happens.

I didn't stare at my phone for hours, hoping for a phone call, like I am now.

The rain calmed down a little and that resulted in my lights flashing three different times within thirty minutes, just after I dropped Axel off.

Mrs. Dalton brought me a pecan pie 'to share with Axel later, if we managed to get together.' She wrote it down on a piece of paper and then tore it up into a million pieces after I'd read it. "Don't want that stinkin' Frank finding out," she'd said. I don't know if she was talking to me or to herself, but I read her loud and clear.

David Shapiro's wife came by after that with some mashed potatoes. "Extra butter, yellow like the sun," she'd said dramatically and making sure her face was close to mine when she'd said it. I appreciated the effort.

Poor old Dennis Walker came by with some painkillers just in case I had a headache. He'd stood at the door a second longer than was polite and I got the message. I warmed up the still untouched container of pasta I'd made the night before and handed it over to him with a canister of fresh coffee and fifty dollars. And I only know his name is Dennis Walker because it said so on the name tag of what looked like a janitor's uniform.

Then, when I was sure my weekly dose of River Valley community check-ups was done, I closed my door and dropped myself onto my bed, my phone stuck to my palm.

I could have texted Axel first. It's what I would have done with anyone else in my life. It isn't rocket science. It's simple and logical: If I wanted to text someone, I simply did. But with Axel, there are rules I'm not accustomed to.

Such as this text message debacle I now find myself in. There seems to be a rule about who texts who first. And it feels like I should wait for him to do it. My gut tells me it's important to give him the space and control. To let him lead this thing between us at his pace.

It's new, this *being led* thing, but it's not unwanted. Axel's comfort and his need for safety have become more important than anything in my life.

As for Mrs. Dalton's confession over the weekend about Axel being sick, the only comfort I have is the fact that, well, he didn't *look* sick but I'm not entirely sure how to leave it to Axel to open up on his own. A tight ball sits in my chest when I think about how sick he must have been at some point of his life.

I must have dozed off at some point. The vibration of my phone in my hand rouses me from my sleep with a text from Axel.

Hi, it says.

My heart leaps. An unfamiliar reaction.

Hi, I type back immediately.

*Axel: **Thank you for the phone. It looks so expensive. I'll keep it safe at work until I have to give it back.***

The last part of the text ties my stomach into knots. I answer his subtext with one of my own.

*Me: **You're welcome. I won't want it back.***

*Axel: **I can't keep such an expensive thing after you've gone back.***

I'm not one to beat around the bush, but this time, I'm unsure about my next response. I send it, but without the usual confidence I'd have felt in other situations.

*Me: **I'm taking you with me when I go back.***

He doesn't respond for several minutes and I watch my screen like a teenage boy, filled with dread and horror and panic, and a million questions racing through my mind.

Do I say *sorry, I didn't mean it?* Even when I do?

Do I wait for him to say something first?

This, too, is something new. This... uncertainty. This constriction in my chest telling me that I don't entirely control this situation and the nagging thought that if something went wrong, I wouldn't be able to walk away as easily as I'd done with previous relationships.

He finally responds.

*Axel: **I'm scared, Eli.***

Before I can take in the content of the text, I pause to notice how his use of my first name sends something skating down my spine. This *thing* is warm and makes me smile. It's like I can *hear* him speak my name. Then I respond, using his name, hoping it will have the same effect on him.

*Me: **I'll keep you safe. I promise. I want you, Axel. Every part of you.***

I'm referring to his medical history too, but of course, he doesn't know that.

Axel: ***There's this book I need to finish reading...***

Again that leap in my heart and the uncontrollable smile spreading across my face.

*Me: **I'll bring you those nuts you like so much.***

*Axel: **You don't have to.***

*Me: **And I'll kiss you all night.***

He turns it playful: ***What about my book?***

*Me: **I won't kiss your book.***

*Axel: ***a string of laughing emojis***

*Me: ***a single heart****

*Axel: ***a single heart****

He goes offline and I go off my axis. I've never felt this way before.

Tonight can't come fast enough.

CHAPTER 39
Axel

I don't know if I have everything I need to continue with what I'm doing, but it feels like I have it all under control.

I'm keeping secrets from my best friend, who, since this morning, can't stop complimenting me on how happy I seem.

I have a secret phone which is currently hidden in the bottom drawer of a steel cupboard in the corner of the storeroom. Bank statements from five years ago lie in a stack over the phone and (hopefully) the only key to the drawer is the one tucked into the inside pocket of my parka.

I didn't argue when Frank texted me to say the boys were coming over to re-watch last week's game. If I allowed my conscience to dictate this part of my life, I'd have died of guilt for the glee I felt when he told me. And if not that, then definitely the fact that I encouraged him.

And as for stealing time with Eli, when Frank asked if we needed more money for gas this month, I'd lied and said yes so he'd agree to the night shifts that his co-worker wanted to swap with him for the next three weeks.

"Hey, you good in there?" Ben pokes his head through the doorway.

"Uh, yeah." I act like my little jump was me reaching for a duster on one of the high shelves.

Ben walks in and inspects the storeroom. "Wow, this place hasn't been this clean and sparkly in fuckin' years. Good job, Ax."

"Uh, yeah, no problem." It's incredible how clean things can get when you're looking for hiding places for your affair-phone.

"I'm going out to get us some lunch. You wanna watch the front for a bit?"

"Sure."

"You sure you're okay?" Ben looks back and squints at me.

"God, Ben. Are you looking for a different answer?"

He laughs. "Did Frank die and rise again a new man?"

"No," I mumble.

"Okay, what do you want?" Ben asks from the door.

"Just a water and an avocado salad."

Ben laughs. "Bro, the last time you had an avocado salad, you were in the hospital and I was writing finals in high school."

He stops abruptly, but before he can say anything, I hold up my hand, stopping him. "I'm fine, Ben. Don't say another word. I'm just not in the mood for grease today."

"Okay, if you're sure." He doesn't sound convinced, but he doesn't interrogate me further. "You can have some of my burger and fries if you change your mind."

"Okay," I say, settling behind the counter to sort through next week's orders.

I don't end up sharing in Ben's lunch. The smell made me want to vomit.

I take two painkillers for a slight headache just before closing time and then I slip Casey a new book as she casually passed by the bookstore. In truth, I was more interested in the book than anyone else because it was about a guy who cheats on his husband.

Anyway, Ben was letting down the last of the blinds inside when Casey and I made the exchange.

Ben decided to close an hour early today because the rain had started up again. Just before locking up, I made an excuse to check up on some damaged books in the storeroom and managed to send Eli a text to tell him I would see him later. I may have also told him I couldn't wait to see him.

There'd been no time to change my mind and unsend that last text because Ben had come into the storeroom to tell me that we can finish up tomorrow and that I'd worked hard enough today and can I please bring that same happy face back to work tomorrow.

I watch Ben drive down the street and once he's out of view, I cross the street to the local medical center and climb the stairs that lead to Dr. Shashi's office. I don't need an appointment to see him. We're old friends. But the kind of friends where *not* seeing each other is how we know everything is okay.

"We need to run some tests, but we've talked about this for a long time," Dr. Shashi says, after giving me a big handshake and a comforting pat on my back.

"Yes, Dr. Shashi."

"We'll do everything we can. We'll fight to keep you as healthy as possible."

"Thank you, I appreciate that."

"Let's wait for the results."

The relationship between a doctor and a patient is hard to explain. They're the closest anyone will come to understanding what it is to be told you're *certainly* going to die and that it will happen soon.

"I'll let you know as soon as the results come in. We knew that a relapse was possible and we've been prepared."

I go through the routine tests and then, numb with the news, I make the walk home. If it seems strange that I'm not losing my mind, it's because I already knew this when I had the first headache. I'd had my meltdown back then. I already know what the test results will be.

It's back. I won't get away with it this time. I won't cheat death again.

Tears fall down my face silently. Just like when Frank hits me, there are no theatrics. Just these silent, exhausted tears.

For people who think it's comforting to know the almost-exact time you'll die... it's not. To know that you won't live past thirty-five doesn't make you more prepared for it.

I'd rather not have known. Like someone who dies in a car accident in their twenties. A short life, but they didn't have to spend their living years agonizing over it.

About ten minutes away from home, after I've passed the main road and turned onto our side of town, a car honks behind me. I step off the side of the road without turning to see who it is. I already know it's Kenny. The car's occupants include Frank shotgun and Peter and Scotty in the back seat.

"Hey, Axel, get in," Kenny says.

I peer into the backseat. Whatever space was left had been taken up by packs of alcohol. Scotty says, "Where're we gonna put all the booze?"

Peter just stares at my crotch. I fuckin' hate that guy. What a fuckin' creep.

"It's not that bad," Frank says. "It's just a couple more minutes." Then to me he says, "You'll be fine, right, baby? We'll meet you at the top."

Kenny looks at me again. "You sure, Axel?"

I step back from the car. "Yeah, yeah. It's just a couple more paces."

"Okay, then."

"Let's go," Frank says with a laugh when someone in the back says something I can't hear.

I watch them drive off without a single hint of surprise, but it still hurts, the way Frank simply... doesn't care.

With the rain now pelting, I jog home and as I step up onto our porch, I turn to the sound of a car roaring past. It's Eli's SUV.

I wonder where he's going. A small part of me wonders if he's gone to pick me up from work.

I wait until Eli's SUV disappears down the road, hoping the rain stops enough for me to still use the excuse of reading at the lake later tonight.

CHAPTER 40
Eli

If I knew any rain dances or ceremonies, I'd have performed them right there on my living room floor.

The time says seven-fifteen. Axel usually makes his way to the lake around eight p.m. and stays till around midnight.

What excuse could he possibly give to be out in the rain?

So instead of rain dances, I pray. I mean, I know what it looks like, but desperate times and all that. Glaring out at the rain, I wrack my brain for ways that would let Axel keep the phone I gave him. But taking it home isn't an option and I can't just call him on his own phone, so how? How do we do this?

Eight p.m. rolls by and still no chance of the rain stopping. I set aside my dinner. I don't even know what I'm eating. Chicken penne?

A text vibrates from my phone. It's from Mrs. Dalton.

Switch off the lights, he's scared. He'll come around the back.

I don't even bother responding to Mrs. Dalton. Tomorrow I'll take her somewhere nice and buy her whatever she wants.

I hurry through the house, switching off the lights and then return to the back of the kitchen to make sure the back door is unlocked. Then I pace, wearing the new wood floor back into the ground.

When a minute has gone by and Axel still hasn't arrived, I panic and text Mrs. Dalton. **Where is he?**

She responds immediately. *The path around the back is slippery. Alberta broke her arm down that path once. He's coming. Pepper's with him.*

My excitement knows no bounds.

I watch the door like a hawk and when the first turn of the knob catches my eye, I step forward and fling the door open, almost taking it off its hinges.

Axel stands there, a hoodie over his head and raindrops clinging to his eyelashes. He peers up at me.

I've never been more sure of anything in my life. This is it for me. *He* is it. I pull him into the warmth of the house, his face between my palms, crashing my lips to his, telling him with my kisses how much I want him here, hoping to erase every speck of doubt I find in his eyes.

He wraps his arms around my neck, kissing me back so hard I have to ease back to accommodate his demanding mouth.

Somehow, without breaking the kiss, we manage to get an obedient Pepper into the house, and I kick the door shut.

Axel softens the kiss, and a light suddenly shines on his face. It's from his phone.

"Lock the door, Eli," he says.

I reach around him and lock the door.

"I told Frank I'm helping Mrs. Dalton with something. That I'll be gone for about two hours. I'm sorry I didn't think of it sooner. I'm sorry I'm late."

It's too many sentences in one go, so I don't get everything but I get the apology. I wave my hand, dismissing his apology.

"She knows about us," he says.

I take his phone from him and open up his notepad. *I know, we talked over the weekend,* I type.

Axel takes the phone from me and types. ***We can trust her.***

I pull him into the kitchen, using his phone for light. There, I get Pepper the biggest bone I can find, plus a few treats.

Enough to keep her busy out here for two hours.

Then I gently pull Axel toward my bedroom.

I wish it didn't have to look like this. Like two people in it only for the sex. I wish we could walk down the street together like we belong to each other. I wish I could erase all the links he has to Frank. I wish we had the luxury of getting to know the deep things and insignificant things about each other. I wish these moments didn't have to be stolen.

But for now, this is all we have.

We stand in the middle of my bedroom. I try to make it right.

With the lights all off, I leave the one window's blinds up so we can have the moon at least to guide us in our sins. Axel stands in front of me, shaking. From the cold he's just come from or something else, I can't tell. I reach out to remove his hoodie. He lifts his arms. Underneath is a basic t-shirt. No double and triple layers of clothing today.

I remove the t-shirt and then run the palms of my hands over the outer side of his arms. He shivers. His head tips back ever so slightly, his eyes drift closed and his lips part. I imagine the sound of his exhale. My dick is rock solid. I could take him right now and he'll open for me like a delicate flower.

My hands move, fingertips skimming his shoulders, then flattening again to glide over his pecs, down his abdomen, over his abs. Skating across the skin where the waistband of his sweats hangs loosely on his hips.

Axel drops his head onto my shoulder, his hands reaching for my body. It takes all of me not to wrap him inside me and devour every inch of him on the bed behind me.

Then he takes over.

His fingers slide up into my hair, pulling me close. His teeth sink into my lower lip. I return the favor to his top lip and then we both lick across the place we've marked.

His hands move quickly, harshly over my body, pulling at my sweatshirt with a growing desperation. It's always so beautiful to watch him lose control like this. It's in his loss of control that his confidence truly comes out.

He rubs his naked upper body against mine. I breathe harshly, my fingers gripping his hair, as his lips skate over my jaw, kissing and biting. His tongue swiping over my Adam's apple. Fuck, that's fucking good. I grip him there and he opens his mouth, taking my Adam's apple into his mouth, sucking gently.

Fuck, nothing, *nothing,* felt like this before.

Reluctantly, I let him go and when he takes my nipple into his mouth, I feel the sounds leave my throat. He ascends immediately, cupping my cheek with a smile in his eyes. He always does that when I feel sounds in my throat. He lifts his hand and in the moonlight, I can make out the sign he makes.

Beautiful.

He trails his fingers down the length of my throat and signs again. *Beautiful.*

I sound beautiful. That's what he's trying to tell me.

I crush him to me, wanting to tell him how beautiful *he* is.

CHAPTER 41
Axel

I can't say who moved first. All I know is that somehow we managed to land on Eli's bed. He gets my sweats and underwear off on the way down so when we land, I'm underneath him, naked, and his body is covering mine like a blanket of safety.

It's never far away, the thought that Frank is only a few houses away around the bend. But knowing I have only two hours with Eli is enough for me to dedicate every cell and molecule of my body to this moment. To *Eli*.

His body moves over me, rutting into me with the same desperation I had when I stood at the window of my house and prayed for the rain to stop.

I reach down and push his sweats over his ass, using my feet to strip him, clawing at him while he bites his way from my neck to my hipbone.

Finally, we're both naked and the revelation is reason to pause and marvel at our entwined bodies. Mine pale and small. Eli's deeply tanned, lean and muscular. He settles on his knees between my legs, his hands resting lightly on his thighs, and he just stares at me.

His eyes rove from my face and then track down my body slowly. He doesn't touch me. He just studies my body. I can't take the inspection but I lift my hips anyway, my cock proudly and shamelessly begging for his touch. His fingers dig into my hips, his thumbs gliding along the crease between my inner thighs. He strokes me there and I lift my hips for him again. And when I do, Eli bends and slides his tongue across the crown of my dick, taking my pre-cum into his mouth.

I reach for him, pulling his face to mine, my tongue tangling with his, tasting myself inside his mouth.

Then I push him off me, rolling with him until I'm on top.

Two hours. That's all I have to absorb his tenderness into my soul. Eli is not just a soothing balm for my physical needs. His tenderness, his gentleness, reaches into my soul and calms that frightened Axel inside.

Here in Eli's arms, no one hurts me. No one is kind to me only to exchange it for cruelty later. No one tells me that I am not who I am. That I don't feel what I feel. That what happened to me, didn't.

Here, locked away inside Eli, I'm just Axel. But I'm *all* of me. I'm the *cancer-infested* Axel and I'm also the *healthy* Axel. I'm the uneducated Axel, but I'm also the Axel who knows how to create music, who can create sounds that Eli understands because he listens with his soul.

As my lips move down Eli's beautiful body, I bask and soak in the manly, grunting sounds coming from his throat. If only he knew how beautiful he sounds when he's in the throes of passion. His inhibition gives me the courage to let go. To *feel*, and just *be*.

When I reach his beautiful cock, he bows off the bed, searching out my hands, my mouth.

The feel of his thick, hot flesh in my mouth breaks whatever resistance I might have still had about what I 'm doing. My wedding ring catches my eye, wrapped around my finger as that finger is wrapped around Eli's cock. Not an accusation for touching the body of a man who is not my husband.

No. My wedding ring is a reminder of every promise Frank broke with his abuse. A reminder that what I have with Frank is not a marriage, but a legal arrangement that allows him to control and abuse me within the 'safety' of a marriage.

I keep this ring on to remind myself that I have no marriage. I have no husband. I have an *abuser*.

And with that ringed hand, I take Eli deeper into my mouth, tasting him. Savoring him. Falling, falling so deep into his safe world.

For these few moments, I'll know what it is to be loved with the tenderness of Eli's touch and I'll give him as much of myself as I can.

Eli pulses inside my mouth, his fingers digging into my scalp. His loud moans encourage me, but I want him inside me when he comes.

Crawling back up, I sheath him with a condom, lather us with lube, and then, hovering over him, I take Eli, inch by inch. His eyes hooded from lust, he holds onto my hips, guiding me until I'm fully seated.

I'm so full I can hardly breathe. Slowly, I ride him, my hands behind me for support and my feet planted on either side of him.

Eli swivels his hips, his loud grunts filling the air. I let my vocal cords loose, joining him in a melody of sex-infused sounds. It's the sound of us. Raw, uninhibited. Forbidden, but so innocent.

He grabs hard onto my hips, pulling me down, and the sounds from his throat increase in tempo and volume. He's coming.

"Come, Eli," I whisper into the air. "Come, love of my life. Come, beat of my heart."

If he was hearing, would I have had the courage to say these words? I don't know. But I say them knowing that somehow he knows already.

One day, I'll look into his eyes and tell him, but for now, I tell him with my body and my soul. And with words, I tell myself what he means to me. I hear my own declarations and I know that I'll never give this man up.

He's the stars that explode behind my eyes, the sizzle of electricity racing down my spine. He's the truth my soul knows and I can never give him up, no matter how fleeting our time together.

Eli fucks up into me with all his might, and then, with a shout that matches his, I spill all over his stomach as he jerks deep inside my ass.

CHAPTER 42
Eli

He lies in my arms afterward, a lover, sated and free. His body glistened in sweat, curved to mine and his head resting heavily on my chest. His palm rests against my heart.

Even if words could be spoken between us as easily as two hearing people, it would not be necessary right now. Everything that needs to be said is being said. The beat of my heart against his palm. The press of his cheek against my chest. The possessiveness with which I hold him to me and his willingness to be enclosed inside this possessiveness.

All the words in the world would not convey adequately how much this man is mine. And how much I have become his.

He has given me more life here in this strange town than I ever thought possible. I thought my life was fine before him. And it was but, now I know what my mother meant when she said to find someone to love.

He shifts, turning his face up to mine.

Are you hungry? I sign. He frowns so I sign again: my fingers curved like a C against my chest and with raised eyebrows, I drag my hand down my chest once and point at him.

He thinks for a second and then places his curved fingers on his chest like I did and then points at himself. But before he points at himself, he drags his curved hand back up.

I laugh and shake my head. Grabbing my phone, I repeat the sign, dragging my hand down my chest *once.* Then I type: *hungry.*

Then, I sign the way he signed, dragging my curved hand *up and down*, and type that sign: **horny**.

He laughs or smiles wide. Then, he makes the sign dragging his hand down once, and points to himself, followed by the same sign dragging up and down and points to himself. He's hungry *and* horny.

I laugh until my throat vibrates.

Unbidden, my eyes are drawn to the time on my phone. We have one hour and twenty minutes left.

Reluctantly, I rise from the bed, naked. Axel follows me but takes the sheets with him, covering himself up.

I grind my teeth, fury building inside me for what he becomes when we're not locked inside our lovemaking. He doesn't notice my observations. He's too busy searching for his clothes.

I turn my back to him to give him the privacy he thinks he needs and reach for my closet. From the back, I retrieve the piece of underwear I'd ordered online. A pair of black lace panties. My heart thuds in my chest, unsure if this is the right move. What if I'd misjudged that whole thing at the library when I first arrived?

I look over my shoulder to find Axel sitting on the side of the bed, his back to me. The bedding is still wrapped around his middle and his sweats are clutched in his hands. My eyes dart to the opposite side of the bed, near me, where his boxers lie— the piece of clothing he's looking for.

I pull off the price tag from the underwear in my hand and approach him just as he rounds the bed, wrapped in the sheet. He drops onto the bed and reaches for his underwear. I sink to my knees in front of him. It breaks my heart how he avoids looking at my nakedness. This isn't shyness. This is *shame*. And my resolve to take him away strengthens tenfold, even if I have to steal him away in the middle of the night, and then hide him from that sick fuck down the road.

My hand stills his. He looks at me curiously when I remove his boxers from his hand. Dropping it to the side, I tug on the bedding. He lets go slowly and I see the increased tempo of his breathing in the rise and fall of his chest. He avoids looking at me. Even with only the moon as our witness, our accuser and ally, he avoids looking at me. The moon provides enough light for me to watch his curiosity morph into hesitation and back to curiosity.

Seated naked before me now, he places his hands on the side of the bed. He bites into his top lip and averts his gaze. But when he feels the brush of the silk panties against his foot, his eyes fly down and he breaks my heart with his horrified leap backward.

I grab onto his ankle, my fingers soothing, while I hold him in place. He stills, but his chest heaves.

He shakes his head rapidly. *No. No. No.* His shame screams back at me, reverberating throughout his body with sounds only I can decipher.

I rub my palm up and down his calf, dropping soft kisses along the inside of his thighs and coaxing him back to that safe place where he gives himself to me without inhibition. The place that belongs only to us, where shame and pain and hurt cannot exist.

His body calms down gradually and his stiffened legs turn soft in my hand. And with his head turned to the side and his fists digging into the bed, he lets me slip on the underwear.

I rise as I glide the soft material up his calves and thighs and urge him to lift slightly so I can slip it over his hips.

When I'm done, I bend, bringing my face to his neck to press a kiss there. His face is still turned away, so I place my fingers to his cheek and try turning him to me. He won't turn. So I try to convince him with soft nuzzles to his neck. My nose trailing up and down the side of his neck. My lips brushing his shoulders, my fingers against his neck.

It's the tremble of his throat that tells me he's crying. My chest tightens with compassion, fury and... love.

I inhale deeply. Yes. I love him. My connection with him runs too deep for it not to be true. I'm not in the habit of complicating things. Admitting this isn't any kind of hardship.

As gently as I can, I manage to get him to face me. The tears fall without drama or effort. His face is blank while the tears fall. A soul falling apart inside a body too accustomed to pain to register it in his eyes or his face.

But then everything breaks. The floodgates are smashed wide open. Axel lifts his eyes to mine and bursts into tears. I drop to my knees again, pulling him to me. He hides his face in the crook of my shoulder, his body wracked with tears and sorrow.

He slides off the bed, onto his knees, and I tuck him inside my body. Our bodies—mine naked and his covered only by the silk panties—cling to each other and I hold him to me while he cries and cries and cries.

Axel's sadness is so devastating that I find tears in my own eyes. While his tears pour into my chest, mine mix with his hair.

How could anyone harm this soft, beautiful human being? Why couldn't I have met him ten years ago? I'd have kept him so safe.

The digital clock tells me we still have time, but even so, it won't be enough. I need more than two hours to love this man. No amount of time in all eternity, even, would be sufficient for me to love Axel enough.

The minutes tick by on the digital clock and all I can do is hold him while he cries like he's grieving. I don't have the luxury of sound to honor his pain, so I listen to his body— pulling him even closer when his fingers dig into my forearm, rubbing along his spine when his body shudders against mine. Pressing my hand to his sternum when it seems like his tears would choke him.

We stay like that for a long time while Axel cries for all the things I know nothing about.

And when his body begins to calm down, and he has enough strength to lift his face from my neck, I allow some space between our bodies. I wipe his tears gently, my thumb caressing underneath his eyes, across his cheekbones, massaging gently at his temples. He leans into my palms, his eyes closed, and then he places a soft kiss on the inside of my wrist.

Tears renew, but this time, he smiles through them, touching his four fingers to his chin and extending that hand to me. *Thank you.*

I bring those fingers to my lips, kissing each of them with the reverence this moment deserves.

Then, quietly, I lift him back onto the bed and help him into his sweats. My hands glide over his silk-covered ass and then, slipping between us in front, I caress his length through the silk material of the underwear.

He tries to look away again, but I don't allow it this time. He doesn't fight me. Instead, he peeks up at me, his smile shy and small. I smack those lips with mine, pulling a wide smile out of him and coaxing him into this forbidden lover's kiss.

CHAPTER 43
Axel

Nobody tells you that the rivers of tears stuck inside you behind a great wall of shame and defeat could be the very thing that washes away the ugliness if only you'd let it out.

Eli's chest is still wet with my rivers of tears. He doesn't wipe them away and in some esoteric twist, it feels like I've become joined to him on some spiritual level through these tears. He takes my face between his palms. I'm so scared, so *hopeful* for what Eli might feel for me. So frightened of how in love with him I might be.

This might be the most humiliating moment of my life, sitting here with these panties on and crying like a baby, but Eli is watching my face, his eyebrows furrowed like he's *listening* to me.

I'm ashamed that I'm the one that can hear, yet he's the one listening to me like no one else has listened before. He's listening to the words I cannot utter. He's listening to my tears; to my unspoken sorrow.

He leads me to the kitchen in the dark. Not once did he question why I needed the darkness. My terror that Frank will find out had long crossed over into the realm on *psychotic* by the time I made the plan to go over to Mrs. Dalton.

Now, I watch him from the bar stool at the counter while he stands at the microwave in the dark, warming up food.

I have two choices: I leave Frank and go away with Eli, or I stay here and cheat on Frank for the duration of Eli's stay. Not being with Eli isn't an option.

Eli brings the food to us. I love how he makes us eat from the same plate. Even when we're eating, it seems we needed to be connected. My marriage is a mountain separating us so the least we can have is this simple sharing of food.

There's also only one fork. I smile up at him when he brings his stool so close to mine we might as well have both sat on one.

It's not pasta today, to my surprise. It's sticky rice and chicken with diced vegetables and a sauce that produces the most incredibly delicious aroma. Eli brings a fork to my mouth. I open, deliberately deciding to put all accusing thoughts about us out of my mind. These moments are *right*. They are *meant to be*.

Eli reaches forward and kisses the corner of my mouth while I chew. It's delicious and I tell him so with a sign. He tells me he's impressed with my sign with a thumbs up. When I'm done chewing, I slide the plate closer to me and take the fork from his hand. Then I lift a forkful of food into his mouth.

He doesn't eat much, saying he's full after three bites, so I finish the rest, insisting that I feed myself.

When I'm done, we both check the time. Forty minutes left.

Eli gathers the dishes to the sink and then pulls me into the living room. He adds a few logs to the fireplace and soon a small bright fire warms up the air.

He sits on the floor in front of the fire, his back to the couch, and pulls me down between his thighs. I curl into his chest sideways, tucking my legs underneath me. Pepper sits next to Eli.

I never knew it was possible to be with someone, not say a single word, and still feel like you've said a million things. And yet, here we are, me and Eli, wrapped in the warmth of the fire and each other, and it's like I have known him my whole life. Like I'd known him even before I'd ever laid eyes on him. And then when I did, it was as if I was only recognizing... and claiming... what had always been mine. He is the lover from my dreams. The one I escaped to when Frank touched me. The one who had protected me from the emptiness of sex with my husband.

He's real. Eli is real. And he's mine.

We stay there, touching, caressing and watching the digital clock on the side table. The debate to tell him about my doctor's visit tosses back and forth in my head. Fear wins, and I put it out of my mind.

When I lift my head ten minutes before our time is up, Eli tightens his arms around my waist. I squeeze him back. It feels like I'm leaving him forever.

But reality runs on a tight schedule. I have to go.

The fire still burns brightly, so I can see his face clearly and he can see mine. "I'll come back," I say.

He nods stiffly, his arms not budging an inch. I push gently and he finally releases me.

Pepper circles us, her bone now dry as a stone. Eli retrieves the rest of my clothing. I change into them quickly, making sure to remove the panties and put on my regular underwear. Eli takes the panties from me and slips them into his pocket.

Seven minutes.

I stand in front of the fire, desperate for my last few minutes to slow down.

Pepper sits at my side and Eli comes up behind me, inhaling into my neck and then pressing soft kisses there. He reaches around and presses a key in my hand.

I turn in his arms. He points to the back door. "Your house key? For me?" I ask.

He nods.

And then, out of nowhere, I blurt out, "I'll grow my hair back out."

He frowns. Maybe I spoke too fast. I open my mouth to repeat myself but he places his finger to my lips and kisses me with so much tenderness, I feel heartbroken over the insignificant fact that I no longer have the long hair that he liked so much. This is the most intense it's ever been between us. I'm so scared. So scared of us. *For us.*

One minute. My head begins to ache.

I cup his face between my palms, the same way he's holding me, and I kiss him back with a terrible joy and an incurable sadness.

Pepper and I walk quickly up the road and disappear into Mrs. Dalton's property. Then, around the back, where Mrs. Dalton has left a treat for Pepper. We grab it quickly and then emerge onto the road again, as if we're coming up from Mrs. Dalton's house.

I turn the doorknob just as Frank swings it open. I'm stunned into a stupor when he glares at me.

"Jesus, Axel. The fuck you creeping up like that? You almost killed me. You done with Mrs. Dalton?"

"Yes, sorry, Frank," I reply, the lie sliding out easily. Pepper barks once, asking to be let in. "Can Pepper sleep inside today?" I ask, still standing on the threshold.

He peers outside to inspect the rain. "Yeah, okay, but if I find that mutt on my side, it's getting kicked out of the house, you understand?"

Pepper barks and I nod. Frank doesn't even care that Pepper is so smart, she's answered him too.

He opens the door wide. Pepper and I step forward, only to be almost run down by Frank's friends who come slurring through the kitchen. "C'mon, get your asses home. I'm tired now," Frank says.

Pepper and I step aside to let them pass. Peter slaps my ass before I can move out of his reach.

"Bust that pussy *goood*, Frank," he slurs. I cringe when Frank just laughs it off.

"Well, what're you standing out there in the rain for? Get inside," Frank says.

Pepper and I get inside. The place is a disaster. Dishes strewn across the kitchen sink and empty beer cans overflowing in the trashcan. I mentally kick myself for not emptying it out earlier. If I had, it wouldn't be overflowing now.

The living room has more empty beer cans and someone hadn't finished their pork chops. Pepper sprints for it and today I let her clean the plate. She hides the bone from Frank on her way to the bedroom. "On my side," I murmur when she passes me.

Then when I notice Frank heading for bed too, I pull her back. "Whoa, wait. Stay with me." She listens, settling under the coffee table to protect her bone.

I work quickly, starting in the living room, only stopping to take two Tylenol. Then I work my way through to the kitchen. Every single thought about the increased frequency of my headaches is incinerated before it fully forms. Not tonight. I'm not going to be a cancer-ridden cunt tonight. The test results are not yet in, so just for tonight I'll be the *in-remission* guy.

Just for tonight, I'll refuse to believe that God would be so cruel and let the cancer come back. Not now. Not when I've found Eli. Before, it didn't mean much to think about dying. Beside Ben, who promised to always keep my memory alive, there hadn't been really anything else to live for. Until now.

Until Eli.

Thirty minutes later, I'm done cleaning. I consider showering before going to bed, but the thought of washing Eli off my skin makes me physically ill. I wash my hands and softly call for Pepper.

She doesn't answer, so I go to get her from the living room.

Oh fuck. *Pepper, you little shit.*

I switch off the lights and hurry to the bedroom. Sure enough, she's on the bed. On Frank's side. With her damn bone. And as if on cue, Frank draws his leg up and *boots* Pepper off the bed.

Flying onto the floor with a yelp, she comes to me quickly. I guide her to my side, making sure her bone is hidden behind the curtain, or she'll get another booting from Frank for scraping the bone the entire night.

And as I drop off into sleep, I make dreams in my head about Eli, thinking about the key he gave me. Yet another piece of evidence of my affair. I slip the key into my pillowcase, another hiding place for the various things I keep from Frank.

Not even the increased tension in my head can sour my thoughts or remove the smile from my face. A smile that belongs only to Eli.

CHAPTER 44
Eli

My mother rubs her chest repeatedly and rolls her shoulders back every now and then on our video call.

"Are you okay?" I sign.

"Yes, just a bit of discomfort. I'm not young anymore, Eli," she signs back with a smile.

I don't like it. *"You should have that checked out."*

"I will. How was your grand opening yesterday? I wish I could have been there."

Yesterday had been great for the town's people. The house is now a historical landmark as far as the residents are concerned. Mrs. Dalton will take up her manager's position as soon as I return to the city. My father's childhood home will now be open for anyone passing through to enjoy. He'd be happy. I think he'd be proud.

"You're not well. I wouldn't have wanted you to make the trip, anyway. I'm a little worried about you."

She smiles. *"I'm fine, Eli darling. I love you for worrying, but try not to."*

"Okay, I'll see you soon. Take care of yourself."

"You too. I'll see you soon."

After the call, I lose myself in thoughts about Axel and what I need to do. I hate the weekends when I can't text him. I could just text him on his own phone, but that's exactly the reason I don't have his regular number—so I'm not tempted by such reckless thoughts.

I touch my hand to my chest where Axel left his sorrow a few nights ago. I don't know if there's ever been a day when he was truly happy. I have every resource at my disposal to give him everything he could possibly want or need and I would love him for all of eternity until he forgets his every sadness. We just need to get past this fucking marriage issue.

So, I place a second video call to my lawyer. I give him hypothetical scenarios and he gives me answers without asking me if I've lost my mind. But he does highlight the fact that I can't simply make arrangements for someone's divorce the way I'm suggesting. Of course I know that, but I need everything out on the table. I need to cover all bases before I go to Axel. I need to be able to answer every question he might have for me.

I need a foolproof plan.

It's the Annual Book Fair today and I receive at least sixteen texts on the community group chat, confirming that I would be at the park. I confirm that I would and that I'm looking forward to handing out the Benson Bookworm Award. Axel will be there with the *Till Books Do Us Part* book stand and I agreed to help Mrs. Dalton manage her cappuccino stand.

I get ready and drive around to Mrs. Dalton to load everything up.

She greets me dramatically, with kisses to my cheek and great big hugs. Then, inside her kitchen, she fidgets unnecessarily. I'm sensitive enough to body language to know something's wrong. I still her hands with mine. She grabs a piece of paper, but I stop her. *Speak*, I sign. Whatever she wants to tell me, I don't want it filtered.

"I heard some shouting last night," she says.

My fists clench.

"Has he agreed to go away with you?" she asks.

I type on my phone. *We haven't talked about it properly yet.*

"Please do it soon, Eli." Mrs. Dalton takes both my hands in hers. "I always told him to find someone who would love him endlessly and then run away as far as possible. I told you that before, right?" I nod. *Yes.*

Is Axel okay? I can't talk to him on weekends, I type.

"He seemed okay this morning when he went out. I called him up for some tea, but he was in a hurry."

Did you notice...? I delete the sentence. I don't have the stomach to even ask. I feel so helpless.

She answers me anyway. "I didn't notice any bruises, but I was too far away, so I can't be sure."

The drive to the park gives me time to think. I'll have to find a way to deal with the possibility that Axel may not *want* to go away with me. The thought makes me sick, so I put it away for later.

At the park, things are in full swing already. The park is filled with bright colors and happy people. It never ceases to amaze me how happy these people become when they come together for an event.

I'm greeted by several stall owners, who do their best to speak to me in sign language.

It's heart-warming, the effort they've made for me, these people who barely have enough to get by every day.

I search through the crowd for Axel. The book stall is set up, but it's a young girl who's managing it. And just barely too; she has her head buried in a book, hardly paying attention to potential customers.

I search for Pepper next and come up with nothing. Mrs. Dalton comes up behind me with the last of the polystyrene cups and gives me her phone.

A text conversation between her and Axel is open.

*Mrs. Dalton: **Axel, where are you?*** Sent seven minutes ago.

*Axel: **Hey, Mrs. Dalton. We had to turn back for petty cash. Ben forgot. Casey is there in the meantime with the first load of books. Is everything okay?***

*Mrs. Dalton: **Yes, everything's fine. We're almost set up. Eli is here.***

*Axel: **Okay. I'll be there in a few minutes.***

And then, a minute later:

*Axel: **Can I talk to him?***

Mrs. Dalton smiles and cocks her head toward her phone and makes a *go on* sign.

I feel like a schoolboy. With trembling fingers and my heart beating right out of my chest, I type.

*Me: **Axel?***

*Axel: **Hey.***

*Me: **You'll be here in a few minutes?*** I suddenly forget how to text people.

*Axel: **Yeah.***

*Me: **I miss you.***

*Axel: **I miss you more.***

I glance up to look for Mrs. Dalton. I don't need anyone witnessing my reddened face.

*Me: **Are you okay?***

*Axel: **Yes.***

And then:

*Axel: **Thank you. For everything. I'm almost there.***

*Me: **Hurry.***

Axel: You can come round the front and help me with an extra crate of books if Mrs. Dalton will be okay without you for a few minutes.

Me: Okay. Are you texting and driving? Please don't do that.
Axel: No. Ben is driving. I don't know how to drive haha.

I frown. Why doesn't Axel have a driver's license? Even around here, it's still a basic skill.

Axel: I'll see you just now. Delete this chat.

Me: Okay, you too. Delete this chat.

I delete the chat and hand Mrs. Dalton's phone back to her. She gives me a smile that tells me she's for me and Axel all the way. I type on my phone, asking if I can go out to help Axel.

She slaps my arm playfully and shoos me away.

The girl at the book stall turns the last page of the book she'd been reading. Then immediately picks up another one from the table and begins to read. Wow. People in this town love their books.

It's no surprise that my father had a whole library in his office *and* at home.

CHAPTER 45
Axel

When I look at him these days, it's like I'm looking at the love of my life. I *am* looking at the love of my life.

To counter the cold weather, he has on a light sweater and jeans.

Ben hops out of the car first and lets Pepper out of the backseat. She bolts across the parking lot. Ben and I both watch her sprint.

"She knows Eli Saxon?" Ben asks while he opens up the trunk.

"Uh, yeah. She goes up to the woods for the squirrels remember? Yeah, so he gives her a treat whenever she's up there."

"Oh, yeah. See, you should have married a guy like that. Look at how nice he is to Pepper." Ben watches as Eli swoops down and takes the sixty-five pound golden retriever into his arms, carrying her like an overgrown baby.

I'm not sure I want to comment on Ben's observation. Mostly because I agree with him and admitting it would bring a whole host of questions.

Eli reaches us with Pepper walking right against his leg like someone would steal him away from her if she walked an inch away from him. Or it could have something to do with the treat in his pocket, since she can't stop sniffing there.

Eli lifts his hand in greeting. Ben and I return the sign.

Eli signs. I frown because I don't get it.

Ben claps his hands. "Help you," he exclaims. Eli grins (and that makes me swoon secretly) and gives Ben the thumbs up.

Ben gives me the proudest smile I've ever seen and then repeats the sign to me. "This means, *can I help you?*" I try it out, and then to Eli, I sign, *yes, please.*

Making sure I'm still facing Eli, I tell Ben, "Eli is helping Mrs. Dalton with the coffee stand. They're next to us."

Ben holds up his palm to Eli for a high five, which Eli returns. He looks at me again, but I'm worried his infectious gaze would last too long and people would notice us stargazing at each other out here in broad daylight. So I look away, hating how I have to pretend that him being here means nothing.

But he understands and when my eyes go back to him, he's already at the trunk with Ben, and with Pepper still stuck to his side.

I join them.

"Ben, you go on ahead with this one," I say, handing him a crate of hardbacks.

He takes it from me and tells me to not to forget the petty cash box.

I watch Ben leave after failing to convince Pepper to walk with him. Hidden behind the open trunk, my eyes devour Eli. I'm aching to lean over and kiss his lips and, from his hungry eyes, I know he's ready for anything.

With a frustrated sigh, I hand him a crate of paperbacks and then reach over for the petty cash box and the last crate of children's picture books.

Eli slams the trunk shut while balancing the crate in one hand, and we make our way through the crowd. Frank said he'll turn up later when the sun comes out. I encouraged him to get in some extra sleep because if Frank got some extra sleep, then I got to be in the same vicinity as Eli for a few hours without having ongoing panic attacks.

Eli looks over at me several times as we walk. It's damn near impossible to avoid returning his quick gazes.

We reach our stalls. Eli sets his crate down and then turns to relieve me of mine. He slides his hand underneath the crate, over mine. His touch, right here in front of everyone, sends bolts of electricity racing through my body.

When both crates are set down, I clutch the petty cash box, desperate for *something* to hang on to. In a moment of crazed madness, I scour the park, looking for an escape. A place where Eli and I could go for a few precious moments.

"Axel." Mrs. Dalton's voice carries across our stalls.

She eyes me curiously, silently asking, *Are you okay?*

I nod and give her a thumbs up.

But I'm far from okay. I didn't anticipate that being here with Eli just a few yards away, in this public place, would be this difficult. The urge to grab his hand and run as far away as possible grows at an alarming speed.

"I should get things going," I tell Eli, waving over at our stall. He nods and moves out of our stall and into theirs. Pepper follows him.

"Look at the fuckin' cheater," Ben says, coming up behind me. My blood freezes and the bones in my face crack. I whirl around, my eyes wide with fear and every blood-draining emotion you can think of.

Ben has his hands on his hips, shaking his head disapprovingly. "Let's see her come crawling back when Eli leaves back for the city in a couple months. Don't take her back." He laughs.

I follow his eyes and only the table next to me keeps me from fainting with relief. *Pepper.* He's talking about Pepper.

Not me. Not Eli.

Ben goes to the back of the stall where he'd been unpacking the paperbacks with no inkling of the heart attack he nearly gave me.

"Hey, you need some water or something?" Casey's voice breaks into my almost-heart-attack stupor.

I blink. "Uh, no. Thanks, Casey."

She leans forward, looking back conspiratorially at Ben and then around at the crowd, before bringing her eyes back to mine. "I'll deliver notes if you let me have the *Garry Michael* hardback."

The reflexes in my face give me away before I even have a chance to deliver a denial of any kind.

"I mean, Pepper's not the only one, right?" Casey's eyes sparkle and she cocks her head to the next-door stall, where a delighted Pepper is lying flat on her back with Eli rubbing her belly.

"W-what?" I sputter, but it's no use. So, I go with pathetic. "Hardback?" I ask in a tone pitched too high.

"Do you know how gorgeous hardbacks look on a bookshelf?" she asks in a low voice, looking back at Ben. I look too, to make sure he hasn't caught us making deals in the front.

"C'mon, Axel. I already promised you the manager's position when I get the bookstore. Just give me the hardback, make a plan with the stock control sheet, and I'll square you up when I get my allowance." She fidgets for a second and then adds, "In three months' time."

"You got your allowance taken away, too?"

Casey rolls her eyes. "I mean, do *you* people even understand math?"

"Us people?"

"Yeah, you great and mighty adult people. So I failed math, big deal. Ben manages the bookstore and I'll bet even he doesn't know what math is."

"Uh, I—" I don't even know what to say.

She grins. "Look, I'm not gonna say anything, okay? I'm a hopeless romantic and Eli Saxon is soooo hot and sweet and sexy, so I want him for you. But—"

She looks back at Ben. He's nearly done. "But Ben is such a stick-in-the-mud gold star employee. He'll just say I already have the paperback, so I gotta do what I gotta do. You understand, right?"

"It's not what you think," I say desperately. We both stand in front of the sales table, facing the crowd. We must look like two secret agents exchanging new information at the park bench trying to look like we don't know each other.

Casey laughs. "Bro, the way he looks at you? You're lucky most of the town will be too drunk or too high soon enough to notice."

My body trembles with fear. I've never been so grateful for my depressed, drug addicted community before.

"I'm not blackmailing you just for the sake of it, Axel. If I didn't need the book, I'd still keep your secret. You have my full support, but like I said, I gotta do what I gotta do. So just give me the hardback and we can forget this whole conversation."

I feel like the second half of a secret agent pair. The one who's always late, or the one falling off the bridge and right into the enemy's meet up place. The stupid one.

With a casual look over my shoulder to make sure Ben is at a safe distance away, I slide over the hardback she's after.

Casey greets a few folks walking by and slides the hardback over the table and into her backpack.

"You look hot together, by the way," she whispers. "You two must have the hottest sex, too."

My eyes round. "Casey, you're seventeen!" I hiss.

She laughs, backing away from the stall and slinging her backpack over her shoulder. "Dude, with the number of monster romances I've read, I'm freaking *eternal*."

"And where are you going?" I call out as she walks backwards.

She pats her backpack. "I have some math homework. I'll be over there by the oak tree."

"Math homework, my ass," I mutter.

"Hey, where's Casey?" Ben drops a few books onto the table.

"She has math homework, apparently."

"That's a big fat lie."

"Probably."

CHAPTER 46
Eli

By lunch time I'd served probably five thousand cappuccinos but not one to Axel.

Each time I looked over to their stall, he'd been busy with swarms of children grabbing picture books or answering questions from the Senior's softball club about some autobiographies they were interested in buying. Axel answers them patiently, sometimes needing to tell them that he unfortunately can't get to read every book they sell, he'd never get anything done, even though he wishes he could just sit and read all day.

Lip reading comes in handy sometimes.

I spot Frank and his buddies just past noon, sauntering around with packs of beer. The way they act, I'm sure they were troublemakers as teenagers. Even now, they act like overgrown schoolboys looking for trouble. Still, the people milling around greet Frank with pats on his back and some even stop for what looks like easy conversation.

I don't know how or why Axel ever ended up with someone like that.

Around three p.m. I hand out the Benson Bookworm Award to a little six-year-old boy who'd read three hundred and eighty-five books this past year. That's more than a book a day. I don't think anyone was more impressed than me.

Finally, around five p.m., just as the park starts to clear out, Axel gets a break and the townspeople have finally gotten tired of free cappuccinos.

Frank is in close proximity to our stalls, facing mostly ours. He looks drunk, as do his friends. Mrs. Dalton sends a disgusted look in their general direction.

I watch him carefully from this distance and I know it's the worst kind of eavesdropping, but I'm not even sorry.

"Like a fuckin' corpse, I'm not kidding," he tells his friends who laugh their heads off.

"What's it called where those psychos want to fuck dead people?" another one asks between what looks like belches.

Each of them speaks, but I can't make out some of it. From the looks of it, they don't manage to find the word *necrophilia*.

Frank, whose mouth is in my direct line of sight, has no trouble shit-talking Axel. "Looks like I need to find me another hole to keep me happy," he says with a sneer in Axel's direction.

I don't get every word but from the body language, their facial expressions and Frank's surprisingly clear enunciation, I'm able to sufficiently gather the jist of the conversation.

Axel has settled on the grass, crosslegged with a little girl and he's reading to her from a book.

And then it clicks. *I'm like a corpse. I'm not any good with this type of thing.*

If I could have summoned up demons to help me rip this pathetic human being to shreds, I would have.

My eyes move back to Axel. He's pointing at the book and smiling. His shoulders shake slightly, so perhaps he's laughing.

The little girl points to the book too, with a smile on her face.

I'll take Axel away from that fucking bastard.

I follow their conversation closely. "And what about that deaf cunt, huh?" Frank carries on. I sneer. *That deaf cunt is fucking your husband so fucking good.*

"Coming round offering Axel lifts to work and making it like I'm not good enough to take care of my bitch."

The friends sneer in my direction, as if I'm not only deaf but blind too. I glare back at them, but they're stupid enough not to realize that I can read nearly every word spewing out of their fucking mouths.

"You should keep your eye on that man of yours," one says.

Frank laughs. "That man of mine doesn't even know how to add two and two. He's too stupid to cheat. Besides, he's a church boy. He's not gonna go to hell just for some deaf dick."

I've had enough. I don't even care about their insinuations about me and Axel. If I could, I'd scream it from the tallest tree in this park.

I swing out of my chair. Mrs. Dalton slows me down with a worried expression. Her eyes bounce between me and Frank.

"Don't ruin it for Axel," she says. "Just be patient."

Her worried eyes dilute some of my fury. I give her a clipped nod, grab two cappuccinos, and walk over to the bookstall.

Axel looks up at me just as a young woman steps close to us. She gives me a nervous smile and says *hello* in sign. I greet her back.

"Amy, you done, honey?" she asks the little girl. Axel stands with the child and hands her over to the woman.

"Can you say thank you to Axel in sign?" she asks. With a broad grin, the little girl tips her fingers to her chin and then back at Axel. He smiles and signs back, *you're welcome.*

Every evil thought from before evaporates as I watch this exchange. This hearing world that has chosen to speak my language with each other, just to make me feel welcome. And I'm reminded that Frank's toxicity and cruelty is his burden to bear. I can't let him ruin all the good in the world. Not even when I'm committed to stealing his husband away from him.

The little girl and her mother look to me for approval and I provide it with a big smile.

Alone with Axel now, I stick out my hand, offering him the cappuccino. He dusts his hands on his sweats. My eyes drop to his crotch. The bulge there makes my mouth water. He catches me staring and although his eyes tell me differently, his face remains a mask of nothingness. A quick flick of his eyes in Frank's direction is code for *please be careful.*

He takes the cup from me and says, "Thank you."

I lift my hand to sign but change my mind when I remember this whole town has been taking sign language classes for the last few months. They'll hear everything I say.

Frank appears out of nowhere. "Are you done with this deaf cunt?" he asks. I don't know how loud he's speaking and if anyone else besides Axel can hear him, but I'm hearing him like a hearing person with how smoothly he enunciates his words, each one sliding out of his mouth on full display.

Axel's eyes widen and he gives me a look, pleading for forgiveness.

"Eli can lip read," Axel says tightly.

Frank flicks his eyes at me and then back at Axel. Then he just grins and shrugs. His friends gather around, tipping their heads up at me as if that's meant to be some sort of greeting. I give them deadly stares, which seem to make them squirm. "I'm working extra time this coming Tuesday and then Thursday, so get me some extra sodas from the store when you go back into town," Frank tells Axel.

Axel nods stiffly.

"I'll do the Thursday shift first and then the Tuesday shift."

"You mean the Tuesday shift first and then the Thursday shift," Axel says.

Frank frowns. "No. Thursday first, then Tuesday. Thursday comes before Tuesday, Axel."

Axel argues back unnecessarily, and I watch this exchange with amusement at first. I'm surprised I'm able to catch these long sentences. Even with my above average lip reading skills, getting this many words is nearly impossible.

"Frank, Tuesday comes before Thursday."

His friends' mouths hang wide open as their bodies shake with laughter. Frank's frown deepens. "The fuck you know, you dumb fuck. You didn't even finish high school."

I set my cup of cappuccino down on the table next to me, my fists clenched at my sides. Axel steps back, his anxiety radiating from his body in waves. "Yeah, okay. Thursday shift then the Tuesday shift."

"What's with the attitude suddenly?" Frank steps into Axel's personal space.

We both move at the same time. Frank's hand rises to Axel's chest. My hand gets there a second faster and I deflect Frank's hand and push him back hard at the same time.

He must not have been expecting it. He's bigger and more muscled than me. So his initial non-response is more the result of surprise than from a lack of strength.

Axel stares, horror exploding all over his face as he watches Frank recover from his fall. But Frank doesn't come for me. The crowd has mostly dispersed, and whoever is left aren't paying any attention.

Frank's lips move. "You think you're so smart, huh?" He lunges for Axel, but I jerk Axel to the side and out of the way. Frank glares at me. I don't know why he won't come after me.

His friend pulls him back. "C'mon Frank. Stop this. If you're going to hit someone, hit me."

Frank gives his friend a pat on the cheek. "Hit you?" he says. "Kenny, you're my brother. I could never hit you."

He gives me a disgusted look, then pins a terrified Axel with a glare and lets his friends pull him away.

Axel turns away from me and I'm left seething.

CHAPTER 47
Axel

I'm shaking with the most evil fury. With the most sickening humiliation. I want to run away and hide. Die even, maybe. So I wouldn't have to hear Frank's voice ever again.

In my madness, I stalk over to Mrs. Dalton. "Is everything okay, Axel dear?"

"Yeah. Just Frank. He's a little upset."

"Is he causing trouble?"

"Not yet, but I need to get out of here, Mrs. Dalton. But please can I borrow your phone?"

She digs inside her pocket, unlocks it and hands it over to me.

I bring up Eli's name and type. *The bookstore? As soon as possible?*

Mrs. Dalton looks over at the screen. "Sorry, I didn't mean to see, but I'll make sure we get done quickly."

She smiles at me sadly. "You deserve happiness, Axel darling. And sometimes, you have to steal it."

I force a smile and thank her. When I look back at Eli, his phone is in his hand. He looks up and nods faintly.

"Hey, I saw Frank spitting fire in the parking lot. What happened?" Ben comes up behind me.

"He's drunk. He tried to push me around a little. But it's fine. Nothing happened."

"I hate that fucking asshole."

"Yeah, anyway, the books we didn't sell? Why don't you drop me and Pepper off at the bookstore? I'll sort them out. You can leave me there, and me and Pepper will walk back."

"Nah, don't worry about it. I'll leave them in the car and we'll sort it out in the morning."

Fuck.

"Uh, actually, Frank asked for extra soda for his late shifts, so I'll pick some up and walk home when I'm done, so it's no problem."

"Okay, come on then. But I'll help you and drop you off at home."

Mrs. Dalton, who'd been standing there listening while Eli moved around the back of the stall packing up, seems to be tired of listening to us.

"Ben, dear," she calls out. "Don't you have to go fetch your mom for prayer meeting tonight?"

"Yeah, but that's at seven. It's not even six yet."

"Well, she's part of the prayer warriors, so we need her there early. Please finish up dropping Axel off and make sure she gets to the church on time."

Ben shrugs and agrees, not knowing how complicit he is in my affair right now.

When we're all packed up, I scout the emptying park for Frank. He's nowhere to be seen. Probably made plans to drink at one of the guys' places before going home. The thought makes me sick. He was embarrassed today when Eli blocked me and when his friend corrected him. And then when he realized he was wrong, he'd tried to deflect it by coming after me. I'm not surprised, but fuck, in front of people? Frank loves for people to think he's amazing. Eli must have really pissed him off.

I don't even know why I bothered to correct him. It was such a stupid thing to fight over. It wasn't worth it, that's for sure.

But as I pack Ben's car and I watch Eli pack his car, it's easy to forget everything when, in a few minutes, I'll be where I belong. Underneath Eli, with his cock deep in my ass.

Ben rants about Frank all the way to the bookstore, finishing with, "Why the fuck doesn't he get his own fucking soda, anyway?"

"We can talk about it tomorrow," I say. And then, with the bookstore keys digging into my palm, I remind him, "Your mom's a prayer warrior, remember?"

"Oh yeah. It's only the one crate left. You want me to help you?"

"Nah, it's fine." I pop the leather handle of the petty cash box into Pepper's mouth and she trots to the bookstore and waits for me.

I grab the crate and only relax my nerves when Ben's car disappears down the road.

Opening the door, I let Pepper and myself in.

Pepper drops the box gently onto the floor. I return the money to the cash register and carry the crate to the storeroom. Then I retrieve my secret phone to let Eli know I'm at the bookstore.

He replies with, *I'm nearly done. On my way. No cameras, right?*

Me: No cameras. Can you park over at David Shapiro's parking space and come around the back?

Eli: Anything for you.

The smile caused by Eli's last text is still there, even after I've packed all the books back into their places.

My heart joins in the happiness when Eli's next text comes through. *I'm near the back door.*

I rush to the side where we receive stock and unlock the door just as Eli steps up on the last step.

There isn't even half a second of greeting.

Eli drops a bag onto the floor and then pushes me back, slamming the door shut with his foot. Crushing his lips to mine, he kisses me so hard I feel the grind of his teeth against mine.

He drops his hands from my face, dragging them down my sides, and pulls my hips into his.

His erection presses into my stomach and I push into it, wanting, needing his hot, naked flesh on me as soon as possible. My hands race over his body, and I pull him with me toward the storeroom, our lips still locked together.

Pepper whines softly, but Eli came prepared. He pauses long enough to get the massive bones out of the bag, and Pepper is no longer guilty of third-wheeling.

I push the storeroom door closed and reach for Eli again. We come together like two oceans meeting—you can't tell one from the other. We're one, fused and flowing.

"Here?" I ask. "Is here fine?"

He nods and signs rapidly. I don't understand. So he does it slower. *You are mine. You're beautiful. I'm hungry for you.*

I laugh. "I'm hungry for you too, Eli. I'm starving. I've been starving my whole life. Starving for this. Starving for you."

He smiles and drops his mouth to mine again. I reach into my pocket and then press a condom and a packet of lube into his hand.

We're about to fuck in a bookstore. How many dreams is *that* made of?

CHAPTER 48
Eli

He'll get carpet burn. It's a weird thought to have when I'm about to rail this man all the way into fucking next week, but also very appropriate, given our lack of bedroom furniture.

I rip his clothes off his body. No finesse, no time, no gentleness. What we have here, right now, is a kind of brutality that can only be understood by people like us. Who steal moments from those who don't deserve to have what we have.

Axel pulls at my hair, ripping into my clothing, his desperation for me more, it seems, than mine for him.

If what we have was borne from the violence that Axel has faced, then it isn't gentleness that he needs now, but the brutality of our passion. Not a soothing balm, but the fierceness of the fire that roars between us. Burning everything around us until all that's left is us. Just *us*.

Fury for Axel's abuse is so great I can hardly stand it, so I claim him with the brutality of my love for him, and praying from somewhere deep in my soul that his days with Frank will soon be over.

Naked, he drops to the carpeted floor, pulling me down with him. His teeth graze mine as he kisses me. I feel his sounds vibrate in his throat, the urgency in the rapid movements of his hands.

I settle on my knees between his thighs. He sits up, easing the condom from my hand. He rips it open, his movements jerky and choppy and his chest heaving. He sheathes me and then pulls me down onto him. I lube us both, and guided by our desperation and our limited time, I push into him, slowing down only enough to offer him the minimal comfort needed.

When I'm deep inside him, he lifts his hips, his body asking me to take him all the way. I move, stroking him gently at first, grinding my way through the pleasure from the way his hole grips me so tightly.

Axel's fingers dig into my hips, pulling me in closer to him. With one hand braced on the floor next to his head and the other wrapped around his throat so I can hear him, I drive into him. Moving in and out of him like a demon is sitting on my back, urging this carnal act of love and lust. Of pain and sorrow. Hopes and dreams.

He reaches down and grabs his dick, pumping himself while he lifts his hips to meet my thrusts.

It doesn't take long. Fast orgasms are a mandatory part of adultery.

And with my fingers now entwined with his above his head, I pull almost all the way out and then drive all the way back in, where my orgasm meets his prostate in a pleasure so intense I feel the vibration of my own shout reverberating throughout my body.

The warmth of his semen spills onto my abs. I lower my body until we're pressed chest to chest, abdomen to abdomen.

We lay like that for a long time. In reality, it must have been no more than two or three minutes, but for us, those minutes somehow always feel like forever.

I eventually slide off him, pulling him into my arms. He faces me, tracing the angles of my face with his index finger. "I think I'm in love with you," he says.

I choose the easiest words to tell him in sign. He'll understand because it was the one they already learned at the sign language classes.

He watches my fingers as I move them slowly. *I... love... you.*

Tears gather in his eyes. His face is expressionless, and he lowers his lashes when they fall down the side of his face. I feel them gather at my chest. I let him look away from me for a second. Because for just a moment, I'm preoccupied by the lack of emotion in Axel's face when he cries. How he lets his heart bleed through his eyes with such numbness. As if his soul can cry without the need for physical reactions.

When we can communicate quicker in the future, I want to ask him about it. I want to know how I can bring out those parts of him that are so hidden away. I want to bring this silent part of him back to life.

When I've had enough of my musings and not being able to see his face, I gently lift his face back up to mine.

He signs back. *I love you.*

I press light kisses to his fingers.

So there it is. The truest declaration ever made between two people who can do no more than steal each other inside the storeroom of a bookstore.

But it doesn't matter. Nothing will keep us apart. He's chained to someone else, but that doesn't mean he belongs to me any less than if it were *my* ring on his finger right now.

"What are we going to do?" he asks.

I reach over to my discarded pants and retrieve my phone. I type. ***I'll get you the best divorce lawyer in the state.***

He nods and I almost shout with relief and joy.

"How soon?" he asks.

Immediately. We can leave for the city as soon as you are ready.

Another nod to add to my increasing confidence that this man could be mine sooner than I imagined.

"I don't have a high school diploma, so it'll take some time to get a job and pay you back."

I'll give you a job.

He sits up, seeming to forget his nakedness. I remain still so as to not remind him while letting my eyes rove over his body as casually as possible.

"What do you mean?" Axel asks.

I'll hire you. I'll pay you a million dollars a year.

His shoulders shake with laughter, but he stops when he notices I'm not laughing.

"Stop talking like that," he says.

But the more I think about it, the better it sounds. There are some jobs at the company that can be done without a high school education.

I'll hire you at my company.

He laughs. "I'll be fucking the boss?"

Yes. I laugh too. And then, *Can you get away this week?*

He nods. "Frank's got two night shifts this week."

So you can spend the night?

He smiles shyly and nods again. "But I'll have to leave before four a.m.."

His phone lights up with a text. He turns the screen to me.

Frank: Where the fuck are you?

My teeth grind together, cutting into the flesh inside my cheek.

"We have to go," Axel says.

No, we don't. I can drive us to the airport right now.

Axel palms my cheek with a gentle smile on his lips. "Soon. Trust me," he says.

If he hurts you again, I'll kill him.

"I'll stay out of the way. I won't make him angry." Then, after a pause, he says, "Will you call your lawyer?"

I nod. It's the first thing I'm going to do.

He reaches for his clothes, and we dress without speaking again.

Axel opens the door to find a patient Pepper leaning against it. Her bone lies across the floor.

I help Axel straighten out his clothes and then we leave through the back door. When Axel turns in the opposite direction from my truck, I grab his wrist and look at him questioningly.

"It's not safe. Frank will ask questions if you drop me off at home."

I type on my phone. *I'll leave you close to home.* I hate all of this sneaking around.

He thinks for a minute and then says, "Okay, there's a dirt road this side—" he points behind me, "—if we take it, we'll end up at the back of your place. I'll walk back home through the woods."

That's better than walking all the way from here or dropping him off on the side of the road.

"But first, let me get Frank's soda," he says.

CHAPTER 49
Axel

The tick in Eli's jaw tells me how upset he is that not only am I stopping at the store for sodas for Frank, but that I have to go back to Frank at all. I try to reassure him by slipping my fingers between his as he drives us through the back.

We don't communicate much in the car. Pepper sits in the back quietly with two more treats than she's allowed on one day, thanks to Eli spoiling her.

My hand remains inside his and on his lap the whole way home.

I direct him and soon we come upon the other side of the woods, headed toward Eli's place. Eli rolls to a stop not far from the lake.

Pepper is going wild in the back seat, after having spotted a few squirrels. I jump off to let her out.

Eli follows. We are far enough into the woods and close enough to his house that no one will see us. Dusk has fallen, the darkened sky offering us mercy in the form of a dark cloak, hiding us. Pepper goes racing up the grassy bank, sending small animals fleeing in every direction.

Eli leans against the truck and pulls me into his arms, my back pressed into his chest. His fingers lock together low on my abdomen. It's perfect, this moment. It's these moments that show me just how empty my life really is without Eli.

I tilt my head to the side, allowing Eli's chin to nuzzle into the crook of my shoulder. He pulls my sweater back to place soft kisses to the exposed skin there. I place my hands over his and lean deep into his body.

I can't tell you why other people cheat. I can't tell you why people who are in happy marriages cheat.

And I can't tell you how some people in abusive marriages have the courage to walk away before breaking their marriage vows. I don't know how those people have that amount of integrity.

I have neither courage nor integrity. And my decision to divorce Frank with Eli's help is motivated only by my desperate need for Eli. All I know is that this very moment is the reason I did what I did.

This moment of nothingness and everything—no tightness in my chest every time Frank's boot drags across the floor, no constant awareness of how I eat, what I wear, when my next haircut is due, none of the alertness to when I might feel the crack of Frank's palm across my face. That's the nothingness I feel when I'm with Eli.

And then the *everything*. When I'm with Eli, the pain goes away and I can live again. However briefly, I can *live* when I'm with Eli. I can live and laugh and love and be loved without fear for my physical safety, my heart or my mind. All these parts of me that are alert to danger when I'm with Frank are safe here with Eli.

This moment. It's everything I ever dreamed of for myself.

Warmth. Smiles. Happiness. Safety.

I turn in Eli's arms, wrapping myself around him. If I could have absorbed myself into him, I would have. I would hide so deeply in him no one would ever find me. He wraps his arms around me, burying my face inside his chest, kissing the top of my head.

Frank is six foot five. He could have held me just like this and kissed the top of my head a million times if he wanted to, but all Frank ever did with my head was bash it into the headboard and the kitchen table.

Pepper comes bounding down, stopping to sniff Eli's pocket. Like magic, he pulls out a treat and hands it over to her. Then he pulls out his phone and types. ***Pepper's coming with us, right?***

I turn the screen to my face so he can read my lips. "You have space for her, right?" He nods.

I hug him back to me and then pull away to ask another question. "How long will it take?"

We'll talk to my lawyer tomorrow.

My phone pings with a text message. It must be Frank. That familiar tightness in my body returns.

Frank: ***You better be home in five minutes.***

Eli reluctantly lets me go and when I turn around at the top of the path, he's still standing there with his hands in his pockets, watching me. Turning away from him gets harder each time.

Pepper nuzzles my pocket several times as we walk. "I'm not Eli." I laugh. "Don't think I'll fall for your tricks. Even if you're the guard dog of the century, keeping my and Eli's secret."

I find Frank drunker than he was at the park when I get home and I know this by the clicking sound he makes with his tongue as he lays sprawled on the couch watching T.V. There's a beer in his hand.

Tsk tsk.

My body closes up—my back tense, toes and fingers tingling, my heart beating at a pace I'm not comfortable with. Every nerve in my body is on high alert. It's not Friday, but it might as well be.

Tsk. Tsk.

"*... and you can get your very own robotic mop for the one-time only price of...*"

Frank switches the T.V. off. I have a ridiculous thought that I would love to have my very own robotic mop at the one-time only price of—

But I don't know the price. I might never know. Frank might put a bullet through my head right this minute and I'll never know how much the mop would have cost.

"So, you had a good time over at the park, then?" he asks with a nasty smile. If Frank was kind, he'd be a strikingly handsome man. And I guess he is—to the people who don't know him like I do. Frank's politeness and kindness and gentleness are reserved for people out there.

"It was okay, I guess," I say, keeping my voice gentle and neutral.

"And that deaf cunt had some nerve, huh? Trying to come between me and you."

God, how to answer this question? I try carefully. "He doesn't know how things work around here." It's a sucker punch. A pathetic betrayal to Eli, but I promised him I'd do whatever was necessary to avoid a beating until... until I can run away with him.

Frank seems satisfied with my answer for all of one second. Something about Eli must has really triggered him. His face twists and his fingers move like little snakes at his sides.

My mouth is dry. I shoo Pepper away with my foot. She doesn't move. I try to move her with my foot again, but she stays planted to my side, her eyes on Frank. It hasn't stopped him before, Pepper being in the way like this. He's thought nothing of kicking her out of the way before. Which is why I need her to move.

"I mean, I'd have laid a thick one into him if he wasn't some kind of disability case. And anyway, I'm not the type."

My blood boils. Not the type? To what? Beat people? He's right, anyway. I'm the exception. "Yes, Frank."

"But that was his one chance. Next time, I don't care if he's got himself cancer even, Ima fucking rearrange his fuckin' face."

"Yes. Frank."

His eyes refocus on mine. "The fuck is this *yes, Frank, yes Frank,* fuckin' shit? You also dumb like that cunt, too?"

I hesitate, but I know to engage more than this will make things so much worse. I answer eventually. "No, Frank."

"Yes Frank. No Frank. Yes Frank. No Frank. Shut the fuck up for a while, Axel. You're such a stupid fuckin' cunt. And if he ever comes between us when we discussin' things again, he's fuckin dead, ye hear me?"

Oh, God. How do I agree? "I hear you."

"And did you get my soda?"

Blood drains to my feet. I'm absolutely fucked. The sodas are in Eli's car. *Think. Oh, my fucking God. Think!* "Uhm, well, I—"

"Fuckin' speak up, Axel."

"I forgot," I breathe.

At first, I'm convinced he's going to send one right across my cheek, but then he laughs. "Ax, you're really something." I don't miss the sarcasm and his infamous smirk.

He cups his balls vulgarly. "Now get that dog outside so you can make it up to me for forgetting my soda."

When I don't move for the sudden shock of the fact that I have to sleep with Frank, he walks over to me and slaps the back of my head. "You a statue or something?"

I move my feet, my mind completely detached from my body. I can't go through with this. There's no place deep enough in my mind where I can go that would protect me from this. Not after Eli. This is a betrayal of the truest love I've ever known. The situation is the opposite now and no piece of paper can make it any other way. I belong to *Eli*. It's *Eli* I'd be betraying.

I shove Pepper out of the house and then enter the bedroom with legs made of lead. Palms tingling like they do when you stand too high up on something and you look down.

One time, the fair came through town. Ben was going on the Ferris wheel. I wanted to go too but Ben was worried I'd get sick, but I was fully committed to my *life is too short* and *you only live once* approach to life so I went, anyway.

I did get sick, and it had started with the tingling in my feet and hands when I looked down.

This is the same, but so much worse. Frank and I hadn't had sex since I said no the last time. Tonight will be a punishment for that, too.

Frank saunters into the room. I watch him from the corner of my eye, pretending to straighten the bed, fluff up the pillows. And when he just stands there looking at me, I move to the window to draw the curtains shut. Pepper is outside the window, whining softly. I put my finger to my lips, telling her to shush. It breaks my heart to shut the curtains on her face, but I'm sure she's more heartbroken than me.

"But I'm not done with you for acting like you're all so much smarter than me," Frank says. "It really hurt my feelings when you did that, Axel. I expected more from you as my husband."

I stiffen, making work out of straightening out the curtain.

I don't know which Frank to be more afraid of. The angry one? The sorrowful one?

"You shouldn't forget that I made you, Axel. If it were not for me, you'd have been six feet under before you even turned twenty-one."

His voice has that loud pridefulness about it. Confident and superior. He truly believes every word he's saying.

I'm self-preserving as much as I can, but Eli has given me small pieces of courage over the last few months.

"You didn't make me, Frank. I was just fine before you came along. With or without the cancer."

"You wanna turn around and say that to my face?" he says. The lightness in his tone is a decoy. I don't buy it. I don't turn around.

"You been gettin' cocky these days, huh Axel? You been taking lessons from old Mrs. Dalton next door? That why you goin' over there every other night? She teachin' ye how to disobey your husband?"

The slight change in Frank's dialect is my measuring stick for how far I can go. And as of now, not much further. So, I take my last shot before my time is up.

"Frank, our marriage isn't working." It's my first step toward Eli and away from Frank.

He laughs. My heart hammers in my chest. My boldness is going to cost me.

The harsh handling of the nightstand drawer makes me whirl around so fast I trip on the bottom of the curtain and grab onto the edge of the bed to break my fall.

Frank is fast. Before I can straighten up, he's behind me, pushing me back down onto my knees, his thick hand around the back of my neck.

His fingers curl painfully into the sides of my neck. He pushes down until my forehead is pressed into the bed. I can hardly breathe. Even if I *could* have taken air into my lungs, I wouldn't have. Even the tiny movement caused by breathing might set Frank off further. Silent screams echo in my head as if on a mega speaker.

You provoked him.

You shouldn't have provoked him.

Now, the cold, metal butt of his gun is pressed into my nape. I brace myself and when the first hit into my shoulder comes, my head sinks further into the bed and I howl silently into the bedding.

Pain explodes in my shoulder and immediately engulfs my entire body. I cry into the bedsheets like a baby because Eli would never do this to me.

I breathe deep and controlled to ease the pain, but Frank isn't done. I'm so scared of that gun, I'd choose a beating with it any day as long as it doesn't go off. I don't have any confidence that he knows how to hit me without accidentally killing me, even though I've received plenty of hits from this gun.

"This marriage is not working?" he spits close to my ear. "You see this gun over here, Axel? The next time you decide on the state of our marriage, will be the time you get a bullet right through here." He licks inside my ear. "I'll blow your brains out right through your ear. You fucking hear me, you sickly fuckin' cunt?"

I'm shaking with fear and fury. Before, it was usually just the fear. Today, fury takes up residence, too. If only I could just turn around and tackle him to the ground and get that gun away from him. But he's too strong. I'd never be able to.

Frank's tongue curls into my ear again. "I'll fuckin' decide when and if this marriage isn't working."

He pushes me upward, hauling me onto the bed by the back of my pants. Then, with the gun still in one hand, he yanks my pants down.

Pepper whines outside.

I'm slammed onto my stomach and then Frank's cock is pushing into my ass.

"I'll fuckin show you something, you dumb fuck."

I lay on the bed with the gun clutched in Frank's hand next to my head and his cock inside me, aided only by his pre-cum.

Tears fall silently.

Only thoughts of Eli take me through the eight seconds needed for Frank to come. My flaccid cock is squashed between my stomach and the bed. *It's only eight seconds*, I repeat in my head over and over. It feels like eight seconds of eternity.

When it's over, Frank brings me a warm cloth and cleans me. The cloth is white. Faint red marks stain the warm material. I inspect the red marks, and all I can think about is I wish Frank had used a condom so I wouldn't have had to feel his raw flesh rubbing against mine.

And how much I wish I could feel Eli inside me, flesh to flesh.

CHAPTER 50
Eli

My mother doesn't look well on our video calls. She insists she's fine, but I want her to see the doctor. She says she has a doctor's appointment set up.

I consider flying back to see her, but... I can't just leave Axel. Maybe I can take him with me. We can make it a one-day visit and be back without anyone noticing.

I'm anxious about not being able to communicate with Axel and between that and my concern for my mother, I find myself at Mrs. Dalton's door just before eleven p.m. She takes pity on me, and, after insisting I have a late night cup of tea, she calls Axel. There's no response after three tries. Texts are undelivered.

"I'm sure he was tired and got to bed early," Mrs. Dalton tries to reassure me. She tries one last time as I finish my tea.

No response.

I thank her for her efforts and make my way back home. The walk is more of a trudge. Not my usual look, but this town has taught me that it's okay to look like how you feel sometimes.

Right now, I feel defeated.

As I come down the path, a movement near my house catches my eye. I pause, then remember, this is not the city. The likelihood of someone trying to rob my house is very low. Still, I walk slowly while I inspect the area. Pepper comes into view and then I'm immediately sprinting down the path. Axel is at the window, banging. As I run, I watch him alternate between the doorbell and the window. His movements are jerky and quick. Desperate.

Something is wrong.

His back is to me when I get to him. I reach for his arm and spin him around. The one second of shock on his face is immediately replaced by a relief so profound I have a hard time not going into a full-scale panic over what's put him in such a state.

His lips are moving, but I don't understand because he's talking too fast. Babbling. He's *babbling* and I can't keep up. I manage to get something about forgetting his key for my backdoor but nothing else.

Pepper circles us, rubbing against Axel's thigh. Axel throws himself into my chest, but I hold him off at a small distance, holding him by the shoulders and inspecting his body for signs of an attack. He almost drops to the ground when I tighten my grip on his shoulders. I release his shoulder immediately and his hand goes up there to rub.

I half carry him into the house with the way he clings to me. I've never felt so helpless in my life. I can't hear him. I can't detect his cries. I can't follow his pain fast enough.

Inside, Pepper jumps onto the couch and settles down. I set Axel on the couch and sit beside him. Taking his face in mine, I force him to look at me. I frown, asking him silently to tell me what's wrong because I can't risk letting go of his face to sign or retrieve my phone to type.

He lifts his hand, his face soaked with tears. Then he signs. R. P. E. The second letter between *r* and *p* is wrong; it isn't a sign, but I don't need it. Axel watches my face and when I make the connection, he bursts into tears.

A scream tears through my throat. "*No*". It must have been loud because Axel's eyes widen before he collapses into my arms. I hold him together while my helpless fury tears me apart. My very first word uttered in his presence and it had to be this? This agonizing sound, breaking the silence between us?

How did I not know that people could be this evil? That innocent people could be tortured like this?

My body vibrates, my breath moving in and out of my chest in short gasps.

Axel shifts and lifts his head. I keep my arms banded around him tightly. "How soon can you call your lawyer?" he asks.

I reach for my phone and dial.

Axel stops me. "We don't have to do it right this minute. It's late."

I gently remove his hand. What is all the power I hold worth if I can't use it to protect him?

Howard picks up on the first ring. The screen is darkened but comes sharply into view a second later when the light on his side is switched on. His hair is ruffled. I've woken him, but he knows I wouldn't have placed this call if it wasn't urgent.

The screen jerks for a second while he sets it up on a flat surface and I do the same, placing the phone on the coffee table. Axel takes my hand in his, squeezing hard. I rub my thumb over the back of his hand.

Eli, good to see you. Is everything okay? Howard signs.

I gently remove my hand from Axel's and sign back. *Good to see you too. I need some help.* I tilt the phone to the side so Axel comes into view. He drops his head, picking at his fingernails.

This is Axel, I sign.

Is he hearing?

Yes. He's still learning to sign.

285

Howard drops his hands, and my eyes move to his lips. "Hi, Axel," Howard says.

Axel's head jerks up and he greets Howard.

I sign quickly. *Axel needs a divorce lawyer. We need to initiate divorce proceedings and have it finalized within the next few weeks. We can't wait longer than that.*

Howard is the best in his field, understanding his place, but even he can't help his curiosity. *We?* He signs. While I watch, his face connects the dots from the last conversation I had with him about my hypothetical situation involving a divorce.

I give him a clipped nod, taking Axel's hand in mine and placing it on my thigh.

Since we're speaking in sign language, Howard moves his eyes to Axel and confirms, "Axel, Eli tells me you require the services of a divorce lawyer, the urgency of which requires for your divorce to be initiated and finalized within the next few weeks."

Axel gives me a nervous look and then nods at Howard.

"I'll get the paperwork started, Eli, but sixty days is usually the best we can do. Be prepared for that. The divorce proceedings will have to take place over there, that's how it usually works, but we'll see what we can do." Howards tells me. I nod and then look to Axel for approval. He nods, some light returning to his eyes.

I thank Howard and end the call.

Then I turn back to Axel. He clings to me again. All I want is to go down the road and murder Frank in cold blood, but Axel's fear radiates from him like an unbearable heat. So, I settle back into the couch and pull him into my lap. He curls into a ball and I hold him to me, stroking his hair with one hand and rubbing lightly across his chest with the other. I don't know how much time passed before the rise and fall of his chest settles into a deep, steady rhythm and then I know he's fallen asleep.

I rise with him, noticing his frame is slighter than before.

He's definitely lost some weight.

I lay him down on my bed carefully and climb in next to him.

A little while longer and this hell will be over for him.

CHAPTER 51
Axel

It's the warmth that wakes me. The soft, pleasant warmth I experience only when I'm with Eli. I'm settled deep in his chest, his body curled around me and his arms keeping me hidden. The way Eli's body surrounds me, you'd never guess I'm here if you looked at his sleeping posture from behind.

This could be my life. I push all thoughts of cancer and chemo and treatment and death sentences and guns out of my mind. Like Frank said one time, if I was going to die, I'd have been gone by now.

The time on Eli's alarm clock says three-thirty a.m.. I've been gone just more than three hours. Frank must still be sleeping. He still had the gun in his hand when he fell asleep. It's the gun I'd been so desperate to get away from. The thought of dying in general has become beyond frightening since Eli came into my life, but to die at Frank's hand is the worst kind of injustice.

Eli's hand is heavy. I try to slip out of his grasp, but it's almost impossible without waking him. I need to get back so Frank doesn't come looking for me. I just need to survive the next few weeks, but even I've noticed that I've become too bold for my own good recently. I'll have to be more careful until I can go away with Eli.

Somehow, I manage to slip out from under Eli's arm.

Pepper's tail thumps softly on the bed. I catch a glimpse of myself in the mirror as Pepper and I creep out of the bedroom. I look surprisingly well rested for someone who was raped the night before by his husband.

Mrs. Dalton is at her kitchen window when I pass with Pepper. She waves her hand and I can see her concern on her face from all the way over here. I give her the thumbs up and sign, *I'm okay*, to her. She nods and disappears from the window. I hope she hasn't been sitting there all night watching for me.

I check through the windows first for signs of movement. I'd pulled the curtain slightly open before I left last night and when I go around to check, Frank is still sleeping.

So Pepper and I quickly enter the house. I give her some water and something to eat and get busy with cleaning up the kitchen.

Halfway through, I can't get it out of my mind and so I creep to the bedroom and peer inside to see if the gun is still on the bed. It is.

Just get your stuff and go. The thought gives me so much hope. My hands pause over the last of the plates I'd been washing. I could do it. I could tell Eli I'm ready and we could be gone right now. What's stopping me? Mrs. Dalton would understand if I suddenly left. She'd be happy, in fact. Ben too.

That's it. I'll leave. Right now. I'll need only my box of memories.

"Where were you?"

Prickles of alertness immediately engulf me. My back freezes and my feet and palms begin to pulse.

With careful movements, I set the plate down and turn slowly.

Frank stands at the doorway, eyes bloodshot, bed hair and an evil gleam in his eyes. He lifts his hand to scratch his head. Maybe it was to show me the gun in his hand. I don't know. My first thought is that the shiny silver of the gun matches that glint in his eye.

"I asked, where the fuck were you when I got up for a piss?" Words stick together inside my throat. I try for a deflection.

"What you did to me last night was unforgivable, Frank."

"It's part of the terms and conditions of our fuckin' marriage contract. When you signed it, you gave your consent for me to fuck you whenever I wanted. So don't go talking about non-consent and all that new age bullshit. I know my rights."

I'm almost sick with hearing this.

"I still have a say in it," I argue. Anything to keep him away from asking me about my whereabouts.

"Fuck you and your *say*. Where the fuck were you?"

He scratches his head again with the hand that's holding the gun. And just like that, all my courage and plans to run away with Eli in the middle of the night, to tell Frank that I was not just leaving, but that I was leaving him for someone else, that I'd found someone who makes me feel so safe and who lets me be me... everything goes up in flames as I track the gun in Frank's hand.

"If you don't start talking, I'm going to blow out your brains, Axel, I swear to fuckin God."

"You'll go to jail." I have a death wish.

"This ain't my gun." He laughs and turns the gun over to his other hand, admiring it.

Then he points it straight at me.

"I—I was just outside, thinking." I don't know if it's true that just before your moment of death, your whole life flashes before your eyes. It isn't like that for me, unless Eli is my whole life, because all I can see, while I stare down the barrel of Frank's gun, is Eli.

His care. His love. His groundedness. His gentleness and the strength entwined with it.

And it's thoughts of Eli and my refusal to accept that I will never see him again if I don't survive this moment that gives me courage.

"I was worried about us," I lie. "I wanted to clear my head so I can figure how to make us happy again. How to make *you* happy again."

"I checked the fuckin' windows. I didn't see you." He lowers the gun slightly.

"I was down by the flowerbed. Pepper was restless. I didn't want her whining to wake you."

He saunters over to me with the beginnings of a *make-up* smile. A smile you could call kind. And although I knew Frank's kindness came at a devastating price, I still leaned so heavily on it for so many years, calling it *hope*.

Before, when we reached this point during a fight, I'd feel a sense of victory. That I'd gotten him over to my side even for just a little while.

That thing about couples who fight do so just for the make up afterward? It's true for abused spouses too. Before Eli, I'd look at the fights with Frank as nothing more than paving the road for him to show me that he cared about me, that I meant enough to him for him to feel remorseful over what he'd done.

That his efforts in making it up to me was his way of showing his care or his regret for what he'd done.

I held onto the hope that those few moments of kindness would turn into something more and the abuse would stop.

It's possible for someone to break you, destroy your spirit, and still offer you enough kindness to keep you in a constant state of confusion and hope. This has been my life for nearly ten years.

But now, as Frank approaches me from across the kitchen, ready to make up, all I feel is disgust and anger. Anger like I never felt before. Because I finally see this for what it is.

Not just Frank. Me too.

I too perpetuated the cycle of abuse by not recognizing these terrible, harmful patterns.

Frank pulls me into his chest. "You make me crazy, Axel. It's that pretty face of yours, I swear."

Fuck you, I scream internally.

He pulls my head back. "You know what you can do to make me happy?"

I shove down the lump in my throat.

"Wear those nice panties for me. I'll let you wear them. How's that?"

"What?" *Never. I'll never wear them for you.*

Frank laughs and runs the tip of the gun across my cheek. I stop breathing. "I'm giving you permission, Axel. And you want to make our marriage better, right?"

Oh, god. No.

"That's what would make me happy, Axel." Another trail of the gun over my shoulder.

I focus on the bile sitting high in my chest from Frank's proximity. I use my revulsion for him like a shield. "Yes, Frank." *Over my dead fuckin' body.*

"Anyway," he continues, "as I was saying, sometimes I get a little out of hand. I do and say things I don't mean. You know that about me. You understand, right?"

His palm caresses my cheek. Vomit sits in my throat. All I can do is nod and pray he doesn't kiss me.

He does. A sloppy, cold, awful kiss. "Come on. Leave these dishes. I'll help you with them later. Come lie on the bed and I'll rub your shoulders."

CHAPTER 52
Eli

We'll have to wait sixty days at the minimum to have Axel's divorce finalized even with a friendly judge but we don't have to wait that long to get Axel away from here.

I send several texts to his iPhone telling him not to worry, for him to see when he gets back to work tomorrow. Each text ends with *I love you*. A truer thing has never been said.

I've considered several over the top options to keep Axel safe. Pressing charges even though Axel told me to leave it alone, sending a surveillance team to watch over him. I'll have security so tight Frank's head would spin. I even considered having someone rough Frank up a little bit. Desperation is a dangerous thing.

I'm trying to listen to Axel and keep things calm until we can leave together, but the thought of Frank not just touching Axel but *violating* him is not something I can sit on and do nothing.

I make a video call to my mother at around eight-thirty.

"Have you been to the doctor?" I sign. "Tomorrow," she signs back.

"Okay. Are you feeling okay, though?"

She smiles but doesn't answer. "Why don't you fly out for a day or two?"

I've told her nothing of how much my life has changed since I arrived at River Valley.

"I can't..."

"You look tired. What's wrong?" she signs.

"Nothing. I'm okay. I've met someone." Her eyes light up like a thousand lights.

"Oh, Eli..."

"Don't cry," I sign, smiling.

"What's his name?"

"Axel."

"Axel... such a lovely name. Bring him with you. I want to see you. Both of you. I've missed your face and I want to see the person who's found your heart."

"I'll try."

"I'm so happy for you, Eli. I can't wait to meet him."

"Me too," I sign.

I end the call with my mother and send Axel a text. ***Can we see each other tonight?***

I'll find a way to convince him to leave as early as tonight, if possible.

Maybe Axel's nightmare will end tonight. I'll take him home and he'll never have to worry about Frank ever again.

CHAPTER 53
Axel

I'm going to leave Frank. I don't have the courage to stay with him while the divorce is in progress. He might really shoot me. So, I'm going to run away with Eli.

But no matter how much I force myself to focus on being with Eli that awful fear just won't let up. I walk around, tapping my chest because the constant tightness there also won't ease up.

Ben is already at the bookstore when I arrive because the door is unlocked. I make my way to the back to look for him, grabbing a new stock sheet from the counter on my way.

I push open the door and call out Ben's name as I enter. Ben is standing near the filing cabinet and—

Oh, God.

Waves of heat pulse at the bottom of my spine, moving upward and gathering fear at a phenomenal speed.

"It wouldn't stop beeping, so I went searching for the sound," Ben says.

He holds up the iPhone. "The drawer was locked, but I only needed to tug it a few times before it opened."

And when I still say nothing, he offers a further explanation.

"This cabinet is old. The lock must have been loose, you know? Loose enough to open with a few tugs, yeah?"

"Ben..." My voice is only an octave more than a whisper. Is that relief skating down my spine? This is my best friend. I should have told him everything right from the beginning.

"I mean, it has an iPhone message tone. I wouldn't have even noticed, probably, if it was one of our regular android ringtones, you know?"

"Ben... I should have told you—"

He rushes over to me and flings his arms around my neck. I hug him back. I should have told him.

"Eli Saxon?" he says with a massive smile when he pulls away.

I chew on my lip while his grin nearly cracks his face.

He drops to the floor, pulling me down with him. "Ax, dude, do you know how long I've prayed for you to be happy?"

"I'm sorry I didn't tell you," I say hoarsely.

He hands the phone over to me. "When I picked it up, a text was coming in. I saw the last one only."

I open the texts. The last one says *I love you.*

I bite my smile back and Ben shoves my knee.

"I'm so happy for you, Ax. But *please*. Tell me how this happened," he says.

"I really should have told you. I'm sorry."

"Yeah, you should be. I'd have held that torch for you like a fuckin' pro. Now tell me how this happened?"

"You know the lake near Mrs. Johnson's house, right?"

"Yeah, the one Frank sends you to so he won't get mad at you when his friends try to sexually harass you."

I sigh. It sounds so much worse when someone else says it. "Yeah. So, he started coming out to the lake and we got talking."

Ben frowns.

I laugh. "Well, I talk and he reads my lips or we text."

"Okay, and then?"

I run my hands through my hair. "Ben, he's just... *amazing.*"

Ben grins. "He treats you good?"

I nod. "It's so different being with him, Ben. I feel... not scared all the time. Like I can just be me. Not like with Frank where it's always like nothing is ever good enough."

"Frank's a fuckin' narcissistic asshole. I hate what he did to you. Even when you started getting sick, you were always so happy. You laughed all the time, and you were never so withdrawn."

"Yeah. I see that now. I see how much I changed after Frank. I can't believe I never saw it before. I think I was always just so grateful he was there, you know. I finally had someone."

"I know it's not the same, Ax, but you always had us too. Me. Mrs. Dalton." He laughs. "Pepper, too. But yeah, I get it."

"Sometimes I worry I'm just using Eli to feel good about myself. That I've become addicted to his kindness and his care because he's the total opposite of Frank. And that scares me. It's like Eli's... too perfect. I mean, Ben, would I have been attracted to Eli if Frank had been good to me?"

"Who knows? There are a million ways things can happen. We don't get to have a preview of every single possible outcome. *This* is your journey. All the *could-have-been's* aren't relevant. Frank *isn't* and never has been kind to you. He never respected you. That's the reality of it. And that's the only reality you can base your decisions on. And I'm sure Eli isn't perfect. What he is, is just a good human being. We all should just be good human beings."

"Hey, why are you so smart today?" I chuckle.

He doesn't take it so lightly. "Do you know what it's like watching someone you care about get treated like that and there's nothing you can do about it?"

I sidestep the question even though I know it's rhetorical.

"So... you don't think I'm going to hell for this?"

Ben throws a damaged book at me. I catch it in mid-air. "I think you're going to heaven every time you're with Eli."

I throw the book back at him. "Shut up, Ben. Lame." But I laugh because it feels so good to talk to him about it.

"So what now, Ax? What's the plan?"

"I'm going to leave Frank." Saying it out loud doesn't bring the relief I thought it would. All it does is bring more fear.

"I can't say I'm sad about it, Ax. I'll help you any way you need me, okay?"

We're silent for a time and then, Ben asks, "What will you do if he finds out? Like, before you leave?"

"I'll try not to get killed," I joke. But it's not funny. Ben doesn't laugh either.

"How soon can you leave? Will you go with him? Or meet him there?"

"He's going to help me get a divorce as soon as possible. I'm the worst person on earth, right? Living with Frank and planning to leave him like this."

"I don't think there's another way, Ax. And that doesn't make you a bad person. Just someone who's backed into a corner."

I scrub my hand down my face. "This is my story, Ben, but I'm still the villain. There's no version of this story that can exist where I get to be the hero. Because heroes don't cheat, right?"

"Then be the best fuckin' villain you can be. Fuck being the hero. Do whatever it takes to be happy."

"Even betray my own husband?"

"Yes. Because he's never once given you a safe place for... anything. You're sitting here, doing this with Eli because he might literally beat you to fuckin' death if you tried to leave in peace. How does he deserve any kind of loyalty?"

Ben leans against the cabinet, watching me while I contemplate his wise words.

"If you stay loyal to him, it automatically means you're betraying yourself," he says at last.

"Still sounds like excuses to cheat, Ben. Not that I'm trying to be all righteous. I just don't want to be delusional about it, making it something it's not. I'm cheating on Frank with the most amazing man I've ever met, and the two of us are planning my divorce. And I don't even feel guilty about it."

"Then get comfortable with it."

"Be the villain?" The idea doesn't sound as bad as it did a minute ago.

"Yeah. Villains don't give a fuck about what people think. Maybe we should all be villains. That way, people won't fuck with us."

I laugh again. I like that advice. Not only because it's convenient for my situation, but because it's true that sometimes you have to be okay with being the bad guy if it means protecting yourself.

The doorbell tinkles, indicating our first customer.

"I'll get that," Ben says. "Read your texts."

Then at the door, he turns and says, "And Ax, you deserve to be happy. Just remember that."

I check my new email on the iPhone and within an hour, I have several legal documents to start the divorce proceedings. My hands shake with fear as I go through them. Getting divorced isn't as much a relief as I thought it would be. It feels... sad, in a way. But I push through the confusing feelings. It isn't even about Frank so much anymore. It's about how I can't bear to be away from Eli. This divorce is about me and what I *want*.

What I deserve.

I promised Eli I'd meet him tonight since Frank has another overnight shift, so I rush home after receiving the new stock at the bookstore. I lost some time admiring the new covers of some of the books so I have to basically fly home. Not just to get things done quickly so I can go see Eli, but mostly because of that motherfucking wall phone. The fucking thing is already ringing when I get through the door. I almost trip over Pepper trying to get to it.

"You're home," Frank says, when I answer.

"Uh, yeah."

"Yeah, I'll be home around four a.m.. Oh, I have your phone with me."

What? I check my pocket. *Fuck.* I'd become so attached to my iPhone that I'd been neglecting my regular phone. "Why do you have my phone?" I ask.

"I just wanted to see what you were up to."

"Well, can I have it back?" I'm confident because there's nothing incriminating on that phone.

"No."

I shouldn't have let it get to me. I'm the one cheating and I won't be here much longer anyway, but I hate how Frank wants to control everything. "It's my phone," I grate out unnecessarily, but my new awareness of the way Frank plays with me makes my blood boil now that I'm beginning to recognize these awful signs. How blind have I been all these years?

"Yeah? Well, I was the one who paid for it, so..." The line goes dead.

I prepare the quickest dinner in the universe, desperate to get to Eli. He'll be waiting at the lake. The night is nice out. I want to spend it with Eli, looking up at the stars. Let Frank keep my phone. I don't care anymore.

When I get to the lake, Eli is already there. I'll have to tell him about the cancer. But the thought of it sickens me so I put it off one more moment.

I fly into his arms, and he's got me tucked deep in his chest within seconds. Breathing in his scent, I pull him tighter to me. My endless hours of learning sign language are paying off. With the moon offering its gentle light, I can make out what he's saying.

Are you okay?

Yes, I sign back.

We can leave tonight or tomorrow.

Frank is at work, I sign. *I can gather the most essential things. What about Pepper?*

Pepper too. She's a therapy dog, right?

Yes.

We should be able to get her on a plane easily.

Pepper dances around us like she knows she's about to go away with Eli, too.

I have a moment, just one single moment of... sadness. Leaving Frank. Leaving this town. Leaving Ben. It's all I've ever wanted but to be faced with the reality of it happening, it's almost suffocating.

Eli pulls me close, his back against the tree trunk. His lips find mine under the moonlight. Kissing me, owning me like the night owned the moon.

In him, with him, I shine. I shine the brightest when he claims me as his like this. I kiss him back, deep and true. The truest thing I have ever experienced. This tenderness that helps me live even as

I'm dying. This tenderness that will help me die a little less every day.

It feels like an eternity since I touched him when it was only this past weekend. His abs dip at my touch as I explore his body with slow movements.

Frank is the furthest thing from my mind as my fingers trail possessively over Eli's chest, my palms spreading over his shoulders and then back over his beautiful pecs. I lose myself in every inch of skin, of muscle that tightens and loosens at my touch.

His hands move harshly over me, matching his loud, harsh breaths as they mingle with the cold, crisp air.

I tangle my tongue with his, sucking and groaning like I'm *his* husband. Like I have the right to demand more from his touch. He gives me more, biting on my lower lip, pulling on that lip and then releasing it with a pop. The sting is so fucking delicious I go back for more. Over and over, Eli sucks my lip into his mouth, biting hard enough for me to groan loudly against his lips, before he releases it. My bottom lip throbs, but fuck, I need more.

Pulling Eli even closer to me, if it were possible, I smash my lips to his, kissing him like I, too, owned him. The way he owned me. What I'm doing is selfish and villainous and *right*. Fucking hell, this is *right*.

My hands travel fast and harsh to Eli's waistband. We'll go to the house in a minute and there he'll fuck me so fucking good, but I need him, at least a little bit, right fucking now.

He races for my waistband too, and in one second, my cock slides against his as he bends his knees and lines us up. We are so fucking hot together like this. He rubs us up and down slowly and I tilt my hips forward, dying for a harder grip. Eli creates some space, releasing us, and signs. *I love your—*

I frown. I don't understand. He laughs, a loud, uninhibited sound, and then closes his fingers around my dick.

—*Dick*. He loves my dick. Even if it's bigger than his. I swallow down the lump threatening to make me cry because this is yet another thing, like my hair, that I can't change and won't ever again have to feel awful for.

I join in his laughter. Why didn't I ever ask him to teach me the sign for *dick*?

Closing my hand around his cock, I move with him as he massages me from base to tip. So firm and sure, his strokes send me hurtling to the edge of the universe. I close my fingers around his girth, lost in the feel of Eli's cock in my hand.

I don't know how I hear the crunch of twigs underneath boots.

CHAPTER 54
Eli

Axel jerks my sweats back over my cock, his body stiffening with what I've come to learn as fear.

His head jerks to the side. I lift my head and—

I spin Axel around, shoving him behind me. I move to the left, making sure he's completely hidden by my frame.

"The fuck you think you're doing?" Frank stalks toward us, his face twisted. His lips move slowly, letting me read him with clarity. As I read his words, a gleam of metal catches my eye. The moon plays no favorites, shedding its light for anyone who needs it. But it isn't the flash of the gun that makes me freeze.

Behind me, a slight shuffle and then Axel's fingers sinking into the material at the back of my sweatshirt. Its impact is stunning. This man behind me is terrified.

I lift up one hand and with the other, reach behind to make sure he's still hidden behind me.

"Leave him alone," I enunciate as clearly as I can. I hope it's as loud as I need it to be. I hope I've pronounced the words correctly.

In no universe did I ever think that on the rare occasion I would use my voice, it would be in a situation like this.

"You can talk, you fuckin' deaf cunt?"

I read that clearly enough.

"Step the fuck away," Frank says.

"No."

He steps forward. I take a step back, taking Axel with me, pressing him into the tree trunk.

Frank holds the gun loosely in his hand.

"Axel, show your fucking face if you don't want someone to fucking die tonight." Frank looks directly at me when he speaks.

Axel shoves me to the side with some impact, but not enough. I grab him, hauling him back. His wild eyes beg me to let him go, but there's no fucking way.

He stands next to me, his hand trapped in mine and on full display for Frank to see.

Frank's lips move too fast and he seems to have slipped into a dialect I've struggled with from time to time here. I don't know what he's saying, but Axel has one hand up and his face is contorted in fear.

I catch only a few sentences from Frank:

You're fucking him?

You're cheating on me?

Peter was right.

Axel keeps his face turned in my direction.

I'm sorry, Frank. It's not what you think, he says.

Frank: *He had you against the fuckin' tree.*

The headlights of a truck cut through the darkness, forcing us to shield our eyes when it rolls to a stop.

Mrs. Dalton rushes out of the passenger seat, followed by a uniformed officer.

Frank discreetly slips his gun into the back of his pants.

Mrs. Dalton stands between us and Frank.

Frank glares at her and she returns the favor.

The officer tips his hand to the side of his head and I dip my head, acknowledging. Axel is vibrating next to me.

The officer has words with Frank, who argues and points at Axel. His movements are aggressive and Axel can't stop shaking. Whatever they're talking about, he's becoming more and more terrified by the moment.

Then he starts to move away. I grab him, causing him to bang into Mrs. Dalton, who also grabs onto him.

Frank shoves a phone into the officer's hand. From here I can see it's a video.

The officer looks at Axel and then at me. His face twists into a disapproving sneer and then he talks to Axel, who begins to nod his head.

My stomach churns.

I move so I can watch the officer's lips.

"You comfortable going back home, Axel?" he asks. "We'll get you guys to church first thing and talk everything out." He gives me another disapproving look and then asks Axel, "He can lip read, right?" Axel nods.

Mrs. Dalton holds onto him like he might run away at any moment.

"Mr. Saxon. Nobody's perfect and all couples have their problems. I suggest you leave these two alone to sort things out. Frank's a good guy. He doesn't deserve this."

I'm surprised I read all of that with the speed at which he seemed to be talking, but there is no way in hell I'm letting Axel go.

I turn to Axel and sign. Frank's disgusted face catches my eye for one second. "What's going on?" I hate not being in control of this. That I can't protect Axel sufficiently.

"I'll go back," Axel says.

"No." I use my voice.

"It'll be okay. Frank says he's not going to do anything."

Mrs. Dalton shakes her head, which earns her another glare from Frank. Other than that, he's docile, mostly. Like he doesn't have a gun inside his pants. Like he's not going to beat Axel to death as soon as the officer leaves.

He's got a gun, I sign to Axel, emphasizing my signs and facial expressions, so he knows that there is no way in fucking hell I'm letting him go.

He won't use it, he signs back.

"No," I repeat with my voice.

Axel signs. *I'll come back.* He's pleading with me to let him go back to this monster. *He has a video of us.* His face is filled with fear.

I don't care, I sign back.

I need to get him away from you.

He's trying to protect me? At the cost of what? His life? Over my dead body.

The officer speaks. "I'll escort you back, Axel." Axel nods.

I pull Axel back to me. Under no circumstances am I allowing him to go back there. Frank will have to put a bullet through my skull first.

The officer faces me. I think he's trying to intimidate me with his badge. He's got the wrong fuckin' guy.

Frank has moved away, pacing, looking like an innocent victim. The unsuspecting husband who caught his husband cheating. Playing the role of the scorned husband so well.

Pepper starts to calm now, sitting close to me.

Frank comes rushing forward, but he doesn't want to look bad in front of the officer. His face eases up. "Come home, Axel. We'll work it out."

I squeeze Axel's hand. He's not going anywhere, and I've had enough of this.

"Get off my property." I speak slowly, trusting that my pronunciation is correct and the tone and volume of my voice are as intimidating as I intend it to be.

The officer glares at me and speaks to Frank. I catch one word— *trespassing*—before he pulls Frank away.

As soon as the vehicle backs away and disappears up the path, Mrs. Dalton sags against me.

"I called to warn you, but there was no response. I saw Frank head this way with a gun in his hand. I was so afraid. I had to call the police."

I tip my fingers to my chin. *Thank you.*

"You two need to get out of here," she says.

Axel nods. "Let us walk you home, Mrs. Dalton. Then Eli and I can figure things out."

CHAPTER 55
Axel

Eli and I stand in his kitchen. His arms banded tightly around me. My face buried in his chest.

My body is tired. More tired than usual and what is considered as normal. Even without the tests back, I know what's coming. Selfishly, I still can't bring myself to tell Eli. I'm so afraid he'll change his mind about us. About me. Who would want to take on a sickly person who won't even be around to celebrate his mid-thirties?

Thoughts race through my head and I bury myself deeper into Eli.

He pulls back enough to sign, "*We should leave tonight or tomorrow morning at the latest.*"

"Tomorrow morning. I'll go back to the house for my personal items."

He frowns, so I reassure him. "He'll be at work in the morning." "*I'll come with you.*"

I place my hand over his heart. "I'll be quick, Eli. I wouldn't have bothered if it wasn't important. It's something of my mother's. I'll go get it and be back here in no time. In the morning, okay? When Frank is gone."

He's not happy, but he agrees and books us the first flight out.

We sleep in each other's arms. Eli holds me like I'm the most precious thing he's ever held, burying my body inside his as if to hide me away. I feel so loved. So *wanted.*

Eli's soft breathing near my ear tells me he's still asleep.

I slip out of his arms carefully, walking through the house, making sure all the windows are shut and double checking that all the doors are locked. It's not likely Frank will barge into Eli's house, but I still check everything.

I call Ben on Eli's cell and tell him I'm leaving with Eli in the morning. I don't tell him about Frank catching me and Eli because he'll stress about it and he has an exam tomorrow. I'll tell him after his exam.

I ask him to ask his brother, Luke, to check tomorrow's schedule, to make sure Frank is on for tomorrow morning's shift. Ben confirms that he is and then he tells me to send him a forwarding address as soon as possible so he can visit me sometime. Also, he called Casey and asked her to cover for me tomorrow while he writes his exam.

That's when the tears come. I'm leaving my whole life behind. This is all I know and tomorrow this time it will be over.

The elation and the relief is overshadowed by an inexplicable sadness. I know I'll get to see Ben. Eli would never try to isolate me from the people I love, like Frank had for so many years.

But despite having nothing keeping me here in River Valley, leaving is as painful as if I was being ripped away from something precious. I know it's the familiarity. The attachment you develop to something or someone, no matter how damaging or harmful, feels the same as love sometimes. But I know now that it's not true. So much of who I am is connected to this place. To Frank.

My identity is being challenged, and *that's* what the tears are for. If I could just remember that this person I'd become is not really me, but the person I had to create in order to survive, I'll be okay. I'll be fine as long as I remember that there is a world out there. A world with Eli in it. And this new world is so much better than the one I'd gotten used to, the one I'm *familiar* with.

It may seem strange to someone who's never lived with an abuser, but it's possible to feel sad, despite all the cruelty.

You think, *why did it have to happen that way?* It's not that you want things to get better so you can stay. It's that you wish none of it had ever happened at all. Your sadness is for all the *could-have-beens*.

And leaving your abusive spouse doesn't make you immune to feeling sadness for him, too.

I end my call with Ben, promising to get all the details to him as soon as I have them.

Sitting on the side of the bed, I watch Eli sleep. It's comforting watching him sleep. I resist the urge to run my hands through his hair. I don't want to wake him. A smile touches my lips. The worst is over. Frank found out. I'm still alive. I'm still afraid, but I'm more courageous than scared now.

I text Mrs. Dalton, asking her to text back as soon as she sees Kenny's car pass by after picking Frank up, usually around seven-fifteen.

She texts me back at seven-twenty to let me know Kenny's car had just passed by. She also lets me know that she'll be leaving to the airport soon. Her daughter is close to her due date, so can I please come by now to say goodbye?

"You deserve this," she tells me when I sit down with the cup of tea she'd placed in my hand.

"I know, Mrs. Dalton."

"I know it's not easy and sometimes we don't even know why we stay—God knows I asked myself that question every single day for thirty years—but Axel, dear, you've shown me that true love can make you brave."

"I'm sorry for what happened to you," I say sincerely.

She smiles, her wrinkles moving upward. "Thank you, dear." She takes a sip of her tea and adds, "I want this for you. From that first time I saw the way you looked at him, I knew this was meant for you."

"I'll miss you." It's a choke erupting from my throat. Life in River Valley had not been all bad.

She pulls me in for a hug. Her maternal embrace is what I'll miss the most. So many times I'd sat right here drinking her tea, listening to her tell me to find a way to leave Frank while she nursed a black eye.

As the minutes tick by, already it's beginning to feel like this is a different life. A past life. The goodbyes are making this far too real.

"Live and be happy, Axel. Maybe we'll see each other again, but if we don't, always remember you have an old lady out here in this little town who loves you and always wishes every happiness for you, okay?"

Pepper sniffs at my feet. She's hungry.

I want to go, get my things and get back to Eli, but I also want to prolong this visit. I'm having a hard time letting go. I swallow the lump in my throat, confusion keeping me in limbo.

"Thank you for everything, Mrs. Dalton. I don't know what I would have done without you all these years."

"You'd have survived one way or another because you're a survivor, Axel. Don't ever forget that."

"Sh—should I say goodbye to Frank?" I ask suddenly.

She shakes her head. "No. Frank's only interest in this whole situation is how much he can control it. If you try to leave on amicable terms, he'll only use it to try to keep you here. Don't engage with him, Axel. I learned this too late. People like him will do and say anything to keep you under their control. Don't talk to him. Don't try to explain anything and don't try to make amends before you leave. It won't work. These types of people, you've got to cut them off. No contact, Axel. That's the only way you're going to have your boundaries respected."

We hug for a long time. I congratulate her on her almost-here granddaughter and make her promise to send pictures to Eli's phone.

"I'll send you my new phone number as soon as possible," I tell her at the door. We try to keep the tears away, but who can deny them when we share such a special bond? Two abuse survivors, bound together by our shame, our pain, our secret dreams that one day someone would come and love us back to life.

I leave her eventually. She has a flight to catch and she'll be late, so I extract myself from her and rush around the corner with Pepper close to my side.

She sniffs the air and barks. I shush her. Her bark sounds too loud in the still morning and being back at the house is making the hair at the back of my neck stand up.

I get into the house through the back door, using the key from inside the pocket of the ceramic gnome, since the front door is locked.

The house is as I'd left it. The food is untouched. A pang of guilt bounces into my head that Frank didn't eat last night, but I don't let it stick.

Pepper follows me into the bedroom, sniffing the air. I'd dreamed about this moment so many times before. Every night I imagined a scenario where we'd fight and somehow I'd manage to grab my little box of memories and I'd run. I'd run and never, ever stop running until I knew I was so far away from Frank that he'd never be able to find me.

Today is that day. And it's better than any scenario I could have ever dreamed up. I'm not leaving alone and defeated. I'm leaving with the man from my imagination. For ten years, he had no face, but he kept me safe in my darkest, most terrifying moments of utter despair. And today, I can tell you that he is more than the most beautiful thing I could ever have imagined. He is what daydreams are made of. Daydreams and midnight secrets.

Dropping to my knees, I slide my hand into the bottom cubicle of the closet for my black lace underwear, my unwashed clothes from that first night at the lake with Eli and my memory box.

It's empty.

The cubicle is empty.

And that's when I hear the toilet flush.

CHAPTER 56
Axel

How many times can an already dying warrior get up and fight before his body abandons him, leaving him lost for strength to even breathe?

Tears sting at the back of my eyes. Tears made of hot anger and poisoned defeat.

How much more? I scream inwardly toward the heavens. *What more do you want from me?* I question this *God* I've been so faithful to for all my life, like Job from the bible. I feel like Job. But the screams echoing in my head cannot drown out Frank's sneering voice.

Pepper's overgrown toenails *tick-tick-tick* frantically across the floor as she tries to reach me. Frank slams the door in her face. Her scratches on the door and her whines make my stomach turn. Terror returns as if it had never left. I cling desperately to my newfound courage, but my old self claws at me, ripping me to pieces, shedding the blood of my bravery without mercy, trying to protect me the old way.

"You looking for these?" Frank's voice reaches me from across through the room like the twisted arms of the lowliest of demons, hissing and suckling air as the sound sinks into me through my pores.

I calculate my proximity to the nightstand where he keeps his gun. I'm closer to it; he's across from me, at the door. I'll never win but I'll have a head start if he tries to get to it and I'll have a few extra seconds to fight to my death.

I rise as if boulders sit on my shoulders. Heavy and effortful, preventing a confident straightening of my spine as I turn to face him.

Heart banging against my rib cage, air trapped inside my body, screaming for release. My hands, my knees tremble and my teeth clamp together to keep from chattering.

My beaded bracelet hangs from the index finger of Frank's right hand. He lifts his other hand. "Or this?" My black lace womens' underwear hangs from that index finger.

He slips my bracelet over his wrist and, with a smirk, reaches into his pocket. And when he pulls that hand out and lifts his fist in the air, and then opens that fist, a wail leaves my chest. Small, shredded bits of paper flutter to the carpet. My mother's letters, written to me when I was a baby, fall, crushed and defeated. Like me.

Frank's face is calm, but his eyes mock me with the filthiest disdain I've ever seen. I can't believe I'd loved this man for ten years. Called him my husband. Entrusted my heart to his care and believed every promise he'd made and continued to believe, even when he broke them over and over again. Even when he blamed me for breaking those promises, still I believed in him. In us.

Until Eli. And then I realized there was nothing extraordinary about Frank at all. Without my desperate need to be loved by him, he is nothing but a monster.

Even with a handsome face and strong arms and the charm he exuded when he was out in public, I can finally see the ugliness he spewed at me and the weakness he showed by the way he treated me. I can finally see that it was never me. It was always Frank. *He* was the monster, not me.

But despite all my recent revelations, I'm still right back where I started. Shaking in my boots and at his mercy, hardly able to breathe for fear of what he'd do to me and fury that I can do nothing to stop him.

"He been lettin' you walk around with these panties like little Goldilocks?" His question rolls off on a sneer. Why had I never noticed before how the lift on the right side of his mouth makes him look so nasty?

Or the cruel slits of his eyes.

Or how empty his eyes are when he's angry with me.

I stand my ground, shifting discreetly toward the nightstand so I'm directly in front of it.

He laughs lightly. I hate his laugh. His cruel chuckle makes me so angry I want to tear my hair out of my head. "Let me go, Frank," I breathe.

"You're not going anywhere," he says with a calmness that makes me rage. He slips my mother's bracelet off his wrist and *snap*. The beads fall, skittering all over the floor. My body vibrates with madness, but I refuse to give in to the insanity.

Pepper scratches at the door again. My eyes flick to behind him. "Let Pepper in, Frank," I say softly.

Another enraging laugh. "Why, you need her to *therapy* you through this, Axel, you fucking cheatin' whore?"

"Frank, it's over between us," I whisper, forcing his words to bounce off me. "Please let me go." My vision blurs with unshed tears for my mother's letters and her bracelet.

"Let you go?" Until now, he's kept his physical distance from me and... the nightstand. Now, he takes a step forward. I take a step back, an instinctive move, and I hate it.

"Axel, you fucked another man. Do you really think I'll let you go? Let you get away with it? The only way you'll leave is in a body bag with a bullet through your skull."

"Frank, don't do this," I beg.

He shrugs. "What difference does it make, Ax? You're dead in two to five years, anyway."

I swallow. "What?" I whisper.

With a dead straight face, he says. "I talked to your doctor. The test results came back. You kept that away from me, too. After everything I've done for you. This is how you repay me?"

"You talked to my doctor?"

"He called your cell yesterday. I got him to tell me what the results were."

"He's not allowed to..." I choke. Even though I knew, I *knew*, to hear the words from Frank's mouth like this is unbearable. Deep, earth shattering pains begin low in my chest, rumbling up my throat.

"I'm your fuckin' *husband*, Axel. And I'm no stranger to your doctors, something you've clearly forgotten."

I'm not surprised. Frank can be *that* charming. He must have spun an amazing tale to get the information out of Dr. Shashi.

"What did he say?" I ask, through the clogging in my throat, like a masochist begging for more pain.

"It's definitely back." Words spoken with such carelessness, shattering my life and every dream and hope all over again. Except this time the death sentence is offered to me with an aloofness that cuts deeper than any surgical knife. Destroys me more than chemo ever did.

"I'll fight it," I resolve.

Frank stares at me with those dead eyes I'd never noticed before. "The last time they said if it comes back, you won't make it."

Eli would have gathered me in his arms and told me we'll fight it together. That he'll never leave me. That's he'll be by my side through it all.

"You think that deaf cunt is gonna be able to take care of you the way I did?" Frank asks. He takes another step.

I don't even have the strength to move further back.

"I've been here for ten years, Axel. Ten fucking years of my life I spent taking care of you. I sacrificed everything for you, and this is how you repay me? You fuckin creep around behind my back?"

"Frank, please." I don't know how to keep myself safe. Eli will come looking for me when he wakes up. A new wave of panic seeps into my bones.

"How long have you been doing this? How long, Axel, have you been doing this to me?"

"It was just this time." My soft tone and frightened demeanor are all I have going for me right now. As long as I look small and scared, he won't do much damage. As long as he can keep all the control, I'm safe.

"And all the times before that? With James? Is this why he never forgot your dick? Because you never stopped giving it to him?"

"No, Frank. It was only this one time, I swear." Pepper scratches the door and barks furiously from the other side.

Through the haze of my panic, I realize my two lifelines are currently unavailable. Mrs. Dalton must have already left. Ben has his entrance exam this morning. I pray to the god who would forgive adultery to please let Eli come.

Then I remember the gun and I reverse my prayer. I don't want Eli anywhere near Frank.

"How many, Axel? How many men have you fucked since we've been married?"

"It was just you, Frank. I swear to God. I promise." The begging whisper conceals all the hatred I have for him.

He smirks. Another hollow lift of his lips to make my blood boil with rage. He steps back to the door, turning the lock. Then he moves to the small window to... tighten the handle? ... Make sure the curtains are closed until not a peep of space can be seen?

My rage morphs into fear once more. That's the sum of my life: tossed between fear and rage until you felt crazy.

"I've been checking your phone," he says in a dull voice, holding it up for me to see. "I guess you were smart enough not to use the phone I bought you for your fucking affair."

He makes for the door. "I need to go to get something from Peter. I'll buy us something to eat on my way back."

"I'm not hungry. Frank, please let me go," I beg. "Please, Frank." I'm whimpering. "I have to go to work. Ben is away. I have to open the store." Ben and I already made arrangements with Casey, but Frank doesn't know that. Maybe if I remind him about the normal, day-to-day things we do, he'll act less scary.

"You're not going anywhere." His lazy smirk has been replaced with a hard set jaw and empty eyes.

"W—what?" I'm supposed to be with Eli, on my way to my new life.

"I *said*, Axel, you're not going anywhere. What're you, deaf like that fuckin' cunt up the road?"

Oh. God. Vomit sits heavy in my throat.

"I have to open the store, Frank. Customers will be waiting." *Please.*

"I heard you the first time. *I'm* not fuckin' deaf. But I'll show you who's in charge around here. I don't give a fuck about your work."

"What're you doing?" I ask as he shuts the blinds of the side window.

"You'll stay in here until you're sorry for what you did."

I'm not sorry. I'll never be sorry. I want to spit the words in his face.

The roar of an engine comes closer and stops outside the house. *Eli.* A banging at the door shatters the deathly silence and Pepper goes wild on the other side, yelping loudly in between barks.

I rush forward, but Frank beats me to it.

"Frank," I scream, banging on the door as he closes it shut and locks it from the outside.

I bang, tears streaming down my face.

The *tick-tick-tick* of Pepper's nails on the floor tells me she's moving around fast. I press my ear to the door. She must have seen Eli, because her whimpering has been replaced with excited yelps.

"Where is Axel?" Eli's voice booms through the house, thick and strong. He pauses between words, making sure he's spoken clearly. His voice is so beautiful. Its sound gives me so much courage. So much hope.

"I'm here. I'm here. I'm right fucking here." The screams tear through my throat and end in unbearable chokes and my palms sting with my desperate banging on the door. It's ridiculous and fruitless because he can't fucking *hear* me, but I do it anyway. "Oh, God, help me," I cry into the air.

"*Help*," I scream. "*Someone fucking help me.*"

"He took his stuff. Said he was going to stop at the bookstore."
The lie slithers out of Frank's mouth.

"*No.* Frank, open this door right fucking now." I scream and
bang and scream and bang. And nothing happens.

"You owe me an apology," Frank says. He talks loudly so I can
hear. He's enjoying this. His voice is calm. He has all the power
now, and he's working it for everything.

Eli's voice comes loud and clear and thick. "I regret nothing," he
says.

My heart leaps with joy. "I regret nothing too," I scream. "I regret
nothing." I've lost my mind. I race to the nightstand and yank the
drawer open.

It's empty.

My heart slams into my chest, exploding as every scenario
involving a gun races through my mind. I yank the unmade bedding
of the bed in search of the weapon. In a matter of seconds, I turn
the bedroom upside down, but nothing. The gun is not in this room,
which means—

I scramble back to the door, slamming into it with the weight of
my body. "Eli, get out of there. Frank, please. Please, Frank. Leave
him alone."

Pepper's *tick-tick-tick* drives me crazy as I scream until my voice
is hoarse and my screams have died down to a pathetic, sobbing
mess.

Don't hurt him. Like a madman mumbling incoherencies, I beg
every entity, every demon and devil and every god to please not hurt
Eli. To let him go. *Let him go.*

"Frank," I scream, as my throat renews its ability to channel my
raging fear. "I'll stay, Frank. I'll stay. I'm sorry. Tell Eli to go. I don't
want him. I'll stay with you. Please, Frank."

Pepper barks, the kitchen door slams shut and everything goes quiet. The lock rattles and I scramble backward on my ass until my back hits the base of the bed. Drawing my knees up to my chest, I brace myself for whatever is coming next. It's hard to choose Frank's mood. His calm is as terrifying as his fury.

He's calm. Pepper bolts into the room, crowding me, licking my face before she settles in front of me, her eyes following Frank.

Frank gives me a lopsided grin. "I wasn't going to shoot your fuckin' lover, Axel." He lifts both his hands and then taps his chest and pockets. "See? No gun. And what's up with his voice, anyway? He sounds like he swallowed a fuckin' frog."

No gun? I lunge forward. He only stumbles back slightly, more from my surprise attack that the force of it, I'm sure.

"He does not sound like a fucking frog," I scream while my fists make insignificant dents on his chest.

"Why do you do this to me, Frank? Just let me go. Just let me fucking go. I don't want to be here."

Pepper's whines escalate with my screeching. I claw and bite. Never mind he swats me away like I'm some kind of annoying house fly. I fight, losing my mind. Screaming at the top of my lungs. "Just let me fucking go, Frank." I'm going mad. Like I used to in the early days.

He laughs.

He. Fucking. Laughs.

I'm going insane. I'm *screaming*. Long, psychotic screams. "*Aaahhhhhhh. Hhhhhhaaaaaa.*"

And the more I scream, the louder he laughs.

"*Fraaaannnnkkkk.*" No other words come out of my mouth. Only his name. Like I'm trying to purge myself of him. If I can scream his name enough times, I'll be able to vomit out every part of him I'd ingested these last ten years.

"*Fraaaannnnkkkk.*" Every mocking word. Every slice of his palm across my cheek. Every punch. Kick. Every derogatory word spoken over me.

"*Fraaaannnnkkkk.*" Every vile moment when I thought I loved him. When I thought he loved me. Every promise I believed.

"*Fucking Fraaaannnnkkkk.*" My head is exploding. The tight ball in my chest squeezes until I can't breathe.

I gasp for air while he drops onto the bed with a smile on his face, watching me as if I'm giving him a performance for his pleasure.

That satisfied smirk shatters my brain like a physical injury. He's looking at me like he's got me right where he wants me. He does. Frank is the most calm, reasonable, polite human being right after he's berated me into insanity.

Whirling around, I tug at the door handle. "Let me out of here. Let me the fuck out of here." I'm so out of my depth.

"*Fraaaannnnkkkk.*"

"*Eliiiiiii.*"

"*Fraaaannnnkkkk,* open this fucking door right fucking now." Snot flies out of my nose, landing on my lips. I don't care anymore. I need to get out of here. "Let me fucking go, Frank."

"You're fucking crazy, Axel," he says to my back. Anyone looking inside this moment would think he's the abused one and I'm the crazy abuser.

I spin around. "I'm not crazy," I scream. "I'm not fucking crazy."

"Yes, you are," he says with that same infuriating calm. That evil smirk I've come to hate.

"I'm not," I scream. "You do this to me. You make me like this. I'm so fucking tired."

325

"Just calm the fuck down, Ax. You're fucking insane. Look at the way you're behaving. I'm gonna take a video of you and show everyone how fucking nuts you are."

"You have me locked up here. That's a fucking crime. I need you to let me the fuck out of this house, Frank."

"Why? So you can run back to your little deaf fucktoy? Or are you his fucktoy? You're lucky I'm even letting you stand here right now. Tell me something, Ax, how many times did you fuck him?"

I *have* lost my mind. "Every fucking chance I got," I scream. "I fucked him every fucking chance I got." And since I've lost my mind, I carry on. "What about you, Frank? Those condoms? They weren't Peter's. Or Scotty's or Kenny's. They were yours, weren't they? You cheated too, didn't you? You cheated *first*."

"I'd like to see you prove that," he drawls.

Oh fuck me, that fucking calmness of his. "Well, I used them, Frank," I scream. "I fucking used them when Eli fucked me. He fucked me with your fucking condoms, Frank."

"You're a fuckin' disgrace to this town, Ax. What will people think of you when they find out? You'd better tell them you fucking messed up, and that I had the fuckin' decency to forgive you."

"Forgive me?"

"Yeah, Axel. I'm gonna give you another chance. You've talked a lot of shit like a crazy person the last few minutes, but I'll forgive you."

"I don't want another chance," I breathe. "I want to leave."

"No, you don't. You're not thinking rationally."

I've never felt as in charge of my faculties as I do right now.

"You don't deserve it because you fucking cheated on me, Axel, but I'm going to try to make it work. It's the best I can offer you." *What?*

"So you can't see that deaf cunt anymore. I hope he'll leave soon, anyway."

"I want to be with Eli," I say bravely. I'm beginning to calm down. Conviction is beginning to take root.

"Do you really think he's going to care about an invalid in a couple of months?"

"I won't be an invalid. And yes, he would."

"No, he wouldn't. He has a whole life up there. I checked him out on the internet. Lots of boyfriends, none of them like you."

"He cares about me."

"Everyone cares about cancer patients, Axel. It's nothing to brag about."

"I want to leave, Frank. Open the door and let me go." I'll walk out with the clothes on my back. My beloved beaded bracelet and my mother's letters lie scattered on the floor. Yet another thing Frank has stolen from me. But I'll survive that too.

He gets up and in two strides, he's in my face. "You'll fucking stay here. You move when I say you can move. And if you think you can so easily walk out on me and gallop off into the sunset with that deaf fuckin' cunt, you've got another thing coming. I'll fuckin' shoot him while you watch. Do you understand me, you fuckin' ungrateful cock-whore?"

The roar of a truck down the street reaches my devastated ears. Frank doesn't hear it. The sound of Eli's truck means nothing to him.

"My work, Frank," I plead. "At least let me go to work." Desperation finding new heights to climb.

He grins. "Say, *I'm an ungrateful cock-whore* first. Then I'll let you go to work. I *promise*." He flattens his palm on the wall next to my head.

The sound of Eli's car lessens with every second that passes. I need to get to him. To the bookstore at least where I can get hold of my phone. I can't tell which direction his truck went in.

If he didn't go back home, then I need my phone.

"I—I—I'm an ungrateful cock-whore," I whisper.

"Yes, Axel. You're right. I couldn't have thought of a better way to put it. You're not always dumb. You should believe in yourself sometimes."

"I'll tell Mrs Flannigan I had an emergency and that I'll open the store late," I say.

Frank pushes himself off the wall and straightens to his full height. If I wanted to look at him, I'd have to crane my neck all the way up. I refuse to give him the satisfaction of asserting such a power dynamic.

"You're so stupid, Axel. You're not going anywhere."

"You said you'd let me go to work," I breathe.

"No, I didn't." He smiles and flicks my cheek with his thumb and middle finger. "You'll stay in this fucking room until I decide to let you out."

CHAPTER 57
Eli

It had been my phone vibrating in my hand with an incoming text that had woken me up. I'd searched for Axel first before checking my phone. And then, my whole life fell apart.

I'm sorry to do this in a text, Mr. Saxon, but I struggled to get you on a video call. Your mother has been rushed to the hospital. She's had a heart attack. Please return home as soon as possible.

There's terror in my bones that I'll lose my mother while I'm hours away from her and that she'll be alone.

I need to get Axel and Pepper so we can get on our flight.

But I can't find Axel. Frank said he'd left for the bookstore, but I don't trust that motherfucker as far as I can throw him. He seemed too calm for someone who'd caught his husband cheating. Not that I care about how Frank felt or the fact that I'm leaving River Valley with his husband shortly, but something seemed off.

Maybe there was something of sentimental value at the bookstore that Axel needed.

I race to the bookstore.

It's closed. It's past eight, but that's not unusual because today's opening time is not until nine a.m.. But I hadn't seen Axel on the way here. I drive around the back, the way he showed me the last time when we met here at the bookstore. The ride takes me back to the woods and past my house and then his house again. Nothing.

I turn my car back and head into town once again.

Calls to Mrs. Dalton go to voicemail. She must be in the air right now. And the same with Ben. He must be on his way to his exam.

I can't think of anyone else I can ask. I'd try the police, but they don't take kindly to adulterers over here. I park outside the bookstore and cut the engine. The street is busy with workers and residents, but the bookstore is deserted.

Doom enters the pit of my stomach. I check my texts a dozen times. Nothing from Mrs. Dalton, Ben or Axel.

Casey skips over the sidewalk with keys in her hand. She stops at the bookstore entrance. I blast the horn, causing her to jump. Grabbing my phone, I hurry to her, typing furiously as I walk.

She watches me curiously when I shove my screen in her face. *Where's Axel? I can lip read. Please talk.*

"He's probably at home. They asked me to help out today since it's a school holiday. Ben will be back tomorrow."

Something isn't right.

"We already cleared it with my mother, so she already knows. I won't read the new books, I already promised," Casey says.

That makes no sense but I don't have time to ponder.

Frank lied. Of course he fucking lied.

If he comes in today, tell him to contact me, please? I type.

I check the time. If I don't leave for the airport now, if I go back to Axel's house, I'll miss our flight. I pull over to the side of the road. Fuck. *Fuck!* Panic is not a common emotion for me.

I bang my head on the steering wheel. What the fuck should I do? How do I do this?

I inhale deeply. I can do this. I've made hard decisions before. *Not like this.*

I can do this. I just need to think about this rationally, without all these emotions.

I send Axel a dozen texts. Instructions to contact me as soon as possible. Instructions on how to get to me. Reasons for why I had to leave. And that I'd been to his place looking for him.

I turn the car around again and race to the airport, checking my phone periodically in the hopes of receiving a text from Axel.

Nothing.

I return home, going straight to the hospital.

How did this happen? I sign, rushing over to the doctor.

"Blocked arteries, Eli. Thank God it happened in my office. She's already in surgery. We have the best surgeons working on her."

I sit and wait. My mother has lived a long life, as had my father. I can't ask for more than what I've been given, but fuck, it hurts to know she's in there fighting for her life.

I check my phone. Nothing from Axel.

CHAPTER 58
Axel

Frank lets me out of the bedroom, but he bolts the back door shut and then leaves through the front door, bolting it from outside. There's no way out of this fucking house.

Who could have ever known that when Frank's father began to show signs of mental health issues, I'd be the one to pay for the insane security he built around this house? I hadn't even been born when Frank's father started believing people were after them and decided to turn this house into a fortress.

I have never been locked inside before. This is a new low for Frank. I watch through the window until he's disappeared around the corner and then I go ballistic.

Pepper scurries around, following hot on my heels as I destroy the house looking for tools to break through the door. While I'm at it, I retrieve my key to Eli's house from inside my pillowcase and shove it into my pocket.

With my phone taking a walk in Frank's pocket, calling someone is out of the question. Then, remembering we have a wall phone, I dash back into the living room. I'll call 911 on the wall phone—

Fuck! The whole thing has been ripped from the wall.

And these fucking burglar bars. I can't even climb out through the windows. Huffing from exertion, I turn slowly, examining every inch of the house that I can see. It's impossible that I can't get out of this fucking house. Thousands of house break-ins every day in this fucking country and I can't get *out* of my fucking *own*?

Abandoning the idea of trying to get out, I go on a hunt for the gun. My body shakes at the thought, but what other choice do I have? I search high and low with zero luck. Desperate, I tear the bathroom apart.

The gun is at the bottom of the hamper.

Inhaling sharply, I stare at the object that, in Frank's hands, had brought me so many terror-filled nights.

Now, sitting here on the floor, looking at it, it doesn't seem so scary. I can't help giving this gun a personality. The way it was able to silence me so many times in the past. It's ability to make me so powerless and afraid. How it looks like Frank's best friend in Frank's hand. This enemy of mine that controlled me while Frank controlled *it* now lies innocently amongst its master's dirty laundry.

With shaking hands, I reach into the hamper and pick it up.

Cool to the touch and heavier than I'd imagined for something so small.

I don't even know how to check if it's loaded; where I shouldn't be touching to make sure it doesn't go off.

I stand, holding the gun away from my body like it's a live snake. I don't know where to keep it. When Frank returns, who knows what mood he'll be in? I need the gun to disappear or remain with me.

The time on the T.V. says two hours have passed. I take a look around the house. It looks like there's been a robbery. Like the place was ransacked. A thought begins in my head to clean up. Because Frank hates clutter. What he'll do when he gets back and sees the place like this. I steel myself against the thought. I don't plan on being here when he gets back.

And as the thought forms, the kitchen door handle rattles. Pepper circles me, weaving between my legs and whining softly.

I shove the gun into my pocket and step out of the bathroom.

Frank smiles from across the kitchen with a bag of Chinese food in his hand. "You done with your *episode?*" he asks. Someone might think he was referring to a tantrum I might have thrown over not getting to watch my favorite show.

I don't answer him.

He inspects the place with a roll of his eyes. "Guess not. You just gave yourself extra work, Ax. You're so dumb. You'll be cleaning all fuckin' night."

No. I won't.

I'm ashamed to say that in a country whose soil cries for the blood spilled by gun violence, Frank's taunts feel different now that I have a gun in my pocket. I hold on to it by the tips of my fingers, assured and afraid in equal measures, but there is a sense of power as my finger grazes that cold metal.

"Where'd you go?" I ask.

"Just down to work. I put in a last minute leave day but Peter owed me some money. I also wanted to go thank him for being a good friend and telling me about you and that deaf cunt."

Peter. That fucking creep.

"I got us some Chinese on the way back. You should thank me. Now where the fuck am I going to find my lighter?" Frank gives the place another disapproving once-over as he sticks a cigarette between his lips.

"On the microwave," I reply quickly. Because the few steps it will take him to get it will get him a few steps away from the door. And if he doesn't remember, he will leave the door unlocked.

Fuck. Frank locks the door and gets his lighter. But my eyes have a hard time staying off the keys he's left dangling from the keyhole. The other two locks above the main one are unlocked.

334

He's had a drink. Not enough to be drunk, but enough for him to mellow out just a little. I don't know how long it will last, but I've got to think quickly. My finger strokes the gun. Frank lights his cigarette and goes into the bathroom and just like in the horror movies, when I reach for the knob, it's stuck and Frank comes flying back out of the bathroom.

On instinct and with the will to just fucking not die, I pull the gun out of my pocket and, with my hands clutching the weapon clumsily, I lift and aim directly at Frank.

He freezes and the power oozing out of the weapon and into my very fucking *bones* gives me the courage to keep my hands raised. The weight of the gun is almost unbearable, but the look on Frank's face is priceless.

"Axel, the gun is loaded. You don't know how to handle it. Put it down."

His voice is calm, kind. *Rational.* Like a mother talking her beloved child off the ledge. I'm the crazy one with a gun pointed at another human being and one wrong move could end up with *both* of us dead. Safety catch? I've heard that phrase before. Not a fucking clue what it is. Fuck, I should have paid more attention to the intricacies of this weapon that had plagued my life for so long.

But, I reason, as long as it is in my hands and not Frank's, my chances of not dying are better.

"Put it down. Axel. Let's talk about this. So we had a little problem. You got a little carried away with the newcomer. I get that. It could have happened to anyone, but we're gonna make it through. I *promise*, Axel."

Tears fall from my eyes and I scream with an instant rage. Not for what Frank is telling me, but because of these fucking tears. He doesn't deserve my tears.

"I already said I'll give you another chance, Ax. You want to hear the words?" His hands are still up, palms facing me, and his eyes soft and gentle. "Okay. Fine. I forgive you. I forgive you for cheating on me. You wanna know why, Ax? It's because I can't imagine my life without you. I'll forgive anything to make sure we're together. You're the only ray of sunshine in my life, Ax. You understand me like no one else. You know about my rotten childhood, about my crazy father. You know everything, Ax, and you still accept me."

"Lies," I hiss.

"It's the past that fucked me up, Ax, but you understand me. You're the only one who gets me. No one understands me like you, Ax. I'll die without you. If you leave me, I'll kill myself. I swear, Ax, I need you that much."

"Stop calling me *Ax*," I shout. I don't know what else to say to make him stop talking.

"Okay. Axel. I'll call you Axel, okay? Axel, give us another chance. We can make it. I'll go to therapy for all that childhood shit you were always telling me about. I'll be better, Axel. Don't you see how I'm already trying? I'm not ever going to talk about you and that deaf— about Eli Saxon. You'll never have to worry about me bringing it up."

Liar. The roar lies heavy on my chest. He could never let me forget my fling with James, and that happened long before he ever knew me.

"I love you, Axel."

"This is not *love*," I scream.

Mrs. Dalton's words smash into my mind. *Don't engage. Set your boundary and leave. The only solution is to leave. Even if it's with just the clothes on your back.* Leave *or it will never end.*

Don't engage. Set your boundary.

"I want to be with Eli," I say with a pathetic tremble in my voice. I have to say at least this.

"You'll gradually get over the novelty," he says calmly, but I have too much experience with this. The flash of fury in his eyes doesn't escape my seasoned observation.

"You're dying of cancer, Axel. No one wants that responsibility. But me? I'll take care of you."

"Eli will be with me while I die," I choke out.

"He won't. I promise you that, Axel."

I shout again, my hands shaking from being raised up. His voice is so soft and sincere, so filled with compassion. If you didn't know Frank. But I know. Another mangled shout slips through my teeth.

"He *will*."

"Okay, then if he cared so much about you, where is he, Axel? Why isn't he here? He just needed a holiday fuck. Someone to keep him warm while he did god-knows-what down there by the lake. It's not your fault, baby. You're so innocent. You couldn't have known."

"He came looking for me."

"Well, he left. I went down there with some of my buddies. There was no one there. No truck, nothing. Someone saw him take the highway and you know when someone takes the highway from here that means only one thing, Axel, right?"

The airport.

I refuse to buy into these lies. And even if they're true, I still can't stay here.

"I'm leaving, Frank. Not just for Eli. For me, too. For me, *especially*."

My hands drop. I straighten them again. "Go into the living room, Frank."

I need to get this fucking door unlocked.

"You're making a mistake, Axel." But he takes a step back.

"I don't care."

"You don't have to do this."

I hold the gun in one hand and reach behind me with the other. I don't know if Frank's obedience is because he's afraid I have the balls to actually shoot him or if I might accidentally shoot him because I'm so unhinged.

I manage to get the door open with the keys in my hand.

Pepper bolts outside, barking at me like crazy.

By some miracle, I get out of the house, shoving the door shut and locking it from the outside. It won't make a difference because he has the keys to the back door, but at least he won't be able to come straight through the front.

CHAPTER 59
Axel

Maybe some people leave their husbands with a well-packed bag, a goodbye to their neighbors and their dignity intact.

I leave with tears streaming down my face, a loaded gun dangling from my hand and fear chasing me down me like a ghoulish, living nightmare.

Mrs. Dalton's house is quiet and the curtains are drawn shut.

I don't have the stamina to run all the way to the bookstore. Frank will catch me and I can't risk hiding in the woods, so I run toward Eli's place.

Pepper is already ahead of me, sprinting down the bend. She stops now and then to urge me forward, but I'm slowing myself down by constantly looking back for Frank.

Pepper barks.

I practically slide down the path with the momentum of my speed, flying to the backdoor where my key will fit.

Pepper flies into the house. I follow her in and lock the door.

Eli's security since his upgrades to this place is impeccable, but after laying the gun down carefully on Eli's counter, I still race through the house, making sure every window is shut and every curtain is drawn closed.

Then, I search for any form of technology to connect with the outside world. Eli's dresser, the kitchen cupboards, nightstand drawers produce nothing.

The lights start to flicker as I race through each room. The simultaneous ringing of the doorbell turns my legs to lead.

I drop to the floor right there in the hallway. Pepper sinks between my legs with her paws on my ankle.

The ringing won't stop. I squeeze my eyes shut and clamp my hands over my ears.

Frank's voice booms through the concrete walls and lands in the pit of my stomach. Nausea rises in my chest and my body goose bumps from the back of my thighs to my scalp.

Go away, I scream internally. *Just get the fuck away from me.*

Everything Mrs. Dalton and Ben had said was true. Frank is a narcissist. He never takes responsibility for anything, always blames me for everything, even when it's not my fault. He's controlling and cruel.

Frank bangs on the door and his finger remains on the doorbell. The lights flicker like a horror movie and I play the part of a paralyzed victim to the letter.

The gun.

If he breaks through the door, he'd be closer to the gun than me. With tears streaming down my face, shameful and humiliating, I slide on my ass, inch my inch, down the hallway toward the kitchen. My faithful, unjudging dog follows me, low and quiet.

I can't believe this is my life.

The banging stops as I reach for the gun. The absence of the noise is as terrifying as the banging. What if he found another way in?

Gripping the gun in my hand, I crawl under the island, doing my best to breathe slow and deep. Pepper never leaves me. Her body remains pressed to mine. The weight of her body against mine calms me. The silky feel of her fur gives me some comfort.

I don't know how long I sit there, waiting for the next bang or the next flicker of the light.

There's nothing for a long time. The time on the microwave says ten minutes have passed. But I still sit there, convinced he's found another way into the house and is creeping through it, looking for me.

Twenty minutes. Pepper licks my hand. She must be hungry.

Thirty minutes.

My legs are numb. My tears have dried up.

Pepper and I creep out from underneath the counter. Pepper looks between me and the cupboard that contains the treats Eli buys for her.

Sniffing my tears back, I keep my footfalls as soft as possible as I make my way to the cupboard. Pepper walks close to my side, pressing her body to the side of my leg.

I give her a rub behind her ear, and she settles on the floor with her treat.

What do I do? I need to get to the bookstore. I need a fucking phone.

It takes me ten minutes to get myself to the window. Frank is nowhere in sight. He'll check the bookstore next. It's been forty minutes; he must have gone there and seen that I wasn't there. I let myself out of the house with Pepper, locking it and stuffing the key into my pocket. The gun lies in my pocket, heavy. I feel like a criminal.

We race through the woods, but I have to stop now and then to catch my breath. When we come out by the back of the bookstore, I almost pass out. I'm so fucking tired, but there's no time to rest. Easing myself and Pepper in through the back door, I rush to the steel cabinet, opening it as quietly as the old cupboard would allow.

Twenty-seven missed calls and eighteen text messages. I hit dial so fast my thumb vibrates.

FUCK. Voicemail.

I scroll through the texts, reading as fast as possible.

He woke up to me gone. His mother's doctor had contacted him about his mother's—oh my god—*heart attack.*

His mother had a heart attack.

He'd looked for me everywhere.

He'll come back for me if I need him to.

His home address, his work address, the details of the hospital where his mother is having surgery.

And then... thirty minutes ago:

My mother is still in surgery, but they think she'll be okay.

I'm sending you new flight details. It's the earliest I could get. I just need to know you're okay and that you and Pepper can get to the airport.

I'm so worried about you, Axel.

Five minutes ago: *Please be safe, Axel.*

I shove my fist into my mouth to keep from crying out loud. I don't deserve this. I don't deserve *him.* I'll give him nothing but pain and sorrow. I'll be just a burden to him.

With fingers shaking, I open my emails.

Two tickets for Louisville for eight a.m. tomorrow morning.

My body wracked with new tears, I type.

I'm okay.

I'm so relieved your mom is going to be okay.

I'm coming to you, don't come back.

I have to believe him when he says he cares about me. God knows he's all and everything I ever wanted.

Pepper scratches at the door, but before I could stop her, the door swings open.

"Axel." Casey's eyes round and she pushes the door shut.

"Eli came in here this morning. He told me to tell you to contact him as soon as possible if you come in and then your husband came in here about twenty minutes ago, asking where you are. What the fuck is going on?"

"Are there customers out there?" I ask.

"No."

"Okay, Casey, I want you to listen to me carefully. I have a gun in my pocket. It's loaded."

She jumps back. "Axel, what the fuck—"

I hold up my hands, palms out. "It's not mine. It's Frank's." I shake my head. "It's not even Frank's."

She stares at me like I've lost my mind. I think I have. "He said he was going to file a missing person's report."

"Fuck. Casey, I'm sorry to do this to you, but I need to get rid of this gun. I was going to throw it in the woods, but I got scared that Frank would find me before I got here."

"Oh my God, Axel. We need to call Ben. He'll know what to do." Casey digs into her pocket for her phone.

"No, he's in his exam; he doesn't know what happened. I didn't want to stress him out."

"He hasn't yet started," Casey says. She puts the phone on loudspeaker. "Ben? I'm sorry, I know you're getting ready to write—"

"Casey? Everything okay? I start in five minutes. I asked to make an emergency call."

"Don't freak out. Axel's with me. And Pepper. Something happened."

"Don't tell me not to freak out when you start like that. What the hell happened? Axel?"

I take the phone from Casey. "Ben, Frank found out. He found out last night. I'm sorry I didn't tell you. I didn't want to stress you out."

"Oh my fuck."

"That's not the worst part. Eli's mom had a heart attack, so he had to leave. I was gonna leave with him, but Frank locked me in the house. I managed to get away, but I have his gun."

"Gun? What fucking gun, Ax?"

I can't believe I lived with that gun for nearly ten years and I never told anyone. Not even Ben.

"He has a gun, Ben. But I took it so I could get out. But now I don't know what to do with it and I need to get onto a flight at eight a.m. tomorrow."

"Okay. Don't panic. Take Pepper and the gun and go to my house. Wait for me there."

"Okay."

"Dude, it's like a movie," Casey says. "You better go out the back. Your husband said he'll come back to check. He sounded so worried."

I scoff. Worried? That was just so people don't guess what a monster he really is.

CHAPTER 60
Axel

I have a suit," Ben says.

I survived the night. Ben came and got rid of the gun. Once he knows I'm on the plane, he'll call the sheriff and let them know he found a gun somewhere in the woods.

Frank came banging on Ben's door around ten p.m. But Ben sent him away with a stern warning that he'd better find me, and in one piece. Frank bought the whole thing.

Now, at four a.m. I'm getting ready to go to the airport. Pepper, after eating almost half of Ben's chicken without permission, sits at the corner of the room feeling guilty and probably hoping she can still come with me.

"He gave you all of his addresses, right? What if he's at work? You don't want to show up all casual. You want to look professional, right?" Ben says, while he lays out his only suit. A brown coat and matching pants with a blue shirt and matching tie. It's the suit he wore to prom. It doesn't fit him anymore, but it'll fit me.

"You're right. I should make an effort," I reply.

Ben comes to sit on the bed next to me. "Don't ever come back here, no matter how much that asshole begs. Do you hear me?"

"I hear you."

"No matter how many promises he makes, you make sure you stay there with Eli. *He's* the one you were meant for."

"I won't come back. But you? You'll come see me, right?"

He smiles and squeezes my shoulder lightly. "Definitely."

"You're my very best friend, Ben. I'm so grateful to have you."

"I'm always here, Ax. I'm just so happy you get to have your happily ever after."

Ever after? I have to tell him about my relapse.

"The cancer came back, Ben," I say.

He swears softly. "Fuck, Ax. I'm so sorry."

We take the mandatory minute to let it sink in. It's not Ben's first time, but I know it's just as hard as if it was.

"Does Eli know?"

I don't have to answer him and like the best friend he is, he says, "He's going to love you through it all, Ax. I just know he is."

"He will, right?"

"He will."

He leaves me to get dressed and then fusses over an oil stain near my coat button all the way to the airport.

Ben cries the most, all the while telling me to quit my tears.

I can't. They won't stop.

My phone buzzes inside my coat pocket. Eli. He'll be at his office from ten a.m. to attend a meeting his mother had planned before she was hospitalized. If my flight is not delayed, I can go straight to his office and if my flight is delayed, I can go to his home and he'll meet me there.

"I'll send you all the details once I'm there," I promise Ben over and over. Pepper gets a thousand hugs, which she returns enthusiastically, and soon we're in the air.

Pepper sits quietly at my feet.

I don't know how to feel. So many things run through my mind. It doesn't seem real that this is happening. I'm finally free from Frank. But this doesn't feel like the victory I thought it would. Deep guilt seeps through my bones, and all I want to do is cry. I hadn't even felt this kind of guilt when I was cheating on Frank.

Doubt is a living thing inside my head. If I'd tried harder, if I'd been more insistent that Frank go for therapy. Something. Anything.

But then...

I think about Eli. And I know that I've made the right decision. I made it while trembling in my boots, with so much fear and shame and uncertainty, but I did it.

Desperate to keep my mind from frazzling any further, I take out a notebook and a pen from my coat pocket. And then I write down everything I want to tell Eli, but may not have the courage to form the words when I see him.

Eli wanted to pick me and Pepper up at the airport, but I insisted that I can take an Uber. I want to do at least this for myself. I want to go to Eli on my own. Unaided.

I'm not sure if dogs are allowed in Eli's office building, so I ask at the front desk after the Uber drops us off.

Wiping my hands down my coat, I try to get rid of some creases that may have been caused by my seated position during the flight.

"You're here to see Mr. Saxon?" the woman at the front desk asks, eying Pepper.

"Uh, yes, please?" She doesn't answer about Pepper.

"Do you have an appointment?" she asks. I think she disapproves of me if the several once-overs are anything to go by.

"Uh, he's expecting me," I reply, hoping that qualifies as an appointment.

The woman gives me another once over, then leaves her desk. Pepper and I watch her from the front as she talks to the security guard softly. I don't know what she's saying, but I'm a little worried. I don't think they're going to let me or Pepper in.

I consider calling Eli, but what if he's in his meeting?

The security guard leaves through the elevator. I sit on a chair in the fancy waiting area nearby while the woman returns to her desk and talks on the phone. She casts several looks in my direction.

Suddenly, everything in her face changes. The security guard comes rushing out of the elevator and talks to the woman at the desk.

I'm sweating blood. A thousand thoughts race through my head. Did they find out about Frank? Maybe Frank is here. He found his way to Louisville, and he's going to kill me.

The elevator doors click open again and—

I'm sitting down, but I still feel like I've been knocked off my feet.

Eli exits the elevator. To his left, the woman at the desk apologizes in sign. She repeats the sign several times, her eyes darting to me every now and then. Eli gives her a hard look and searches the expanse of the lobby. He spots me about the same time Pepper spots him.

I rise from my seat and Pepper bolts across the lobby, barking and wagging her tail. People at the front desk, security guards and employees stop to stare as Eli bends to grab Pepper. I'm a little embarrassed that she's so shameless, but also a little jealous. I wish I could have rushed into Eli's arms like that.

A small distance separates us. Eli lifts his eyes to mine. A lump forms in my throat. I can't move. He's so beautiful.

As he walks toward me, I take all of him in.

The sweatpants and sweatshirts I'd become accustomed to seeing him in have been replaced with black pants that fit him like a glove. A white shirt tugs at his biceps and stretches across his chest as it competes with the muscles there.

My mouth dries and my heartbeat flies up to the heavens.

His eyes are worried as he walks toward me, Pepper trotting happily next to him.

I wipe my hands on the sides of my coat, acutely aware that we have an audience. And it dawns on me that these are *Eli's employees*. He's their *boss*.

Feelings of shame and doubt beat down heavily in my heart. I try hard to ignore them, but it's almost impossible. It's easy to forget everything when you live in a town like River Valley and everyone is the same as you.

But this? This world is the one people like me get to watch on T.V. I don't belong in this world. Frank said that Eli had a lot of boyfriends, and none of them were like me. Inadequacy finds its way into my blood.

Eli reaches me and, right there in front of all the people who work for him, he gathers me in his arms.

My shoulders shake with traitorous tears. I didn't want to cry. I wanted to be strong, like him. Not this spineless nobody.

He pulls back to inspect my face. *I'm okay*, I sign.

He takes my hand in his and walks us across the lobby. My face burns with the stares, but Eli doesn't seem to notice.

Inside the elevator, Pepper sits quietly next to Eli. I look up at him, devouring his face, hardly able to believe I'm actually here.

He pulls me to him, enveloping me in his arms. I go so willingly. Lifting my face to his, I part my lips for his mouth, sighing into his kiss when his lips meet mine. Soft and beautiful, I sink into him, moving my lips against his. Eli deepens the kiss. His scent, his touch, all of him permeate my senses, filling me, fluttering over me like a gentle wind. And I hold on to it. God, do I hold on.

The *ding* of the elevator pulls us out of this moment. Eli takes my hand and walks us across another lobby, smaller than the one downstairs.

A framed photo of an older man is flanked by a frame of a woman on the right and Eli on the left. His parents? There is a resemblance to the older man.

A well-dressed woman sits at a desk off to my left. She stands, signing to Eli quickly. I catch only one word, *Tea*.

Eli gives her a nod and pulls me in through a set of large mahogany doors.

Pepper's toenails *tick-tick-tick* across the floor. As she sniffs out the place with her tail swishing from side to side, I let go of Eli's hand and turn a slow one-eighty.

I feel like Beauty, who's just been shown the library. The side I'm looking at has a bookshelf that goes from floor to ceiling and, fuck me to book heaven, a whole goddam ladder.

On the other side is a smaller bookshelf, but fuck, still bigger than any bookshelf I've ever seen.

It's only when my eyes return to Eli that I notice the massive oak desk in front of the window. A black leather couch is adjacent to the desk. My eyes immediately switch to the floor to ceiling bookshelf, and I make to step in that direction when I realize where I am and why I'm here.

I smooth out my coat and turn back to Eli. This place is Eli's world. So calm, so organized. Not anything like the world I come from.

He's smiling at me and then, after giving Pepper a treat, he takes my hand and walks over to the big bookshelf.

"This was my father's office," he signs. *"He loved to read."* He pulls out a book from the middle shelf—Edgar Allan Poe's *Tamelane and Other Poems.* He presses it into my hand.

"A first edition?" I ask, shocked and suddenly feeling like I've contaminated the book simply by touching it.

Eli's smile broadens. He nods.

Delicately, I open it, eating the words up from the page. But this is a very expensive book, so I give it back to him.

Eli sets the book on the desk behind him and pulls me back into his arms. I stay there for a long time. It's quiet but for the gentle whirr of the air conditioning and the occasional grunt from Pepper as she finishes her treat.

"How is your mother?" I ask when he lets me go an inch.

Recovering well. It was a scare, he types on his phone.

"I'll do my best to speak to you with my voice," he says with his voice. "I hope I'm not too loud."

I'm amazed at the sound of his voice. I've heard it only a few times before and then, I was not in a position to appreciate it. Now, the deepness of his voice and the hint of a lisp wraps me in a kind of safety I've never felt before.

I wrap my arms around his waist and smile up at him. "It's beautiful. Your voice. It's so beautiful, Eli. And I'll get better at signing."

He kisses my smile. A light brush of his lips over mine. ***We'll meet my mother soon. She's been looking forward to meeting you,*** he types.

"She knows about me?" He nods.

I drop my eyes. I couldn't give Eli a decent start to our relationship. I should have left Frank before starting anything with Eli. Now, he'll be forced to explain to his own mother that the person he's with is married.

I remember the letter in my pocket and push gently against Eli. He lets me go but keeps his hands loosely around my waist.

I dig into my pocket and hand the paper over to him. Smoothing out the creases as much as possible before letting him take it.

He looks at me curiously. "I wanted you to know everything," I explain.

He opens the letter. I wipe my hands over the pockets of my coat.

CHAPTER 61
Eli

I've been told my whole life how *grounded* I am. So mature and diplomatic. Never one to panic. It's what has made me so successful in everything I do. I'm watchful and silent in more ways than the obvious one, and that's what keeps people in their place.

Yet, that person was nowhere to be found these last forty-eight hours. For the first time in my life, I felt like the most unstable human being on the planet. The hours at the hospital during my mother's surgery, combined with not knowing where Axel was... I was losing my mind in chunks.

The light flickers. I walk to the door and open it for my assistant. Theresa gives me a small dip of her head, but her eyes shine with happiness when she can't help sneaking a glance at Axel.

Axel is so nervous, it makes my heart swell.

She signs, "Hearing?" referring to Axel.

I nod.

She speaks to Axel, angling her face so I can still lip read.

"Hello, I'm Theresa, Eli's assistant. It's nice to meet you," she says, extending her hand.

Axel takes her hand and tells Theresa it's nice to meet her too.

She leaves with a smile, and I set the letter down and get to making Axel some tea. He scoots over to me to help.

I gently shoo him away, setting him down on the couch, and then hand him a cup of tea. I make it the way Mrs. Dalton makes it for us—extra sugar.

He takes the tea and watches me nervously as I lean my ass against the desk and open his letter.

Dear Eli,

Hello. My name is Axel St. James. That's the name I was born with.

I reach behind me for a pen and strike out his name. Then, above it, I write *Axel St. James Saxon*. Because I will make him mine, but not at the cost of who he is.

The letter goes on.

My father left when me and my mom when I was a child. My mother tried to take care of me, but she struggled and became addicted to painkillers around the time I was first diagnosed with Acute Lymphoblastic Leukemia. She died of an accidental overdose when I was eighteen. She was a good mother.

I lift my eyes from the letter to gaze at the man I want to spend my life with. He's staring into his tea. Compassion for him mixes with my hurt for him.

Just after she died, I went to a New Year's church event. Frank asked me to lie down next to him. I fell asleep. He touched me inappropriately. I let him.

My fingers tighten around the paper. My world has been so small, so sheltered. I never would have imagined that people suffer like this. Frank needs to be in prison.

He asked me to marry him after two weeks. He was kind and loving. I was so desperate for someone to love me that I never saw the warning signs. If it were not for you, Eli, who showed me what love and kindness really was, I might still never have seen Frank for who he truly is.

I endured ten years of abuse. I made so many excuses in the past because I wanted to believe that Frank loved me like he said he did in the beginning. But now I know he never loved me. I think he is a narcissist, but I don't think I'm qualified to throw around such big words. All I know is that he was cruel in ways I couldn't even comprehend. His kindness after his cruelty confused me, and I now know the price I paid for those moments of kindness.

He blamed me for everything that went wrong. I was never good enough, no matter how hard I tried. He kept me away from my friends and people I cared about, and I didn't mind at first because it meant he wanted me all to himself and that's all I ever wanted too, to be wanted. It's only when I met you, Eli, that I realized that being wanted didn't have to come with so many sacrifices.

I pick my head up again to look at Axel. He's still looking into his cup of tea, both his hands wrapped around the cup. I want to gather him in my arms and never let anything from this awful world touch him ever again.

Frank threatened me with his gun repeatedly over the years. I was beaten with it several times. I lived ten years in fear for my physical safety.

Frank broke my spirit. My mother always called me a diamond. Frank took a diamond and turned it into a stone, and I let him. Until you, Eli.

You gave me the courage to see my life for what it was and what it could be.

I like to wear womens' underwear. You know that already. I don't know why except that it feels good. I'll try to understand that part of me more. I also don't have a driver's license or a high school diploma, as you know. Frank told me I didn't need those things because I had him.

Eli, I have to tell you something else. And after I've told you, I'll respect any decision you make.

I've been in remission for a long time and I was sure I'll remain that way. I felt strong and healthy. Recently, I'd been getting headaches and my skin began to bruise easily. My joints began to ache, and I wasn't feeling well.

I wish there was an easier way to tell you this, Eli. There isn't. But I know that I never want to keep anything from you.

I've relapsed. My cancer came back. I must start treatment immediately. I may not make it this time. I don't know how long, but I'm not expected to live past my mid-thirties.

I am now twenty-eight.

My hands shake. There's not much more of the letter left. Only a thousand apologies for being sick. A thousand more reassurances that he'll understand if I want to end our relationship.

I don't read half of his martyr-style ending. I get to the end, where the only thing that matters has been penned.

I don't have forever, Eli. I have only now. And what little of me is left belongs to you. Even when I'm nothing but a distant memory, I'll belong to you. You are the only person in this whole world who has loved me the way I'd wished to be loved. Even when I can no longer share in your breath, I'll love you. I'll love you now, in this moment, enough for a hundred lifetimes.

I'm sorry.

The lump in my throat causes enough pain to travel to my temples.

Axel trembles on the couch, his eyes still cast downward. It's only when his tea ripples that I realize he's crying. His tears fall into his tea, disturbing the calmness of the deep brown liquid.

I gently remove the tea from his hands and set it on the coffee table. He folds his hands on his lap. I close my hands over them, stilling them. Finally, he looks at me. "I'll fight, Eli," he says, his tears falling from his eyes and onto our joined hands. "I'll fight so hard, you'll see. I'll try hard to live. I'll be brave and I'll fight like a warrior right till the end, I promise."

His anguish that I would leave him is unbearable. My tears join his, mixing and creating one tiny river between our clasped fingers. "*We'll* fight," I correct him with my voice. His eyes lift to mine.

"I—I can stay?" he asks. His question so sincere, his relief so heart breaking it makes me want to kill Frank over and over again. One death for a man like Frank is not enough.

I hand him his letter. He gives me a quizzical look and then inspects his letter. When his fingers slide over my alteration, he doesn't throw his arms around me with joy like I'd hoped. Instead, he drops his head to my lap. His shoulders shake violently. I can do nothing but soothe him with my hands along his back. Bending, I kiss the top of his head while he cries and cries.

His cancer is only an announcement of what we all must face one day. Axel gets an announcement where the rest of us have to guess.

Nothing, not even this, can destroy what we have. Our truth was borne from lies and deceit. And sometimes, that's just how it must be.

I have no regrets.

CHAPTER 62
Axel

He does nothing more than hold me. I never knew that just the presence of a person could have such a devastating impact on the walls that had seemed to have built themselves around me over the years.

On the outside, my body shakes with this terrible acceptance that I'm safe. Inside, my soul is calm and at peace and I feel this innermost part of me trying to reach out to my confused and still-scared nervous system. Pepper's head perks up, but she goes back to her treat when she finds that I'm okay.

A war finally declared over. Enemies of my soul—pain, sadness, fear—retreating. And my ally next to me, an unshakeable rock. I'm free. I'm finally free to think for myself. The war is over and now it's time to sort through the debris. To pick up the broken pieces and begin to build again. To separate the truth from the lies, the 'me' that I *am* from the 'me' I had to become to survive a life with Frank.

I'd fought a war I hadn't even known I'd been in. I fought my enemy while I fed him every ounce of myself, and he ate and became so strong with my kindness, my compassion, my endless supply of second chances, he almost destroyed me with everything good about me.

But I'm still here. Almost broken, but not quite. Almost driven mad, but not quite. Almost dead, but not quite.

When I finally lift my head from Eli's lap, the tenderness I find in his eyes becomes the first piece of my new life that I pick up. The first remnant of my war for true, authentic love. I'll start rebuilding with this tenderness that I'd never known existed before Eli.

He bends, pressing his lips to mine. My face is wet with tears, but I feel better for them. My tears finally have a place to rest—right here between Eli's palms. He honors them, where Frank not only caused them but shamed me for them, too.

It may seem like I'd broken my marriage vows to be with him. That I'd betrayed my husband to be with Eli. And that's true. But it's also true that I'd broken a dangerous cycle of abuse and this was the only way to do it.

And it's also true that Frank had broken our vows first when he laid his hands on me. It's also true that Frank had betrayed me first when he'd destroyed my spirit little by little every day. He may have even cheated on me during our marriage, but I'll never know for sure, and anyway, who am I to judge?

Eli signs. *"Let me take you home."*

Home? My heart thumps unexpectedly. Joy mixed with dread. Pushing through the confusing feelings and the opposing ideas inside my head of happiness and fear, I nod.

Eli wipes my tears with the pad of his thumb, and then signs, *"You look very handsome today."* He trails his fingers over the material at my shoulder and then down the outside of my arm.

"It's Ben's prom suit," I blurt.

Eli's smile could outshine the sun. *"Beautiful on you."*

I thank him in sign even though I feel stupid, not beautiful.

He signs, but I don't catch it. I frown and shake my head to let him know.

He writes at the back of my letter. *"Can we go home right away?"*

With a smile that feels like the first real one since my mother died, I nod.

Eli's assistant signs goodbye to me and then speaks animatedly with Eli in sign. I'm able to catch some words; it looks like they're rearranging his diary.

We enter the elevator with Pepper sitting quietly next to Eli. Eli holds me close to him the whole way down. His proximity is deliberate, not casual. It's in the way his grip around my waist is so firm, telling me that he's all the way present here, with me. Aware of my current state of being. Letting me know that he's okay here with me. That I'm okay here with him.

A car is waiting for us next to the elevator as we exit and step into an underground parking area.

The driver greets me with a smile, an even bigger one for Eli and an affectionate rub for Pepper. It's fascinating to watch how people just... love Eli. Even back home in River Valley, everybody loved him.

Eli urges me into the back seat and he follows, sliding in close to me. Eli's driver opens the door on my side to let Pepper in. She settles in, pouting over me not letting her sit next to Eli. *I want to sit next to him*, I tell her with my eyes. She barks once to tell me I'm an asshole. I ignore her after that.

A darkened screen separates us from Eli's driver, so I edge closer to him, pressing my outer thigh to his and tightening my fingers through his.

Leaning over, he brushes his lips against mine. So soft, but so possessive at the same time. And again, I'm taken by surprise at how this kind of possessiveness doesn't feel the same as with Frank. With Eli, I'm his, but I'm still me. With Frank, there'd been no space for *me*.

We kiss like that, slow and sweet, but I also know the passion simmering just beneath the surface wouldn't be contained for much longer.

I pull back reluctantly when Eli's phone buzzes. He sends me an apologetic look and I motion for him to please take his video call. He is, after all, everybody's boss and I'm the hurricane that just ripped through his day.

While Eli tends to his call, I turn to the window to get my first real glimpse of... *home?*

I'm still embarrassed to think about it like that, coming out here acting like everything belongs to me. These busy streets with people rushing by, trying to get to wherever it is they're headed; these cars, purchased with money people have around here because they're smart, educated... *employed;* teenagers on a school break, their heads buried in their phones, their earphones cutting them off from the rest of the world, knowing they have their whole lives ahead of them.

They're all so different from me. Their lives, so different from mine.

Eli pulls me out of my downward trajectory toward self-deprecation with a hand on my forearm. I turn back to him with a smile. It's okay. I'm starting over. I'll be okay. All is not lost.

The driver slows down in front of a building that looks like a hotel and then eases out of traffic and down a security controlled ramp. I can't remember the last time I've even seen a building like this. High rise, elegant and very-expensive looking.

The driver pulls into one of the parking spaces and within a minute, we're flying up in an elevator. When the *ding* sound of the elevator indicates we've arrived at our destination, Eli takes my hand and steps into an apartment so large my eyes bug out.

We're in a vast open space, separated into various parts by the furniture. To the left, glass walls with no curtains and a leather sectional off to the side. A coffee table with various books stacked neatly on the carriage underneath. A fireplace with a plush carpet placed in front.

On the right is an open concept kitchen—very state-of-the-art type, separated from the living area by a two-sided book case.

Eli pulls my gaze from the bookcase with a smile. *"Welcome home, Axel,"* he signs.

Pepper doesn't bother with *thank you's.* She scoots through the glass doors, which, as far as I can see, lead to an enclosed balcony. She'll be safe.

"Thank you," I sign back with a lump in my throat when my eyes return to Eli.

"Eat?"

The truth is that as much as I want to eat because I really am hungry, the sight of Eli standing in his own home and me standing here with him, with nothing but a piece of paper of no value standing between us, it isn't food that I need.

He has the same thought because as soon as I give my head a small shake, he advances, stars shining in his eyes.

The light of day changes everything we've come to expect of our time together. Each time before, it was always under the cover of night. Always with the fear that Frank would find out. That the town would find out.

But it didn't stop me then, and it's certainly not going to stop me now.

I step forward and in seconds Eli engulfs me in his arms, kissing me hard and deep. My mouth opens for him, tangling my tongue with his, sucking and nipping at his mouth. Eli groans, loud and lustful.

His inhibition gives me courage once more, and coupled with the fact that, married or not, I am here and I am *his*, I allow deep, salacious groans to slide from my own throat.

Eli's fingers travel up my chest, closing around my throat. He hears my moans with his fingers and I bask in the sounds coming from the both of us.

He lifts me; my legs come around his waist and he walks us through the open space and down a wide hallway.

I'll ask for a tour of *home* later. Right now, the only tour I need is one of Eli's bed. His lips don't leave mine as we make our way to his bedroom.

Inside, I catch a glimpse of midnight blue bedding, curtains. A rug the same color.

Eli's lays me down onto the bed. His movements, so gentle and slow. I shift up, lifting myself onto my elbows and gaze at him as if he'd fallen from heaven, bringing with him a kind of ease and safety only God could provide.

Standing back, he returns my gaze, although there is nothing I could possibly offer him in exchange for what he's given me. It's hard to wrap my head around the idea that he could feel as fulfilled and, well, happy with me as I do with him.

He reaches for the buttons on his shirt, slipping them free slowly while watching me. I watch the gradual exposure of his chest as it comes into view little by little. My mouth dries when he gets to the last one and then shrugs out of the shirt.

Maybe I'd been too high-strung in the past, back in River Valley, to truly appreciate Eli's body. Maybe I was too ashamed to openly admire him. But now, the valley between his pecs calls to me as flashes fly through my mind of my face buried in that valley, my tongue dragging up that space. His abs contract, drawing my eyes down those blocks of muscle, and further. The bulge in his pants makes my mouth water. I can't look away.

Eli unbuckles his belt. My breathing escalates. I sit up and lift my hands, signing, *"Please, Eli."*

He comes to me, knees on either side of my hips, his pants unbuckled. I lift my face to his, sinking into a kiss filled with earnest longing. Eli groans into my mouth and I swallow his beautiful sounds.

The room is suddenly too hot. I'm too clothed. Dropping back onto the bed, I fight with my coat. Eli, with his mouth still on mine, strips me of it. My shirt, buttons popping, goes next and fuck if trying to get out of my pants and shoes doesn't feel like an uncoordinated disaster. Eli's chuckle adds to my dilemma, but finally, I'm naked underneath him. He's still in his half-undone pants and I'm writhing beneath him, my cock pressing up against his concealed erection.

Our lovemaking escalates, kisses become more urgent and less elegant, and soon I'm tearing at the clothing left on his body, until he's naked. His warm skin gliding against mine. I spread my legs wide when Eli's knee nudges them apart. His mouth leaves mine to trail hot kisses down the column of my neck, sucking gently at my Adam's apple, brushing his lips over my nipples.

"Aahh, fuck," I groan, bowing off the bed in search of his mouth. Eli sinks his teeth into my skin, eliciting more deep moans from my throat. I bring one of his hands to my neck, closing his fingers around my throat so he can hear what he's doing to me.

I want him all over me. His mouth over every inch of my skin. I want no part of my body to remain free from Eli's touch. I pull him up to me, reaching for his mouth once more. Kissing him like he might disappear if I let him go, I *devour* his mouth while I rut up against him. My cock sliding against his. Eli ruts into me and together, with obscene, pornographic moans, we rub our dicks together, our balls getting in on it, rubbing together.

It's insane that I can become this person when I'm with Eli.

Eli kisses me slowly, deeply, before leaving my lips once more to kiss my hipbone. He leaves a neat trail of kisses from one side to the other, pressing hard into the lowest part of my stomach. His stubbled chin grazes my cock and my lower body leaps off the bed, demanding more.

Eli obliges me. Pressing his palm into my inner thighs, he spreads my legs even more apart, then slides his hands underneath my thighs and lifts my legs onto his shoulders.

I'm so open, so *exposed*. And I'm okay. I'm *okay*.

I want his mouth on me. Need to sink into the warmth of his throat. I know how beautiful it is there and I need it now.

Eli sinks his mouth over my cock, taking me as far as he can go. He gives me a few long, slow strokes before popping my dick out of his mouth to drag his tongue up the underside of my cock. Then back down, and further down, scraping his teeth down my taint in search of my hole.

Situating my hands under my thighs, I pull my knees up to my ears, giving Eli unrestricted access to my body.

He presses his palms into the back of my thighs and, rocking back on his knees, he gazes at my hole with hooded eyes. I love him like this. Like he's enthralled with my body.

Then he leans forward, spreads my ass apart and with his thumbs he massages my hole. I feel myself loosening, blooming open, as his thumbs play with my asshole, squeezing, stretching me.

And when he drops his head to eat my ass, I scream with the impact.

Eli kisses my asshole, loud, slapping kisses, mixing with his loud breaths, his tongue spearing in and out of my hole like a fucking sword, drawing waves and waves of pleasure out of me.

My cock leaks onto my stomach and I rock into Eli's mouth, asking, begging for more. He gives it to me, flattening his tongue to suck my asshole in long, wet strokes. It's wicked and I deserve to be flung into the lowest pits of hell for how much I love what Eli is doing to my body, but I don't care. Nothing matters but this. No one matters but him.

Eli leaves my weeping hole to reach for a condom and lube.

I lower my legs for a moment to sign to him. *"Fuck me, Eli."* He grins because I got the sign perfectly right.

Sheathing himself, he lathers us both with lube. I can't help noticing that he uses far more lube than is necessary. His way of protecting my body as much as he can, maybe. I swallow a lump in my throat. How is this man real?

Our bodies ready, Eli slides into me, inch by inch. I can take him, but he's still careful, his movements slow.

His breathing escalates and I see how much he's struggling to keep himself together. I'm gripping him tightly, sucking him into my channel and holding him there like a prisoner. But still, he won't push in.

My heart sings for Eli's care. For the care he gives me without me asking for it, so I wrap my legs around him, digging my heels into his lower back and urging him forward. Asking him to take my body. To take his pleasure because it's the least I can do for him, for what he's given me. My nails scrape down his back, telling him in every way I can how much I want this.

Finally, *finally*, he's all the way in.

Eli slides in and out of me, his dick grazing my prostate, taking me to the edge of the universe and then flinging me back to earth when he slides out.

It's only when I'm clawing at him, my shouts vibrating in my throat and screaming against his fingers wrapped around my flesh there, that Eli lets go and truly *fucks* me.

My cock slaps against my stomach with each hit from Eli's pistoning hips. My shouts join his and then—

I join the stars, flying through the blackness, exploding into innumerable pieces of iridescent light. Eli comes hurtling after me, and together we fall.

If this is what home feels like, then I've been homeless my whole life.

CHAPTER 63
Axel

He has a piano in his home. A baby grand, similar to the one he'd had transported to Mrs. Johnson's house months earlier. I hadn't noticed it earlier because it was on the other side of the living room, off to the left. If you sat down to play at night, you'd be able to look outside and count the stars.

Now, dressed in Eli's clothes—a pair of navy blue sweats that ride low on my hips and a t-shirt—since I arrived here with only a pen, notebook and Ben's prom suit on my back, I take a hesitant step forward toward the piano.

Has he always had it here? Does he play, too? Surprisingly, it never came up in all our time in River Valley.

Eli comes up behind me, wrapping his arms around me. I sink into his embrace. It can't be real, this. My life could not have changed so drastically in a matter of hours. I feel like I'm on a different planet. It's so quiet here. Not just the environment. In my head too. I never knew how noisy it was inside my own mind until now. Until its absence provided an unfamiliar sense of safety.

I turn in Eli's arms, looking curiously between him and the piano.

"It's for you," he signs.

"You didn't have to do that," I say.

"Play for me," he signs and then, taking my hand, he leads me to the piano and urges me to sit. With tentative fingers, I play.

A simple tune I'd learned on YouTube. Eli sits next to me and places his hand on the side of the piano while I play.

Pepper finds us and settles next to Eli on the floor. I swear she and I are going to fight over Eli. She's as smitten with him now as she had been the very first day she almost went under his wheel.

Sometimes, when I look over at Eli, I find him watching my fingers move over the keys. Other times, he watches my face and I can't help meeting his gaze. The calm I find in him is mostly unsettling. Like I... miss... the chaos.

Eli retrieves his phone from his pocket and turns the lit up screen to me. It's an article from some medical society site.

I stop playing and take the phone from him.

The article is about small steps to take when coming out of an abusive relationship. There's a list: have supportive people around you, try to recall what you loved doing for yourself before the abuse started, reconnect with old hobbies. Talk about what happened with people you trust. But the one that stands out for me the most is: create a boring, predictable routine.

And so that's what I do.

Eli helps me. More than I ever expected.

I feel like a burden sometimes but Eli makes it hard to maintain such a mind-set. I can't imagine how much his family must have loved and believed in him that he has such a firm hold on... well, *himself*. I'm in awe of just how put-together he is—mentally, I mean. I feel like a psychotic fool sometimes. Eli is what people grow up to be when they have parents who love them and nurture them. He's the evidence of what happens when human beings just do what's right for the people they love.

I was convinced he would find a way to end the relationship after I told him everything. What he did instead was ask me if we could do therapy together. To which I agreed because I believed in such things but could never get myself to seek it out in River Valley. I also grabbed the chance for one-on-one therapy, where it's just me.

Dr. Shashi is working with doctors from the hospital here. I learned that he never told Frank anything about my relapse. Frank had just put two and two together and let me believe Dr. Shashi had told him. Frank hadn't even known for sure about the cancer when he announced it to me. The cruelty astounds me.

I'm getting the best medical care in the world.

Three days. That's how long it had taken for Eli to make all these arrangements. It was strange working with him. He never made any decisions. Instead, he always looked to me to make the final decisions on everything. It was... empowering, having someone by my side like that while I took charge of my own life.

Ben and Mrs. Dalton text every day. Mrs. Dalton said that Frank told everyone that he caught me cheating and asked me to leave. He went on a smear campaign, telling so many lies about me and Eli. The only truth he told was that I'd cheated and he'd gotten buckets of sympathy for it.

Mrs. Dalton told me to leave it alone. That I had nothing to prove to anyone over there. She hasn't stopped apologizing for telling me that Frank had left for work that day when he hadn't, even though I tell her everyday it wasn't her fault.

Eli and I got tested together, clearing each other for sex without protection.

We make love as often as possible, but I'm getting more and more tired as the days pass. Erections are becoming fewer as the days pass, so we make the best of the times I'm able to get it up. Eli won't have penetrative sex if I'm not hard. I love him so much for his consideration.

Eli is still technically on vacation, so he spends most of his days at home with me, afternoons at the hospital, and evenings are spent eating dinner and me playing on the piano.

I ask not to meet his mom in the hospital because I'm terrified of how she might react, despite Eli assuring me not to be. But he tells me he understands and we agree that I'll meet her as soon as she's back home.

Having my choices respected is difficult to accept, and it feels like my brain is broken sometimes. Asking for what I need and then the guilt that follows when I get it, is an emotion difficult to explain.

I fall into a predictable, mundane routine, like the article said. Even the food I eat is the same. Eli shows me a food market two blocks away, a pizza and pasta place two blocks in the opposite direction, and a library around the corner.

"Your first time applying for a library membership," the librarian had asked when I went in the first day with Eli.

After that, Eli encouraged me to leave the house to go to the places I've become familiar with.

I leave the house with Pepper every day at ten a.m. when Eli sits down for his work meetings. We visit the market on Mondays, the library on Tuesdays, and I've learned that Eli loves the pasta from down the road, so we get pasta for lunch every Wednesday. Thursdays is back to the market and Friday, back to the library.

I video call Ben and Mrs. Dalton some days to give them a tour of my new home. Their response is always the same: a resounding *we're so happy for you* and *don't ever come back.*

There's a history museum not too far away. With a credit card issued for my use and Eli's driver, I arrive at the museum early on Friday morning, while Eli is at his office for an in-person meeting.

We dropped him off first. Pepper is at home, upset she couldn't come.

I browse through the museum, listening to the guide. Today, there is an exhibition about bourbon whiskey. I'm mesmerized, not just by the history of this place, but by the fact that I'm out here, doing something I love and I don't have to worry about what Frank would think about it. Or have my phone blow up with him asking what time I'll be home. In fact, I wouldn't have been able to do this at all in River Valley.

I eat lunch at the restaurant outside and the aloneness is invigorating. The sense of independence is both foreign and completely natural at the same time. I notice that I chew my food slowly, not having to rush through so I can get to the dishes in the sink. I can load my fries with ketchup without being asked *how the fuck can I eat like that.*

I receive a text from Eli asking me if I'm enjoying my day out. My first instinct is to think he's being sarcastic, but I breathe through it and remind myself that he's genuinely asking me. So, I respond, saying I was having the best time.

When I return home, something smells... burnt.

Eli stands in the kitchen feeding Pepper charcoaled chicken.

He laughs when I enter and signs, "I wanted to make you chicken wings."

I laugh too but, really, I want to cry with his thoughtful gesture.

We end up ordering sticky chicken wings and we have an early night because I got too tired.

CHAPTER 64
Axel

I meet his mom as soon as she's released from the hospital.

Eli's parents' house is simple for a family that owns so much of the world. It's spacious but not opulent. Elegant but not untouchable. It looks lived in. Like many happy memories is what built this house.

Mrs. Saxon sits on the couch in the living room. It's cold today, and she's seated close to the fireplace. She's the slightly older version of the woman whose picture hangs on the wall at Eli's office. He gets his blue eyes from her. The rest of him comes from his father, whose pictures could be found in frames all over the living room. Eli had a happy childhood. It's evident in the family photos.

Eli holds my hand, his fingers linked with mine. It feels rude to hold on to him like this, but he won't let me go.

"Give us a minute, Eli," Mrs. Saxon says gently. She sounds like Eli. In fact, this whole house... sounds like Eli and now his mother. The calmness is strange. I'm not sure how to respond. Convincing myself that I don't need to be on high alert, watchful all the time, is a more difficult feat than it might seem.

But being asked to have a word with Mrs. Saxon alone, without Eli, invites panic in like an old friend. Eli simply kisses me, right on the lips, right there in front of his mother. My face explodes with heat and I must look like a bright red tomato.

And then he leaves.

"Come sit by me," Mrs. Saxon says, patting the space next to her on the oversized couch. It feels too close, but how can I say no?

I sit next to her.

"Eli told me a few things. I hope that's okay with you," she says.

"Yes, of course. He asked me and I told him it was okay." My voice shakes.

"How are you feeling?"

She means about the cancer. "Uhm, good. So far."

"You're getting tired a lot these days, huh?"

She sounds like a *mother*. Like *my* mother. Like Mrs. Dalton. This place isn't good for me. All I do is cry when someone is nice to me.

"Yes, but it's not too bad. I—I'm managing okay. And, uhm, how are you doing?"

I'm struggling to make eye contact with her. She knows about the abuse, about Frank. All I want to do is hide from her.

"It's not too bad. I'm managing okay." She smiles when I finally look at her with a smile for repeating my answer.

"Are you settling in nicely at home?" she asks.

Home. She doesn't say *Eli's* place. She says *home*. Like it's my home too. I drop my eyes to my lap when I think about how she must know that I'm living with her son while I'm married to someone else.

She reaches over and lifts my chin. "Eli would never have made these difficult choices if you didn't mean that much to him," she says softly.

"I'm sorry," I whisper. "I—I should have divorced my husband first."

"I've lived long enough to know that life isn't that simple, Axel."

"Thank you, Mrs. Saxon." My voice is soft, grateful, daring to sound happy.

"Is Eli being good to you?" she asks.

My eyes fly to hers, stunned. Oh my god, what a question.

"No one's ever been as good to me as he's been," I say sincerely.

She grins. You'd never think she's almost eighty and had just got out of the hospital. "He's pretty great, huh?"

Her smile is infectious. I can't help the upward tug of my own lips. "He is amazing, Mrs. Saxon."

Her smile widens. "Yeah. I really like him, that son of mine. You like him too, huh?"

I laugh. "I like him very much."

I've been in therapy now for just over eight weeks. Eli comes with me once a month and I go alone the other three times a month.

On days when Eli comes with me, Pepper comes too. The only place Pepper doesn't go with Eli is to his work, and even that, I think he would have given in to if I hadn't given Pepper a good scolding. She acts like he's abandoned her every morning and then every evening she sits by the elevator doors, watching the light. She's learned that when the lights flicker, it means Eli is on his way up. Today, he has a late meeting. Pepper doesn't believe a word I say anymore, so when she ignored me after I told her that Eli will be late, I left her there.

I cook dinner for us every night. Eli loves everything I cook. It's an effort not to make the comparison to my other life, but I try very hard. Sometimes, the guilt over what Frank would be eating, how he'd be coping, overwhelms me. But I try to remember all the reasons I had to leave. And not only that, but the *way* I had to leave. Sometimes, I feel like I let him down. Like I abandoned him. But I know now it's my loyalty talking. My *empathetic* nature. It has nothing to do with Frank, except the part where he exploited that part of me to control me. I see the difference now.

I've obtained a whole new set of vocabulary since I started therapy. Narcissistic abuse. Gas lighting. Trauma bonds. Emotional neglect. *Reactive abuse.* I used to have a vague idea about some of these things before, but when you're using those words to dissect your own memories and experiences, it becomes utterly terrifying that a person could endure such pain.

It was liberating to find the word that described those times I'd scream and scream and scream like a madman. And Frank would just sit there and laugh. Or record me. Or tell me that I was insane. There is such a thing as *reactive abuse.* A kind of abuse where you're pushed and pushed and pushed until you snap and your reaction is used to inflict more abuse on you.

My divorce was finalized today. Eli's lawyers were ruthless in making sure everything went through and that Frank didn't try to delay the proceedings. He was also ordered to destroy the video he'd taken of me and Eli at the lake.

When I sleep next to Eli tonight, I'll be Axel St. James again. I'll be me again. And I'll be Eli's, truly.

In the bedroom—our bedroom—I scroll through my phone, accidentally opening my Facebook app. I have over a hundred notifications and sixty-six private messages. Frank has gone through every post and picture dating back ten years and reacted to them. Some comments are just appalling, such as: *good times*, underneath one of me and him just after we got married.

I open the PM's with shaking fingers.

Sure enough, every single one of them is from Frank.

I miss you, Axel. Come back home. I'm begging you.

I'll change. I'll do everything you need me to do. I'll be the man you need me to be. I don't deserve you. You're too good for me, but I'll try.

Then,

It's so tough without you, Axel. I even miss Pepper. How is she? Is she coping well?

My hand balls in a fist. What? Frank hated Pepper from the first day I got her.

More messages. He's been sending them every single day.

I ate sticky wings today, and I thought about you. I even got a recipe book from the bookstore so I can make them for you just the way you like it.

You are everything to me, Axel. I got a card from the medical center for a therapist just outside of town. I'm going to make an appointment. It's all for you, baby. Everything is for you.

And the last one was sent a few days ago.

Axel, baby, I had to sign the papers today. I had no choice. But this is proof, sweetheart, that I'm willing to lose you for a little while so that I can win you back forever. I also got rid of the video to prove to you that I hold nothing against you.

Tears wet my cheeks. I squeeze my eyes shut and breathe through the emotions. *Sit with them,* the therapist had said.

Honor your feelings. They deserve to be acknowledged. And then find words to describe them.

Finding words to describe them feels like talking myself off a ledge. I breathe deeply in and out while I speak to myself, reaffirming my own truth.

I suffered narcissistic abuse at Frank's hand.

He does not love me.

He loves the control he used to have over me.

He misses the control, not me.

His abusive nature will do and say anything to get me back so he can get that control back.

His primary goal is to control me. Nothing more.

It occurs to me that he hadn't asked once how *I* was. Or wished me happiness with the choice I'd made. Nothing in his messages was about me and my wellbeing. Everything was about him.

And it was all the confirmation I needed that Frank was baiting me.

No contact. Mrs. Dalton, and my therapist, too, had said *no contact* is how you deal with this type of abuser after leaving them.

I delete the messages and then block Frank and walk to the closet to get a pair of socks.

Standing in the closet, I trail my fingers over the drawer where my underwear is neatly stacked next to Eli's.

Tears come from nowhere as I let my fingers drift over the rows and rows and rows of silk panties. My mind drifts back to that day behind the library. I'd been so ashamed. But with Eli, there's no such thing as shame. He simply accepts... me. I will never go back to Frank. I will never allow any contact between me and Frank ever again.

Half the rows of panties are black, but the rest are of every color you can think of. This drawer gets more and more full every other week. Eli buys them for me.

The one I have on now is black. Some of them are of the flimsiest material. So easy to tear. Eli must think it's his honorable duty to replace ones he'd—

The lights flicker. Eli is home.

I rush downstairs to meet him, but Pepper beats me to it.

After she's had her one thousand hours of kisses and hugs, Eli rises to his feet and gazes at me from across the kitchen counter. Pepper is on the mat by the sink with a treat.

"Something smells good," he signs.

I shouldn't have, but my response is immediate. *Something smells good.* The sneer in Frank's voice rings inside my head.

My body closes up. Eli catches it. He doesn't move. In therapy, he learned that sometimes the smallest things could trigger me... the way his shoes might drag a certain way, if he made a fist with his hand without meaning to. We both learned that I have ten years' worth of abusive tics to work through.

This man has gone to the ends of the earth to understand me.

"I love everything you cook," he says in sign from where he's standing. "Let's eat together?"

I rush to him, throw my arms around his neck, and hold him close to me.

He slides his hands into the waistband of my sweats, his fingers grazing my silk panties. I pull back, taking his mouth with mine, kissing him deeply.

"Hmm." His deep voice tumbles over my body.

"Let's eat later," he signs.

"You must be hungry," I laugh.

His hand moves to the front of my sweats, taking my underwear between his thumb and index finger. *So sexy,* he signs.

I bury my face in his chest, but he just lifts my face up again and kisses me, wet and hard and full of tongue.

Then, without warning, he yanks down my sweats, exposing me to the cool night.

I'm barefoot, so getting the sweats right off is easy and in point four seconds, we're shutting the bedroom door before Pepper realizes we're missing from the kitchen.

I'm naked except for my panties, sprawled on the bed. I sign to him, *"I'm single and I have a boner."*

He raises an eyebrow. *"You're taken and that's my boner,"* he signs back. I laugh.

He strips quickly and in no time, I'm on my stomach, my cock painfully hard and sensitive against the silk material. I thank the gods for this erection.

Eli kisses me from my nape to the base of my spine, his lips moving carefully over each part of my skin he touches. I bruise easily these days, so sex is careful but no less explosive.

I know where his mouth is going and fuck, I want him there. Frank was wrong. I'm not a *fucking corpse* in bed.

Eli's mouth tracks up my spine again and I squirm, rotating my hips. My fingers sink into the sheets, aching for Eli.

His mouth makes another slow track down my spine and his hands drift up from the back of my knees to my thighs. Up. Up. Up

Hmm. His big hands slide over my silk covered ass. He rubs there, big circles over and over, then sliding between my legs to slip his hand underneath.

"Aahh." My groans join his loud, harsh exhales and the roughened baritone of his groans. Nothing compares to sex with Eli. His uninhibited pleasure is some kind of wonder.

His palms move again up to my ass, finger pressing down, separating my ass cheeks and then—

Ah, fuck. My dick tightens inside the confines of my panties as Eli rips the silk right in the middle, exposing my ass.

His tongue traces along the exposed crease of my ass. Joining Eli's loud grunts, I encourage him into my ass. His tongue is everything, sinking in deep, biting, sucking.

I lift my ass for him, and he eats me through the newly ripped underwear. But I want more than his tongue.

Reaching back, I grab hold of the hand that's on my thigh.

He comes up, lifting my hips and there's that first drizzle of lube. Eli's fingers slip between my ass cheeks. He likes to play with my ass like this, through my ripped panties. And fuck if I don't love it when he wants to play.

He lubes my whole ass. My cheeks, slick with lube, cause his hands to slide erotically over my skin. Then his thumb circles my hole. Mmm. I could come just like this. Eli runs maddening circles around my hole with that thumb, massaging my asshole. He spreads my ass wide open, sliding his pinky in. Ah, fuck. So fucking amazing. Soon, I'm demanding for more than his fingers. I need that fucking cock of his inside my ass.

And then, ohh fuck me to the fucking pits of hell, when Eli's makes the first breach with that beautiful crown of his dick, I lift my ass for him.

He gives it to me, so long and deep and hard. The best kind of burn.

Eli knows how to ride my ass. I take him in all the fucking way and when he withdraws to just his tip inside me, I hold my breath for the—

Fuck me. That strike back inside, hitting my prostate.

Again.

And again.

And fucking again.

We go until Eli is fucking me through the torn silk panties like a grunting beast and I'm coming like a fucking freight train, giving him my ass to wreck in every which way until he too explodes inside me, warm and so fucking beautiful.

CHAPTER 65
Eli

We're not done. He's so damn beautiful like this. Sprawled on his stomach, the sheets totally fucked with his cum, and mine oozing out of his ass.

He reaches back and spreads his cheeks for me. Axel is so sexy when we fuck. It's the only place every single one of his triggers, his insecurities and his demons are banished from his mind, his heart, his body.

Here, he belongs all and only to me. And I honor his trust in me with a kind of lovemaking that transcends just physical release. Here, nothing separates us. Not Frank. Not cancer. Not the painful memories of River Valley.

Now, he lifts his ass for me, and I spread him wide, ripping his panties even more to give me a clearer view of his asshole.

He flexes his hole. Fuck, so fucking gorgeous. My cum oozes from that beautiful little pucker. I catch the dribble of semen in the pad of my thumb and sink my thumb back into his hole. Reaching forward, I close the fingers of my other hand around his neck. The cords in his neck vibrate and I imagine his groans. His shouts of pleasure.

When I've lavished Axel's beautiful asshole sufficiently, I slowly turn him around until he's on his back. He gazes at me with hooded eyes. Running my hands over the front of his thighs, I hook my fingers into the waistband of his silk panties and roll them down slowly.

"You'll have to replace those," he signs.

I laugh, the sounds vibrating in my throat. I bunch up the destroyed underwear in my fist and bring it to my nose, inhaling deeply. I'll never get over Axel's scent.

Then, I take the panties and rub them gently over Axel's semi hard cock. He closes his eyes, lifting his hips. Ecstasy looks so fucking good on him.

His cock lies against his stomach, thick and veined. I reach down and take him in my mouth. Even softened, Axel inside my mouth is a dream.

He doesn't harden again. He's tired. Fatigue is common these days.

I slip him out of my mouth, lifting myself off him carefully. By the time I manage to get a pillow underneath his head, he's asleep. I bring him a warm towel, opening the bedroom door for Pepper on my way back to Axel, and wipe as much of him as possible before covering us both with the comforter from the bottom of the bed. Pepper settles behind Axel, in the crook of his knees.

She may go ballistic for me when I leave or return, but at night, she stays very close to Axel.

Facing Axel, I reach over him and rub Pepper on the top of her head. *Thank you,* I sign. Her tail beats lightly on the bed and she lets out a soft whine.

I switch off the lights with a remote but keep the one on the nightstand on my side on. It's still early for me, so I pick up the book that Axel carries with him everywhere. I don't know how many times he's read it.

All The Battles We Surrender. I've been reading a little every night after Axel's fallen asleep. He reads *Tamelane and Other*

Poems almost every night. At first, he refused to even touch the first edition, but I'd insisted he read from it.

As I near the end of *All The Battles We Surrender*, my heart breaks for Axel all over again. He's looking for his happy ending.

I set the book aside and settle into the bed, facing him. Tracing the outline of his face, I admire him in the near darkness. His small, straight nose. His long lashes. His sweet, pink lips, now open slightly. His hair... I now understand the sorrow in Mrs. Dalton's words when she told me to never ask him to cut it.

I'm not a religious person, but I know Axel has always had faith in God. So, now, while I watch him sleep, I pray to his God and ask him to please let Axel's hair grow out so he can have his curls back. I don't ask for more years than what Axel will have. Only that the years that he is given be filled with every joy he could ever contain in his heart. That his belly will always be filled with the food he loves. That his face will always be radiant with his joy.

Tears fall, gathering at the corner of my eyes. The pillow catches my sorrow, holding them together in the wetness of the fabric.

I'll love him until his last breath and even after that, I'll love him. If there is an afterlife, I'll search for him there and when I find him, I'll never let him go. Then I'll collude with death to let me have him forever.

Even now, if I could bargain with the devil for his life, I would. I would do anything to keep him here, in this world, where I can gaze at his beauty and tell him every day how very loved he is. How beautiful he makes the world. How every good thing to ever exist belongs to him. How deserving he is of every good thing.

I link my fingers with his, and sleep takes me into the place of dreams where Axel is healthy and well and safe with me.

CHAPTER 66
Axel

I'm an expert at whirlwind romances. One experience had been enough to qualify me for such a thing. So, when Eli held an engagement ring to my finger one night in bed, while he made love to me, I knew what it looked like to agree to marry someone after having known them for only six months.

But you can't predict the future. All you can do is count the odds that are in your favor and listen hard to your own intuition. Your inner guidance system, no matter how faint that voice may be. So, that's what I do.

I test my feelings of fear, insecurity, my sense of feeling stifled or uneasy, the way I'd been with Frank. I have none of them. Eli's love for me is the same as him: calm, soft, grounded and sure.

His possessiveness and protectiveness of me isn't the kind that isolates me from people around me. His regular check-ups bring with them a feeling of genuine concern. And my relationship with him isn't some kind of flex to throw around for the public to consume.

So, when he held the ring to my finger while his cock was inside me, there was no answer I could have given, other than *Yes*.

My therapist says they generally don't encourage a new relationship so soon after what I'd been through, but she understood that I don't have a lot of time and that I needed to live *now*. So Eli and I worked on how I could rebuild a relationship with myself while in a committed relationship. He gave me the space I needed to figure out who I am. It's a work in progress. *I'm* a work in progress and Eli supports me, even on those parts of my journey that I must walk alone.

I'm going for driving lessons and I'm enrolled to finish school.

Eli worked relentlessly with me and the doctors to find new clinical trials that we could try. He got doctors from around the world to treat me. And I promised him that I would fight my hardest to live. To remain with him in this world as long as possible.

Chemo is awful. Worse than the last time. I feel like I'm getting sicker, but the results of the new clinical trials are promising. Right now, we don't know, but there is more hope now than there had been before. Eli is the rock next to me that never moves.

Frank was wrong. Eli didn't leave me. He stayed with me through every chemo session. Every doctor's visit. He never missed a single joint therapy session.

I tell him every day how amazing he is. He tells me we shouldn't praise basic human decency. That he's not special for simply caring about me. That it's the most basic thing any human being can and should do.

I know it's that simple for him. Of course, he would love so selflessly. He'd been loved like that his whole life.

But for me, Eli isn't a basic human being. He's the one who saved me. Even as my body destroyed itself from the inside out, he strengthened the parts of me I thought had long been destroyed by Frank.

Never look back, is what Mrs. Dalton told me. It's hard. Even though I'm the one dying, I still sometimes think about how Frank is doing.

My therapist tells me that I must grieve the death of hope. Not of the relationship, but of the hope of all that could have been.

She'd also said I must allow myself to grieve for the person I was when I was with Frank because leaving that version of me behind will feel like I've lost someone close to me. That the old me deserves as much grieving as if someone had actually died.

She told me that sometimes we don't have the answers for why the things that happened to us did, but if that path led us to a place of peace and joy, then maybe we can learn to let go, little by little the pain of the past, and cultivate gratitude for where it's brought us.

Also, that I'd lived in a kind of addictive cycle for so long, it isn't uncommon to feel withdrawal symptoms like an addict might. That it will take time to coax my nervous system out of its default fight-or-flight mode. So, missing Frank and the *good times* sometimes isn't something to be ashamed of. It's just one more way my body and mind had been harmed and needed time to heal from.

I don't know how much longer I have, but the new trials give me hope. With such rapid advancements in medicine and this new treatment, I have a better chance this time around.

"Are you alright?" Eli asks in sign as we dress for our wedding.

I move from the bed and go to him by the window, nodding.

Slipping my hands around his waist, I lift my face to his, studying him. "Are you alright?"

He dips his head. *Yes.* But I know this is hard for him. The person he had loved the most in the world, alongside his mother, is not here to watch him get married. And his anguish is increased tenfold by the recent first anniversary of his father's death.

"He's here," I say softly, but clearly, touching the place where his heart beats.

A single tear escapes his ocean eyes. *"I know,"* he signs.

He swipes at his tears harshly. I take hold of his hands and press them to my heart. "It's okay to cry, Eli," I say.

389

He drops his forehead to my shoulder and his shoulders quake. Taking him in my arms, I hold him as he had held me so many times before.

We'd chosen not to do things the traditional way. Our relationship did not begin and grow the traditional way, so nothing about the way we'll marry will be *normal.* We dress together, drive to the church together, and walk down the aisle together.

Pepper, who rocks a black satin bowtie like any badass girl would, is with us as we walk.

The cheers from the crowd are unbelievable, and I wish for a second that Eli could hear how happy people are for us. But then I realize that he *can* hear. Not the way I can, but the happiness and pride radiating from the crowd is not lost on him on account of him not being able to hear with his ears. In fact, I believe he's able to hear them more than me because he has years of honed in skill to detect and appreciate every single facial expression, every smile, and moment of joy better than I can.

We have vows prepared. Our own vows, not the traditional ones.

I chose to sign my vows. And as I sign, Eli's face shines with adoration and joy. The interpreter types the words on the big screen to the side, to let all the hearing people know what I'm about to say.

I promise to love myself first so I can love you with all that I am.

I promise you the kindness and respect that you deserve.

For every breath that I breathe, I promise to hold you in high esteem always.

I promise to never take for granted your love for me and to always inspire your confidence in my love for you.

I'll stay with you all the days of my life and love you more as each day passes.

And when our time on this earth draws to a close, know that I'll love you into all eternity

I'll love you while I still breathe and I'll love you still when I am nothing but dust.

Know always that you are my safe place.

You are the one who accepts all the parts of me; in you my true self is known and wanted.

And so, today, I am yours, as I have always been

And you are mine, as you have always been and always will be.

The crowd is silent. From the corner of my eyes, I catch a glimpse of Mrs. Dalton in the front row, sniffing her tears back while she clutches Ben's hand. Eli's mom is in a worse situation with her tears.

Eli lifts his hands to sign his vows. My heart thumps in my chest, praying I'll understand everything and wouldn't need to look up at the screen because God knows, I can't take my eyes off this man for even one second.

I promise to be your safe place, as you have become mine.

I promise to embrace every part of you in every stage of our lives together with awe and wonder.

I promise to love all the parts of me so I can love all the parts of you.

I promise to stand with you in all things, to weather the storms together and share in the joys together.

Axel St. James, I promise to cherish you and keep you safe.

To adore you and admire your wings when you fly, to never stifle or confine you.

To honor the freedom you need to be all of who you are.

I'll love you in all the ways you need and more.

And when the priest declares us husband and husband, Eli sweeps me up in his arms and kisses me like no one is watching. I'm no less enthused, kissing him back with everything in me while our audience celebrates our union.

We got our happily-ever-after, but for me and Eli, the future isn't some distant destination. Our *forever* isn't a linear progression to a utopian land of bliss. And our happily-ever-after isn't a goal measured in years.

Our future, our forever, our happily-ever-after, is *now*. It's always *now*. We're not waiting for our happy ending. Our happy ending is in every moment of every single day.

And even if I was not fighting the biggest battle of my life, I suspect this is what it would have been like with Eli. We'd still live like tomorrow doesn't exist.

Now, with a ring on my finger that says I belong to Eli and a ring on his to say he is mine, we enter his mother's backyard, hand-in-hand for our wedding reception.

I'm a little slow and Eli takes his time with me. I smile at the crowd. I don't know all of them. Very few of them I can name, in fact. But I know they are here because they love Eli so much and Eli's happiness means so much to them. And I've been starved for family my whole life, so I accept every one of them standing here today as my family.

We're showered with congratulations as we walk down to our seats. Mrs. Dalton and Ben and Casey rise from their chairs. Mrs. Dalton cries and I wouldn't have if it weren't for her. Tears are contagious at wedding receptions, I keep telling myself, especially after Ben bawled his eyes out while he tried to give his speech.

Casey came to sit next to me, linking her arms in mine. She tells me how hot Eli and I look together.

Eli's mother cries the whole time and I spend half the time locked in her embrace.

After the formalities, Eli asks me to play on the piano.

He comes to sit next to me on the bench as I play for the crowd. Pepper sits under the bench.

I gaze up at Eli, smiling through my unrepentant tears. I have no remorse for my infidelity.

Eli brings his arm around me, touching my bald head before slipping his hand into my dress pants at the back, reaching for my silk underwear. I still have hopes that I'll be able to grow out my curls for him.

I lay the side of my head on his shoulder.

Maybe the question of why people cheat can never be answered. Maybe because one single answer could never cover the vastness of the human psyche and what propels us forward in our quest for fulfilment.

Every affair must begin with a longingness, a yearning for... *something*. Mine was obvious, and maybe I could be forgiven for it. I'd been denied so many things in my marriage to Frank, but maybe it's not so obvious for others. Maybe they haven't yet figured out what they're longing for and follow blindly after what they feel in that moment of betrayal.

It's true. We are the villains in our own story and, often, society will never let us forget it. So villains we will be, then, hunting for the source of our emptiness and destroying everything in the process. But maybe we didn't know another way. Maybe there *wasn't* another way.

Frank was looking for the source of his emptiness, too. But he refused to face his demons and I know now that it was not up to me to fix him and that role had never been mine to start with. I destroyed the sanctity of my marriage. Frank destroyed *me*, and I paid dearly for his quest to find peace. I don't know if he'll ever find it.

If anyone were to think my story is a sad one, I'd want to tell them not to be too sad. Because I have loved and have been loved in all the ways I'd dreamed of. I had loved Eli in all the ways I knew how, and when I'd loved him like that, I'd begun to search for more ways still that I could love him. Because I'd wanted to love him into eternity.

With Eli, I get to have my happy ending every single moment I am able to breathe. My test results show positive signs that I'll be okay, but I've learned that it doesn't matter anymore. Whether I live another five years or fifty, I've already lived a hundred lifetimes with Eli. He's loved me enough to take me through every lifetime.

We are sound and silence and when we are together like this, those two things are the same.

I know I stole my happiness, but if you had been loved the way Eli loved me, maybe you'd have stolen yours too, because after Eli loved me, I lived. I *lived*. I was dying, but I was also the most alive I had ever been.

I am grateful for every breath I've been given since I was diagnosed when I was eighteen but I never knew what it was to be alive until Eli.

And after being loved like that, what more could I ever have asked for?

THE END

Dear reader,

If you've come this far, thank you for staying. This story might have been hard for you to read, so I am extra grateful for your time.

If you liked Axel and Eli's story, please consider rating it and/or leaving a review. It helps me get this book in front of other people who might also enjoy it. If you didn't enjoy it, I promise to try harder in the next one.

If you've suffered abuse of any kind, know that it's not you. It was never you. May you find the child in you and love yourself back to the raging inferno you were always meant to be.

For a time, you may have to remain still while you gather your strength, but the time will come for you to roar from the mountaintop. They lit the match hoping to turn you to ash, but you will rise and you will burn as bright as the sun. Lift your chin and straighten your shoulders. Your time is now.

xoxo
Jen

Please stalk me across my social media pages:

Instagram: @jen_samson_author
Email: sharewithjen7@gmail.com
Like my Facebook page: www.facebook.com/AuthorJenSamson
Friend me on Facebook: www.facebook.com/JenSamson
Amazon: www.amazon.com/author/jensamson
Join my reader group: www.facebook.com/JenAndTheHotGirls

SAY YES
Jen Samson

It began the very first moment their eyes met across that boardroom table, at a meeting Colt Hanson should never have been at in the first place.

Sebastian Stone is unlike any man Colt has ever encountered and his quiet, innocent world is rocked when Sebastian discovers his secret and then reveals his interest in him.

But Sebastian has rules that Colt will have to accept if he wants to get close to Sebastian. Colt agrees, and both men enter into a sexual arrangement that will have Colt questioning everything he knew about himself, while he uncovers, layer by layer, Sebastian's painful history.

Kindle e-book OUT NOW
Paperback edition coming soon

BEHIND THESE EYES
Jen Samson

"If this is a sin, then I'll burn in hell for all eternity. I'll never deny you, not in this life and not in the next."

When Chase Batton's wild ways land him six months away from failing to graduate from college, he is forced into a remedial program with the university's academic star, Jaxon Lee. Either that or answer to the heads of the third richest family in the world: his parents. The latter is no choice at all.

Jaxon is distant and cold, and unimpressed by Chase's social and economic rank. On the other hand, Chase couldn't be bothered by the opinions of the supposedly hottest gay guy on campus. He was, after all, a long way up the food chain, not to mention straight as an arrow on the bullseye.

But something happens during a vicious argument, and everything changes.
Chase is left reeling, and he soon learns that Jaxon is keeping secrets too...

Kindle e-book OUT NOW
Paperback edition coming soon

HOME, THEN
A.E Jensen

Colton

After being in the army for more than 20 years, Colton returns to his home town in Nebraska. His estranged uncle has offered him a job at his auto shop. With nothing to his name, he hopes to start over and build some sort of life. Preferably a quiet life where he doesn't have to deal with the rest of the world. And everything is going pretty well except for the fact that he keeps running into the local vet, Henry. With his charm and boyish good looks, he stirs feelings inside Colton, which he hasn't allowed himself to feel in a long time.

But what does a middle-aged ex-soldier with a bad case of PTSD have to offer a hot, young doctor with a college degree and the whole world at his feet?

Henry

It was never part of his plan to come back home to small town Nebraska after college. But when the only person who had ever really been there for him - his grandma - became ill, he had to. Now, two years later, Henry is living with his grandma, working as the town vet. Life is okay. Hayley's Peak doesn't exactly have a vibrant gay scene like the city, but at least no one seems to mind him being out. Then one day, Colton Dietrich arrives out of nowhere. Tall, dark and brooding he is the embodiment of every wet dream, Henry has ever had. And maybe, just maybe, things can go from okay to earth-shatteringly amazing. Henry just needs to get Colton to talk to him.....

OUT NOW

Made in the USA
Middletown, DE
16 May 2023

30669979R00243